Lizzie Lane was born and brought up in one of the toughest areas of Bristol, the eldest of three siblings who were all born before her parents got round to marrying. Her mother, who had endured both the Depression and war years, was a natural-born story teller, and it's from her telling of actual experiences of the tumultuous first half of the twentieth century that Lizzie gets her inspiration.

Lizzie has had a long association with our canine friends, which began with a puppy she named Rusty, a pedigree Irish Red Setter. Encouraged to show him, she became more and more involved in the canine world acquiring more Irish Setters, including one who became a British champion and one, Swiss. Besides showing and breeding dogs, she ran dog training classes and even presided as a dog show judge. It's from this background and knowing dogs so well that she is now including them in her books.

LIZZIE LANE

War Orphans

Don't know if you have read this book?						
If you wish, add your initials here to keep track!						

EBURY
PRESS

1 3 5 7 9 10 8 6 4 2

Ebury Press, an imprint of Ebury Publishing
20 Vauxhall Bridge Road,
London SW1V 2SA

Ebury Press is part of the Penguin Random House group of companies
whose addresses can be found at global.penguinrandomhouse.com

First published in the UK in 2016 by Ebury Press

www.penguin.co.uk

A CIP catalogue record for this book is available from the British Library

ISBN 9781785037924

Printed and bound in Great Britain by Clays Ltd, St Ives PLC

Penguin Random House is committed to a sustainable future
for our business, our readers and our planet. This book is made
from Forest Stewardship Council® certified paper.

To my friends Sally and Mike, for all the kindness and fun times we had together, and to Sharon, Chris and Mary for being there for me in a time of trouble.

AUTHOR'S NOTE

At the outbreak of war between Britain and Germany, the government advised that parents' evacuated their children from the nation's cities to the safety of the countryside.

Less is known about another government directive advising that all household pets are destroyed. Their advice was based on the likelihood of an enemy blockade of food supplies and the severity of rationing. There would be no food to spare for pets.

The government surmised that, following intensive bombing, packs of maddened dogs would form, attacking and eating anything they could.

The majority of pets were put down humanely, but a lot were abandoned, knocked over the head with a hammer, drowned or left tied up in sacks to slowly starve and suffocate to death.

It is estimated that 300,000 were destroyed in the first ten days following the outbreak of war. This does not take into account those less than humanely killed or abandoned to die. It is estimated that 750,000 dogs and cats were put down by the end of the war.

CHAPTER ONE

'Five hundred and one, five hundred and two, five hundred and three . . .'

Joanna's whispered words hissed softly into the darkness, her lips barely moving. Even at the tender age of nine, she knew from experience that if she opened her mouth too much she would breathe in the dusty air and swallow the gritty coal dust.

The coalhouse was not underground as it was in older houses, but beneath the stairs and adjacent to the kitchen. Being locked in here was the ultimate punishment, the one she hated the most. The sound of the normal life of the house continued on the other side of the door.

It was light and warm on the other side of the door. In the coalhouse it was dirty, dark and she was very alone.

Elspeth, her stepmother, had told her it was all her own fault, that she was bad and nothing but a nuisance. 'I've got things to do without bothering with a cocky little kid like you.'

Joanna couldn't recall exactly what she'd done wrong. Elspeth always turned nasty after she'd put on her makeup, curled her hair into the latest style and put on her best costume – a tightly fitted jacket and skirt. It was a mixture of red and green, like paint splashes, though ordered not random. Last on was the strong-smelling perfume that Elspeth favoured, but which made Joanna retch. Perhaps that was the reason for her punishment, retching and wrinkling her nose. Sometimes she thought she heard a man's voice beyond the door, though it didn't sound like her father's.

She'd been locked in the coalhouse under the stairs for so long she'd counted to one thousand again and again, her eyes tightly closed, the smell of coal in her nostrils and dust clinging to her throat.

Keeping her eyes closed helped her maintain an illusion of normality, that the darkness was of her own choosing and not because her stepmother had yet again found an excuse to lock her up.

Counting helped her cope. Counting and closing her eyes had become a habit, even in school.

Her teacher had noticed she did it, but merely commented that if it helped her count then it was a good thing. But her teacher didn't know about her stepmother. Neither did her father.

Elspeth – she couldn't bear to call her 'mother', and Elspeth couldn't bear being called that except when Joanna's father was home – twisted her stepdaughter's arm up behind her back and made her swear never to tell that she was sometimes locked in the coalhouse. Joanna had cried. She used to cry a lot until Elspeth began throwing her under the stairs even for doing that.

Now she only cried at night, and even then silently so neither her stepmother nor her father would hear.

Sometimes she fancied a soft hand stroked her hair before she fell asleep, a gentle voice telling her not to cry, that she was loved and everything would be all right.

Her mother had died three years before. Her happy face became pale and drawn, and she began spending more and more time in bed. Joanna had no idea of what her mother's illness was called, only that it took her away from her when she was young and still in need of her.

Lonely, and thinking his daughter needed a mother, her father had met and married Elspeth. She'd presented a caring picture, even bringing Joanna sweets and ribbons, cooing and fussing over her as though she was the most precious thing in the world.

But once she became Mrs Ryan her behaviour changed.

Joanna's father knew nothing of how his new wife treated his daughter, or perhaps he couldn't face the fact, preferring to bury himself in work than see how difficult life had become for his only child.

He'd worked long hours as a lathe turner at the aircraft factory in the weeks before war was declared; they'd known even then there was going to be a war. When he came home from work Elspeth went out of her way to behave differently.

She made a point of making herself look good even on those days when she didn't lock Joanna in the coalhouse and she went off to meet one of her fancy men. There was nothing like making a bit of extra money and, anyway, old habits died hard.

Housework and looking after Joanna took second place to being dressed and made up as glamorously as possible even if she was only going shopping, and certainly in time for Tom Ryan coming home from work.

Sometimes she made Joanna wash and change too. At other times she didn't bother, and if Tom did frown and look concerned she put the blame on Joanna's shoulders, blaming the girl herself for being dirty and ragged.

'Out playing with the boys again! Mark my words, young lady, boys will only get you in trouble!'

Then she'd smile her best smile and laugh as though they were the happiest family in the world.

Joanna had to laugh too. There'd be hell to play if she didn't.

The darkness was total. Her stomach began to rumble which was not surprising seeing as she'd only had a piece of bread and dripping for breakfast. Elspeth had been too busy to prepare lunch. It was Saturday and she'd had a hairdressing appointment.

There were few women in their street able to spend money on hair appointments but Elspeth was a regular at the tiny shop that smelled nasty and was very hot.

Elspeth's hair never looked that different when she got back from a weekday appointment. The only time it did look different was when she went to the hairdressers on Saturdays.

On the one occasion Joanna had been brave enough to ask why that was, Elspeth had slapped her face and told her not to ask questions. She'd also demanded that she say she was sorry for criticising her hair.

'After all the trouble I take to make it look nice! Just like this house. It was never like this when I first came here. Right rubbish tip it was.'

Joanna thought it felt like home with its comfy sofa and mismatched chairs, a standard lamp throwing its yellowish glow over her father's chair and the Bakelite radio that sat on a small table with bamboo legs.

Elspeth liked ornaments. Lots of ornaments, mostly of ladies in crinoline dresses wearing poke bonnets, and gentlemen in tight trousers with curly moustaches. She also liked brass plaques and fire irons. It was Joanna's job to clean these, a job she hated. Her father had called her a little trouper when he'd come home early one Saturday and caught her doing it. She'd smiled and thrown her arms around him, only barely holding back the tears. She'd so wanted to tell him she hated cleaning the brass but that Elspeth would punish her if she didn't.

'Seven hundred and seventy-seven . . . seven hundred and seventy-eight . . .'

On hearing the sudden rattling of the key in the lock, she stopped counting, blinking as bright light fell from the narrow gap onto her face.

The gap widened. Her stepmother, hair bleached the colour of light honey, appeared in the doorway.

Unlike Joanna who had dark hair, her stepmother's dyed hair replicated that of Joanna's mother. Even her features were similar to those of her mother. Joanna knew this from the black-and-white wedding photograph she'd found in the back of the sideboard drawer one day. The one thing Elspeth couldn't change was the hard look in her eyes. She also wore too much makeup, and had yellow fingertips thanks to incessant smoking.

A cigarette dangled from the corner of her bright-red lips.

'Right,' she said, reaching in and dragging Joanna out. 'I'm out of spuds. Get down to Gingell's and get me five pounds. Here's the money . . .'

Joanna blinked. The light was still too strong for her eyes but she dared not complain. She was just so glad to be out.

'You can keep the change, but only if it's a few pennies. And spend it right away. I don't want your dad thinking that I'm a wicked stepmother – like that Goldilocks . . .'

'Snow White,' Joanna corrected her. 'It was Snow White.'

Seeing anger flare in her stepmother's eyes, Joanna knew it was time to make a quick exit. She grabbed the brown leather shopping bag set aside for vegetables. Elspeth rarely shopped for vegetables. That job she either left to Joanna or bought from Charlie Long, who came round on a cart pulled by a brown-and-white horse named Polly. Joanna was fascinated by the dependable old horse who waited patiently while Charlie served the street with vegetables. Polly had even let her stroke her muzzle and Joanna had been fascinated by its softness.

'Like velvet,' she'd said to Charlie, smiling up at him.

Charlie had said the horse didn't let everyone touch him like that. 'It means she likes ye. Animals know who they like and who they don't like.'

Joanna had felt so privileged she thought her heart would burst.

Her stepmother was always willing to puncture any sign of happiness.

'Leave the animal alone. You might get fleas,' she'd snapped, a comment which brought a surly look from Charlie.

'My horse ain't got fleas, missus, and don't you forget it. Say it again and ye won't be buying any of my potatoes, I can assure ye of that.'

Charlie always said ye, thou or thee. Joanna didn't know why and didn't care to ask. She liked the way he spoke.

It wasn't Charlie's day to come clopping up the street with Polly so the potatoes had to be bought from the shop at the bottom of the hill. Joanna didn't mind running downhill to the shop, her hair flying behind her and arms outstretched as though she could fly. Running downhill felt like freedom. She wished there was some kind of magic that would turn her arms into wings and she could fly away.

There were a few people in the vegetable shop when she got there. One or two looked at her with pity in their eyes. She was careful to look away. Fifteen minutes later and she was off back home, shoulder sagging one side as she lugged the heavy bag, a lollipop stick hanging out of her mouth. Slogging back up the hill with a heavy bag of potatoes was slower and the prospect of arriving home far from liberating.

Halfway up The Vale, as their street was named, she looked back down the hill, half expecting to hear the rattly roar of her father's motorbike coming up behind her. He'd been called up to fight in the war just a week ago, yet she still expected to see him riding up that hill between the red-brick council houses.

Ever since she was a little girl she'd always ran halfway down the hill to meet him, riding pillion for the remainder of his journey home.

Her mind went back to the time when he'd brought the kitten home for her. She could still see him now, wearing a leather flying helmet, gauntlets and goggles even when the weather was warm. His smile was always there and his voice always rang with the same invitation. 'Sweetheart! Hop on!'

On the day when he'd brought her the most wonderful gift of all, he couldn't seem to stop grinning.

'Tell you what,' he'd said, 'you hold something for me, and I'll heave those potatoes up here between me and the tank.'

Joanna stopped, making the lollipop stick twist and turn as she remembered what he wanted her to hold. She'd handed him the potatoes, which he bundled up in front of him, the weight resting on the tank.

'Here,' he'd said, reaching inside his jacket, his smile undiminished. 'Her name's Lottie.'

Joanna had gasped. 'It's a cat!'

'A kitten,' he'd corrected. 'Just a little snippet of a thing.'

The kitten had purred as she wrapped her arms around her.

'It'll be your job to look after Lottie from now on,' her father had said.

'Where did she come from?'

'Well, she belonged to Fred, the night watchman at the factory. His cat had kittens and then Old Fred died, so Lottie here has nowhere to go.'

Joanna had been dumbstruck.

'Well, can you look after her or can't you?'

Too surprised for words, she'd nodded her head vigorously.

'Come on then. Get on the pillion.'

Tucking the purring cat inside her cardigan, Joanna had scrambled on behind her father, wrapping her arms around him tightly enough not to fall off while at the same time being careful not to squash the cat.

On hearing the sound of the approaching motorcycle, Elspeth had appeared at the front door, done up to the nines, ready to play the ideal housewife. As usual her lips were painted bright red, her dress was clean and glossy curls bounced around her shoulders.

She'd waved a manicured hand, the fingernails the same bright red as her lips. 'Darling!'

Joanna always winced at the sight of those bright red nails and that waving hand, bringing to mind as it did the slaps she'd often received.

Her father had steadied the bike so Joanna could get off first.

'Look what my dad's brought me,' had said Joanna, unable to control her happiness.

'A cat. That's nice for you. Make sure you look after it.' She'd thrown a disapproving look at Joanna's father. 'Tom. You shouldn't have.'

Joanna interrupted what could have been the beginning of a quarrel. 'It's a girl. Her name's Lottie.'

From then on the cat had shared her bed and Joanna had looked after her, feeding her and bringing her in from outside when Elspeth had shut her out at night, even when it was bitterly cold. Once she was sure her father and Elspeth were gone to bed, Joanna would sneak back downstairs and let Lottie in. Together they had fallen asleep, Joanna's arm around her very best friend.

One week ago, her father stood there on the doorstep, wearing his brand-new uniform and looking in two minds to go.

'It'll be just you and me, darling,' her stepmother had said just before her father had left.

Joanna had trembled at the thought of it, though she didn't dare say a word. Her stepmother had made a show of being kind to her that day. Her father was not to know that things were not always like that – not that there were ever any bruises to show, bruises would have to be explained. (Joanna feared that would change once her father was gone.) – instead, she endured cutting words and cruel treatment. But now, there would be no shoulder for Joanna to cry on, no kind voice to soothe the loss of her mother.

Elspeth had tolerated Lottie while her father was around, but once he was called up to serve his country, her stepmother took to throwing the cat out even during the day.

'It's just a mangy cat,' she snarled at Joanna.

Joanna was brave in the defence of Lottie, her little chin firm and her eyes bright with intent. 'My dad brought her home for me.'

'Well,' snapped Elspeth, pushing her face close to Joanna's so there was only a hair's breadth between them. 'Your dad is not here. He's off fighting in the war. Animals are of less importance now than they've ever been. The whole lot of them should be put down!'

CHAPTER TWO

The first Joanna knew that something was horribly wrong was as she was walking home from school up The Vale. Her friend Susan was with her, prattling away about her day in school as though she were the only one who went there.

Joanna heard her but didn't really take it in. Going home today, the first day of school since her father had gone to war, had left her feeling very apprehensive.

All the way up the hill red-brick houses sat behind privet hedges. The houses had been built in the late twenties and early thirties for people who had been moved out from the city centre when their homes were demolished to build a chocolate factory. Some of the privet hedges framing the handkerchief sized front gardens were neatly trimmed. Others were left overgrown until the occupants were shamed into taking action by their neighbours. People took pride in their gardens as much as they did their houses. Her father had been no exception. He'd taken care of his garden.

Joanna admired the little gardens and particularly liked the smell of the privet flower, its blossom a sign that hedge trimming time was imminent, the perfume hanging in the air as the shears did their work. She wondered who would take care of theirs now her father was away fighting in the war. Elspeth hated gardening, saying it destroyed her fingernails. She resolved to do what she could, though because the shears were so heavy cutting the grass and hedges was out of the question.

Although it was September, the smell of privet flowers still hung in the air, resurrected by the crisp freshness of the first month of autumn.

Normally Joanna would be elated, but the thought of going home to a house without her father's presence made her subdued. When she got home only Elspeth would be there, and as soon as she walked in the door, she'd tell her to get her own food, that she was too busy to bother with the demands of a child.

Joanna's only solace would be that her cat would be there, greeting her with a purr the moment she entered the garden gate.

The Vale had been bustling for days with people delivering sandbags and Anderson shelters. Some people whose back gardens were bigger than average had been ordered to have a block-built shelter erected for the benefit of those who didn't have room for an Anderson or were too old to or incapacitated to install one.

Joanna forced herself to tune in to what Susan was saying.

'That Miss Hadley told me I should think more before I read aloud,' Susan said petulantly. 'I don't care for reading. I don't care if I never read another book ever again.'

Joanna laughed. She didn't understand Susan's reluctance to read. She herself loved books and Miss Hadley had commended her on how well she read.

'I like her,' said Joanna.

'I like her too,' Susan admitted grudgingly. 'It's the books I don't like.'

Joanna's attention had shifted to Mrs Goodson in number 15, a formidable woman most of the time, the sort who refused to give a ball back when it bounced into her garden. She was leaning on the garden gate, crying into her handkerchief and blowing her nose.

'What's up with her?' muttered Susan.

Joanna had never seen Mrs Goodson be anything but fierce; never, ever had she seen her crying. She couldn't help but stop and ask her what was wrong.

Mrs Goodson's glare of recognition that these were some of those badly behaved kids was short-lived, riddled by sobs. 'It's the war. The filthy war! How would I have been able to feed him?'

'Clarence? Do you mean Clarence, Mrs Goodson?'

Clarence was a Pekinese with short legs, a snub nose and sharp teeth. Just like his owner, he didn't like children, and the children didn't much like him, but old Mrs Goodson had doted on him. Joanna had even glimpsed her feeding him a square from a Fry's Five Boys chocolate bar.

Joanna glanced over the garden gate to the front step where Clarence usually lay stretched out with his eyes closed, until somebody chanced to walk past. At the sound of footsteps he was always up, racing to the gate and yapping until the intrusion on his territory had passed by. Once he was sure no threat lingered, he went back to lying on his step.

'Is he dead?' Joanna asked. She had got used to his noisy ways, his squashed face and his needle-fine teeth.

Mrs Goodson dabbed at her eyes. 'The man from the Animal Committee told me he'd be found a home in the country, a place of safety, he said. He pointed out that with a war on I wouldn't be able to feed him and also the noise of bombs falling and guns firing might send him mad.'

Joanna felt Mrs Goodson's pain. The old lady had loved her dog. 'I hope he'll be happy there,' she said.

Impatient to be going, Susan tugged at her arm. Together they continued the long trek up the hill.

'Imagine living in the country,' said Susan. 'I know our Bertie would like it. He chases cats and if the cats get moved to the country he'll chase them there.'

'I'm not letting Lottie go to the country,' Joanna said adamantly. 'She's staying with me. We'll both get bombed together!'

Her tone was defiant, but inside she was scared. And her fears were intensified when she saw the van outside John Baker's house. John, a freckle-faced lad with a thatch of auburn hair, was in the same class as her and had a scruffy old dog named

Dandy. He and his mother were standing by the gate, looking sad.

Joanna's heart almost stopped when she saw Dandy being led to the van. The van shook and echoed with barking of dogs. Joanna glimpsed a cage, saw the man reach in and open it. Dandy was loaded into the cage. From the heart of the frenzied interior she glimpsed the fear-filled eyes of caged cats and dogs, staring out at the world where they'd wandered free.

'Come on. Hurry!'

Joanna tugged at Susan's sleeve. The two girls quickened their pace and caught up with John.

'Is he going to country?' Joanna asked him.

John shook his head sadly. 'He's a bit too old to move so they say it'll be kinder to put him to sleep.'

The knot of fear Joanna had been feeling inside grew tighter.

They were running now, Susan lagging behind and calling for Joanna to slow down. But Joanna was desperate to get home to Lottie as fast as she could.

The van caught up with them. Breathless from running and fear, Joanna saw it pass, a black shape swaying from side to side. A sick feeling of dread swept over her as it stopped outside her house. Elspeth, her stepmother was at the gate, a closed cardboard box in her arms.

Lottie hated Elspeth as much as Elspeth hated her. Somehow her stepmother had lured the cat into that box and taped down the lid. Joanna ran faster.

'No!' she shouted. 'I don't want Lottie to go to the country.'

'Take no notice,' Elspeth said to the man to whom she gave the box. It wasn't lost on Joanna that her stepmother was giving the man her most winning smile. But most of all her heart was breaking. She could hear Lottie mewing pitifully from within the cardboard box.

Susan, who had always feared Elspeth Ryan, backed away. Joanna was vaguely aware of her saying she would see her in school tomorrow.

She lunged towards the van, but firm hands dragged her backwards. Sharp nails dug into her shoulders. Her stepmother jerked her back before she could attempt to snatch the box from the man's hands.

'Now now, young lady,' he said, his thin lips stretching into a lax smile. 'It's all for the best. There's a war on and it ain't fair for animals to be in the city. Your cat will be fine.'

Elspeth smiled at the man and pressed more forcefully on Joanna's shoulders. 'This gentleman represents the National Air Raid Precautions Animal Committee. It's his job to take animals to places where they'll settle away from the chance of being bombed.'

'Can I go with her?'

Her stepmother gave her what was supposed to be an affectionate shake. 'Of course not, silly.'

Joanna knew her stepmother well enough to know that she'd get more than a shaking of shoulders when they were indoors. Likely she'd be sent to bed with no chance of getting herself supper. But she didn't care. Not if Lottie wasn't there.

The doors slammed shut and the van eased away from the kerb.

Joanna sobbed as she saw the van carry on up The Vale, stopping to collect a dog here, a cat there, even a guinea pig from the Connor twins at the top of the hill.

'Inside, young lady.'

Joanna almost tripped over the front step as she was pushed into the house. Once the door was closed she was spun roughly round to face her stepmother. Elspeth's eyes were narrowed and her teeth were showing between her bright red lips, a sure sign that she was very angry.

'You will learn to do as you are told, young lady. Do you hear me?'

Elspeth shook her far more violently than she had outside the front door. Once they were in the house and without Joanna's father around, she was capable of doing anything.

'I want Lottie!' Joanna cried out.

Her shoulders were gripped even harder, and there was a pleased smirk on her stepmother's face. 'Well, you can't have her. Do you hear me? She's gone and that's that!'

'I'll tell my daddy about you,' Joanna cried, her face wet with tears, her whole body shaking from the force of her sobs.

Elspeth pursed her red lips, her eyes blazing. 'You do that, little miss, and you will rue the day you were born! Off to bed with you and no supper for a start.'

'I don't want any supper!'

Elspeth let go of her shoulders and placed her fists on her hips.

'Then go without. Now get out of this house.' She clouted Joanna's ear as she reached for the catch and opened the front door. 'I don't want to see you until bedtime. And even then I don't want to see you. Straight to bed with you. Now get out of my sight.'

'It's raining.'

'I don't care.'

One more smack across the back of her head before Joanna gladly ran from the house, tears streaming down her cheeks.

She ran unseeing down The Vale, heedless of anyone who called out to her. She ran past the rank of shops at the bottom of the hill before skidding dizzily into Gibbs Lane and onto the stony path leading to the allotments bordering the railway line.

Lottie was gone! No longer would she snuggle up to the comforting furry bundle lying beside her. No longer would she hear her cat's satisfied purr as she whispered about her day at school or confided her fear and loathing for her stepmother and her sincere hope that the war would end and her father would be home soon.

Her rain-soaked hair flying out behind her, Joanna headed downhill past the allotments with their neat rows of vegetables and tall canes supporting the last plump runner beans of the year.

The path was steep and grew more slippery but she couldn't stop running

Stones slid out from beneath her feet and she was running so quickly only the fence bordering the railway line at the bottom of the slope stopped her from tumbling out onto the track.

A train hurtled past, steam billowing from beneath its wheels and out of its stack, its brakes hissing and clanking as it slowed on the approach to Bedminster Station.

Breathless and totally despondent, Joanna squatted down between the bushes that grew there and buried her head in her hands. Lottie, with her soft black-and-white fur, had been the only way she could bear life with her stepmother.

A sudden rustling of bushes and a sprinkling of water startled her. She looked up to see the cheeky grin and tousled hair of Paul Green.

He slid down beside her, wrapping his hands around his dirty knees. 'What's up then, Jo?'

Paul was her best friend. He wasn't the tidiest of boys, being from a family of seven children – six boys and one girl. He was the youngest boy, so the clothes he wore, hand-me-downs from his older brothers, had seen better days. His sister was a year younger. It was a tight squeeze in their three-bedroom council house.

Joanna sat with her arms slouched across her knees, her head bent forward. Paul's cheeky grin and freckled face were usually enough to make her smile, but not today.

Paul attempted to cheer her up. 'Come on. It can't be that bad.'

Joanna rubbed at her eyes. Although she attempted to stifle her sobs, they kept coming. 'Lottie's gone. A man came and took her.'

Paul's grin wavered then vanished. 'Is that so?'

Joanna nodded. 'He took Mrs Goodson's dog too. And Dandy.'

Paul's eyebrows rose in surprise. 'Good riddance to Clarence, but Dandy?' He shook his head sorrowfully. 'Who would ever have thought it?'

'The man said that he was taking them to the country to be rehomed.' She turned her tear-filled eyes on Paul. 'Do you think they would let me visit her?'

Paul swallowed. Joanna wasn't to know it but when she turned her big eyes on him his insides turned to mush. She was the only girl in the street that he really liked. He'd do anything to make her smile again.

'I knows where they takes them,' he said, his accent as careless as usual. 'How about I go there and see about gettin' her back? I mean, she's yer cat, not yer stepmother's.'

Joanna managed to stifle a sob. Her eyes were wide with pleading.

'Could you really do that? Do you really know where she is?'

Paul had only an inkling of where Lottie might be but he was desperate to help. 'Leave it with me. I'm like a cat meself, you know. Can climb and go anywhere I please without anyone noticing.'

Paul's father was 'away', as neighbours whispered to each other, and not in the army. Rumour was that he was a cat burglar, so to Joanna it followed as only natural that Paul should be following in his father's footsteps and rescuing a cat.

Despite the sorrow still gripping her heart, Joanna smiled through her tears. Paul had given her hope.

CHAPTER THREE

Victoria Park Junior School had been built at the beginning of the twentieth century. It was a red-brick building surrounded by a large playground segregated into infants, junior boys and a separate school and playground for junior girls. Boys and girls were segregated once they reached eight years old.

The infants entered through the gate on Raymond Road. The entrance to the girls' junior school was on St John's Lane and the boy's entrance was further along.

Miss Sally Hadley had only been at the school for two years, but to her it was like coming home. She'd grown up around here and attended both the infants and junior schools before winning a scholarship to Colston's Girls' School. Having obtained a degree in English at Bristol University, followed by a teaching course at St Matthias Teacher Training College, she had completed a few student teacher assignments before acquiring the situation at her old school.

In some ways the school had remained the same as it had when Miss Hadley went there, and so had the children attending it. Some were very badly off and lived in the old Victorian terraces close by, some in the bay villas surrounding Victoria Park. The remainder lived in red-brick council houses built in the twenties and thirties on what had been a green hill.

It had been a long hard day in a long hard week, and although she firmly believed in keeping her worries at home separate from those in school, she didn't always succeed.

Worrying about her father was like a toothache, throbbing and untreatable. When would he be his old self again? Why couldn't he see how much she worried about him? She sighed. No matter how much she'd tried to help him, he just would not be helped. He would not adjust to life as it was now.

Her mother had died sixteen months ago. Grace Hadley had been a fine figure of a woman, very typical of the late Victorian and early Edwardian age in which she'd come to womanhood. And yet, her fine physique didn't stop her from collapsing on the street one day when she was out doing her shopping. It was instant, the doctors told Sally and her father, she would have been dead before she had even hit the ground.

She missed her mother a great deal, but had steeled herself to get on with life. Unfortunately, her father was still in deep mourning for his beloved wife. He barely spoke, ate little and sat staring into the distance, an unlit pipe in his mouth.

No matter what Sally did, she could not get him to snap out of his despair and get on with his life. He was retired and had no interests, nothing to fill his days.

Before her mother died he'd loved his garden and a piece of allotment down near the railway line. Seb and Grace Hadley had gardened together, growing the most beautiful flowers, enjoying the exercise and the effort, and working side by side.

He still went down to the shed down there. She'd assumed he would resume his gardening, looking after it as well as he had done so when her mother was still alive. Hoping it would be so, and keen to encourage him, she'd taken him some sandwiches and a Thermos flask. To her profound disappointment she'd seen nothing had been done. Where once brightly coloured blooms had grown there were now only straggly plants, their flowering long over, their leaves brown and tangled with woodbine. Other weeds besides woodbine grew in profusion, thistles and nettles thrusting and spreading between rotting flower stems. The allotment hadn't been touched for a very long time and nature was claiming it back as its own.

Yesterday, she'd gone down there because he hadn't been home for his dinner – brisket, roast potatoes, cabbage, carrots and parsnips followed by rice pudding.

'Dad, I've got dinner on the table. Are you coming now?'

'I'll be right there once I've finished this.'

He was sitting on an upturned water butt pretending to read the paper, which he was holding upside down, his mind obviously elsewhere.

Sally tried to blank out the fact that all the other allotments were already devoid of flowers and turned over for the sowing of seedlings. Potatoes, cabbage, beans, carrots and onion were in far more demand than flowers.

She was aware that a few of the other allotment holders were glaring in her father's direction.

'When you going to get rid of them flowers and grow something useful?' one of them shouted out.

'And do some weeding,' shouted another. 'One year's seed is seven years' weed! When you going to do some weeding, eh?'

'When hell freezes over,' muttered her grim-faced father without looking in the direction of the speaker.

Something else shouted was drowned out by the piercing whistle of a passing train.

Sally sighed. 'I'll wait until you've finished,' she said.

Her father grunted something inaudible then looked up at her. She noticed his eyes were red-rimmed.

'Your mother loved these flowers. I can't rip them up until she's ready to let me.'

Every week when her mother was alive he had carefully dug around each of his flowerbeds, where dahlias, moon daisies and chrysanthemums grew in ordered glory. His flowers had won prizes, and despite the urging of government to turn all available land to the growing of vegetables, he'd held out. They were his Grace's choice. She'd helped him plant them and he saw them as the last link with her and with the happy times they'd had together.

A lump in Sally's throat drowned any chance of retorting. She hurried away. If her mother had still been alive she would have insisted that they dug up the ground to plant vegetables. But her father refused to move on, at least for now. All Sally could do was hope and pray that he'd return to his old self before very long, though she had no way of knowing when that would be.

And she had someone else to be worried about now. Joanna Ryan loved reading and always put her hand up to be the next to read out loud. Today she did not and had seemed quite distracted all day.

Sally had harboured misgivings, but every child could have an off day. What happened next confirmed that something was indeed very wrong.

'Please, miss.' Susan Crawford, a pink-cheeked girl with dark hair, looked at pointedly at Joanna sitting beside her. 'Jo's crying. The man in the black van came and took her cat.'

The four o'clock bell rang announcing that school was at an end for the day.

Sally dismissed the rest of the class but before Joanna could leave, she walked between the desks and laid her hand on Joanna's shoulder.

'Stay a moment, Joanna. I want to talk to you.

The sound of slamming desk lids was followed by that of scrabbling feet and excited chatter as the children fled the classroom and headed home.

Joanna had remained sitting at her desk, her head in her hands. Even though her face was half hidden, Sally could see it was wet with tears.

Joanna's friend Susan lingered, shifting from one foot to the other in her leather sandals and baggy socks, settled in wrinkles around her ankles. Sally told her to go outside and wait for her friend there.

Silence reigned in the big square room, the smell of ink and chalk hanging in the air. The classroom was full of light. One wall was occupied by a series of tall windows. Dominating the rear wall was a map of the world, upon which the countries belonging to the British Empire were shaded in red: Canada, Australia, New Zealand, India, Africa and many more. The map was surrounded by pictures painted by the children and diagrams of fractions, shapes and the whole sequence of times tables, all the way from two to the twelve times table. A huge radiator occupied the wall nearest the door, and the blackboard the other wall behind Sally's desk.

Sally squeezed herself into the space beside Joanna, vaguely aware that this might have been her desk when she was a pupil here.

'Why are you crying, Joanna?' She didn't repeat what Susan had told her but preferred to hear it from Joanna herself.

Joanna kept her face hidden. She liked Miss Hadley a lot but even her soft words failed to heal the hurt in her heart.

Sally had always considered Joanna a smart girl and on the whole well cared for, but that was before her mother had died and her father remarried.

Just of late her hair, her clothes and the spark she'd seen in her eyes seemed to have faded. She'd also noticed she was usually the last to leave the classroom, and the last to leave the playground at four o'clock when the children swarmed like bees towards the school gate and home.

'That's a girl who doesn't want to go home,' she'd once remarked to Miss Burton, the headmistress.

Miss Burton was a solid figure with a gentle face framed by cotton fine grey hair. A misty look came to her eyes. 'There are many children with a less than ideal home, Miss Hadley,' she said. 'I've learned over the years that it's best to keep focused on one's vocation. It's difficult not to get emotionally involved, but one has to try.'

Sally stroked the girl's hair back from her eyes, aware that her attention was above and beyond the call of her profession.

'Is it really so bad?' she asked gently.

Joanna came out from behind her hands, sniffed and nodded.

Sally felt her heart lurch at the look on the little girl's face. Joanna had seemed markedly different when she returned to school on Monday. Perhaps it was time to have a talk with her parents, even though Miss Burton had warned against that too.

'I'm warning you. They won't thank you for it.'

Sally pushed Miss Burton's warning to the back of her mind.

'Tell you what,' she said, placing an arm around Joanna's shoulders. 'How about I walk home with you and you tell me exactly what the matter is.'

Joanna nodded. Her foremost hope was that Miss Hadley could persuade her stepmother to get Lottie back. If she could do that she didn't care about anything else.

'Did you bring a coat today?'

Joanna shook her head. The cardigan she was wearing had holes in the elbows and was hand knitted from thin wool. Her dress was of cotton and faded from many washes. Sally wondered whether she actually owned a coat.

'Never mind.' Sally went to her desk to pack the last of the children's exercise books into her attaché case. She buttoned her jacket, part of a teal-coloured costume that was her daily uniform. 'The rain's stopped now. Come on. Let's go.'

She held out her hand. The little girl took it pensively, her big blue eyes still moist but her sobs less than they were.

Together the two of them crossed the empty playground. Joanna looked towards the school gate to see if Susan had waited for her. If she'd been alone she would have been disappointed to see that Susan had not waited. Miss Hadley's presence helped her cope with that too.

'Feeling better now?'

Joanna shook her head.

'Has someone been nasty to you?'

Joanna bit her bottom lip. Should she tell her about her stepmother?

Sally had enough experience to sense that Joanna was the victim of neglect at home. There were no signs of bruising on

24

the child's arms and legs, but she didn't doubt that Joanna was victim to some form of cruelty. It did occur to her to ask Susan, but children were often loath to tell tales on their classmates. She tried again, concentrating on school rather than home.

'Joanna, you must tell me if anyone in school has been nasty to you. I can make it stop.'

Joanna shook her head avidly. 'No. It's Lottie. They took her away.'

Sally looked down at the bowed head. They were halfway up The Vale and Joanna had only just begun to unload her unhappiness.

'Who's Lottie?' she asked gently, even though Susan had told her it was a cat. In these situations it was always best to let the child concerned tell what was the matter in their own words.

'My cat. They took her away because of the war. Elspeth said they had to.'

Sally gritted her teeth. Official notices had been appearing in newspapers and on the wireless besides falling through every letterbox in the country. The directive was explicit: it was best to put your pets down rather than have them starve to death or be upset by bombs. They even offered a 'humane' gun that fired a bolt into the brain. Goodness knows what other damage these guns could do if they fell into the wrong hands.

Sally swallowed hard as she thought about her next move. She couldn't possibly upset Joanna by telling her the truth that household pets were being put down in their thousands. Others were being abandoned and left to die in out-of-the-way places.

'I hear they're being found places in the country away from cities,' said Sally. It was just one of the euphemisms for being put to death, the fate that would befall most of them.

Joanna looked up, a desperate look in her eyes that made Sally's chest tighten. 'Will there be other cats in the country?'

'Lots. She'll have lots of friends there.'

Sally almost choked on the lie but told herself it was necessary. It was the only answer she could give without exposing Joanna to the absolute truth: Lottie was probably already dead. And Joanna was upset enough as it was.

Joanna got out her key at the garden gate.

Without asking, Sally already knew this meant nobody was at home – or at least that was what she thought.

'Goodbye, miss.'

'I'll come to the door with you.'

A scared look came to Joanna's eyes. 'No. You'd better not, miss.'

'Just to the door. I'm not going to come in,' Sally added brightly.

She remained on the doorstep while Joanna stepped into the tiny hallway. A set of stairs arose on the right-hand side. Numerous coats and hats hung in a space behind the door at the bottom of the stairs.

Looking both cowed and embarrassed, Joanna pushed open the living room door. From where she stood, Sally saw a blonde-haired blowsy woman sitting in an armchair. Red fingernails held a magazine. Judging by the glossy paper it was an old issue. Since the outbreak of war both the quality of paper and size of publications had decreased phenomenally.

'About bloody time. Get and put the kettle on. I could do with a cup of tea, you lazy little cow!'

On seeing Sally she sat bolt upright.

'Who the bloody hell are you?' Her tone was nasal, raspy from tobacco smoke.

'Elspeth, it's my teacher. Miss Hadley.'

For a moment the woman in the chair seemed to freeze. Once she'd recovered she threw an accusing look at Joanna before turning her attention to the slim young woman standing on the doorstep.

'Oh,' she said, pasting on a deceitful smile. 'If I'd known we were having an important visitor I would have laid on cocktails and put on me best frock.'

Smoothing her dress and fluffing up her hair she came to the door knocking Joanna aside with her hip in the process.

'What do you want?' Her manner was less than polite.

Miss Burton had advised Sally to always adopt a professional veneer – even a superior one – when dealing with some parents.

'It's the only way to deal with latent aggression. Show weakness and you won't stand a chance.'

With Miss Burton's advice ringing in her ears, Sally held her ground. 'Are you Joanna's mother?'

'Her stepmother.'

'Is her father here?'

'No. Thanks to that bloke Hitler he's gone off to serve his country. He needn't have gone. He was in a reserved occupation up at the aircraft factory, but wanted to go off and do his bit. Stupid sod. He left me with the kid.'

It crossed Sally's mind that any sane man would prefer to leave a woman like Elspeth and go off to fight. The downside was that Joanna was also left behind. Did her father know how his daughter was being treated? Obviously not, she decided.

'Joanna was very upset in school today. In fact, she hasn't been her usual bright self for a while.'

Elspeth folded her arms over her large breasts. The neckline of her dress was cut very low and showed her ample cleavage.

'So what? Her dad's gone to war. She's upset.'

Sally took a deep breath. 'It's not only that, Mrs Ryan. It's her clothes and general appearance. She's a lot thinner than she used to be.' She said all this very quietly but firmly and only once she'd ensured that Joanna was out of earshot. The poor child had enough to cope with by the looks of her stepmother.

Elspeth Ryan stiffened. 'Look. I've only got so much to keep her on. Army pay.'

'You don't work yourself?'

'Certainly not. If a man can't keep his wife and family then there's no point in being married. Not in my book!'

Sally pointedly cast her gaze over the peroxide-blonde hair, the red fingernail polish, the dress with its scattered flowers and lace borders. The state of the house was much the same as Joanna: dirty and neglected. Elspeth shone in the midst of it like the brassy piece she was.

Sally decided the time was right for her to lay down the law, to be professional and non-emotional.

'If you feel you can't keep her, then I can make a recommendation for her to be evacuated.'

Elspeth shrugged. 'Do what you like.'

'Fine. Then you won't mind if I get in touch with her father and explain to him that Joanna is being removed from a home where I suspect neglect. Only you can say what his response might be to that!'

'You cow!'

Recognising she was in the ascendant on this, Sally carried on. 'Of course, sending Joanna away will mean a cut in the your husband's army pay, which I'm sure will decrease the allowance that he sends to you . . .'

Elspeth's expression turned panic-stricken.

'You wouldn't dare!'

'Oh yes I would! And if I don't see an improvement in that child's health and general well-being, that is exactly what I will do. First things first: does she have a winter coat?'

Mrs Ryan's features stiffened before she answered, less stridently this time. 'She did, but grew out of it. I can't keep up with her.'

'You should buy her one. See that you do.'

She could have offered to find a coat among parents' donations of items of clothing their own children had grown out of, it was sheer cussedness that she did not.

Elspeth's nostrils flared and red pricks of colour dotted each cheek. She prided herself on being able to stand up to authority, but this young woman with her flawless complexion and shoulder-length auburn hair had boxed her into a corner. Tom had always been good where money was concerned. Half the time he'd hardly been left enough for petrol in his motorbike. The sooner she got rid of this woman the better. With that end in mind she made an effort to look as though she were eating humble pie. 'All right. I'll see she gets a new coat and stuff. Is that all?'

'No. It's not.' Sally glanced down the hall to see that Joanna was busying herself in the kitchen. She lowered her voice anyway. 'She was crying today because her cat was taken away. I know it's a very hard time for everyone, but pets being destroyed is enough to make anyone upset. I've told her the cat has gone to stay in the country until the war is over. For now she seems to believe that. It might be a good idea if you reassured her too.'

Elspeth chewed the inside of her cheek as she looked over her shoulder, aware that Joanna had taken the opportunity to make herself a jam sandwich. She was saving that last bit of jam for herself and had intended giving Joanna dripping tonight. Not that there was much left of that either.

Mouth full of jam sandwich, Joanna returned, gazing in adoration at Miss Hadley, the only person she'd ever seen face up to her stepmother.

Elspeth pasted on a false smile. 'There's biscuits in the tin if you want some. Help yourself, love.'

Joanna winced at the touch of her stepmother's hand as though expecting a slap rather than a pat.

Sally was shocked. She knew the look of a frightened child when she saw it. She had the measure of Elspeth Ryan, who was keeping Joanna short of food while making sure that she herself had all the comforts she could get. But there was nothing she could do and she was loath to get the local children's officer involved, at least for the time being. Taking a child into care was never an easy decision.

'Enjoy your biscuits, Joanna. I'll see you in school tomorrow.'

She refrained from reassuring her that her cat was probably very happy wherever she'd been taken. It wouldn't be true, and it might help Joanna get over it more quickly if the cat wasn't mentioned.

When she got home her father was sitting in his chair staring at the fire. He hadn't done anything about preparing dinner. So far she'd been patient, but she was tired and her patience was running out.

'I thought you might have put the potatoes on,' she said as she unbuttoned her coat, trying not to sound as though she were nagging.

'I'm not that hungry.'

'Oh, Dad.' She draped her arms around his shoulders, her cheek resting against his. 'You've got to eat something. Bangers and mash. That's what we've got tonight.'

'I told you: I'm not hungry.'

Her tone became firmer. 'Well, perhaps you could work up an appetite by digging up your dahlias and planting vegetables? That's one sure way of taking care of us both.'

His face showed a glimmer of interest, but it was short-lived. Sally sighed. He needed somebody or something else to fill his life, but no matter what she suggested he showed no interest.

'You could do with company of your own age,' she said to him.

He looked at her askance. 'I'll have no other woman! Me and your mother were like two sides of a coin. That's the way a good marriage should be!'

'I wasn't suggesting you get married again. I was suggesting you get out a bit more. There's plenty of your own age down at the allotment. And let's face it, the allotment does look a bit bedraggled at present. The Ministry of Food are urging everyone to dig for victory. Vegetables, not flowers.'

Perhaps this war might have a positive side if it helped her father rebuild his life, making him feel useful, if still a bit lonely.

The only problem was persuading him to plant vegetables instead of flowers. She told herself that it was just a case of being patient. He was bound to come round in time.

He sighed. 'I might go down to the allotment tomorrow.'

'I think you should.'

He grunted something inaudible.

She kissed his cheek before starting on dinner. 'Can't wait for you to tell me what you plant.'

Leaving him sitting there, she walked stiff shouldered into the kitchen, worrying and hoping for him to improve. In the meantime she had an evening meal to prepare.

People were planting vegetables in every scrap of earth available but it would be some time yet before they had the benefit of home grown vegetables – if ever. It all depended on when her father stopped grieving and started living again.

CHAPTER FOUR

Elspeth Ryan set a slice of streaky bacon and a piece of toast on the table in front of her stepdaughter.

Wide eyed with surprise, Joanna wondered if this was some kind of trick. Would it be snatched away from her the moment she tucked into it.

'Well, get on with it! And don't you run telling tales to that teacher that I don't feed and clothe you proper.' Elspeth used the butter knife for emphasis, pointing it directly into Joanna's face.

Joanna didn't wait to be threatened a second time. It was rare she had anything to eat except bread and dripping. If it hadn't been for Mrs Allen next door bringing in the odd piece of pie or pot of stew, she'd have starved by now.

Elspeth watched as she ate, her jaw clenched. It was against her character to be kind to the girl. Joanna was the whipping boy that she used to be, growing up with a bullying stepfather until she'd ran away from home. Being cruel had become second nature.

Unlike her stepfather, Elspeth had a conniving mind. From the moment she'd left home she'd put herself first. Even Tom had been a means to an end, giving her the home she'd never had and the money to go with it. The last thing she wanted was for her stepdaughter to be taken into care because that meant losing the money Joanna's father would be sending via the army paymaster. And she had appearances to keep up.

The neighbours called Elspeth Lady Muck, because she never went out unless she was dressed to kill. Plus she had her own teeth and wore earrings. Most of the other women in The Vale,

Susan's mother included, wore curlers in their hair all day long and big flowery aprons that crossed over their ample chests. A lot of them had bad teeth, never wore makeup and their standard jewellery was a wedding ring, which for some of them was pawned on Monday and redeemed on Friday. That was before the war began and they started to get regular army pay – or at least a good portion of it. But they were proud to be able to put dinner on the table every night, and keep their houses clean, unlike Elspeth, who although she dressed to the nines, was known for being a slovenly housekeeper. Even when she did put out a line of washing, it never looked that clean.

Later that night, not trusting her stepmother's good humour to last, Joanna kept her head down, carrying out her household chores as usual.

It was another big surprise when Elspeth bought her a winter coat – not a brand-new one, but at least it fitted though it came with a warning. 'And don't get it dirty or torn. Money don't grow on trees you know.'

Joanna thanked her. Elspeth threw across a bundle of clothes. 'There's a few other bits and pieces.'

Judging by the smell of mothballs the source of the clothes was probably the Salvation Army. They certainly weren't new.

'I'll wash them,' she said, wrinkling her nose.

It was the wrong thing to do and say. She realised that when she saw the sudden stiffening of her stepmother's face. 'You ungrateful little cow!'

Fearing a slap Joanna stepped swiftly back. 'I can't wear smelly things. My schoolfriends will make fun and Miss Hadley might notice.'

That was definitely the right thing to say. Elspeth's expression changed immediately. 'Well, that's me. No sense of smell. You wash them then. Do I get a hug?'

Joanna hid her surprise and did as she was instructed. Elspeth hadn't asked her for a hug since her father went away. Even

33

then it was only for show so he wouldn't suspect the woman she really was.

Elspeth sat on the opposite side of the table, smoking as she watched Joanna eat a portion of liver and onions with potatoes.

'Hope you're enjoying that. There wasn't enough for me. Still, I've got to watch my figure.'

'Did Mrs Allen cook it?'

Elspeth's face dropped, her real character bursting through. 'What if she did? I still gave it to you didn't I? I didn't eat any for myself!'

'Thank you.' Sensing her stepmother was returning to type Joanna ate quickly glad that tonight she would have a full belly for a change.

For a moment Elspeth put on the persona she most certainly was not, even reassuring her stepdaughter about Lottie the cat. 'Probably having a whale of a time. All that country air.'

Joanna kept her eyes lowered and her head down.

'Now off to bed.'

'It's only—'

She'd been about to point out that it was only seven o'clock and she wasn't usually in bed until eight.

Her stepmother grabbed the dirty plate. 'Don't contradict me!'

'But what about the dishes?'

'I'll do those!'

Joanna couldn't believe it. Her stepmother didn't usually do the dishes, though she had done them a few times in the last few days.

Elspeth thrust a small glass of dark liquid under her nose. 'Drink this. It'll help you sleep.'

Joanna eyed the glass. The liquid had a strong smell. She didn't want to drink it but didn't dare say no.

'Drink it,' Elspeth ordered, more determined this time.

Joanna did as she was told, pulling her face as the dark red liquid slid over her tongue.

'Sherry,' said Elspeth in a cheery voice and drank some herself. 'See? I'm not trying to poison you.'

The liquid did indeed help her fall asleep. It also made her head throb and she had strange dreams. At one point she thought she heard a man's voice in the living room downstairs, the sound of him laughing and her stepmother joining in.

For one brief moment her spirits soared. *It must be Daddy!* She thought in her half-asleep state. *He's come home. He's home!*

The glass of sherry did its work. She tried to wake up but her eyelids and her head refused to obey. She fell back into a heavy sleep and didn't wake again until the morning.

The next morning dawned chilly and grey. Raindrops drummed on the windowpanes driven by a westerly wind. Condensation misted the windows on the inside and the living room smelled strongly of beer and cigarettes. Dirty plates, dirty glasses and empty beer bottles shared the table with an overflowing ashtray. Joanna had a headache and a strange metallic taste in her mouth.

There was no sign of Elspeth, just of the mess she'd left from the night before. It was Joanna's job to clear it up. There was so much to do before going to school.

Her stomach rumbled. The meal the night before had been much enjoyed but she needed something for breakfast. But much as she needed to eat, first priority was to light the fire. Before the war, that had been her father's job but became hers immediately after her father had been called up. If she didn't do it then it wouldn't get done and although Elspeth had not lost her temper so much of late, Joanna suspected her good humour was only temporary.

'Everyone has to do their bit,' her stepmother constantly barked.

In the week after war had been declared lots of government leaflets had dropped through the letterbox, mostly about air-raid precautions, rationing and where to collect your gas mask. Joanna's stepmother had kept those she'd deemed most important and placed the rest in the orange box where she also kept kindling for lighting the fire.

'Only fit for lighting the fire with,' she'd declared regarding the pamphlets. 'Waste not, want not.'

Joanna staggered in with the orange box. First she screwed up the newspaper and tore up bits of leaflets. She'd almost finished piling on the bits of kindling, when the two halves of one particular leaflet caught her eye. Her breath caught in her throat as she began to read.

This country is at war and as an island the enemy will attempt to blockade our food supplies. Rationing will be introduced and humans must take precedence over pets. There will not be enough food for pets, much loved as they may be. There is the strong possibility that loud explosions will affect their nerves. Also when homes are bombed there is the likelihood of stray dogs forming packs and becoming a danger. It is deemed kinder therefore that both dogs and cats are put to sleep rather than suffer unnecessarily . . .

A number of organisations were listed on the last page. One of them was the one who had taken Lottie.

Her heart felt as though a set of icy fingers had gripped her heart. The man had lied. Her stepmother had lied. Lottie hadn't been rehomed in the country. She'd been put to sleep. Killed.

Engrossed in reading the leaflet, she didn't realise her stepmother was up and about until she suddenly appeared at the door. 'Ain't you got that fire lit yet? I'm bloody perishing.'

Her stepmother's face was blotchy and smeared with yesterday's makeup. She was still wearing her dressing gown. Even this early in the morning a cigarette dangled from the corner of her mouth and it was hard to tell which smelled worse, her or the overflowing ashtray.

Joanna's eyes blazed with anger. Outright despair gave her courage. 'Lottie's dead! You lied to me. That man lied to me.

It says so in this leaflet!' She waved the leaflet, her expression defiant though she trembled inside.

Elspeth Ryan jolted awake. If there was one thing guaranteed to make her angry it was Joanna standing up to her. She'd married the child's father for the house and for security, not to pander to a nine-year-old brat.

Joanna immediately regretted her outburst. She saw her stepmother's face change from slovenly sleepiness to grim-faced anger and knew instantly that the effect of Miss Hadley's visit was wearing off. Elspeth was sliding back into her true character.

'You and that bloody cat!' In a flash of pink quilted dressing gown she was across the room and standing over her. A yellow-stained finger stabbed at Joanna's cheek. 'Don't you cheek me, my girl!'

Joanna winced. Her stepmother had long scarlet fingernails that she spent hours keeping trim and painting and their sharp points left indents in her cheek. But despite her fear and the sharp pain caused by the fingernails, Joanna remained defiant. 'You lied! Lottie's dead!'

Her stepmother laughed, a great hooting laugh from deep in her throat. Smoke exhaled out of her mouth and down her nostrils. Her face came close, haggard with shadows and the smell of old face powder. 'So what! It was just a bloody cat. There's a war on. Cats are not important.'

'Lottie was important to me.' A lone tear rolled down Joanna's face. 'She was to me,' she repeated, her voice trembling with emotion.

Tears and sad words broke no ice with her stepmother. She raised one plucked eyebrow and her small red mouth pursed sourly. 'Right! That's it! Get that fire lit then get off to school.'

'I haven't had any breakfast.'

Her stepmother's face loomed close again. Joanna balked at the sickening smell of her, stale sweat and cheap perfume.

'Then let that be the first lesson of the day. This is how it would be if the cat had stayed here. It would have to be fed.

You're the one who'd have to go without. Only food enough for one of you so today would have been the cat's turn, not yours. Now get out of my sight. Now!' She said it gloatingly not hiding the fact that she enjoyed being a bully, or the fact that she resented that Joanna had ever been born. 'I want you to be a mother to my girl,' Tom had said to her. She'd smiled and accepted while choking back the suggestion he should have hired a nursemaid!

She gave Joanna a rough shove that almost sent her into the kindling box and went out into the kitchen. Joanna heard the sound of the kettle being filled and the teapot being emptied.

By the time flames were licking around the coals, Joanna's stomach was rumbling loudly. If her stepmother hadn't been in the kitchen she would have found something to eat, even if it was only a crust of bread. But Elspeth Ryan was still there, pouring herself a second cup of tea and eating a bacon sandwich, the smell of which filled Joanna's nostrils and almost made her wish she'd kept her mouth shut.

The fire roaring in the grate, she cleared the table and took everything to the kitchen sink. There was just enough hot water left in the kettle for the washing up.

'And don't hang about.'

Her stepmother left her while she went to the lavatory.

Joanna waited a moment until she heard the bolt slide across on the downstairs bathroom. Once she was certain she had a few minutes, she wiped her hands, took a bite out of her stepmother's bacon sandwich, then found a crust of bread which she wiped around the frying pan, the fat transferring to the bread.

There was no time to eat it there and then so she swiftly wrapped it in a piece of newspaper and stuffed it into the pocket of her new winter coat. It might make a mess but she didn't care.

On arrival at school she lingered at the gate to the junior boys' school waiting to catch a glimpse of Paul.

He was not in the playground, though that was not unusual. He was always late for school.

Suddenly she heard his cheery voice.

'You looking for me?'

The bell rang, summoning them to get into orderly lines before entering the school. The boys in the playground ran in all directions before finding their places. Joanna knew that the girls would be doing the same and if she didn't hurry she would be late and perhaps get detention.

She hurriedly told Paul about the leaflet she'd found. His cheery face turned solemn. 'I know. I told you I'd make enquiries and I 'ave. They've been round the whole street.' He began counting on his fingers the dogs who'd been taken. 'Clarence, Dandy, Poppy, Bonzo . . . and that's only the dogs. Cats have gone too. They didn't take my rabbits, but then my mum said they weren't pets. They were food.'

Joanna gulped and hung her head. She couldn't imagine eating Twinkle and Silver, Paul's pet rabbits. She imagined bits of their flesh in a stew and couldn't believe Paul would eat them either.

Despite the fact that the school bell was sounding for a second time, the last one before it meant a black mark in the register, Paul leaned back against the red-brick wall of the school and sighed. 'People are doing really stupid things. Just cos the government says pets are going to be a nuisance, they're believin' every word. Nobody wants to starve and some people can't be bothered to get them collected or take them to the collection places. There's so many dogs and cats that some people are dumping them anywhere or killing them themselves. They can even buy a special gun to do it.' He shook his head, a deep frown furrowing his boyish brow. 'I couldn't do that. Not to an animal. Could shoot a Nazi though – if they gave me the chance.'

Joanna fixed her eyes on Paul's knees. Today, Monday, they were clean but would get grubbier during the week. Sunday night was bath night for his whole family but nobody seemed to bother much with washing during the week, except for face and hands.

Despite the piece of bread she'd dipped into the fat and the stolen bite of sandwich, her stomach rumbled and Paul heard it.

'Here. Have a humbug.'

Paul's grandmother in Railway Terrace kept him stocked up with sweets.

She took the sweet gratefully, rolling the sweet over her tongue and doing her best to keep sucking and not crunching it. It would last longer that way.

The bell jangled for the third time.

Paul dashed off into the boys' playground while Joanna ran swiftly along the road to the girls' gate, unable to resist crunching the sweet before she got there. Her stomach rumbled again. The evening meal seemed a long way away.

Susan was already standing in line. They'd missed each other this morning because Joanna had left a bit later thanks to having to wash up. Susan's mother did everything like that and Susan hated being late for school.

'In here,' Susan hissed having saved a place for her friend. As usual Susan started chatting about anything and everything. 'Last night I dreamed of custard and jam sponges piled high with cream. It was just like the Mad Hatter's tea party in *Alice in Wonderland* though I was the only one sitting at the table and all the food was for me . . .'

Susan prattled on and Joanna listened. Food figured in her own dreams, but so did Lottie. She would never forget her. War had turned both her world and that of animals into a nightmare and she was helpless to do anything about it.

That morning something astounding happened. The smell of boiled potatoes and other food began circulating at around ten o'clock. The whole school was summoned to assembly to be addressed by their headmistress. Judging by the trampling of feet in the playground next door, Junior School boys were being assembled too.

The light from the school windows reflected on Miss Burton's glasses as she gazed out over her pupils, her hands clasped in front of her, the light making her fluffy hair shine like a halo around her head.

'Girls. As of today all of you will be entitled to a midday meal. This action has been instigated by the Ministry of Food in the event of your mothers being called up to do war work. I'm sure you'll agree it will be too hard for them to run a home as well as working a factory or keeping the railways and buses running.' She glanced swiftly at the piece of paper she held in her hand. 'Today's menu consists of liver and onions with cabbage and potatoes followed by semolina pudding.'

A huge gasp of approval ran throughout the assembly. One or two girls muttered how much they hated liver and onions and semolina was not favoured by everyone.

Joanna, so hungry she would have eaten the whole lot on one plate, promptly fainted.

When she came to she was sitting on a chair outside in the playground. Miss Hadley was holding her hand. Joanna blinked at the cool touch of Miss Hadley's palm.

Her teacher smiled. 'How are you feeling now, Joanna?'

Her smile was so sweet she looked just like the angel on the Sunday school wall. Her hair was a lovely soft reddish colour. Her eyes were blue and beautiful, and she smelled fresh and wholesome. Yes, she was wearing makeup and perhaps a smidgeon of scent, but anyone could tell it had been put on fresh that morning. Elspeth could never be bothered to wash the night before so ended up with patchy skin and a stale smell in the morning.

'I think I dreamed we were going to have dinner here in school. Was it a dream, miss?'

Sally Hadley smiled. 'No, Joanna, it was not. School dinners will be provided for all, although it's really supposed to be restricted to those whose mothers are already out at work. However, Miss Burton has decided, and I agree with her, that many more women will be called to work shortly so all children who want it can have school dinners. Miss Burton believes in being prepared.'

Sally glanced down at her wristwatch aware that Miss Burton was overseeing her class while she dealt with Joanna. Much as she wanted to help the little girl, she had to get back.

'You fainted. Are you feeling better now?'

Joanna nodded.

Sally paused before asking the next question, already guessing what the answer would be. 'Did you have any breakfast this morning?'

Again Joanna nodded.

'What did you have?'

'A piece of bread. And some bacon fat.' She was too embarrassed to tell her about the bite of bacon sandwich, and she supposed the humbug Paul had given her didn't count.

Sally tried to picture the meagre repast but couldn't. 'So you will have room for lunch?'

A soft smile lit Joanna's pale face. 'I don't mind liver and onions, miss. Or semolina.'

'Does your mother make you them too?'

Later, Sally would describe Joanna's look to her father as old beyond her years.

'She's my stepmother. She mostly makes bread and dripping.'

Sally recalled the blowsy blonde, her perfume fighting a losing battle with her body odour.

'Never mind.' Sally smiled in an effort to gloss over her anger and her pity. 'At least you can look forward to a decent meal every day you're at school. Now. Shall we go back to the classroom? It's only an hour until dinnertime.'

Joanna slid off her chair. Fearing the little girl might still be a bit wobbly Sally took her hand. The child would have at least one decent meal each weekday. Weekends and school holidays were a different matter, but hopefully Joanna's circumstances might have improved by the time the long summer holiday came around next year. Perhaps her father might come home on leave and see what was going on, or a relative perhaps.

'Do you have any aunts and uncles?'

'No, miss.'

The answer was as she had feared. In her heart of hearts Sally couldn't see much changing in Joanna's circumstances, just as she couldn't see anything changing in her own father's disposition. All she could do was hope that both of them would fare better in future.

CHAPTER FIVE

The six puppies were ripped away from their mother's teats and went into the sack first. The seventh had been exploring the outer reaches of the litter box and, being the strongest of the litter, had climbed over the edge.

On hearing his mother's yelps of alarm his little heart was filled with fear. He'd never been afraid before and his mother had never sounded so distraught.

The other sounds he heard were equally as frightening: loud human voices and the tread of heavy feet, so heavy the floorboards beneath him shook and made his legs wobble. Not liking all this noise, he scooted behind a pile of sacks in the corner of the shed.

The vibration from heavy footsteps advanced towards him. A voice growled with impatience.

'Come 'ere you little whippersnapper! You ain't gettin' away from me.'

A hand as rough as the voice snatched him up by the scruff of the neck. He struggled and yapped as he was shoved into the sack with his siblings. He heard his mother whining plaintively, then a yelp, the crack of something very loud, and then nothing.

The inside of the sack was dark and smelled of something rotten and the puppies squealed with fear.

Puppy number seven had landed on top of his brothers and sisters and felt the bodies of his siblings wriggling around beneath him. His heart raced but rather than expending energy as his brothers and sisters were doing, some ancient instinct inherited from wild ancestors came into play. Instead of wasting energy on struggling, that instinct told him to listen, to sniff, and to wait and see what would happen next.

His nose, so much more sensitive than a human's, twitched as above him a draught of fresh air came through a hole in the sack.

Bracing his back legs against his siblings brought whines of protest, but his instinct to escape and survive was strong.

The puppies tumbled about as the man carrying the sack gave it a violent shake. An angry human voice warned them to shut their racket.

The sack bounced roughly against the man's back and the puppies continued to tumble about as they were carried to their fate.

The poor little creatures knew nothing about who this man was or where they were going. They only knew they had been dragged away from their mother.

If they had been able to understand, they would know that the man was not their mother's owner but a man employed to get rid of them all. The real owners did not have the heart for it, but this man had told them he would dispose of them painlessly. He had lied.

The puppies kept up their whining and howling, squirming against each other as they fought for air.

The man muttered. 'Shut yer bleedin' noise.'

The puppies neither heard nor understood. Terrified for their young lives, they cried and whined their hearts out.

There was a shifting of breeze as the sack was swung through the air. The puppies at the bottom of the sack screamed as they impacted with something hard. The man, nervous their yelping would be heard before he finished what he had to do, swung them against a brick wall.

The yelping became less as some of them were already dead or too injured to survive. The puppy at the top of the heap and closest to the man's hand had escaped the worst of the impact. The breath was knocked out of his little body, though only for a moment. The same instinct as before kicked in. Keep small. Keep quiet. Keep immobile. But he was scared. Very scared.

Preferring not to be seen, the man waited until it was dark before picking the spot where he would throw the sack into the swirling water. It wasn't a wide stream but deep enough to drown the puppies in the sack. Hopefully the flow would suck the puppies down before the sack got caught in eddies and floated downstream.

Once he was sure, he swung the sack around his head and let it go. The splash of it hitting the water was enough confirmation that he'd done his job.

'And now for a pint,' he said cheerfully, fingering the ten-bob note in his pocket as he walked off whistling a merry little tune.

He failed to see that the sack had jammed in deep water, between stepping stones the kids had placed in order to ford the stream more easily. The top third of the sack had flopped onto one of the stones. He was long gone by the time those puppies still clinging on to life at the bottom of the sack had drowned. Only one remained alive.

That lone survivor whimpered. He was wet, frightened and alone. He knew from the silence that his siblings were dead.

The hole in the sack became wider, ripped open by a sharp edge on the rock. He poked his nose out, sniffing the fresh air, smelling water, plants and the tangy whiff of creatures he did not recognise.

A sly and curious rat slid into the water close by. A duck quacked just once before resettling for the night.

The hole was big enough for the puppy to poke his nose through. His brothers and sisters were dead, but his survival instinct was strong and he was an intelligent little chap. He would not join them.

Outside the rat circled, waiting for the opportunity to investigate further, but he held back. His keen sense detected movement plus the unmistakeable scent of man, always a threat to the likes of him.

The puppy barked sharply. The rat retreated. Now was not the time. When the scent of man diminished, along with what little life was left in the sack, he would come back, keen to feed on whatever was left.

Bracing his little legs against the dead bodies of his brothers and sisters, the puppy shoved his nose further into the hole.

The ripped sacking cut into his muzzle. Much as he tried to push his way through it just wasn't wide enough.

Tired and wet, he pulled his muzzle back and then began chewing, his sharp little teeth ripping at the sacking, turning it from a small hole into a bigger one.

His teeth were sharp and he went on chewing for as long as he could until he became too fatigued to continue, then he rested and would begin again.

The hessian sack was strong, but although he only had milk teeth, he chewed his way through driven by fear and the will to live. Scrabbling with his front paws and pushing with his rear legs, he steadily hauled half of his body out of the sack.

All around him was darkness and the strange sounds of night creatures. He sniffed again and barked at something he saw in the water. Whatever it was moved away at the sound of his bark.

Scared and tired he lay spent on the rock, unable to chew any more. He was just a puppy. He needed to sleep.

CHAPTER SIX

The rain had stopped and a rainbow arched from the green slopes of the Novers, a hilly expanse where sometimes ponies grazed, to the gasworks in Marksbury Road.

Joanna sat hugging her knees beside the Malago, the shallow stream that ran at the bottom of the expanse and disappeared into a culvert in St John's Lane.

Never had she felt so miserable. Paul tried to cheer her up but to no avail. Disappointed that he had failed to move her, Paul got to his feet. 'I'm off with Lenny Scott to see if we can find any conkers. Want to come?'

She shook her head.

The reflection of the sky on the water made her think of heaven. Hopefully there was a special one for cats where there were no dogs and Lottie would be fed cream and kippers. She hadn't tasted cream herself for a very long time, though she had eaten the occasional kipper.

'I've got a kipper for you,' Mrs Allen from next door had said to Joanna that morning as she'd wandered past. Joanna had declined, too upset to eat. Not only was her beloved Lottie no more but her stepmother had accused her of telling tales to 'that toffee-nosed bitch from your school'.

Joanna had denied doing any such thing, but had earned a smack around the back of her head all the same.

The sudden splash of something entering the water caught her attention.

A rat? She knew there were plenty around here and even more over towards the gasworks.

She looked around in case Paul was still close by, but he was off to find conkers with Lenny Scott and the other boys. Even at this distance she could see that his hands were tucked his pockets, his elbows poking through the holes in his jumper.

Joanna considered herself as brave as a boy, but still wished he was here just in case it was a rat. She didn't like rats. She'd heard they would bite if cornered and attack anything small enough to eat. She hoped she wasn't small enough to eat.

There was no movement among the reeds in the water or in the grass growing thickly on the bank. The only thing that drew her attention was the pondweed streaming like green hair in the water's flow.

The weed had fanned out over something surrounding what seemed to be a small rock in the middle of the river. On second thoughts, she decided it wasn't a rock because it fluttered slightly, as if a piece of cloth had been caught there.

Curious, she got to her feet, stepped closer to the bank and narrowed her eyes.

Whatever the lump, rock or mound of cloth was, it seemed half in and half out of what she now guessed to be a sack. The object – whatever it was – anchoring it to a stone.

The local kids had placed a series of flat stones at frequent intervals so they could more easily cross from one side of the stream to the other. Whatever this was had landed on one of those rocks. To Joanna's eyes looked like a brown blob, shapeless, slick and still.

Intrigued she sat down on a dry mound of reed and took off her shoes and socks.

The stones were wet and moss covered, but she dug her toes into the wet slushy surface and made her way from one stone to the next.

All around her was movement. The water formed chortling eddies and a small fish darted out from beneath the third stone. That was where she stopped. The first thought to cross her mind was that the brown blob she had seen was a dead rat. If so she would turn back immediately.

But you don't know for sure.

Bracing both hands on her knees, she peered more closely. It was not a rat. The colour of the fur was too rich, not the dull brown of a river rat but copper-coloured, brown but tinged with a touch of dark red.

The wet moss was cold beneath her feet and the next stone wobbled. Flinging her arms wide, she held her balance, her toes dug in to stop herself from slipping.

The fourth and fifth stone were solid beneath her feet and gave her chance to see more clearly whatever it was on the sixth stone.

Joanna gasped. All the pity she might have felt for herself evaporated at the sight that greeted her.

The little lump was soft and soaking wet. There was a shiny black nose and one paw was crossed over the other.

'A puppy!'

The exclamation came out in a soft squeal. The puppy dog's eyes were closed. The possibility that he might be dead frightened her.

She stooped down on the stone she was standing on, her elbows resting against her knees. Should she touch him? She was almost afraid to do so. And what was he doing here? How come he was lying on a stepping stone in the middle of a stream?

When she saw the sack again, she remembered what Paul had told her. Pets were not just being put to sleep, they were also being abandoned. People were being panicked into destroying those things they had once loved.

Kneeling down in the wet moss, she stretched out her hand to touch the damp fur.

'Poor thing,' she whispered. 'If only Paul were still here. We could sing a hymn for you.' It didn't seem right for just one person to sing a hymn.

She didn't doubt that the poor creature was dead, drowned in a stream where children played.

'But at least I can give you a proper burial,' she added softly. 'Jesus will take care of you.'

Joanna's gaze wandered warily to the rest of the sack submerged in the water. Instinctively she knew there were more dead puppies in the sack. They too deserved a decent burial. Perhaps it might be best if she did run after Paul and get him to help. She couldn't bear the job of burying them all by herself.

Hot tears pricked at her eyes and she hardly noticed how hard she was biting her bottom lip as she ran her hand over the waterlogged coat of the puppy.

How could people be so cruel? This horrible war was making people do horrible things that they wouldn't contemplate doing in peacetime.

Her tears grew more copious, running down her face and dripping off her jaw. Some of them landed on the tiny pink tongue protruding from beneath velvet soft flews.

She was about to close her eyes and recite the Lord's Prayer when she noticed something extraordinary. The tongue flicked. Another tear landed on his nose. The puppy sneezed.

Joanna's jaw dropped and she could barely breathe. Was it too much to hope that he might be alive?

Taking a deep breath, she felt where she thought his heart must be. To her amazement something pulsed like the ticking of a clock beneath her fingers.

He was alive! She could hardly believe it. He was actually alive!

She looked around her. There was nobody about who might lay claim to him. Nobody to see her rescuing him from what would have been a watery grave.

Sliding one hand beneath his head, the other beneath his rump, she picked him up, holding him close to her chest.

The puppy whimpered as she tucked him beneath her coat. His eyes remained closed.

Should she take him home? No. Elspeth would curl her lips, clout her around the head and throw him out into the street – or worse! Either that or the poor mite would go the same way as Lottie, her beloved cat.

But what should she do with him?

Joanna cast her gaze around her, seeking somewhere suitable to hide him.

Away from here, she decided, tucking him further beneath her coat. Fear of losing what she had found made her secretive. She didn't want anyone to know about him. Ears could be boxed and secrets shared betrayed. *Even Paul*, she thought to herself, *I can't even tell Paul. Nobody will know.*

Before she got too far away she took one last look at the sack left in the stream and shuddered. She would tell Paul about the sack and ask him to bury it. However, she had made her mind up to keep secret the fact that one puppy had survived. Nobody would know. Only her.

She reached the rows of allotments adjoining the railway line at the bottom of the park. All manner of vegetables were presently growing, green shoots piercing the dark rich earth. It seemed deserted, most of the allotment owners were at work, and the few that were on the allotments were too intent on what they were doing to notice a small girl.

The allotment owners came down frequently to tend their plants, taking their tools from out of their sheds to dig and weed and plant vegetables, all following the government's entreaties to dig for victory. At the end of each allotment was a shed used by the gardeners to store their tools. All of them were well looked after, except one. It was ramshackle and neglected, and its scruffy windows looked out over a patch of tangled dead plants, thistles, nettles and elder saplings. It was made of wood, had dirty windows and a rusted corrugated iron roof. The door was lopsided and held closed by a rusty hook. She prayed it wasn't locked.

She'd never seen anyone there so it stood to reason that it was as abandoned as the piece of overgrown land. She made up her mind. If nobody else made use of it then she would.

Gritting her teeth, she hugged the puppy closer, pushing the thought away that no matter what she did, the puppy still might die. First she had to warm him up and then she would gather all the things he needed – something snug to sleep in, bowls for food and water, a blanket to wrap over him . . .

Although she had no idea how to get those things – or whether she could get them – she would do her best to save the little chap even if she had to give it all her bread and dripping!

She looked down inside her coat, glad to see the puppy nestled against her chest. Its eyes were still closed. Fearing he might have died on the short journey from the stream to the shed, she put her finger up to his noise. To her great delight she could feel him breathing, his little heart beating time against her chest. His body felt warm now, not icy as it had been. She smiled, thrilled to see him sleeping so contentedly.

She was loath to disturb the sleeping bundle, but disturb she must. The hook holding the door closed was very rusty and she would need both hands to open it.

Carefully, she took off her coat then her cardigan, first one arm then the other, and wrapped it around the sleeping puppy. Once that was done and the puppy still did not wake up, she placed him in a patch of long grass growing between the shed and the flowers and put her coat back on.

Just as she'd guessed, the rusty hook was difficult to budge. Again and again she tugged it, doing her utmost to push it up from the metal eye it slotted into.

Tears of frustration sprang to her eyes and she muttered bad words under her breath, words her stepmother sometimes used when she was angry after coming home late, calling somebody a bloody sod, a bastard only out for what he could get – whatever that meant.

The sudden sound of the puppy whimpering drew her attention. She fell down beside him, stroking his silky little head just as she used to stroke Lottie's.

'Please don't die,' she whispered to him, her heart breaking at the prospect that he might. 'Don't die. Don't die!'

A few spots of rain began to fall. Joanna sprang to her feet. The puppy needed a safe hiding place and she was going to give it to him. Taking a deep breath, she used both hands to tug at the hook, shaking the door, kicking it then tugging again, trying to shift it upwards and out of the eye.

Her hands were too soft and she was too weak. She realised she needed something hard to hit it out of the clasp.

A quick look around and she saw a trowel with a wooden handle and a metal blade. She picked it up and with the back of the metal blade gave the hook an upward blow. It sounded so loud she looked around, fearing somebody might have heard.

There was nobody there, just rows of cabbages, leeks, beans and other vegetables dripping raindrops onto the ground. Despite their bedraggled wetness, they had a friendly look, hiding her as they were from the surrounding world of red-brick houses and privet hedges. Their rustling in the breeze seemed to be cheering her on to do her very best: *Give the hook a really good bash!*

This time the hook moved upwards, not by much, but enough to encourage her to hit it again.

Screwing up her face, gritting her teeth and using every ounce of strength she possessed, she bashed it again. This time, to her great delight, it sprang upwards. The door budged enough for her to slide her fingers through and pull it. Bending down, she picked up the puppy snuggled in her old cardigan and slipped into the gap.

Inside the shed was quite dark, light trying its best to break through the curtain of cobwebs covering the cracked windowpanes.

Joanna didn't like spiders at the best of times. There were some in the coalhouse and her stepmother took great glee in reminding her of the fact each time she threw her in there.

'Big and black with long hairy legs,' she would cackle, like a witch.

Joanna's eyes opened wide. The spiders were mostly confined to the window. Small round shapes and bigger ones with long thin legs hung in the webs, along with flies and other insects all forming the spiders' larders.

Joanna shivered. Only the fact that the puppy needed somewhere safe to stay persuaded her to be brave. He mattered far more than anything.

'They won't hurt you,' she said to herself over and over again, in an effort to make herself believe it was true. Of course it was true, but that didn't make seeing them there easier to bear.

Dragging her eyes away from the spiders, she took stock of the rest of the interior. A rough table stood against the wall underneath a window piled with old seed trays and plant pots. Shelves lined the opposite wall, and beneath them garden hoes, spades and forks hung from hooks.

There were a few galvanised-steel buckets plus an old deckchair and wooden seed boxes, some of them quite large and looking as though they might once have been part of a chest of drawers. There were also old sacks that might once have contained daffodil and tulip bulbs. These were folded neatly and placed on top of the table in front of the window.

Joanna hugged the sleeping puppy closer. She heard him murmur contentedly and sensed he was beginning to stir. 'Just a minute,' she whispered, her chin resting gently on his head. 'I'm going to make you a bed so you'll be warm and comfortable and can sleep all you want. Will that be all right?'

The puppy snuffled weakly. His eyes remained closed.

Holding him beneath one arm, she dragged one of the larger seed boxes from the other side of the room and pushed it beneath the table. At least that way the tabletop would shelter him from the draught coming through the cracked window.

After that she filled it with old sacks and once that was done she placed the puppy in it. He didn't stir. In a way she wanted him to wake up, look up at her and wag his little tail. In another she wanted him to sleep so he could regain his strength.

Her biggest fear was that he was very hungry. She'd given him warmth, but food would keep him alive and she had nothing to give him.

'What will I do?'

Her chest felt tight and tears misted her eyes. She'd lost Lottie. She didn't want to lose the puppy.

Her despair turned to anger, anger with grownups, anger with cruelty and anger that she'd had to bring the poor little creature here instead of a nice comfortable place by a living-room fire.

'And just look at this place! It's filthy.'

Just as she said it, the sun peeped out from behind a cloud and a ray of sunshine shone through a chink in the dirty window. Though dust motes swam in that ray of sunshine to her it was almost magical, as though her mother, her real mother, was saying, *'You can clean it up. Sweep away those spiders' webs. Spiders won't hurt you. The puppy will sleep until morning. He knows he's safe here.'*

CHAPTER SEVEN

Sally Hadley watched the last child leave the school gate before making her way there herself.

The plight of her brightest pupil had preyed on her mind most of the day. Joanna Ryan was hardly the only child with a far from ideal home life, but there was more than that going on. There'd been no love in her stepmother's eyes, only selfishness and the bitter twist of envy on her lips. *Whatever had possessed Joanna's father to marry her?* she asked herself. Probably because he wanted a mother for his child; it wasn't easy coping with a child and holding down a job. Money had to be made if they weren't to end up destitute.

'A penny for your thoughts.'

She looked up into the concerned expression of Arnold Thomas, headmaster of Victoria Park boys' school.

'A pupil,' she said laughingly. 'What else?'

'Care to discuss your concerns over a cup of tea at the park?'

Sally glanced at her watch. Her father would be his usual grumpy self, so why not be an hour late home? It would serve him right.

Arnold Thomas was married and had been headmaster for about five years. He was well respected and, although he seemed to enjoy his work, there was a sadness about him. His wife was an invalid and confined to a wheelchair and he had to look after her as well as hold down his very responsible job.

Despite being bespectacled, he wasn't a bad-looking man in a homely kind of way. He was about forty-five, pink complexioned, with wispy sandy-coloured hair peppered with grey and an amiable manner. His eyes were a chill blue behind horn-rimmed glasses.

Roses spattered the wallpaper in the Park Tearooms and oak-backed chairs were set in groups of four at each and every table. Sally was about to sit at a table near the window so she could look out.

'Best if we sit at the back,' offered Arnold with a nervous smile as he took hold of her elbow. 'There's quite a draught from the door opening and closing.'

Sally followed him to the table he preferred but couldn't help smiling to herself. Arnold was clearly embarrassed to be seen with her, hence sitting at the back of the tearoom away from passers-by. Not that there were many. Poor Arnold. She couldn't help wondering at his home life. Still, no point in starting unnecessary gossip.

They waited until the waitress had set two cups of tea and a buttered teacake on the table. The teacake was for Arnold. 'I have to cook my own meal when I get home. This will help sustain me until then,' he explained. 'So are you going to tell me the essence of your thoughts?'

Sally sighed, folded her arms and looked down into her tea. Arnold had added milk to it, but she had declined sugar.

'Very wise. It's a distinct advantage if you can go without. Sugar will be first to go on ration.'

She smiled weakly before explaining what she had on her mind.

'It's about one of my pupils. I feel I could get very involved with her life if I'm not careful.'

He nodded at her in understanding. 'I take it her home life is not exactly ideal. Father away is he?'

'Yes. She's been left in the care of her stepmother.'

'Ah! The wicked stepmother! Every good fairy story should have one.'

Sally knew Arnold was attempting to be reassuring and she had to smile at the comparison. However, wicked stepmothers between the pages of storybooks were a world away from the real thing.

'I find this particular stepmother quite objectionable. She has cruelty and selfishness written all over her.'

Arnold looked at her over the top of his teacup as he took a sip, wincing as he did so. 'Weak but wet,' he muttered. 'Oh well . . .' Yesterday's sweet strong brew was no more. Everyone was cutting down. 'I'm glad you confided in me, but you know very well what I'm about to say.'

She nodded and replaced her teacup back in its flowery saucer. 'Miss Burton has already told me not to get involved.'

'It's best not to.'

Arnold looked at her longingly, disappointed that she didn't seem to notice how he felt about her. He had never broached the subject of how much he liked her. Neither had he told her that he and his ailing wife despised each other. His wife had once been the love of his life. It had come as a cruel blow when her illness had affected her limbs until she could no longer walk and had to have almost everything done for her. Losing her independence had changed her; the loving woman had been replaced by one he no longer recognised.

It was because of his wife that he didn't go out much, not because he didn't want to but because she'd cause a scene if he did.

Their relationship had become something of a battle and was now the bane of his life.

At first when the more intimate part of their life had ceased, he'd been philosophical, but as time went on he sorely missed the physical side of their relationship. He still wanted that intimacy but had to content himself with fantasies or, on those rare occasions when she let him out, he would go to the seedier side of the city where what they called 'French Fancies' were hidden beneath the counter, black-and-white photographs of naked women.

It was all he could do to feed his yearnings. In the meantime she was his wife and he would stick by her.

However, there were times when he thought about what he would do when she was gone – as she inevitably would. The doctors had assured him of that.

Sally had gorgeous auburn hair and his wife was dark, but ultimately they were out of the same mould. They were both tall and graceful. If ever he should wish to remarry, Sally Hadley would be the woman he would propose to. They were of the same profession, both intelligent and well educated. She would be his soulmate.

Sometimes he dreamed of her at night until his wife nudged him in the ribs, demanding a glass of water or assistance to be taken to the toilet.

He continued to gaze at Sally's face, tuning himself back into what she was saying.

'The father is away fighting, of course, but I'm not sure Mrs Ryan is spending her time keeping the home fires burning. She's not that type.'

Arnold placed its cup back in the saucer. 'Are you sure you're not letting your prejudices get the better of you?'

'Absolutely! Joanna has gradually looked more and more neglected since her father went away and I'm sure she's not being fed half the time.'

Arnold fingered a cigarette from a tin case and regarded her as he lit it. Sally didn't smoke so he didn't bother to offer her one.

'Perhaps we should be contacting the children's welfare officer up at the council offices. If the case is proved, the child might have a better life placed with foster parents.'

Eyes downcast and looking thoughtful, Sally fingered her teacup. 'I'm not sure if that would be the right course, Arnold. I'm just not sure.' She glanced at her watch. 'Goodness. Look at the time. I have to go.'

She fumbled for the clasp of her handbag so she could pay for her tea. Arnold's hand touched hers.

'Please. Let me.'

She looked up at him, saw his expression and immediately knew how he felt about her. She kept her voice calm as though she'd noticed nothing. 'Are you sure?'

He nodded. 'Although times are hard I can just about manage to buy a colleague a cup of tea.'

Again the warm smile, the kindness in his eyes, plus the other look, the one she couldn't truly read but didn't quite trust.

Sally headed for the door first, Arnold right behind her.

'You really are excellent company,' he said to her, at the same time patting her posterior.

Sally froze. 'I'd rather you didn't do that.'

He blushed profusely. 'Sorry. I didn't mean to.'

She glared at him. Of course he had. 'Please don't do that again.'

Once outside he walked her a few hundred yards along the main road.

At first they both remained silent. *So much for professionalism*, thought Sally, her cheeks burning.

It was him who broke the silence, mentioning the likelihood of him landing the job of air-raid warden for Jubilee Road.

'I do have to run it past Miranda first, as it does mean her being left alone a lot at night.'

'Very commendable of you,' said Sally a trifle sarcastically.

'My age, my job and the fact that my wife is an invalid means I won't be called up. Still, I have to do my bit somehow.'

'I understand you fought in the last war,' said Sally, glad to change the subject.

A haggard, haunted look suddenly dimmed Arnold's customary cheerfulness.

'Gallipoli.'

'Was it bad?'

His expression turned grimmer. 'A blood bath. I was a medical orderly.' He flexed his fingers before putting his hands back in his pockets. 'I can still feel the stickiness of the blood. Such a lot of blood . . .'

Sally walked on silently and he did the same. They said goodbye at the junction of St Luke's Road and St John's Lane. They shook hands. He held on to hers just too long. She snatched it away.

'Sally! I'm sorry . . .'

'Goodbye, Arnold.'

She turned sharply away, her shoulders rigid. She was overwhelmed by the desire to put distance between them. No more after-school cups of tea at the Park Tearooms, or anywhere else for that matter.

Arnold strolled on towards Redcatch Road where private houses swept upwards to an area of green grass recently made over for yet more allotments. Jubilee Road was a left-hand turning halfway up.

Sally headed for the Victorian bay villa she shared with her father where they had a view of the park from the front room.

She wondered where her father would be and what he'd been up to all day. Hopefully he'd taken her advice and gone to the allotment. She sincerely hoped so.

As usual, the heavy wooden front door with its ivory porcelain knocker was wide open. It was only firmly closed at night or if it was raining. Only the inner door remained closed all day regardless of the weather. The dark blue glass of the inner door was trimmed with a red border and a cut glass rosette decorated each corner. The light shining through the door from outside threw blue-and-red patterns over the wall of the interior hall, shimmering like a line of dancers as she pushed it open.

'Dad!'

There was no response. She went into each room expecting to see him asleep in his favourite armchair, his freckled hands resting on his newspaper, the latter spread wide over his lap.

She called him once or twice more, then retraced her steps to the hall door and out into the street.

She spotted him immediately sitting on the park wall, his back against the railings.

'Dad?'

The only sign of acknowledgement was a half turn and a raised hand, before he went back to looking out over the park.

Sally crossed the road entering the small gate, one of many set into the wall surrounding the park.

'Dad. Didn't you hear me come home?'

He jerked his chin towards the park. People were strolling in the late sunshine just before twilight fell. Children were playing.

'Flossie would have enjoyed an evening like this. Me and your mother used to enjoy taking him for a walk, you know.'

Flossie was their old terrier who had died shortly before Sally's mother.

She sat down on the wall beside him reached for his hand holding it in both of hers.

'I know, Dad. I wish both of them were still here.'

'Do you see,' he said, again jerking his chin at the scene before them. 'There's no dogs. Do you see that? And before you deny there's anything wrong, I have read the newspapers. Do you know that woman's cat next door but one had kittens? Yes,' he said, answering his own question, a faraway look in his eyes. 'She had them all killed she did.' He turned his head, his expression one of total puzzlement. 'Why would anyone do that?'

Sally squeezed his hand and bent her head as she sought the right words that wouldn't upset him too much.

'It's a government directive. They're afraid the animals will get frightened and run amok if we're bombed. And then of course there's the food situation . . .'

She was merely repeating the official advice, hearing herself say it without really believing it.

'Rubbish! Animals helped us in the trenches, you know. We used them as messengers. Even used them to take ammunition where we were too afraid to go. A lot of them died doing their duty to their country. Did you know that?'

Sally eyed him intently. Her father's disposition and behaviour had changed a lot since her mother died. Up until this moment getting a conversation, let alone a response out of him, had been like pulling teeth. Even the declaration of war had failed to elicit a strong reaction.

As she sat there in the dying afternoon, her heart lurched in two different directions. In one way she found it odd to accept that his first positive response to anything was with regard to a dog. On the other hand, at least he'd responded to something.

'I loved that old dog, you know. I wouldn't have put him down. He was my pal.'

Sally squeezed his hand. 'Come on. Let's get over home and have some supper.'

She didn't press him as to whether he'd actually made it to the allotment and dug up the flowers her mother had loved. She didn't nag him that he really should be preparing the ground for vegetables. It was enough that, just for a change, he'd made a thoughtful comment rather than mutter a morose response.

They walked together up to the house, each dwelling on their own thoughts.

Joanna Ryan still loomed large in Sally's mind and so did Arnold Thomas. Both of them deserved her pity. She would help Joanna if she could. But as for Arnold, the further she stayed away from him the better it would be for the both of them.

Approaching the front door, Sally was vaguely aware of a man standing on the pavement, a piece of paper in his hand. He appeared to be scrutinising the front of each house, looking for a specific address perhaps?

Suddenly he spotted them and almost sprinted along the pavement.

'Excuse me. I wonder if you could help me. I'm looking for a Mrs Gertrude Evans.'

'Two doors down.' Sally pointed to a bay villa very similar to the Hadley house except that its window frame and front door hadn't been painted for some time.

'You'll have to give the knocker a hard rap,' Sally called out. 'Mrs Evans is a war widow and a bit deaf.

She fancied his eyes swept over her, which only made her cringe: what was it with men today? All she wanted was to be left alone.

The living room at the back of the house was warm and cosy. Adjoining the living room was the scullery. The front room with its polished linoleum floor and woollen rug in front of the fire was only used for best.

Sally laid the square dining table in the centre of the living room while her father gave the fire a poke then took his pipe down from its rack and began stuffing it with tobacco.

Sally turned on the wireless. Once it was warmed up they might have some music before the news came on.

Their normal routine for that evening would have been to eat, drink tea and, while her father listened to the radio, Sally would attend to the homework the children had completed the week before. But tonight a loud knocking on the front door interrupted the evening calm of their routine.

The inner door, the one glazed with blue-and-red glass, was closed but she could see a figure on the other side, standing on the doorstep. The fragile glass trembled as she pulled it open. She recognised the man who had asked for directions to Mrs Evans' house.

'Can I help you?'

Occupied with her own thoughts from their earlier encounter, she hadn't expected to be smitten by the man's appearance. He was quite tall and had broad shoulders. His eyes were like dark pools and had an exotic look about them. His eyebrows were dark too and a small scar nestled like a question mark on his cheekbone.

His smile brightened the evening.

'I'm sorry. I came to see Mrs Evans. Her son said she was distressed about her cat. I believe it recently had kittens. She needed them to be taken off her hands.'

'Oh!'

His beaming smile crumpled. 'Ah. That exclamation sounds like bad news. Am I too late?'

'Are you one of them?' Her tone was brusque.

His eyebrows arched in surprise. 'Them?'

'Yes. A member of the organisation responsible for taking pets away and destroying them.'

'They have already gone?'

'So I've been told. Do you get paid by how many you take for destruction? Or so much per leg perhaps? Four legs multiplied by—'

'I do not.'

'Just a salary then!'

Her anger was unabated. That poor cat. Those poor kittens.

He hesitated as though disinclined to respond, but instead he found himself wanting to impress her.

'I do not need a salary, I have a private income. Though I have tried a number of professions. In time I will find the one that suits me best. It is best to do work at what you enjoy, then it is not work, yes?'

Sally frowned, not so sure now that she should be angry but unwilling to back down just yet.

'And in the meantime you're collecting pets for the government's destruction programme.'

'Not at all. I'm here on behalf of my aunt, Lady Ambrose-DeVere. She has it in mind to rescue as many animals as she can.'

'Rescue?'

'That is her aim. She has a very big house and outbuildings and will take in as many as she can. She is also rich and not without influence. I have come from France to help her.'

Sally took a breath. She'd heard his voice, noted the careful way each word was spoken, but his accent was almost perfect, and she didn't notice the way some of his words were inflected until he called her attention to it.

'I'm sorry. I had no business speaking to you like that. It's just that . . . well . . . all this turmoil. So many have been taken. They're probably already dead.'

The man shook his head sadly. 'I agree with you. It is a great pity. This is a very sad time.'

'I'm sorry I mistook you for one of those people who put them to sleep.'

His eyes twinkled. 'There is no need to apologise. I enjoyed fencing words with you but hope I never have to fight you with a sword. Your words are sharp enough.'

'I'm sorry. I really am.'

She felt her face reddening, not just because she felt a fool but because of the way he was looking at her.

'You said your aunt is Lady Ambrose?'

He nodded. 'That's right. My aunt has set up a facility providing safety until such time as this madness is over. I was going to offer Mrs Evans a place for her animals. We do our best to find homes for them . . .'

Although full of sadness his voice was warm.

'So you're from France?'

He inclined his head. 'That is where my home is, yes. Brittany.'

Feeling tongue-tied, Sally could only nod in response.

He smiled at her. 'I had better be going.' He looked as though a sudden thought had crossed his mind. 'Can I leave you a card just in case you hear of any other person wanting sanctuary for their animals?' He took out a pen from his jacket pocket and scribbled something on the back of it.

Sally wasn't aware of anyone close to her having a cat or dog but she took one of the cards anyway. The name on the card was Lady Ambrose-DeVere. The house was Ambrose House, a place she knew was surrounded by acres of land and a high wall; she had only glanced at from the top of a double-decker bus.

'I will bear it in mind. I only knew of her as Lady Ambrose. I didn't know there was a French connection.'

An intoxicating laugh rumbled in his throat. 'For better or worse, there really is. I am from the DeVere side of the family.

I know France better than I know England. In fact you could say that I am a stranger here. I know nobody.'

'Hopefully you won't be a stranger for long.'

What he said next took her completely by surprise.

'Excuse me for asking, but would you like to have dinner with me one night?'

To her own surprise, Sally found herself saying yes without hesitation.

He looked pleased. 'Tomorrow? I have a car. We will go into town? Yes?'

Yes. She couldn't help herself. She said yes.

After he'd gone she turned back into the house, heading for the living room at the back in something of a daze. What in heaven's name had happened out there on the doorstep?

Her father was sitting in his chair reading the newspaper and so failed to notice the dazed look on her face. For him, nothing would appear to have changed. Jerking herself back from romantic musings, Sally turned her attention to the mundane surroundings that she was so used to. The potatoes were boiling away on the stove, the steam rising in a thick fog to hang in cooled droplets on the ceiling. The fact that he'd done nothing to save them from being overcooked annoyed her, yet she didn't have it in her heart to reprimand him. Her mind was preoccupied with the dark-eyed man she had only just met who had asked her out. She had so readily agreed. What was happening to her?

Her father didn't bother to look up and ask who it was at the door. Usually she accepted that this was the way he was and didn't bother to tell him. On this occasion she couldn't help herself. She had to share the experience with someone.

'That was a Frenchman at the door. He's the nephew of Lady Ambrose-DeVere. She's opened her doors to unwanted animals. He's asked me out to dinner and I've accepted.' She glanced at the card he'd given her. He'd scribbled his name on the back. 'His name's Pierre.'

Her father grunted his familiar response but didn't look up. She knew from experience what he was plotting to do. Since the death of her mother, her father had shadowed her movements, petulant if she should dare leave the house on an evening. A night at the cinema, a dance or even an evening at a friend's house, she could guarantee her father would be waiting outside for her. On some occasions he had insisted on escorting her there.

'He has a car,' she said boldly. 'So there's no need for you to chaperone me there and back.'

She fancied the fingers holding the newspaper stiffened appreciably.

Although he said nothing, she knew he was displeased. She also knew this behaviour had to end – whatever it took.

CHAPTER EIGHT

School dinner consisted of slivers of gristly meat, potatoes and cabbage. Dessert was baked apple and custard.

Joanna very carefully cut the beef into portions before sliding each piece under the table and into the handkerchief nestled in her lap. Once that was done, she bolted down the cabbage and potatoes, mashing it into the gravy.

'I could do with seconds,' she said to her friend Susan after hiding the handkerchief in her pocket.

The two girls put up their hands when the teacher supervising the meal asked if anyone wanted seconds.

'Only those with a clean plate,' Miss Hadley stated, her keen eyes surveying the flock of upraised hands.

Joanna's plate was as clean as clean could be and Sally noticed her upright hand. 'Only six at a time to come out for second helpings,' she added nodding in Joanna's direction.

Joanna couldn't believe her luck when she was one of the first to be picked. Once she had secured a second portion of meat, potatoes and cabbage, she hurried back to the dinner table she shared with fourteen other children. Just as before she cut the meat up into cubes and, after eating one or two herself, took the handkerchief from her pocket. After scraping off the gravy a few more portions of meat went into the handkerchief. After that she wolfed down the second helping of potatoes and cabbage.

'I hope you're going to have room for apple and custard after all that,' said a voice.

70

Joanna started. Miss Hadley was behind her looking very pleased indeed.

'Yes, miss,' murmured Joanna. The fact was that, having only eaten potatoes and cabbage, she had plenty of room. The meat was for the puppy. He hadn't eaten since she found him and she was desperate to get to him.

The afternoon lessons seemed to drag. Joanna glanced at the wall clock, willing its hands to move faster. The days were drawing in, October fast turning into November. There wouldn't be much time to clean the shed today, but at least she could feed the little puppy. Hopefully he would find his way to the clay pot tray where she'd poured some water, but she couldn't help wondering how he was. He hadn't opened his eyes when she'd left him. What if he didn't recover? What would she do then?

She thought of the dead flowers on the allotment at the front of the shed. Here and there an odd bloom was still flowering bravely, though not very many. One or two flowers would be nice to place on his grave, if she had to.

Susan called out to her as she raced away from school. 'Hey! Wait for me.'

But Joanna couldn't wait. She ran faster, keen to get away from Susan's chatter and the possibility she might ask questions and tag along with her. She spotted a familiar figure playing conkers outside the entrance to the boys' school.

'Can't stop, Paul,' she shouted as she ran past him as fast as her legs could carry her.

She was vaguely aware of his puzzled frown before he returned to knocking out his opponent. But still she couldn't stop. Not even for him.

By the time she got to the allotment a thick fog had descended turning what greenery remained from the long hot summer to a chill dull grey. The air was still. Even the crows in the bare branches of the trees were silent. Sheds containing gardening tools loomed out of the mists like lopsided sentry boxes guarding nothing more than rows of vegetables and gooseberry bushes.

She tripped over an upended bucket used to force rhubarb to grow. The handkerchief containing the bits of meat fell out of her pocket, the contents scattering on the ground.

'Oh no!'

The earth was soft beneath her knees. It was all about the meat and keeping it clean and wholesome for the puppy to eat – if he was still alive. Diligently, her breath steaming from her mouth, she picked up every last piece of meat and gristle retied her handkerchief – more securely this time. Cupping it with both hands, she hurried for the shed.

Due to her efforts the day before, the hook lifted more easily.

Thanks to the fog, the interior of the shed was darker today. The cobwebbed window didn't help. She vowed it would be her next job once she had fed the puppy. The puppy came first.

It occurred to her to leave the door open for the sake of extra light from outside, but she didn't dare. One of those horrible people who killed pets might be out there. Or even somebody out late to dig the damp ground. She couldn't risk being seen. She couldn't risk the puppy's life.

There was no sign of movement. Her chest tightened.

'Here, boy,' she called softly. 'See what I've got for you.'

She untied the handkerchief, laid it flat on the ground and peered into the box where she'd placed the puppy the evening before. The layers of sacks were still there inside the wooden seed box, the puppy was not.

Alarm clutched at Joanna's heart. Had the man who owned the shed and worked the allotment come back and discovered him and handed him to those who would kill him?

Tears sprang to her eyes. She'd lost Lottie. Finding the puppy had given her something to hope for. It would be so unfair if he was gone too.

Despair and anger mixed in equal proportions. She had nothing and nobody else, only her father and he'd gone off to fight in the war.

The pottery dish used to place beneath a plant pot to retain water was still there. She remembered filling it to the brim. The pain in her heart shifted. There was less water now. Had the puppy found it?

She looked around the shed, seeing dim shapes leaning against the wooden walls, the hoes and other implements hanging from hooks and piled on the shelves. Nothing had changed since yesterday.

Her attention strayed to the dark and dingy corner of the shed to a pile of sacks and a bucket. Something moved.

He was still here! Her spirits soared. She went down on her knees, a small piece of fatty meat quivering between her finger and thumb.

'Here, boy. Here.'

She stayed on her hands and knees, her attention riveted on the furthest end of the shed.

'Come on. See what I've got for you.'

Nothing happened for a moment, but suddenly, sensing the smell of food, the black spot that was his nose quivered. The nose was followed by a muzzle, which in turn was followed by two bright eyes.

The puppy regarded her warily. She smelled similar to the man who had tossed him and his siblings into a sack and then into the cold water. The little creature shivered at the thought of it. But his nose continued to twitch. One paw stepped forward, then a second.

The smell of food was so tempting. He hadn't eaten for over twenty-four hours and the fear he'd felt on hearing his mother yelp, then the cries of his siblings as the sack had been smashed against the wall, were still fresh in his memory.

The human he saw before him was smaller than he'd been used to. Following a second sniff of the air he perceived she didn't smell quite the same. She also spoke softly, urging him not to be afraid. But fear still made his blood race. The instinct to survive was strong, but the gnawing in his stomach was impossible to dismiss. He was hungry and the meat smelled so appetising.

He took a third hesitant step, then another. Nothing bad happened so he darted forward, snatched the piece of meat from her fingers and darted backwards.

He watched the girl from a safe distance as he swiftly chewed and swallowed. His milk teeth were sharp enough for him to chew. The meat had tasted good. He licked his lips. The small human was yet again holding out another piece of meat.

The smell was so enticing and he was still so very hungry.

Taking a hesitant step forward, he snatched it and swallowed, too hungry to chew before doing so.

'You shouldn't bolt your food,' the little girl said to him. 'You'll get a tummy ache if you keep doing that.' He sat down and regarded her with his big soulful eyes, his long ears hanging like golden pads from his head. 'Here you are. There's plenty more where this came from.'

The girl held out another piece of meat. This time he was less hesitant. Nobody had hurt him and he heard no cries of fear from other dogs.

When she wasn't speaking there was only a great silence, except when a steam train went by which set the old shed rattling and shaking.

When he'd first woken it had frightened him, but now the little girl showed no sign of being afraid and was feeding him, so he took no notice, accepting it as just a noise and not an intrusion into this dingy shed.

Joanna was elated, delight shining in her eyes. She couldn't stop smiling.

The puppy was getting braver and braver. Three or four pieces of meat and he was close to her now, willingly taking more from her outstretched hand.

When it was gone she let him lick her fingers. By now he was used to her and showed no fear.

'There. That was good, wasn't it?'

His velvet brown eyes regarded her solemnly and when his stumpy tail wagged happily, she knew she'd won him over.

'Shh,' she said, her finger in front of her lips. 'You have to be quiet while I get you some water.'

The watering can she'd used to fill his dish was empty and there was no supply inside the shed. She realised she would have to go outside and dip the can into the water butt.

The puppy attempted to follow her as she headed for the door.

'No,' she said firmly. 'You have to wait here while I get you some water. I won't be long.'

The puppy sat on his haunches and whimpered, its big eyes fixed on her.

Joanna crept outside carefully, pulling the rickety door behind her so the puppy could not follow.

The water butt was quite tall and only three-quarters full despite all the rain they'd had. It was hard to reach the water and there was no tap to make the job any easier.

Joanna pulled a stone close to the butt and stood on that, stretching her arms over the side of the butt until the can was immersed enough in the water so some could trickle in.

The watering can was made of galvanised steel and very heavy, so she had to use both hands to heave it out and carry it back inside.

The puppy had not moved from where she'd last seen him. He was shaking slightly but on seeing her stopped immediately and got onto his feet, his stump of a tail wagging enthusiastically.

'Hey,' she laughed, feeling happier than she had in months. 'You nearly tripped me up. Let me put some water in your dish then we can play, you little puppy, you!'

The puppy lapped at the water as it splashed from the water can and into the dish. Once there was enough, Joanna placed the watering can back where she'd found it.

In order to keep the water clean she laid a sack over the top so it wouldn't become a bath for spiders.

'There,' she said happily, getting back down on her knees. 'Would you like to play?'

Not understanding, the puppy eyed her expectantly. There was something interesting in her tone of voice so he waited to see what would happen next.

She rolled up a piece of newspaper into a ball and for a while she rolled it across the floor, the puppy chasing it then bringing it back, enthusiastic for her to do it again.

Eventually he made the decision not to give it back to her and proceeded to tear it into pieces.

Joanna immediately remembered an old tennis ball she had at home. That would be her first present to him.

Replete with food and tired out from play, the puppy snuggled up against her, his chin resting on her thigh. She heard him make little comforting grumbling noises before he fell asleep.

Joanna continued to stroke his head, thinking how lucky she was to have found him. As long as nobody came to this shed and she could bring him some food, the puppy would survive.

Suddenly aware of how dark it was getting, Joanna knew she had to go home. Elspeth used any excuse to punish her and being home late – although really she couldn't care less – was too good an excuse to miss. Unless she was out, of course, then she wouldn't notice. Elspeth, it seemed, always had somewhere to go. Joanna hoped that she would be out by the time she got home. It would give her the opportunity to find food for the puppy.

'I have to go now,' she whispered to the puppy as she gently lifted him into the wooden seed box that was now his bed. 'But I'll be back tomorrow morning. I swear I will.'

Breakfast, if I can. And lunchtime, she thought. And after school. Somehow she had to try and feed him first thing in the morning and immediately after school. This would mean leaving him enough at breakfast time to last him through the day.

Stealing food from home would be difficult. Half the time she didn't get enough to eat herself. But she had to try.

Nothing was going to be easy, but this puppy was hers and he had nobody else in the world. *Like me*, she thought. God had sent her this puppy to replace Lottie and she was going to look after him.

When she got outside she could barely see her hand in front of her face. An evening fog in November was bad enough, but the fact that all the streetlights were out because of the blackout made the night darker.

The only reason that Joanna could find her way home at all was the fact that she was familiar with the path she was walking on and the area she lived in. All the same, the dark shapes of sheds and the scurrying of night creatures was a little unnerving.

She did her best to ignore them, fixing her mind on the little creature she had saved from the river. He was dry now and his flesh was warm, his little tummy round and hard with food.

She found herself smiling at the thought of him, snuggled safely in his box beneath the wooden workbench. She would do her best to take him some breakfast and later on save something from her school dinner. She hoped it would be liver tomorrow. Her puppy would like liver . . .

Her puppy. She rolled the words over in her mind before saying it out loud.

'My puppy.'

She felt she was walking on air. The puppy had come to her via dreadful circumstances but she determined they would become good friends. Like Susan and Paul, and like them he had to have a name.

She had no doubts the puppy was a boy. She knew enough about boys to know that, so it had to be a boy's name.

She considered her father's name, Thomas Henry Ryan. Naming the puppy after him would make him feel less distant. She pulled a face as she considered her options. Thomas? She didn't want to call the puppy Thomas. That would just be too confusing once her father *was* home. Neither did she want to call him Henry. That was too formal. But for her father, the man who had once given her a cat and had been kind before Elspeth had come along, she decided on Harry. Yes, she thought, smiling into the foggy night. His name would be Harry!

CHAPTER NINE

Seb Hadley twisted a thick knitted scarf around his neck and reached for his overcoat. He heard the irritation in his daughter's sighs, but did not meet her eyes, fearing that if he did she would lose her temper and tell him to stay at home.

No matter how much he tried to persuade her that she needed protecting in case the Germans decided to bomb the country within the next hour, she still refused to let him accompany her to school.

'Anything could happen. It's just in case.'

'What do you mean by "just in case"?' she'd asked him. 'It's a dangerous world. There's no knowing what might happen. You could get run over by a bus.'

'I know all about safety first. Look left, look right and look left again,' she'd replied impatiently.

'You might get taken ill.'

When he'd said this she hadn't snapped the obvious, that she was feeling and looking perfectly well. Like him a pall of sadness seemed to fall over her. Her mother had dropped dead while out shopping. There'd been no sign of her being ill, in fact she'd seemed a picture of health. Apparently a blood vessel had burst in her head. The doctors said she would not have known anything about it.

'And then there's the Germans.'

'Ah,' exclaimed Sally, somewhat contemptuously. 'The Germans! Dad, I really don't think Hitler has a plan in place to bomb Victoria Park girls' school. I don't think the park itself is a target either.'

The corners of her father's mouth turned downwards. She immediately regretted her sharpness, but this really was getting too much.

'Dad,' she said, touching his arm. 'You have to let me live my own life. Mum wouldn't want you fussing over me like this and neither do I.'

Grace Hadley's death had left her husband a changed man. Seb Hadley was a few years older than his wife and just a few months off retirement when she'd dropped dead. He'd fully expected to die before her. It had come as a terrible shock when she went first.

The protectiveness he'd had for his wife shifted on to his daughter. He'd always loved Sally, of course, but now his love became stronger. She was all he had in the world.

Fear that something might happen to her dominated his life. She was all he had left, and although he knew it irritated his daughter no end, he couldn't stop himself from being over-protective. It was hard to accept that he should occupy himself. What was there to do without Grace? Who else could he dote on?

Her jaw clenched so she wouldn't let out what she was thinking, Sally buttoned her coat and grabbed the briefcase full of pupils' homework that she'd brought home the night before.

She didn't ask her father if he was coming with her. She knew he was and there was nothing she could say or do to stop him.

Their walk to school was silent as it always was on those days she couldn't dissuade him, Sally seething with inner thoughts, her father resolute in his determination to protect her.

For the most part she accepted his company, though refused to let him collect her from school.

'Collect me! I am not a curly haired tot from the infants' school,' she'd snapped at him. He'd given in, probably because she did sometimes have meetings after school or join the horrendous queues for food.

He'd almost been persuaded not to escort her to school. Today she had relented because tonight she would be leaving him alone. Tonight she was going out to dinner with the dashing young Frenchman. On the night before she had studied his name on the card he'd given her again and again, turning it over in her hand before going to bed. Pierre DeVere.

Sally glanced at her father. His expression was as stoic as usual.

'You've remembered I'm going out tonight?'

There was silence for a time, the only sound the clicking of her heels and his heavier footsteps a beat or two behind.

'Sally, I don't think you should go—'

Sally stopped so suddenly, he overtook her before coming to a standstill, turning and seeing the determination in her face.

'Well, I am going, Father. I am going and there is nothing you can say that will make me change my mind. Now go back home. I'm here at school and I'm safe at school.'

Although his hurt expression gave rise to a moment of guilt, she held back from saying anything soothing. She needed to remain firm. She had a life to lead and she couldn't allow him to ruin it.

'Now, please, Dad. I have to go.'

She glanced at her watch, gave him a quick peck on the cheek, and went through the school gates.

A host of children gathered round, wishing her good morning and showing her treasures they'd found in a field: a red autumn leaf, an abandoned bird's nest, a fish in a jar taken from the Malago, a slow flowing stream close to St. John's Lane.

Seb found it hard to turn away from his daughter. The sight of Sally being in such great demand from the children gave him mixed feelings. He was proud of her but also jealous that she had the attention of others, even if they were her pupils. She was his baby and he could not easily let her go. Today was bad enough. Tonight she was going out with a man. He had no objection to the young man's nationality, but he had objections to any man who came between him and his daughter.

Not wishing to return to an empty house, his footsteps led him down the cobbled path leading to the allotment. He stopped some distance away noting the bowed heads of dead flowers, raindrops dripping miserably from the withered leaves.

The rain had grown stronger since earlier that morning though it still fell in a fine mist from a leaden sky. Everything looked grey. November had been wet and foggy so far. It wasn't likely to get any better.

Rain trickled from the brim of his hat, from his eyebrows and off the end of his nose. His scarf kept the water from getting inside his coat.

Once at the allotment he surveyed the plot where flowers had once grown in riotous colour. The remains of dead blooms barely held their heads above the forest of weeds. If he followed the advice from the government, as clearly all his fellow allotment holders were doing, he would pull them all out and plant vegetables instead.

The truth was he couldn't bring himself to do it. When Grace was alive he'd come down here with a Thermos flask and sandwiches and enjoyed digging the earth, the dark loam crumbling between his fingers. If she wasn't too busy around the house, Grace had come with him. *What times they'd had*, he thought to himself, *and damn God for taking her!*

He pursed his lips as he took in the sad-looking allotment. The dead flowers could stay until he was ready. In the meantime he would go for a walk in the park. At one time he would have also called in at the Park House, the pub on the corner of Merioneth Street, not the larger Engineer's Arms where factory workers gathered. The Park House was small and intimate, no more than a small room with a bar, darts and a shove ha'peny board. He hadn't been in there since his wife's death. Neither had he been to church. They'd used to go, the two of them, but he no longer attended. God was in disgrace because he'd taken Grace away from him.

Head bent, his eyes watering, he turned away from the shed but something made him stop. Had he heard something? Or had he only felt that he heard something? Perhaps just the rain.

Narrowing his eyes he took a longer look at his shed. He and Grace had laughed themselves stupid when together they'd built it from odd bits of wood and a window they'd found abandoned on the side of the road.

'A good wind and it'll be blown to bits,' she'd said, laughing as they stood side by side admiring their handiwork.

For a moment it seemed as though she was yet again standing beside him, her laughter ringing in his ears.

'There's nobody there,' he muttered, shrugging his shoulders against the rain. It was just the creaking of old wood and second-hand nails slowly falling apart.

Over a period of days Joanna cleared away the spiders' webs from the solitary window so she could see a bit better. She also used an old broom she found to sweep the floor and brought a shabby rug from home. The rug had lain curled up behind the back door for ages and was in need of a good beating. Once she was sure nobody was around, Joanna bashed it against the outside of the shed until it was as clean as she could get it. Unable to take the solitary torch from the house without Elspeth noticing, she found her father's old bicycle lamp. The light came on when she flicked the switch. Thankfully the battery was still charged. She'd have some light to see better in the shed.

At the same time as sneaking things that would not be missed from home, she brought food. She'd taken to saving some of her supper from the night before. The bits of bone and bread soaked in gravy formed Harry's breakfast. Things saved from her school dinner was his evening meal, plus a third of the pint of milk she was given at school just before morning break. Unused milk was left in a crate outside the kitchen door. When she could Joanna had taken one of these, making sure she wore her coat at breaktime so she could hide it in her pocket.

Harry was becoming more and more confident, and had started to bark the moment he heard her coming, which was beginning to worry her.

'Shh! Harry, you've got to be quiet,' she said to him, softening her voice in the hope he would understand her tone if not the words she was speaking.

Harry, full of youthful energy, bounced around in response, his stumpy tail wagging happily, pink tongue lolling and eyes bright with mischief.

Joanna smiled. She didn't have it in her heart to scold Harry. Having her very own puppy had made such a difference to the emptiness of her life and the coldness of the house that was supposed to be home.

Harry loved her because she was the first human to be kind to him. She loved him because she had nobody else. And he was so very cute and affectionate

Food played a part in Harry's affection. He was filling out and getting bigger thanks to the food she scraped from her school dinner. His coat was shiny, his body rounder than it had been and to her great delight, his coat was a coppery brown. So far he hadn't gone outside, but once he did she was sure his coat would shine like gold in the sun.

When she turned on the bicycle lamp Harry attempted to catch the circular beam it threw on the floor, patting it with his paws, dancing from one leg to the other when she moved the lamp and the beam moved too.

Joanna laughed at his antics. She laughed here in this shed more than she had ever laughed at home, more even than she had ever laughed at school.

Once he'd eaten his fill and finished playing, Joanna settled him down among the dry sacks in the seed box. When she'd first placed him here he'd fallen asleep quite quickly, but he was getting older now, and his energy increasing accordingly.

Joanna looked up at the window. She'd had the foresight to cover it with yet another old sack just as everyone was doing because of the blackout. In her case it wasn't so much about German bombers seeing her. Occasionally a man might come down to inspect his allotment following a hard day at work and she greatly feared being discovered. She would do everything in her power to ensure that Harry did not meet the same fate of so many other animals.

December was approaching. Twilight seemed to begin around three thirty in the afternoon and all was pitch black by five o'clock.

Before the imposition of the blackout, streetlamps would have lit her way home, orange halos piercing the darkness. A little light would even have filtered down from the street lamps on the road running above the allotments, falling like strips of gold cloth from amber globes. Since the outbreak of war the world had turned more densely black than it had ever done before.

Now there was only darkness and because of this and Harry's increased exuberance she was arriving home later and later. With sudden panic she realised tonight she would be later home than ever. Hurrying was impossible. The only way she might gain more speed was if she took the bicycle lamp to light her way.

She wasn't sure of the time but knew this was something she had to chance. Once she'd reassured herself that Harry was asleep, she picked up the lamp, shut the door firmly behind her and hurried up the slope.

The lamp's flickering glow picked up the shininess of the frost-covered cobbles. Her feet slid, but she hurried towards home, her breath turning to steam before hanging like ice in the frozen air.

Worries about Harry stayed with her all the way home. Would he be warm enough? She thought about his silky coat and the sack she'd covered him with. Hopefully he would be fine, though his water was bound to turn to ice. Never mind, she thought to herself. I can deal with that in the morning.

She'd taken to going down to light the fire and put the kettle on half an hour earlier than usual. One advantage of this that she had not considered was that it gave her the opportunity to grab something to eat before her stepmother came down. Not bacon or eggs, which would be instantly remarked upon, but a slice of dry bread fried in fat saved from the meal the night before. She even managed to grab herself the first cup of tea from the pot, carefully washing the teacup afterwards so the evidence wouldn't be so obvious. Her stepmother would be drinking from the same teacup but would not know that. It was a small triumph but pleased Joanna no end.

By the time she got to the bottom of The Vale, she knew she was in for it. Although all the shops at the bottom of the hill would be in darkness anyway, she knew by looking at the shop doors that they were closed for the night. She was very, very late!

The hill was steep but she ran as fast as she could, her legs kicking out behind her. She was a good runner but The Vale was steep, so steep that buses refused to go up there following a fall of snow or a thick layer of ice.

Here, where houses and hedges protected them, the pavements were less icy than the cobbles leading up from the allotments. She didn't slip but she did get breathless.

By the time she pushed open the front gate her breath was coming in quick, snatched gasps. The door was left on the latch as usual – few people in the street ever locked their doors, a habit they'd brought with them from the Victorian back to backs in the heart of the city.

Elspeth was standing in front of the fireplace when she went in, her lips turning ruby red as she applied the tip of a fresh new tube of lipstick.

'About bloody time,' she shouted.

Joanna kept the dining table between them. The dining table was square and filled the middle of the room. Two armchairs sat either side of the fireplace and a settee behind her. A nice smell wafted in from the kitchen. Had her stepmother turned over a new leaf and prepared an evening meal?

'Sorry. I didn't know it was so late.'

It was best to be like a mouse when Elspeth was having a tantrum and she didn't want her asking any awkward questions, get suspicious and beat the truth out of her. Not that she would ever tell. Not now she had Harry.

'There's stew in the kitchen. Help yourself. I'm off out.'

So that was the smell. 'Thank you.'

'Don't thank me. It was that daft old cow next door. "Made too much," she said. "Would you like some," she said. "Would your lovely little daughter like some."'

Elspeth had nothing but contempt for Mrs Allen next door even though the old lady occasionally handed a pot of stew, pork bones or a slice of fruitcake over the back fence.

Joanna's spirits leapt at the thought of pork bones, a little bit extra for a growing dog.

Elspeth pushed past the table, her scarlet fingernails flashing as she reached for the door.

'Things are going to be different in future, my girl,' she said, pointing one scarlet nail in Joanna's direction. 'Tomorrow I'm starting a job so you'll have to fend for yourself. So get used to it. Starting from now!'

Joanna didn't dare say that for most of the time she fended for herself anyway. Her stomach was churning. As usual, she had saved some of her school dinner for Harry and today, of all days, there had been no chance of having a second helping, in fact, there was barely enough to go round.

'Are you going to work now?' Joanna asked timorously.

Glassy eyes glared from Elspeth's painted face. Her bright red lips parted in a contemptuous smile. 'No, you silly bitch. I'm off to celebrate. And make sure you do the dishes before I get back or you'll be gettin' what for. Is that clear?'

Joanna nodded that she understood. She stayed very still until she heard the slamming of the front door then the squeak of the rusty springs on the garden gate before it clanged shut. Even her grumbling stomach couldn't send her running to the kitchen, not until she heard those distinctive sounds. She was home alone and she couldn't have been happier.

After helping herself to a large portion of stew and a chunk of bread, washed down with a cup of tea, she began the dishes.

There weren't many and her stepmother had had the good grace to leave two chop bones on the edge of the plate. No stew for her stepmother, then. The butcher in North Street was always giving her bits of extra meat.

'Fancy a nibble on a nice pork chop, Mrs Ryan? Or how about a couple of fat sausages? One for tonight and one for tomorrow night.'

His suggestions were always accompanied by a salacious wink. Joanna took it that his comments were some kind of joke. If it was she didn't understand it.

Normally Joanna would gnaw on whatever Elspeth had left on the side of the plate. Tasting meat was a rare occurrence since her father had gone away.

On this occasion the chop bones ended up wrapped in a piece of newspaper. She also found some broken biscuits at the bottom of the tin, though she was careful not to take too many in case her stepmother noticed. Elspeth only always ate whole biscuits. The broken ones were for Joanna though she was expected to make them last. The bones from Elspeth's plate would form Harry's breakfast in the morning along with a small sliver of cheese rind and a spoonful of pork dripping. There were also the bones from Mrs Allen's stew which she would place within the puppy's reach in case he got hungry.

Once the dishes were done and everything for Harry was safely stored in her satchel, Joanna made her way up the stairs to bed.

She was careful not to turn the light on without drawing the blackout curtains. Once she'd switched it off she opened them again, her face glowing in the silver light of the moon, her eyes scanning the stars, the only lights she could see.

Before the blackout had been imposed she used to gaze out of that window, wishing she could be far away from The Vale. She'd read of faraway places with strange-sounding names but had never been anywhere except a Sunday school trip to Weston-super-Mare. It had rained most of the day, but she hadn't cared. The distant horizon was spread out before her and she couldn't help wondering what was beyond.

In the morning she woke up early, washed, dressed and went downstairs to light the fire. She'd already laid the kindling on top of screwed-up newspaper so it was just a case of fetching coal from where it was stored in the cupboard beneath the stairs. The door to the coalhouse was next to the kitchen, a big improvement on the lot of some people who still had to bring it in from outside. The coalman had to come through the house to tip it in but everyone in The Vale, unless they were the end ones on a block of four which had a side entrance, had to endure the same.

Joanna shuddered as she lifted the door latch. For a moment she could go no further forward. She'd been shut in there so many times. She could cope when the light from the kitchen flooded through the open door onto the heaps of black coal. The times she was locked in there when all was darkness were an entirely different matter.

By the time Elspeth put in an appearance the fire was lit and the tea was made.

Her stepmother was still wearing her dressing gown. The remains of red lipstick were smeared around her lips and congealed lumps of mascara hung from her eyelashes. A cigarette drooped from the corner of her mouth and her dressing gown gaped open, revealing what looked like purple pinches on her breasts.

Seeing Joanna's gaze, Elspeth slapped a hand across the back of her head.

'What the bloody hell do you think you're staring at?' Her voice was coarse and loud as she pulled the gaping garment around herself. 'They're just bruises. That's all they are. Right? Just bruises. I bumped into a door. Several doors.' She grinned as she said it and then laughed.

Joanna had experienced enough bruises in her time to know her stepmother was lying. The purple marks were very much like the purple blotches that came up on your arm if you sucked it long enough. The older girls at the big school in Marksbury Road called them love bites. She dared not ask if that was the case.

Bowing her head she shrugged her shoulders into her coat. The multi-coloured knitted scarf she wound around her neck had been knitted by Mrs Allen from odd bits and pieces. Joanna pulled on her wellington boots, the only footwear that didn't pinch her toes. The day was too wet to wear the second-hand shoes purchased at the same time as the coat.

Elspeth went out in the kitchen to pour herself a cup of tea and fry herself some bacon. Two fresh rashers had been placed in the pan. Two slices of bread were already cut. Joanna knew better than not to have Elspeth's breakfast ready.

'It'll have to be earlier next week,' Elspeth shouted after her. 'I'm on early shifts.'

Joanna reached for her satchel and headed for the door, relieved to be going outside whatever the weather might be. She was also relieved her stepmother would require her breakfast earlier next week. It would give her more time to gather things for Harry's breakfast.

'Just a minute. I want a word with you.'

Joanna stopped in her tracks and did her best to look innocent as she placed her hand over her satchel.

'Is something wrong?'

Even though Elspeth couldn't possibly see into her satchel, it was as though the bones, the biscuits and the other bits and pieces had jumped out and were dancing on her shoulders.

Elspeth's smeared lips widened into a self-satisfied smile. 'I'm on early shifts next week but late shifts today. Do you understand what that means?'

Joanna waited expectantly.

'What it means, you stupid kid, is that I won't be here when you get home, so feed yourself, wash up, and don't wait up. I begin my new job this afternoon. We get given our shift schedules one month in advance. This means working tonight as well.'

Joanna said nothing, her eyes as round as marbles in the pallor of her face, her fear replaced by relief. Her mouth was too dry to say anything.

Elspeth peered at her through a pall of cigarette smoke. Her smile slackened. 'Well, you could at least congratulate me.'

Joanna swallowed and wasn't sure what to say.

'Will it be interesting?' she asked in a small voice, hoping to God her comment met with favour.

'I don't suppose it will, but the money's good. I would have preferred a job as usherette down the Rex.' A dreamy look came to her face. 'Three matinees a day, five days a week. I would have been seeing all the latest pictures before anybody else had the chance. Clark Gable, Gary Cooper, Errol Flynn, you name them I would've been seeing them. And Jean Harlow. People say I look like Jean Harlow. Now there's a thing. A job at the Rex would have been nice. Still, I suppose in these times you've got to be grateful. And in any case, the factory pays better. I'll probably be making bombs to dump on Hitler. Anyway, this factory job means I won't be here when you get home for five nights of the week so you'll have to manage without me. Any problems, go see the old bag next door. She'll look after you. Got nothing better to do than poke 'er nose into other folks' business. Just don't go telling 'er anything about me. Right?'

Joanna nodded. She wasn't quite sure what secrets her stepmother required her to keep, but Mrs Allen was not a nosy person. She was kind and had twinkling eyes and was very generous with her cooking. If it hadn't been for her she would have starved.

It never occurred to Elspeth to question why her stepdaughter left for school when it was still dark and Joanna was thankful.

Her stepmother was full of the new job and when she spoke of coming home late – very late – her eyes had gleamed with excitement.

Joanna too was excited. The new job meant she wouldn't have to worry about getting home late.

That morning, despite the fact that it was still dark outside, she skipped her way down the garden path, too happy to care if she tripped over something or knocked into the dustbin.

With her satchel slamming against her hip she ran all the way to the allotments, slipping and sliding on the frosty pavements and cobbles. Even the hard-baked mud paths around the allotment were capped with frost and the intermittent puddles slicked with a thin layer of ice, but she danced around them, glad to be out and extra glad that she'd have the house to herself this evening.

Harry was wrestling with a sack that he'd managed to pull out of his bed, twisting his little head this way and that and growling as though the sack was a living thing.

He left the sack in the heap the moment she entered, jumping up at her, sniffing at her satchel and wagging his rump and little stump so much she felt sure he would wag what little he had left.

Once she was on her knees, he rained sloppy kisses upon her with his little pink tongue, jumping and dancing all over and around her.

Joanna took out the lamb bones, the cheese rind, the scraping of dripping and the broken biscuits and placed them in a cracked plate she'd brought with her.

Harry woofed all of it down without a moment's hesitation, then continued to lick the plate, making it rattle as he pushed it around the floor with his tongue and his nose.

Joanna took the sack he'd been wrestling and remade his bed. Once that was done, she refilled his water dish from the watering can which she had had the foresight to fill the night before.

The chill light of a winter's day had barely pierced the dirty window frame when she left.

The bones and gravy from Mrs Allen's stew she left within Harry's reach. He tucked in immediately.

'You have to make them last all day,' she said to him.

He continued to gnaw, sucking and chewing, completely oblivious of her presence.

Joanna was worried. There was no food left in her satchel only the old bicycle lamp, a few school books and a clean piece of newspaper into which she could place a few scraps from her school dinner.

She took more than she used to now, storing some of it in an old tea caddy she'd found inside the shed. The extra food was for Harry to eat on the weekend when the school was closed. She also poured him some milk from the third of a pint bottle she'd taken yesterday.

Soon it would be Christmas and she would no longer be able to bring him food from her school dinner plate. Somehow she would have to store even more than she did for a weekend to last him over the whole of the Christmas season.

'I shall store extra bits and pieces in the tea caddy,' she told herself, but was not reassured by this decision. The fact was Harry was quickly growing bigger and eating more and more. Somehow she had to figure out a way to get hold of more food. She frowned at the prospect. There were so many plans and decisions to make. Sometime in the spring she had to teach him to walk on the lead, to let him out into the fresh air. She certainly couldn't keep him indoors for ever.

At the sound of his plaintive howl she looked nervously around her, casting her eyes over the vegetables the flowers and the fruit bushes. Harry wouldn't eat anything she could see growing, but she had to do something or he would starve to death.

'I have to go now,' she said to him, holding his jowls as she gazed into his button bright eyes. 'You'll have to make those bones last all day until I come later. Promise me you will.'

Harry whimpered.

'Good,' she said, kissing the top of his head. 'I'll see you later.'

After carefully closing the door behind her, she set off down the path that would lead her back to the main road and eventually to school.

A rabbit awake from hibernation and out searching for breakfast chose that moment to run out from cover and cross her path. If Miss Hadley was right, rabbits should be hibernating. Obviously this one had grown tired of being confined in a dark hole in the ground. Definitely a wild rabbit, not domestic like the ones Paul had owned.

She thought of Paul's pet rabbits being killed for the pot. Paul had been loath to eat them though he openly confessed to snaring the rabbits that plagued the allotment holders around here.

A plan busily formed in her head. Paul could be the answer to her problem, though it meant she would have to let him in on her secret. But Harry could not stay in the shed for much longer. Neither could he live on scraps for ever. Catching a rabbit and cooking it seemed the ideal solution.

The junior boys were congregated around the school gate where they entered into their playground. Joanna headed for the girls' entrance but waved to Paul as she went in.

'I want to see you later,' she shouted to him.

He waved back, a cheery smile lighting his face. She'd avoided his company since finding Harry, but now she needed him. Everything would be fine, she told herself. Paul wasn't the kind to tell tales. It was her only option.

CHAPTER TEN

Seb Hadley was not just angry, he was confused, and although he knew he shouldn't lean so heavily on his daughter, he just couldn't help himself.

Although Sally was positively blooming since meeting her Frenchman, he couldn't get over the feeling of being discarded in favour of a sweetheart.

That evening he stayed up waiting for the sound of her key in the lock.

Much as he tried to rein in the jealousy that brewed inside, it burst out of him.

'What sort of time do you call this?' he demanded when she dared to walk in the door after half past eleven at night.

The sparkle in Sally's eyes vanished. Her happy expression disappeared too. Only the pink flush of her cheeks remained.

Without her needing to say a word, he knew she was in love. He could see all the signs. If Grace were still alive they would both be glad for her. Although he knew it was wrong, he feared losing her.

There wasn't a day went by when he didn't wake up and immediately reach over to the cold half of the bed where Grace had slept beside him for thirty-odd years. There wasn't a day went by when he didn't mourn her loss and resurrect vivid memories of their years together. The past meant everything to him; the future seemed only bleak and empty. At least he had his daughter, his life raft between the past and the future. He couldn't easily let her go.

Sally was dismayed though not entirely surprised. 'Dad. You can't go on like this. I miss Mum as much as you do, but I have my own life to live. You can't keep clinging to me like a drowning man.'

'So you're off, are you? Yes! I can see it in your eyes. Don't lie. I know you want to go off with him and leave me all by myself!'

'Dad! You've got to snap out of this. Other men have lost members of their family and with this war going on there will be a lot more. Think of the children who are likely to lose parents, the parents likely to lose sons. We're all in this war together, Dad, and we all need to pull together. So why aren't you? Why aren't you growing vegetables instead of flowers to the memory of a woman who would tell you the same as I am telling you? Get out there and dig for victory.'

Seb was stunned. Never before had Sally so vehemently stated the facts.

'Well,' he said, looking disconsolately into the fire. 'Now there's a way for a daughter to speak to her father!'

He waited for her to say sorry just like she always did. But on this occasion she did not.

'Stay here feeling sorry for yourself if you like. I'm going to bed,' she said grimly. 'See you in the morning.'

The door slammed behind her.

For a while Seb sat in front of the fire, his hands clasped tightly together, his eyes staring at the glowing embers but seeing nothing in them.

Although his heart was heavy, he didn't cry as he had on many other occasions when he dwelt on the memory of his dearly departed wife. Tonight Sally had voiced a truth that could not be denied: Grace would have pulled all those flowers up herself if she thought it could help feed the population and bring an end to a terrible war. Tomorrow he would do his best to honour her memory and begin doing what had to be done.

* * *

Sally lay awake for a while, listening for the sound of her father's footsteps coming up the stairs.

Before she'd met Pierre she would have felt guilty about spouting those words; in fact, she might not have said them in the first place. Things had changed.

Just one night in his company and Pierre's measured phrases and she knew him well. The way he looked at her, the half smile that lifted one corner of his mouth, had been familiar to her as breathing.

She knew beyond doubt that her life would never be the same again, and yet, not so long ago, he'd been a stranger in the street.

Falling asleep was difficult that evening. In her mind she was still in Pierre's company, going over what he'd looked like, what he'd said, what she'd said.

She could see Pierre smiling at her, his brown eyes warm with affection, his hair glossy and unsullied with Brylcreem.

When he smiled it was reflected in his eyes and when he spoke, his English slightly accented, his voice deep, she was lost.

And what he spoke. That floored her.

'Is this love at first sight?' he'd asked her.

She'd been speechless. Not because it surprised her that he'd asked, but because she'd been thinking the exact same thing. That's the way they were, saying the same thing at the same time.

Her response to such a surprising comment was equally surprising, even to her.

'No. It was love before we even met. We were just waiting for it to happen.'

And there it all was in front of her, as though they were the leading parts in a Hollywood romance. Not really, of course. The screen she was watching was in her mind. She replayed it time and time again, hardly believing that a doorstep conversation regarding a neighbour's cat could lead to this.

'I will take you to meet my aunt,' he'd said before they parted that night. A sad look had come to his eyes. 'She is very stalwart on the surface but beneath it her heart is breaking. There are so many animals being abandoned. There has been little forethought behind this action and everything has happened too quickly. The aftermath has been quite horrible. So will you come with me,' he'd asked, the warmth returning to his eyes. 'Would you come with me to meet my aunt?'

Her heart had raced at the prospect. 'To meet your family?' It was so soon. 'I would love to.'

His smile turned mischievous.

'Ah. In England meeting the family is a precursor to marriage, is it not?'

Lying there in her bed, Sally lay her palm on her cheek, recalling how she had blushed and stammered some kind of reply that said nothing either way.

'I am not asking you to marry me,' he said, looking amused at her discomfiture. 'Not yet.'

Absorbed in her thoughts that were swiftly becoming dreams, she never heard her father climb the stairs to bed. Instead she dreamed of Pierre and her up on the silver screen, two lovers kissing passionately and living happy ever after.

Seb wasn't sure whether it was surprise or relief he read on his daughter's face the following morning. She looked surprised that he hadn't insisted on escorting her to school or given any appearance of doing so.

'There's more bacon if you want it,' she said to him.

'One slice is enough, under the circumstances.'

To Sally's surprise he began piling dishes into the sink. He was an old-fashioned man, the kind who had set tasks and took it for granted that washing dishes was woman's work.

'You don't need to do that.'

'It's not as though it's never been done before. In the last war, gender was no barrier to what job you ended up doing. Likely as not it won't be any different in this war.'

Sally wasn't convinced but held her tongue. She glanced at the wall clock. Time was getting on.

'I'll see you later,' she said, before slipping out of the door.

Once he'd washed and wiped the dishes, Seb looked at his overcoat hanging on the back door. From there his gaze descended to a cast-iron boot scraper and the two pairs of boots standing next to it. He gazed at the larger pair of wellington boots, big and black with a thick sole. Grace's boots were still where they always had been when she was alive. They were black too, but lighter and shorter. He could almost imagine that she'd be along in a minute to pull them on – or off as the case might be.

He remembered laughing with her as they attempted to pull off each other's boots.

'You're pulling my leg off!'

'It wouldn't be the first time I've pulled your leg.'

Her ribald laughter faded like the echoing of a stone rattling along the gutter and into the distance, a moment lost for ever.

Then he thought about what Sally had said to him, about the war, about people needing to eat and what Grace would say about that: '*Come on, Seb. We can't sit around here leaving it to the youngsters. We have to do our bit.*'

He stared at the spot where the coat was hanging above the boots. He reached for the pair that fitted him. They felt comfortable, as though his toes were returning to greet an old friend.

Next was his overcoat, his scarf and his battered old trilby. With a feeling of anticipation that was almost fear, he opened the blue glass inner door, closed it behind him, then left the house, closing the heavy exterior front door behind him.

The early-morning gloom of November was beginning to dissipate, a weak sun attempting to break through a misted sky.

The street outside was deserted. So was the park. Most people had already left for work and a few chattering children were heading along the main road to school, heads bent against the early-morning chill, book-laden satchels bouncing on their hips. Another half an hour and the sound of children's voices, laughter, shouting and screaming, would come from the school playground.

Seb looked in the direction of the school for some time before turning away. He set his attention towards the cobbled lane, then the hard-packed mud track down to the allotment.

The ground had thawed a little from the last frost and he smelled rain in the air. Ideally he should wait to clear his patch. The roots would be difficult to pull up with the ground this hard, but the work would do him good. It had been too long since he'd done anything very physical. His tools would need cleaning of course, the fork and the spade a little rusty without the application of oil.

The sound of a train heralded a cloud of steam rolling in like sea foam over the railings and on to the allotments, shrouding the finer details from view. He watched the heavy iron giant sweeping along: powerful and noisy also a little dirty. Before retiring, Seb had worked on the railways. It had been Grace's suggestion to acquire one of the allotments next to the railway line. Memories swirled around his head as he breathed in the pungent smell of burning coal and boiling water.

The steam hovered in the morning air, a veil between him and his old shed. Not that he needed to see the shed to know what condition it was in. No doubt the dilapidated construction would need a bit of a clean after almost two years of neglect. It had never been built to last.

Then he saw the shed door open and a small figure appear.

He heard her – for it definitely was a little girl – speak to somebody in the shed. Soft words. Comforting words.

Someone was in his shed! His first inclination was to demand what this person was doing invading his personal property. Instead he stood absolutely still, waiting to see what she did next. If she came his way he would challenge her. But the little figure ran off in the opposite direction, disappearing in what remained of the steam.

Feeling confused at his own inaction, Seb headed for the shed, the dried-out stalks of what remained of Grace's flowers snatching at his overcoat as he passed close by.

He'd heard the girl speaking to somebody inside the dilapidated structure. He presumed it was another child, perhaps a truant taking a day off school or even a runaway hiding out until the coast was clear. He had to discover who it was before making a decision what to do with them.

Cupping his hand over his eyes, he looked through the window. The panes were surprisingly clean and although the inside was dingy there was just enough light to see his workbench and the shelf on the far wall. There was, however, no sign of another person.

He glimpsed his implements hanging from hooks and the trowels, tins of linseed oil and other bits and pieces on the shelves looking dusty and forgotten.

So who was it she'd been talking to?

Perhaps he'd misheard. Kids talked to imaginary friends, didn't they?

After casting a critical and somewhat guilty look over his allotment he lifted the metal hook from its fastening and entered.

For a moment he stood there in the middle of the shed, frowning at his surroundings. It all seemed as he had left it. Nothing moved. Just as it had appeared from the outside, the inside was most definitely empty.

Not able to believe it truly was, his eyes swept over his surroundings for the second time. He had the distinct impression he was being watched. There was also a sound that he couldn't quite identify.

At first he thought a small steam train was close by – a very small one. *No*, he thought to himself. *That's too soft a sound for a steam train. It's more like* . . . He thought hard. *Panting!* It sounded like somebody panting, not a steam train at all.

The sound was coming from somewhere down near his feet. He looked down and found himself gazing into the most endearing little face he'd seen in a long time.

Two glowing eyes looked up at him. A long pink tongue hung from the puppy's mouth. The creature was sat on its haunches, gazing up at him with those velvet brown eyes and panting, perhaps in fear.

Seb had never been a hard man, but neither was he a soft one. Yet seeing the vulnerable little animal his heart skipped a beat and something heavy, as stout as an old oak door, seemed to creak open. The reason for it opening was as light as a feather, an ecstatic feeling, like a bright light shining into a dark corner.

He bent down to take a closer look.

'You're not afraid, are you?' he said, keeping his voice low so as not to frighten the little chap.

He held out his index finger. The puppy's tongue was wet and warm and at its touch Seb felt that oak door creak on its hinges and finally crash to the floor.

The puppy came out of his bed, stepping over the board that penned him in, wagging the whole length of his body from wet nose to stubby tail.

It had been a long time since Seb had felt so wanted and his heart melted.

'And who might you be?' he asked, softly going down on one knee.

The puppy, obviously glad of company, wagged even more vigorously than before. Seb knew enough about dogs to guess that this was an English cocker spaniel and he didn't need to see the docked tail to work that out. Poor little chap. He must have had that done at a very young age. He'd heard two weeks was the norm, usually before their eyes were open.

The puppy's coat was fluffy and golden. When he grew up it would be glossy and as bright as a newly minted copper penny. His ears were low set and draped around his face like a young girl's hair. His eyes were deep brown and soulful.

He spotted the old pottery dish and the name written in crayon around its side in a childish hand. Harry.

He smiled, his eyes remaining fixed on the little dog.

'So you're Harry, are you? I wonder if you're hungry. Are you hungry?' Seb undid the buckles on his rucksack. 'Let's see what we can find for you, eh?'

Harry gobbled back a piece of the sandwich Seb had made before leaving home. Bread and cheese, and the puppy didn't seem to mind the pickle even though afterwards he did lap up all the water in his dish.

Seb's lips twitched from one side to the other as though smiling too broadly might crack his face.

'That mustard pickle a bit too hot, then, Harry?'

The little dog sneezed in response, his ears flapping as he did so.

Seb took all his sandwiches apart, scraping aside the pickle until he was left with just cheese and bread.

Harry ate everything, despite sneezing every so many bites. Once everything was devoured, the little dog looked up at him expectantly licking his lips. Seb guessed he wanted more water. His dish was already empty.

He saw the watering can and guessed there was water in it beneath a layer of ice. He immediately thought of the flask he'd brought with him.

'How about a drop of milky, sweet tea? How would that suit you, young Harry?'

Understanding Seb's tone and deciding it held no threat, Harry licked his lips in anticipation, watching as this new human in his life unscrewed the top of a Thermos flask.

'Just a minute. Give me chance to pour it in,' said Seb, one hand holding Harry back while he poured the tea into his dish with the other hand.

Harry made great big lapping noises as he drank until there was nothing left except a droplet hanging on the end of his nose; that too was swiftly dislodged and swallowed.

As seemed to be his custom, Harry wagged his whole body, his little face upturned and looking at Seb, his newfound friend.

'There's no more,' said Seb showing him the empty paper bag. Harry promptly shoved his nose in the bag, snuffling as he licked up every last crumb of food.

Tummy bulging after the unexpected feast, he ignored the piece of fruitcake Seb offered him from a separate paper bag. His eyes were drooping and his wagging tail was not so vigorous as it had been.

'Tired out old fellah?'

With a quick hop over the side rail the puppy returned to his bed beneath the table.

Seb watched, heart brimming over with affection as the little fellow curled himself into a ball and fell asleep. Tears brimmed in his eyes as something deep inside broke open, something that had been closed for years.

He stayed there watching for a while until finally reminding himself of the reason he was here.

He spent the next two hours clearing the ragged remains of straggly plants from the allotment, piling most of it onto a heap he intended for compost, weighing it down with a piece of heavy slate. He'd never put in so much effort since Grace had died, and the morning went fast.

Lunchtime he spent with Harry, sharing the piece of pie he'd wrapped in tissue and placed in the same paper bag as the fruitcake. There was only enough tea left for Seb.

'You'll have to make do with water, old chap. I've only got enough for one.'

Harry didn't seem to mind.

Once lunch was over and Harry had again settled down to sleep, Seb did another two hours pulling out more of the old plants before looking up at the sky and rubbing his back. The rain wouldn't be long coming if his aches and pains were anything to go by.

By four o'clock he looked at the bare expanse of allotment and told himself he'd done a good job. Grace would have been proud of him. The dark brown rectangle of earth was cleared and ready for planting, though this time only with vegetables.

Methodically and purposefully he cleaned his gardening tools, then entered the shed and proceeded to put them away.

If he'd thought he was getting away with a quiet end to his gardening day he was very much mistaken. Harry had woken up, yapping with delight on seeing that Seb his new friend was back and running round and round Seb's legs.

'Steady on, Harry, my boy.'

He almost tripped over the puppy and eventually was forced to pick him up so that Harry could welcome him properly, washing his face with his darting pink tongue and wagging tip of nose to tip of tail.

He laughed as he put him down, wiping the earth off his hands on a piece of old rag, as he considered clearing away the little chap's litter tray and making him comfortable for the night. Something stopped him. He didn't want the little girl to know he'd been here. If she did find out she might very well remove Harry from his little nest beneath the table and he didn't want her to do that. Already he was certain he would miss him.

He reconsidered his decision but still arrived at the same conclusion.

It had taken him a long time to return here and what he'd found had surprised him. Harry had decided to love him despite him being a total stranger. Now they were strangers no more.

The government were full of advice nowadays and, although some was helpful, he found their suggestions regarding beloved pets totally abhorrent.

So many had died and so many others had been abandoned. He guessed that Harry was one of them and that the little girl was keeping him hidden.

For the foreseeable future he would respect her secret.

Harry watched him with soulful eyes as he put on his hat and coat.

'I expect I'll be seeing you tomorrow,' he said, speaking to the little dog as though he could understand every word. The puppy looked up at him with his big mournful eyes. One look from those eyes and Seb knew there was no expect about it. He had to come here. He had to make sure the puppy was thriving, besides which he enjoyed his company.

He didn't go home straightaway. He wanted to ensure the little girl was coming back with Harry's evening meal. The little chap must be feeling hungry by now. He grinned as the realisation hit him that Harry was always hungry. He was a growing lad.

Still, it won't hurt to check, he said to himself.

With that in mind he hid behind the shed on a neighbouring plot, waiting to see if the little girl dropped by.

Sure enough, a small figure bobbed out of the descending twilight, running down the path, her pigtails flying out behind her, her arms pumping like the pistons of a steam train.

Once at the shed, she heaved upon the door to the sound of excited barking coming from within. The puppy sounded very pleased to see her and Seb was almost disappointed at that.

'You old fool,' he muttered to himself. In the blink of an eye he had grown fond of Harry and was almost jealous that the puppy's first loyalty was to the little girl.

The girl would have brought Harry food, and Seb pictured the puppy jumping up and down with excitement as he waited to be fed.

He smiled as he turned away, glad that he'd left everything more or less the same as he'd found it. The girl would be none the wiser and tomorrow he would attend his allotment again and share his food with Harry. He was very happy.

CHAPTER ELEVEN

It was Friday night. The saloon bar of the Engineer's Arms throbbed with conversation and the air was thick with cigarette smoke. The fug and noise was louder in the public bar where the men piled six deep, shoulder-to-shoulder and elbow-to-elbow.

An unwritten rule prevailed that only men drank in the public bar while those women who were out and about were confined to the saloon bar.

The saloon bar had a certain ambience about it, due in no small part to the tinkling keys of the piano and the fact that the floor was wood-block rather than sprinkled with sawdust. The seating too was more comfortable.

A crowd were gathered around the piano, drinks in hand, fingers and feet tapping. Eyes that had become tired, thanks to long hours working a lathe or measuring the dimensions of engine parts, regained a little sparkle as they sang along, glad to have finished their shift, escaping for a moment into another world.

Elspeth Hadley studied the scene with half-closed eyes. The smoke from her cigarette only added to the fug already there.

Before she got the job, working in an engineering factory making bits for artillery shells had never appealed as much as working as an usherette, but now she reckoned it the best thing she'd ever done.

Why be stuck at home with a kid that wasn't yours when you could be working among all these men? She loved being in male company and didn't complain when one gave her the wink or pinched her bottom; she loved that kind of attention.

Friday night was the best night of the week. All those that could headed for the bar of The Engineer's – mainly single women and what men were lingering on the way home to their nearest and dearest.

Elspeth loved it.

'Penny for 'em, Elspeth, me love.'

Elspeth smiled. Every man here called her 'me love'. Not all the women got the same attention she did and it made her feel special. The woman she worked next to had got quite irate when the foreman had slapped her bottom.

'It's not right,' she'd protested. 'It's disrespectful.'

Elspeth didn't agree. She loved what everyone called 'a bit of slap and tickle'.

'I was thinking about when war broke out,' she said, smiling sweetly at the man who had asked the question. 'Never thought I'd get involved in it.' She shrugged. 'But there you are. None of us can see what's coming, can we?'

When Tom, Joanna's father, had gone off to war, Elspeth had had no intention of getting a job and to her great delight her husband had agreed with her.

'You just keep the home fires burning, love. The army pay should do you proud. In the meantime, here's a bit to spend on things you need. You might include a new coat for our Joanna. She's growing that fast. Her old one won't last.'

Smiling seductively, Elspeth had got him on her side without any fuss. She could read her husband like a book, and in that respect was no different from many of the other men she met. Elspeth Wood, as she used to be before marriage, had always had a way with men. Her hair colour was not natural and she was in the habit of over-painting her face. However, her figure was her own, she knew how to dress to entice, and knew that she had eyes that were full of promise.

Without her needing to say a word, a man knew what was on offer and how good she was at delivering it. She could cook a bit, enough to feed a hungry man, and her skills in bed made up for her slovenliness around the house. Still, she had Joanna to do the housework. Even before Tom had gone to war, she'd bullied Joanna into doing as she said.

'You're not my kid. I don't have to look after you. All I've got to do is to tell your dad I don't want you and you get put in an orphanage. That's why he married me. Just so you wouldn't end up in an orphanage.'

Joanna had believed her. Elspeth sniggered to herself at the memory.

'What you laughing at, darling?'

The bull-headed docker was hardly the most handsome of men but he was generous with his money.

'I was just thinking I'm glad I never had kids.'

Her companion – she remembered his name was Fred – pulled a face before tipping the last of a pint of bitter into his mouth.

'Fancy another? Port and lemon, ain't it?'

She smiled at him and nodded. He was married. Even if she hadn't already known it – gossip was rife at the factory – she could tell that by the way he swigged back his beer rather than comment on her statement. He had kids too. Not that she cared. He could buy her all the drinks he liked. But he wasn't her type. He was too coarse. She did like a bit of refinement. She had her sights set on something better, a more refined man who didn't stink of sweat and wore cologne. She wanted somebody to spoil her, take her dancing or to the pictures, at least until Tom came home.

Of course there was always the chance that Tom wouldn't come home and then she'd have to quickly find a replacement. The truth was she couldn't live without a man. She loved the smell of men, their strength, the way they towered over her, the feeling of security they gave. Of course, men always thought they were in control, that they were the dominant partners in the relationship. She let them believe that. She could play a man like George Formby could play a ukulele.

Her head jerked round the moment a blast of cold air came into the bar from outside. It was her date, a respectable-looking man who didn't smell of engineering grease and always drank in the saloon bar.

The moment she saw him, the anxious tightening of her stomach relaxed and she smiled at him.

'Here you are, love.' A drink was set down on the table. The man who had bought her the drink made a move to sit down but Elspeth slapped her handbag onto the seat of the chair and smiled up at him 'Sorry. My date's arrived.'

The man scowled, his bushy eyebrows meeting in an angry V above his nose, but Elspeth kept her composure.

Arnold Thomas sat down, took off his hat and placed it on the table. He was nervous, as usual, glancing around him in case he was recognised. Elspeth knew that this was another married man, and again she didn't care. This was the man she wanted.

'So how is she?' He'd told her all about his wife, Miranda, that she was an invalid and not in the best of health.

'Not good. I made soup for her dinner, but she didn't eat much of it.' His eyes were downcast as he sipped at his drink.

Elspeth patted his hand. 'I bet she's asleep now. Best thing for her, I'd say. Sleep is a great healer.'

'You're probably right.'

He nodded at her, his pale blue eyes bright with appreciation and a smile came to his face.

Drawing on her vast experience of men, Elspeth had worked out that possessing her body did not appeal to him, at least for now. It didn't mean he didn't want her physically, but Arnold Thomas was not the sort of man to grope her in public or take her in a back alley against a dirty wall. He was a schoolteacher, with a house in Jubilee Road, and he had a sick wife. Bearing in mind they both had spouses who might not make old bones, she would snap him up at once if the chance arose. All she had to do for now was appear to be his best friend, the person with time to listen.

His gaze strayed, a faraway look in his eyes as they travelled to the saloon bar door.

Elspeth read his expression. He was in two minds whether to go or stay. The last thing Elspeth wanted was for him to think too deeply.

'Are you a good cook?'

Her sudden question brought him back from his reverie. He made a so-so gesture with his right hand and gave her a nervous smile. 'I do what I can.'

'Well, if you ate it yourself it must have been tasty enough,' she said.

He shook his head before sipping at his beer and swallowing. 'By the time I tucked her in and made sure she was asleep, my appetite was gone.'

The sudden growling of his stomach made them both laugh.

'Sounds like you should have lingered and made yourself a sandwich. It don't do to drink beer on an empty stomach.'

Arnold sighed. 'I suppose you're right.'

Despite his rumbling stomach they had another drink each. The conversation continued to centre round his wife.

Absorbed in his woes, it didn't occur to Arnold that he was being selfish. He always talked about himself and his wife, their humdrum lives in their semi-detached house in Jubilee Road.

Elspeth knew better than to let her annoyance show. Maintaining an expression of sympathy wasn't easy, but it seemed to please him.

After two more drinks each, they both declared themselves finished for the evening.

Each had their own reasons for calling a halt. Arnold didn't have a head for drink, but Elspeth had another motive.

A plan had formed in her mind that excited her almost as much as the time she'd set her cap at Tom. In a war situation it played to hedge your bets. Tom might not come back and Miranda might die. It might or might not happen. In the meantime she had no intention staying in by herself night after night. She adored male company too much to do that.

It might be a bit too soon for snaring him, but she decided to play her first hand.

'Fancy coming back for a sandwich?'

He shook his head laughingly. 'You don't need to do that, Elspeth.'

'Sorry I'm sure,' she said petulantly.

Arnold Thomas knew instantly that he'd upset her. His conscience pricked him to make amends. He was already feeling guilty for leaving his wife at home ill in bed. Now he had upset the only person who listened to his troubles.

'Look, I wasn't being rude and I don't want to put you to any trouble . . .'

'It's no trouble,' Elspeth interjected. 'You're alone. I'm alone and we're friends. That's all.'

In normal circumstances she would have ran her hand through his sandy hair, but guessed he'd find it embarrassing.

For a moment he looked indecisive but she knew that as long as she maintained her sugary smile and the look of concern in her eyes, he would tumble.

It turned out she was right.

'I will accept your kind offer though it does rather depend on what you're offering. A cheese sandwich would not be welcome. Not at all!'

Elspeth raised her puzzled eyebrows. On seeing them Arnold began to explain. 'Because Miranda eats so little, I tend to cook as little as possible and usually end up with a cheese sandwich.'

'Bacon?'

He shook his head. 'I don't eat meat.'

She thought that peculiar, something that in time she would change once she had her claws in him, but for now she would pander to his every predilection. In the meantime she mentally scoured her larder.

'How about fish? I'm sure I've got a tin of pilchards in the larder.'

112

It took her by surprise when his face lit up. 'Yes, I wouldn't mind a plate of pilchards.'

Just like Tom, thought Elspeth. How disgusting men could be.

Outside the frost-covered ground sparkled beneath the light from Arnold's torch as arm in arm they made their way along St John's Road and up The Vale.

Feigning a fear of slipping, Elspeth clutched Arnold's arm tightly, her steaming breath as much due to excitement as to the exertion of walking uphill.

They had little conversation. Both were saving their energy so they might get up the hill safely, a fact Elspeth was grateful for.

He was hardly the first man she'd brought home since Tom had gone to war, but he was the most special, and with that in mind the last thing she wanted was for a nosy neighbour to hear them come home.

Before leaving the house she'd told Joanna to wash up and tidy the house. With hindsight she wished she'd done a bit more herself but if she had to put up with the child she might as well got some use out of her.

She so badly wanted to make a good impression and she'd done all she could. Joanna was suitably cowed to be obedient, and she knew beyond doubt the child would have followed her instructions to be in bed by nine o'clock.

It was ten o'clock and as she pushed open the front door. She was pleased by the silence that met her. A little bit of discipline and the girl did as she was told. That was the trouble with Tom. Her husband had been too lenient with the kid.

The living room was warm and the fire was banked up, the fireguard placed in front of it. All was neat and tidy. Goodness, but she almost felt it in her heart to praise the girl in the morning.

Arnold stood nervously by the living-room door.

Elspeth waved at a chair. 'Take a seat.' She was about to add that she wasn't going to bite him, but sensed he wouldn't appreciate such a vulgar insinuation. He wasn't the type of bloke she usually picked up. Arnold was the closest thing to a gentleman round here therefore she would make the effort to watch her Ps and Qs.

'While you make yourself comfortable, I'll put the kettle on and make us a bite to eat. Pilchards, you said?'

'If you could,' he said, as he removed his hat and slid his arms out of his overcoat.

A thrill of excitement shot through Elspeth. Even the dingy kitchen seemed that bit brighter. This man excited her. He was so special, and even though he was married, she reminded herself he had good reason to seek company. Yes, she'd do all right by him.

Out came the best teacups, the ones that used to belong to Joanna's mother. They had red flowers on them and a wavy edge trimmed with gilt. There used to be six but she'd taken four to the pawnshop. She had planned to take the other two before very long, but was now glad she had not. Arnold wasn't the type to drink from a chipped enamel mug.

There was milk, tea and enough sugar. She sliced the bread, scraped some butter on each slice, then went to the larder.

Because of her dislike of all things fishy, the tin of pilchards had been pushed to the back of the larder. Bottles, tins and packages were moved around the shelf like chessmen on a board, but no matter how hard she looked there was no sign of the pilchards.

Elspeth frowned. The excitement she'd been feeling was severely dented. Her dismay intensified when she realised the only suitable sandwich filler was a piece of mouldy cheese. Arnold was fed up with cheese. What could she do?

Not a cheese sandwich. He was well and truly fed up with that, but how about if she toasted the cheese?

Taking a deep breath she picked up the two teacups and went into the living room, her beaming smile ably hiding the burgeoning disquiet she was feeling inside.

'Arnold, I am so sorry. It seems as though my daughter had eaten the pilchards for her supper.' She shrugged apologetically. 'You know how it is. I'm working all these hours so she has to fend to herself to a great extent.'

He nodded and waved his hands, a sign she took as dismissal of the problem. 'We all have to manage with what we have. Forget what I said. Cheese will do nicely.'

Thank goodness for that! She almost felt like singing. He certainly wasn't one to be inconvenient! All the same she made the instant decision to still go one step further.

'How about cheese on toast? At least it's warm and I can mix a bit of butter in it and top it with . . .' She laughed. 'Silly me! I was going to say I could top it with bacon, but you've already said you don't eat meat.'

'Cheese on toast would be very welcome. And thanks for the tea.'

She made him two pieces of cheese on toast even though it would leave her short for the morning. Although she had considered rewarding Joanna for having the place looking so clean and prepared for visitors, it was Joanna who would have to go without. No toast. She would have to make do with porridge

Oh well, she thought to herself as she listened to Arnold go on and on about his job. He didn't seem very put out not to be eating pilchards for his supper. Veiling her thoughts she listened with a smile on her face while in her mind she made more plans to get to know him a bit better.

'Bit of music?' she asked brightly.

'That would be nice.'

'And another cup of tea?'

He handed her his cup and saucer. 'Only if you can spare it.'

'Of course I can. My daughter doesn't drink tea so we have enough.'

'Does she go to my school?' he asked.

'I thought you were the headmaster of the boys' school?'

'I am. I meant does she go to Victoria Park?'

115

'Yes. She does.'

Elspeth handed him his second cup of tea. She'd used the same tea leaves, merely adding water to the pot and it a good stir. She'd also poured into his cup first, ensuring he would get the strongest.

'Is she doing well?'

'Well, I couldn't really say. She never tells me anything about school, and quite frankly she is a bit wild. Sometimes I just can't break through. In my opinion she needs a bit more discipline than she's getting. A few raps across the knuckles never did me any harm when I was at school.'

Arnold looked down into his tea as he took a slurp. 'That's a pity. We don't like inflicting corporal punishment, even on the boys. I'm sorry to hear your daughter has gone off the rails. Still, there are places you can put her where they are trained to deal with problematic children.'

'Are they very far away?'

Arnold shook his head and drained his tea before answering. 'The children live in. It's a wrench sometimes for both the children and the parents, but in certain situations it's all for the best.'

Her face fell. Arnold winced.

'Elspeth, I didn't mean to upset you.'

Her eyes were very wide and bright and there was an odd serene expression on her heavily made-up face.

'You didn't, Arnold. You could never do that. And as you say having her sent away might do her some good. Sad but true.'

The sigh she heaved was too intense to be real, but Arnold didn't seem to notice. He was too worried he might have upset her.

The fact was his life had become more lonely and routine over the past few years. His job lasted most of the day. The time he spent with his wife when she stayed awake long enough to listen to the details of his day and relate the details of hers, such as it was, was minimal. It wasn't that he had actively sought the company of a woman. He'd just needed a little company and some time away from his home that smelled of carbolic, disinfectant and sickness. Something was bound to break and, although he had held his natural urges at bay, he wanted company, and when he was at his lowest ebb, along came Elspeth.

'Shall we meet again?' she asked him as she handed him his hat and helped him into his overcoat.

He looked a little guilty. 'Well. It's been a wonderful evening, but . . . I wouldn't want people to talk . . .'

Elspeth pressed a finger against his mouth.

'We're just friends. That's all.'

The tension left his face. 'In that case I see no reason not.'

Whatever guilt he might be feeling, she thought she knew the antidote. But not yet. She told herself to give him a little more time.

He paused before she opened the living-room door and looked down into her face. 'Thank you again for a lovely evening. I've really appreciated your company.'

Her bright red lips spread in a smile that displayed nicotine-stained teeth.

'You're welcome. I enjoyed it too. Goodnight,' she whispered, keen for her neighbours not to hear as she switched off the light before opening the door.

Arnold said goodbye in similarly hushed tones. He had no wish to be seen frequenting the house of a woman who was not his wife.

And then he was gone. She couldn't watch him striding off down the path because of the darkness and there was no point in waving. The night took him.

Smiling to herself she ran her hand down the closed door. Everything had gone very well. Very well indeed, though it was a shame about the pilchards.

The smile faded from her face at the thought of them. She'd told Joanna to have cheese on toast for supper. Obviously the child had fancied the pilchards – the tin of pilchards that Arnold Thomas would have enjoyed.

The sparkle that had lit her eyes was replaced by a hard look that failed to reflect any light at all. The corners of her mouth turned down. Joanna had defied her. Luckily she had charmed Arnold into eating cheese on toast and he'd seemed genuinely pleased with her offering. But that was hardly the point. From the very start of her relationship with the child's father, she had deeply resented the child. She had wanted a man to herself, but marrying Tom meant she would have a roof over her head and three square meals a day, unlike where she had come from.

From a very young age she had lived on the streets, too scared to go home to her drunken father and her violent brothers. There had been no question of procuring a respectable job. She had been trained to live on her wits, to smile at the stupid sailors and Lascars that came aboard ships to Tiger Bay, Cardiff. She'd known what they wanted, but had been swift on her feet. Sometimes she had stolen their money and legged it before their befuddled brains realised what she was doing. Sometimes she exchanged the money they offered for her body.

Fed up with her life Elspeth had taken it on her head to strive for better things. She wanted nice clothes and a roof over her head that wasn't letting in the rain. She'd also wanted a man who wouldn't beat her if she refused to go out and sell her body on the streets.

Just a few months after running away and coming to Bristol, she was pretty well set up. She had a job as a bar maid in a pub called The Hatchet in Bristol city centre.

The customers had liked the singsong Welsh lilt of her voice and her sweet voice.

Her hair had been mousy back then and her skin clear. The landlord she worked for had queried whether she was old enough to serve behind a bar. Not wishing to lose her job she'd dyed her hair and used more makeup. The overall effect was to make her look older. Nobody questioned her age again.

There had been no shortage of suitors. Young as she was, she knew the difference between those who were genuine and those who wanted merely a bit of fun.

Then she'd met Tom. She had recognised at once a lonely man who missed his wife and had a guilt complex about how best to look after the child. He accepted that a man alone was useless at being a mother as well as a father. Recognising a man in need of a companion rather than straightforward sex, Elspeth decided to reel him in.

She'd told him she was from a small Welsh village in the Wye Valley and that she had no living relatives. 'Died in the mines you see.' She wasn't sure there were any mines in the village of Tintern, the one she'd selected, but he didn't press her for more details.

Elspeth never told Tom about Cardiff and her real life. Nor did she ever admit that she disliked children and he never questioned her on the subject. Like most men he assumed the maternal instinct came naturally to every woman. He couldn't have been more wrong. It was cruelty that came naturally to her it having been the norm in the shamble of a home she was raised in. Tom would never have understood that.

Her thoughts went back to the tin of pilchards. She was livid that Joanna had eaten the lot, but how come there was no half empty tin? She went to the larder to double check.

Nothing. Nor was there anything in the meat safe or any empty tin in the rubbish bin.

Elspeth stood at the bottom of the stairs. The house was in darkness and, although she was keen to know the truth, she knew it was best to leave it until daylight. Just for once she would get up early.

CHAPTER TWELVE

It was late afternoon on a Friday when Pierre took Sally to meet his Aunt Amelia, Lady Ambrose-DeVere, picking her up in a two-seater sports car the top pulled up firmly against the cold weather.

Butterflies were performing aerobatics in Sally's stomach. She'd rather stand in front of a class of screaming nine-year-olds, each throwing a tantrum. What if Aunt Amelia disliked her on sight?

Noticing her nerves, Pierre did his best to reassure her. 'You will love her. I know you will.'

'But will she love me?'

Pierre was adamant. 'Of course she will. She loves me. I told her I loved you and so she will love you.'

Sally was stunned. Pierre had just uttered the most thrilling three little words he could ever say. He loved her! She knew he was a man who made up his mind quickly. He oozed confidence, fully convinced that his opinion would be instantly echoed and agreed with by other people. A niggling voice at the back of her mind pointed out that he might very well be the kind of man who insisted on having his own way, that he was convinced he was always right and expected everyone else to fall in line.

As fast as the thought formed, she dismissed it. He was perfect, her very own Prince Charming.

Ambrose House was a rambling mid-nineteenth-century building with medieval turrets at one end, a Georgian portico slammed right in the centre, and a neo-Elizabethan black-and-white gable at the opposing end.

Sally eyed the building with foreboding that was coupled with a good dose of criticism for whoever had designed it.

Either the original place had been added to or successive generations had favoured one era. It occurred to her that the former was the most likely. The Victorians had a reputation for mixing styles with no regard for good taste.

Instead of pulling up in front of the imposing main entrance, Pierre followed the road around the gabled end to the rear of the property, drawing up at the back door and a far plainer entrance than at the front.

On alighting from the car, Sally noticed a painted sign, ordering tradesmen to ring the bell and wait.

She bristled at the insult, that she was relegated to the tradesmen's entrance as befitting a member of the general public. That was before Pierre opened the car door, grabbed her hand and proceeded to drag her in the opposite direction to the house.

'This way.'

He led her away from the rear facade to where a collection of single storey buildings stood in a separate courtyard opposite a series of very large greenhouses.

The sound of barking told her that whatever the old stone buildings might once have been, they were now converted to kennels. It sounded as though a whole pack of dogs were housed there.

Pierre, excitement lighting up his delicious brown eyes, pushed open the door of what might once have been a dairy where maids spent all day churning milk into butter or cheese – the milky smell long gone and replaced with the smell of dog.

'Auntie's favourite place,' Pierre whispered.

Ahead of them Sally spotted someone bent down. All she could see of them was a wide bottom and a worn seat of a pair of dark green corduroys. The corduroys were tucked into a man-sized pair of wellington boots.

'Aunt Amelia!'

At the sound of Pierre's voice the figure turned round. Sally was confronted with a weather-beaten face and the brightest blue eyes she'd ever seen. She flinched as they swept boldly over her in a swift act of evaluation. Most people would take their time weighing up a visitor, possibly not making their mind up until a bedrock of familiarity had been established. Pierre's Aunt Amelia had made up her mind in a moment.

'Right,' she said, her jaw-clenching stiffness vanishing in an instant. 'So you're the little poppet Pierre's been rabbiting on about. Pleased to meet you.'

Sally shook the proffered hand, the roughness of which surprised her.

Suddenly a gust of wind blew a cloud of steam between them. Sally wrinkled her nose at the smell that came with it.

Her ladyship beamed. 'Intestines! That's what you can smell. Tripe,' stated Pierre's aunt, with a sideways jerk of her head. 'Though unbleached, so not fit for human consumption. And it comes from a horse! The knacker's yard is quite happy for me to buy it. Different for a cow's tripe, of course. Or a sheep's, for that matter. Have you ever tasted mugget? That's the name they give sheep's tripe.'

Sally admitted that she had not.

Perhaps because they could smell that evening's meal cooking, the dogs began to bark.

Pierre, who had been watching Sally closely, suggested they take a look at his aunt's menagerie.

Without waiting for Sally to answer, Lady Amelia Ambrose-DeVere, who looked more like a farmer than a titled lady, strode off, her boots slopping slightly as though they were too big for her.

Sally exchanged a smile with Pierre and he squeezed her hand reassuringly. All they could do was follow.

They stopped in front of a little black-and-white dog yapping for all his worth and bouncing up and down on his hind legs.

Amelia pointed to him. 'I've named him Jack. You can see why, I trust?'

Under Amelia's hard stare, Sally felt as though she were a butterfly being pinned to a display board.

'Because he's like a Jack in the Box?'

'Correct. He was also left in a box outside my gate. Unfazed by his experience. He's that sort. One of the lucky ones to be so.' Amelia's manner was abrupt but her expression was soft.

She went on to introduce Sally to other dogs she'd rescued, including a greyhound.

'It's supposed to be a bit like horse racing, though more favoured by the common man, rather than a sport of kings. Once he ceased winning for his owner and reached the end of his racing life he was destined for the scrap heap. The war hastened this. He was abandoned, though not before they'd cut off his ears. Racing greyhounds are tattooed with an identification number. The owner would have been found. Then I would have cut off *his* ears – or something more painful,' she added.

Judging by the look on her face, Sally had no doubt she was being deadly serious.

'I used to concentrate on greyhounds, but the war has changed all that. This is now a haven for the unwanted: cats complete with litters of kittens, placed in a sack, weighed down with bricks and thrown into a river. A dog found hanging from a tree, another tied to a railway line. Not all the animals that come to me have been mistreated. Some of the owners are just at their wits' end. War or not, they do not wish for their pets to be put down. I'm their last hope.'

Feeling genuinely moved, Sally patted and stroked those animals she could reach. 'You're so wonderful to be doing this.'

Amelia shrugged. 'As I've already said, I've always done it. Anyway, I prefer animals to humans.' She glanced at her nephew, her look firm and forthright. 'Some of them anyway.'

From the kennels they returned to the house, Amelia stripping off her boots and man's ex-navy duffle coat at the back door. From there she led them into the drawing room.

The house turned out to be a hotchpotch of different styles, mirroring the outside. The furniture was heavy and old but in excellent condition. The smell of lavender polish hung in the air.

A teatime spread was set out on a low table, sandwiches and a cake taking centre stage. A maid who looked almost as old as the house came in with a tray of tea and a vacuum flask of hot water.

'That will be all, Iris.'

Iris tottered out, her back bent, her feet carefully treading to support her bandy legs.

'Knowing you were visiting I've done the best I can with what we have here,' Amelia explained. 'Can't cater on a large scale nowadays. I used to have full-time servants, but no longer. Just Iris in the house and Fred the gardener. Everyone else is casual and part-time. All keener to get to fight and die or help the war effort in other ways rather than keep house. Oh well . . .' Sighing she began to pour the tea. 'Push the animals off the chairs. Sit down and help yourselves. I'm not here to wait on you.'

Pierre encouraged two cats and a black-and-white English pointer off the chairs. Looking very disgruntled they all headed for a sofa at the further end of the room and settled there.

'Can't keep them outside in the kennels. They're always in the house. Getting old. Like me,' Amelia said with a chortle.

'You'll never get old, Aunt Amelia,' said Pierre, raising his aunt's hand to his lips and kissing it.

Amelia snatched her hand away. 'Flatterer!'

Sally thought she saw a twinkle in Amelia's eyes. It made her think she'd been quite a girl in her youth.

'Are only cats and dogs brought to you?' Sally asked, while accepting a piece of cake from Pierre.

'Mostly. Pet mice and suchlike are merely set free. Rabbits, well, you can guess what happens to them so they're not likely to end up here.

'There is Poppy the pony,' Pierre pointed out. 'And Big Ears.'

Sally smiled. 'Big Ears? That has to be a donkey.'

Pierre's aunt smiled benevolently at her. 'Quite right. He's a donkey. The hurdy-gurdy man brought him. Said he was afraid his family might insist on eating him if he kept him. People were content enough to hear his music without having a donkey to pet. As for Poppy, she's the pony Pierre used to ride when he was small. She's old. We might well end up eating her, but not until she keels over of her own free will.'

Before leaving, Sally excused herself to go to the bathroom. Amelia directed her to the far end of the corridor. All the way along the corridor Sally felt she was walking on air.

Pierre had been right. Lady Amelia clearly approved of her and once she'd got over her ladyship's bluntness, she loved his aunt. As for Pierre, well, she loved him most of all.

After Sally had left the room, Pierre questioned his aunt as to why she'd directed Sally to the bathroom at the end of the corridor when there was one much closer.

His aunt's amiable expression became challenging. 'You know why. I want a word.'

'Ah!' he said, looking disconcerted as he settled himself back in the chair. 'Might as well ready myself for a verbal mauling.'

'You're not going to lead her up the garden path, are you?'

Pierre smiled in the way he knew usually got him his own way. 'No. Only up the aisle. If things all work out.'

Unimpressed, Amelia drew in her chin. 'You can't mean that. Not until you know Adele's whereabouts.'

Pierre sighed impatiently and met his aunt's forthright gaze with one of his own.

'Adele and I did not part on friendly terms. We differed in our views of what was happening in Germany. She thinks it's all quite wonderful and that France should follow its lead. I, on the other hand, feel we'd be making a pact with the Devil!'

'I am aware of your views, also of hers. All the same . . .'

'Enough! I'll get round to it in my own good time. When the time is right.' Eyeing his aunt intently, hands clasped, he leaned towards her. 'You're not going to tell her, are you, Aunt Amelia? Please. Give me time. I will do what's right. Just give me time.'

Amelia felt her heart softening. Pierre's mother had died when he was nine years old. Rightly or wrongly she had plunged wholeheartedly into the vacant position. It occurred to her that every woman who had ever come into contact with her nephew swiftly fell under his spell – including her.

Conceding defeat, she shook her head. 'I won't tell her. It's none of my business. It's all down to you.'

CHAPTER THIRTEEN

When Joanna opened her eyes on Saturday morning she sensed that something had changed. The room felt very much colder and her breath came in white clouds from her mouth.

Driven by the necessity to feed Harry, she arose from bed at the usual time and pulled on her old woollen skirt, pairing it with a patchwork jumper knitted by Mrs Allen next door from scraps of unpicked adult jumpers.

Frosty patterns covered each windowpane, so solid that even the heat of her finger failed to melt them.

After making her bed, she shot down the stairs to the kitchen before her stepmother put in an appearance.

The kitchen was in darkness so she switched on a light. The blackout curtains were still drawn and there was no point in pulling them back, not in December at this time in the morning, though she did peer out just to see how intense the frost might be. Although it was dark she could see a white crust covering that piece of garden where her father had planted vegetables before leaving for war. They were all wilted now. What remained of the unkempt straggly grass was white; the shed, the fence and the gate at the end of the garden that led out on to the lane all crusted with white too.

Her bedroom had been cold enough but outside would be even colder. She would need to wrap up as warm as she could. It occurred to her to get the fire going first so she could spread the coat in front of it. Even its early smouldering would warm the inside of her coat.

Once at the bottom of the stairs, she attuned her ears to the sound of her stepmother stirring. All was silent.

The larder held little except for the remains of the cheese and some bread.

Disappointed, she eyed the leftovers disparagingly. From there she delved into the pig bin and found the remains of two-day-old pastry and the gristle and bones from a pig's head. The gristle and bones were grubby with old tea leaves. She swilled everything off beneath the tap. It wasn't enough for a growing dog. He needed meat and biscuits, scraps of fat if she could get hold of any.

Getting hold of anything suitable was not easy. The food that pets had been fed was now in short supply. A piece of meat might be a bit gristly, the biscuits a bit damp, but the government was encouraging everyone not to be wasteful. Scraps of fat were rendered down and kept for frying. Marrowbones, once bought for the family dog to gnaw on, now formed the basis of many a nourishing soup.

Joanna swallowed her dismay, her eyes once again searching the shelves for something that she could feed Harry. There was no alternative but to give him the tin of pilchards she'd found the night before, which she'd hidden in her coat pocket.

At the back of her mind a small fear niggled like a stomach ache. She really didn't want to be found out, but surely her stepmother wouldn't want them?

The tin of pilchards had been there since before her father had left to fight in the war. Her father had liked them. Joanna remembered her stepmother turning up her nose as he'd eaten them. She'd seen them out in the garden, her father's arms around her stepmother, him laughing and Elspeth wrinkling up her nose at the smell of pilchards on her father's breath. She'd heard her exclaim, 'Disgusting!'

'Fish is good for you,' he'd said, throwing back his head in laughter.

Elspeth had slapped his shoulder playfully. 'Not if they smell like that.'

Elspeth didn't seem to mind the smell when Tom smothered her mouth with his.

Joanna had felt a pang of jealousy at the sight. She and her father would have been better off without Elspeth. She'd never wanted another mother once her own was dead. Living alone with her father would have suited very well indeed.

She didn't mind if his breath smelt after eating pilchards and she had no doubt that Harry would wolf them down quickly. It wasn't meat, but it was the best she could do today. With the tin in her pocket and a newspaper tucked beneath her arm for Harry's toilet training, Joanna unlocked the back door with great care. The front door wasn't so stiff but it had a tendency to squeak, besides which it was situated at the bottom of the stairs leading up to her stepmother's bedroom so was best avoided.

'And where do you think you're going?'

Joanna nearly jumped out of her skin, her breath catching in her throat. Her mouth turned dry and a little time passed before she mumbled something about going to the park.

Her stepmother's makeup was smudged. She flicked a chipped finger nail at a piece of tobacco that had stuck to her bottom lip.

'That newspaper.' She pointed accusingly at the bundle Joanna carried beneath her arm. 'For what reason are you taking a newspaper to the park?'

'Something . . . to . . . read . . .' Joanna stammered.

As her stepmother's face loomed over her the smell of cheap face powder flooded Joanna's nostrils. 'You're lying!'

The force of her stepmother's shout hit her forcefully.

'Now. What else is going to the park with you?' She moved like lightning, her long fingers taking hold of the collar of Joanna's coat and tugging her forward. 'Let's see what's in your pocket, shall we!'

Her sharp fingernails dug into Joanna's coat pockets, scraping the girl's hands. 'Aha!' She held the tin high in the air. 'Now what might you be doing with a tin of pilchards in your pocket?'

Joanna attempted to explain. 'I . . . I . . . wanted them for later on – in the park . . . with my friends . . .'

'Friends? Now look here, my girl. It's bad enough with this rationing to feed you without feeding the whole bloody street. It goes back in the larder. Now!'

Her stepmother shoved the tin into her face. Joanna took it with a trembling hand, her stepmother's hand slapping the back of her head so hard that she stumbled and almost dropped it.

'You're a thief! Do you hear me, Joanna Ryan? Thieves end up in prison, and that's where you'll end up, my girl. Mark my words!'

Joanna's mind screamed because she knew so well what would come next.

'Please,' she said, her eyes wide after she'd returned the tin to the larder. 'Don't put me in the coalhouse. I won't do it again. Honest I won't.'

Her stepmother's eyes narrowed in that old familiar way. Joanna knew without a moment's hesitation what was coming next. Like bands of steel, her stepmother's hands closed around her shoulders. Her heart thudded against her ribs as she was frogmarched towards the door beneath the stairs.

'Please! It's Saturday and I have to see a friend! Please don't put me in there . . .'

Her stepmother pushed her roughly into the coalhouse. She went sprawling over a pile of coal delivered just the week before. The door slammed behind her. The rough edges of the coal scratched at her palms and knees. She managed to turn round, ending up sitting on the top of the heap.

Tears flowed as she sobbed out her heartache. Squeezing her eyes shut she wished and wished that her father would come back soon. Then she would swallow her fear and finally tell him how things really were.

'Count to ten, Jojo,' he used to say to her. 'Count to ten and everything will be on top of the world.'

Keeping her eyes tightly shut, her father's smiling face imprinted on her mind, she began to count.

'One, two, three . . .'

CHAPTER FOURTEEN

It was Saturday morning and Sally felt as though she was walking on air.

Pierre DeVere was the most romantic man she had ever met. His Gallic charm had a lot to do with it, of course. How could any Englishman compare with the natural easy-going manners of her wonderful Frenchman?

She hummed a tune the two of them had danced to some weeks ago as she prepared a breakfast of sausage, egg and a piece of bread, fried in the fat the sausage produced in the pan.

Arnold Thomas, the headmaster of the boys' school, had taken to keeping chickens in his back garden. The eggs were from him, one each for her and her father for breakfast and the rest for an omelette tomorrow night. She was in no doubt that Arnold was trying to make amends for his behaviour. A work colleague and a friend, that's all he would ever be to her, and she'd gone out of her way to make that plain.

It did not escape her attention that her father cleared his plate in the time it took her to plate up her own breakfast.

'Goodness, Dad,' she said brightly. 'You've got a good appetite this morning.'

It seemed too good to be true. Pierre had made her happy and it now seemed that that her father was recovering. This might indeed be a turning point in both their lives.

Sitting herself down on the opposite side of the table, she began to tell him about her visit to Ambrose House and the eccentric woman who was Pierre's aunt.

'Being a titled lady I was fully expecting her to come out dressed in a lavender ball gown and wearing lace gloves. Instead she wears men's corduroy trousers, tweeds and thick sweaters. Not at all what I was expecting!'

'Sounds like a very sensible woman to me,' her father remarked. 'Given what she's doing.'

'You're right, Dad. Those poor animals.'

She told him about the greyhounds and the cats with their kittens. 'If Mrs Evans had known her ladyship was willing to take them in, I could have taken her cat and kittens there. As it is . . .'

Her features became downcast as she waited for her father to make some comment about that was the way of the world and that was that. He surprised her when he responded differently.

'It's a good job there are folk about with a bit of common sense. If less people ran around like headless chickens, we'd get through this war a lot happier than we are at present. A dog is a man's best friend. I saw that in the last war. Without them a lot more men would've been killed.'

Sally couldn't believe her ears and hope soared. Since her mother's death his sentences had been short and decidedly pessimistic. It did seem indeed that a milestone had been reached.

'Right,' said her father, hastily rising from his chair and grabbing his coat. 'I'm off to the allotment. I'll take what's left in that teapot, if that's all right with you.

'Of course it is.' The fact that he was going to the allotment gladdened her heart. Was he actually going to do something there? 'Do you have anything planned?'

He nodded as he pulled on his old coat and hat. 'I've cleared the ground. I'm thinking I might plant carrots, onions, spring greens and runner beans. They should grow well as long as the frost keeps off. Then we'll see where we go from there.'

Sally beamed at him, her heart skipping at the news. 'That's wonderful. We could do with some fresh vegetables. Just you make sure to take something for your indigestion.'

Her father's eyebrows rose quizzically. 'Indigestion? What makes you think I'll be suffering a bout of that?'

Sally turned her attention to the dishes she'd left piled on the draining board in an effort to hide her smile.

'You ate that sausage very quickly. You deserve to get indigestion.'

She heard him grumble something about the young having no respect for the disposition of their elders. She was bemused. He never usually did that unless he was hiding something, though she couldn't think what it might be.

When Seb arrived at the allotment, a few other figures were tending their own narrow patches, hoeing and digging and pulling out weeds. One or two turned their heads at his approach, or they might have heard the sound of yapping coming from his shed. Not that anyone seemed at all concerned.

Turning his back on the other allotment holders, he looked through the window just in case the little girl was inside tending her pet. There was no one, so he lifted the metal hook and opened the door.

Harry was panting and wagging fit to burst. On seeing Seb his yapping subsided though the panting and wagging continued. And no wonder, thought Seb on checking his water dish. It was empty. So was his food bowl.

Anger bristled in the depths of his soul. So did disappointment and surprise that he'd misjudged the little girl, thinking her conscientious and caring. It seemed she hadn't called in and it grieved him to think the little girl had neglected her puppy. Perhaps there was a good reason, but his anger was slow to subside. He smiled down at the bright eyes looking up at him. 'Never you mind, Harry. You just see what I've got for you.'

First he poured water into Harry's dish. Once the little dog had drank his fill he brought the sausage from out of his pocket plus a few biscuits from the tin at home. Harry gobbled up the lot.

After refilling the water dish Seb looked at Harry's bed and at his toilet area.

He'd had no reason to doubt that the little girl called in to see the puppy twice a day. Seb's expression darkened. She hadn't bothered to come in this weekend. The little brat! To leave an animal to suffer left with no water and no food was unforgiveable.

'She'll get a piece of my mind when I see her,' he said to the dog.

Harry licked his chops and looked up at him before seeking out an old tennis ball.

Seb laughed. 'I'm supposed to be planting vegetables not playing with you.'

The puppy persisted.

'Oh well.' Seb resigned himself to his fate. 'I'll play with you for half an hour and then I've got to get on.'

CHAPTER FIFTEEN

It was Saturday evening and very late before Joanna was let out of the coalhouse under the stairs. Elspeth told her to get her own dinner.

'Here. Sixpence to go and get fish and chips at Hamblin's.'

Joanna, her face streaked with coal dust and the tracks of her tears, heard her stomach rumble as she took the money. It crossed her mind that Harry might like fish. And chips. Perhaps when she'd bought some she could take them directly to him.

'And you're to come straight back here afterwards. I want your supper eaten and you in bed by eight. Is that clear?'

Joanna's hope was dashed. All she could do was nod, feeling empty and scared inside.

Elspeth rested her knuckles on her hips, her face a disdainful mask. 'You might say "thank you". Money don't grow on trees, you know.'

'Thank you.' Joanna's voice was low. She was frightened and breathing coal dust all day had made her throat dry.

On the surface Elspeth's offer sounded generous enough, but if anyone could have read her mind, they would have seen how selfish it really was. There was purpose in everything Elspeth did, and this action was no exception. If Joanna ever did complain to her father, her stepmother could tell him that she'd given his daughter money for fish and chips. Joanna could not deny it.

Joanna was glad to go the fish and chip shop but dared not take time to visit Harry. It would have to wait for the morning.

* * *

Sunday morning was as cold as Saturday had been, and Joanna was frantic. Not daring to raid the biscuit tin or the larder in case she was found out and thrown into the coalhouse again, she would have to dig around in the pig bin to find something for Harry to eat. She didn't relish the task. The pig bin was where food waste was thrown before being collected to take to a farm to feed the pigs. Not that there was much in there nowadays. Everything that could be recycled into cooking fat, soup or a pudding made from stale bread and cheese rind. It was rumoured that employees of the Ministry of Food peered into pig bins and ordinary waste bins in the middle of the night. Woe betide anyone who had dared throw away something that looked reusable. They would be fined or put in prison.

Her stepmother had been out the night before and this time did not get up early. As she'd crept past her bedroom, Joanna had heard her softly snoring.

She wrinkled her nose as she quietly lifted the lid of the pig bin. There was mainly vegetable waste, plus a few picked bones with very little meat left on them.

Joanna sighed. She had to take the poor dog something, but what?

As she shrugged her shoulders into her winter coat, she searched her pockets for the odd penny. She could buy a bag of broken biscuits for a penny. Her fingers found only holes. Her eyes lifted to the cast iron mantelpiece on which sat a red tin post box, last year's Christmas present from her father. At one time it had been full of farthings, but not now. Elspeth had borrowed them but failed to pay them back.

Joanna frowned. It was nearly Christmas but there was no sign of her father coming home. It was going to be bleak without him. There would be no Christmas dinner, no festive decorations. Her only enjoyment would be Harry. But he needed feeding. Where else could she look for money? Where else could she get food?

Feeling terribly downhearted, she bent down to fasten her shoes. As she did so, the front edge of her coat fell to the side of her knee and something hard knocked against her leg.

Curious, her fingers traced the outline of an object trapped there. With luck it might be a penny. Even a halfpenny would do. Elation swept over her as she delved into her pocket. Whatever was trapped in the lining must have fallen through the hole. The pocket was part of the coat. Anything that fell through it would not fall onto the ground but would become trapped in the lining.

Finding the hole in the silky pocket, she pushed her fingers further down until she'd gained the hem that held the lining in place. The object moved, but her quick fingers moved with it. Eventually she gripped it and carefully, very carefully, she brought it out, up through the lining and out of her pocket.

It was indeed a penny. Hardly a huge amount but seeing it gave her an idea.

Prying her fingers into both coat pockets, she felt the hole the coin had fallen through and another hole in the other pocket.

If the penny, a large coin, had fallen through the hole in her pocket at some time, smaller coins might also have made the journey and whoever had once owned the coat never noticed.

Placing the penny to one side, she delved again into the pockets, burrowing further down into the hem of her coat. First she brought out a sixpence. This was better than she'd expected. One more search her fingers fumbled around the unmistakeable edges of a thruppenny bit. Once the money was safely stowed in the pocket of her liberty bodice, she buttoned her coat, threw a scarf around her neck, grabbed her hat and was gone. There was no way she was going to hang around and chance Elspeth taking the money off her.

Before heading for Harry, she took a detour to the row of shops at the bottom of The Vale. And then she remembered it was Sunday. The shops were closed.

Filled with dismay she stared at the blacked out frontages, wondering whether to bang on the door and purchase what she could.

Just about to do so, she happened to see Mr Lewis, the shopkeeper in the side entry tying up paper with bits of string.

'Mr Lewis,' she said tentatively. 'I'm sorry to bother you, but can I buy something?'

Mr Lewis turned round, his face beetroot red above his brown shopkeeper's coat. 'Well, I don't open on a Sunday – unless you're out of food then I can make an exception.'

She immediately thought of Harry. Should she tell him the little dog would starve unless she got him some food? She decided against it. She didn't want him to work out who she was and perhaps tell her stepmother what she'd bought. If her stepmother could have Lottie destroyed, she could have Harry destroyed too, and that was something she couldn't possibly countenance.

'Oh. I thought you might be – seeing as there's a war on. But our larder is bare. There's only a crust left and no meat or biscuits.'

She bought biscuits and asked him if she could have some bacon bones.

The shopkeeper shook his head and frowned. He knew who she was. Knew her father and had known her mother. Back when her mother was still alive she'd been a lively little thing, really pretty too, and always clean and well turned out. Since her father's marriage to 'the Welsh Rarebit', as his wife called her in very disapproving tones, the child had gone downhill. 'That child is being mistreated and with Tom away it's only likely to get worse.'

His wife's comments weighing heavily on his mind, he smiled and began wrapping up a few bacon bones. He also threw in the remains of a ham bone, the fat hanging white and glistening from the knuckle. A good percentage of the bones would normally go into the stockpot, a base for one of his wife's tasty soups. But he had a soft heart and he couldn't help thinking his donation would be welcome.

'Here,' he said, handing her the wrapped up bones plus a large bag of broken biscuits. 'They're for you and you alone, mind. Don't you tell your stepmother I gave you things without your ration card or she'll want the same treatment. I only make exceptions for people I really like.'

Joanna was more than pleased. He'd only taken sixpence for everything, which meant she had four pence left – the penny and the thruppenny bit.

It was very cold outside, but her cheeks were pink and she felt warm all over thanks to Mr Lewis. Harry would have some very meaty-looking bacon bones to eat, plus the ham bone.

Despite the frozen ground, she broke into a run, each breath rising into the air like white feathery plumes, streaks of white against the black. The darkness was so intense it was hard to see where she was going. On top of that the ground beneath her feet was slick with frost and slippery.

There was only a little battery life left in her torch and daylight was a long time coming. She was determined to save the little she had left so she could better see Harry inside the shed.

It wouldn't have been so bad if there had been streetlights or patches of light falling from the windows of houses as there had been in peacetime. At this time of year the blackness of night lingered into morning. The world had become a more sombre place since September, the blackout more intense, more all-consuming, as winter set in.

As Joanna entered the shed Harry bounced around with excitement and happiness at seeing her.

'See what I've got for you,' she said, getting down on her knees and laughing as he jumped up at her and licked her face with his warm, wet tongue. 'Look!'

She held up the food she'd brought. Harry responded with the usual wagging of his stumpy tail, which made Joanna very happy. She'd expected him to be whining and shaking with hunger and cold but he seemed quite happy.

Once he was settled with the ham bone, she flashed her torch over his dishes. The water dish was not as empty as she'd expected it to be. The remains of some kind of meat clung to the sides of his food dish.

Joanna froze. Someone had fed him. She was sure of it. But who?

She looked over her shoulder, half expecting someone to leap at her from the shadows. There was no one there.

With the childish innocence of not wanting to believe anything was wrong, Joanna pushed the suspicion to the back of her mind and Harry helped her do that.

For a while they played, Joanna screwing up a piece of newspaper into a ball and throwing it for Harry to retrieve. Eventually he tired himself out. A quick drink and he climbed into his bed curling himself into a tight ball.

Sighing with satisfaction, Joanna laid her head against the table leg. She loved watching the puppy sleep, his round tummy rising and falling with each breath he took.

The everyday world fell away and Joanna felt happier than she had in days. All she needed was Harry, somebody to love and somebody to love her.

Her eyelids began to feel heavy and, despite the cold, she fell asleep, curling herself around the puppy's bed beneath the table. It wasn't the ideal situation and her coat didn't really keep out the cold, but her love for Harry and the fact that she was close to him comforted her.

Deep in sleep, she didn't hear the door open or see the elderly man with the kind eyes enter as softly as he could. He came into the shed so quietly that even Harry was not disturbed, though when he opened one eye and saw who it was, he wagged his tail and went back to sleep.

Seb Hadley eyed the thin legs and pale skin of the little girl. The shoes and socks she was wearing had seen better days and by the looks of it her coat wasn't offering much warmth.

The girl moved almost imperceptibly. He knew immediately she was shivering. The shed provided shelter but it wasn't that warm – not like his own cosy living room at home.

The girl needed a blanket. He didn't have one with him, but he was wearing his army greatcoat, a leftover from the Great War, heavy as you like and made from the very finest wool.

Oh well. You're not going to need it, he told himself as he took it off. *You've got gardening to do.*

Gently, so as not to wake her, he placed the coat over the child's sleeping form. One of the sleeves settled on Harry.

Seb smiled. They'd both be warm now.

With silent precision he retrieved the tools he wanted and went back outside. As he gazed out over his patch of allotment he had the strangest sensation that a female hand landed on his shoulder. He knew immediately that it was Grace's hand and that she approved of what he'd just done.

He smiled. 'I knew you'd approve,' he said softly, as though she were right there next to him. He sighed deeply. 'I suppose I'd better get on.'

Joanna opened her eyes to daylight and Harry licking her face. On cuddling him close she noticed the warmth of his body and then realised that she was very warm too.

She pushed at whatever was covering her, certain it hadn't been there when she'd fallen asleep. It was heavy and on closer inspection she realised it was a coat – a man's coat. For a moment she was filled with alarm until she reasoned that whoever it belonged to was also the person who had fed Harry. It had to be the man who owned the shed.

Carefully, she got out from beneath the coat, Harry jumping around excitedly, almost as though he knew who the coat belonged to. Getting to her feet, Joanna made her way to the single window overlooking the allotment.

The tin oil drum used as a water butt obscured one half of the window, but through the other half she could see a man digging at the ground. So intent on seeing Harry she hadn't noticed that the weeds and dead plants had been removed, the earth turned over.

For a moment she watched as the man turned over the clods of rich, dark earth. He was quite tall, and although his hair might have been a different colour when he was younger, it was now white and streaked with yellow. His back was to her, so she couldn't see his face. Although he'd been kind to let her sleep with his coat over her to keep her warm, she was wary of strangers. Her stepmother had told her to have nothing to do with strangers – not ever.

She sucked her thumb desperately, wondering what she should do next. Should she hare out there, or should she make sure Harry had all he required and leave? With a bit of luck the man would not see her go.

The little dog had his head dipped in his bowl, lapping at the freezing water. She reminded herself that Harry had been fed so the man couldn't be a bad man.

It had been so warm beneath the khaki-coloured coat. Her own was big enough but worn on the elbows and the material wasn't half so good as the army greatcoat. Although the thought of confronting the man scared her, she needed to know for sure that he wouldn't betray Harry to either the authorities or her stepmother.

'Stay here,' she whispered to Harry. He looked up at her with big sad eyes and whined. 'It's for the best. I have to speak to that man out there. This is his shed. I need to ask his permission for you to stay here. I have to,' she added, her voice fading away into nothing. Without anywhere to stay Harry would be doomed.

Closing the door quickly behind her so Harry couldn't follow, she went outside. The cold was so intense it was as though she wasn't wearing a coat. Her legs were cold too and her cheeks were blossoming to pink. Tucking her hands into her pockets and keeping to the path, she approached the bent figure cautiously.

The narrow path that ran along the edge of the allotment was of compacted earth and encrusted with a layer of frost that was almost thick enough to be mistaken for snow.

Uncertain of what to say, she stood and waited for the man to notice her. Then she coughed nervously, though only in a small way, as though she were clearing her throat.

The man leaned on his shovel and regarded her thoughtfully. Tufts of the white hair she had seen from a distance stuck out in silky strands from beneath a flat cap. His eyes were a chilling blue but she couldn't tell whether he was smiling or not because of his facial hair. His beard was very bushy and so were his white eyebrows.

'Well, girl. What have you got to say for yourself?'

Feeling a sudden jolt of fear, Joanna stared at him wide eyed.

The man barely moved. He just returned her enquiring look with a steady one of his own.

At last he spoke. 'Cat got your tongue?'

Joanna gulped and said the first thing that came into her mind. 'You look like Father Christmas.'

For a moment he seemed taken aback but recovered quickly, a faint smile softening his features. 'Is that so? Do you really think Father Christmas would be here digging in an allotment? I should think he got more important business at this time of the year than planting cabbages! Don't you?'

Joanna nodded. She wasn't quite sure how to take him and had to keep reminding herself that it was his coat that had kept her warm and him that had fed Harry.

'So,' he said, fixing her with his starry-bright eyes. 'How come you didn't come to feed that dog yesterday? A dog is a big responsibility, you know. It's a living creature that depends on you to keep going. Didn't you know that?'

Joanna nodded again.

His white eyebrows met above his nose in a deep frown. 'Only donkeys keep nodding and that's because they can't speak. I take it you can. So where were you yesterday? Why weren't you here to feed the little chap?' He wagged a warning finger. 'No lies, mind. I want the truth.'

Joanna gulped. She wasn't at all sure of the truth about donkeys, but somehow she just couldn't avoid telling him the truth. 'Elspeth locked me in the coalhouse.'

The man's expression changed and a small frown puckered his brow. 'Elspeth? Is she your sister?'

Joanna shook her head. 'No. She's my stepmother.'

Seb swallowed the remnants of anger he'd had towards the girl. By the sound of it the stepmother was more deserving of his ire. 'Does she lock you in that coalhouse very often?'

Joanna nodded.

He hesitated as he digested the terrible truth. 'Good job I was around then, weren't it, or the poor little chap would have been starving.' His voice was steady and although gruff there was kindness in his words.

Joanna hung her head as unbidden tears pricked her eyes. 'I'm sorry, mister, but when she caught me with the pilchards . . .'

'Pilchards?'

It all came out in a rush, her not finding anything much for Harry to eat except for a tin of pilchards.

'She don't like them. She bought them for my dad to give him when he next comes home on leave. They were at the back of the larder and I thought . . .'

She went on to tell him everything.

Seb listened, thinking her very articulate for a young child. At the same time pity clenched his stomach right until she finally finished her tale.

'Are you going home for your lunch?' he asked her.

She looked at him blankly.

'Your dinner,' he said to her. 'I suppose you call it your dinner.'

Joanna shrugged. 'I suppose.'

'You suppose? What's that supposed to mean?'

'I don't want to go home for dinner. I forgot to make sure the fire stayed in this morning. If it goes out she'll have to do it herself. She'll be angry.'

The man with the white hair and blue eyes stabbed his shovel into the earth and straightened.

'Then we better see what I've got in my coat. Cheese sandwiches I think. Might even have a slice of pork pie if we're lucky. Come on. Let's see what we've got.'

Joanna followed his broad, slow-moving form into the shed, where he picked up his coat and proceeded to delve into the copious pockets.

He brought out sandwiches and other things wrapped in greaseproof paper, plus some apples and a Thermos flask. As he placed things on the table where he also planted and transplanted seeds, Harry jumped up and down around his legs.

'You wait your turn,' he said, looking down at him.

Harry took no notice, continuing to dance up and down on all four legs.

'I've got him some bacon bones,' said Joanna. 'He's already ate a ham bone and some biscuits.'

'That seems like a good idea to me,' said the old man.

Harry began happily munching on the bacon bones while the old man poured milky tea and offered Joanna a sandwich.

Before seating himself on the corner of the table, he upturned a bucket and folded a sack to make a cushion so Joanna would have somewhere to sit.

'Now you sit there and don't move until you've eaten it all up.'

Joanna did as she was told. 'Thanks, mister.'

'Seb. You can call me Seb. Now eat up and once you've done that and got a warm drink down you, you can tell me all about yourself and young Harry here.'

The sandwich of cheese and pickle went down very well indeed. So did the piece of pork pie and the slice of apple cake he gave her.

'Aren't you having any?' she asked him.

He smiled. 'I had a big breakfast and, anyway, I'm not growing any longer. You still are and so is Harry.'

Once she had eaten all he gave her, she told him that on the day she found Harry she had been in tears because her stepmother had got rid of her cat.

'The man who came tried to tell me that she was going to a better place. I thought he meant in the country but then I found out that she would be put to sleep . . .' She paused, alarm in her eyes. 'They don't really mean sleep, do they? They mean Lottie was killed.' Her bottom lip quivered.

Seb shook his head. 'It's a rum do and that's for sure,' he muttered, unsure what to say that could possibly make her feel any better. 'Still, look at it this way. If you hadn't been crying over Lottie, you wouldn't have gone down to the brook and found Harry. He'd be dead along with his brothers and sisters, so there was some good came out of that bad, wasn't there.'

'My friend Paul found the dead puppies and buried them. I didn't tell him about Harry.' She frowned. 'I don't want to tell anyone about him.' She looked up suddenly. 'You won't tell anyone, will you?'

'Cross my heart,' he said, making the sign over his chest.

Satisfied he was telling the truth, she happily passed the last of her pork pie to Harry, who gulped it down quickly. Then she sat up straight as a dire thought came to her. 'I have to get him something for his supper. The bones won't be enough, but the shops are closed.'

Seb's heart was touched by the concern in her eyes. 'Tell you what, how would it be if I brought something from home for him tonight?'

It did his heart good to see Joanna's face light up the way it did.

'Could you, mister?' Her face was a picture of grateful innocence.

'Yep. I can do that,' he said, his joints cracking as he got to his feet. 'And stop calling me "mister". It's Seb. Seb Hadley. All right?'

Joanna nodded emphatically. She had been a little afraid of this man, but then once he'd given her food and she'd learned he'd been feeding Harry when she hadn't been able to come, her doubts retreated.

There was only one thing that continued to worry her.

'Is this your shed? For ever?'

Seb gazed around him at the stout wooden frame, the mismatched bits of wood that formed the walls. 'That it is. I built this myself. Me and my Gracie that is.'

Joanna presumed he was speaking of his wife. 'Do we have to go? I mean, can Harry live here?'

He looked at her in amazement. 'Did I say you had to go?'

She shook her head. 'Not so much me. I mean Harry. Do you mind him living here?'

'I just said I don't. Harry can stay here. Nobody else lives here do they?'

'No.'

'Still,' said Seb as he folded up the newspaper so it would be suitable for reusing. 'I reckon Harry needs to get out and about a bit more. He can't stay in here for ever now, can he.'

Joanna thought about it. 'I suppose not. I suppose I'll have to start taking him for walks.'

'I suppose you will.'

Joanna bit her bottom lip as she mulled over how best to take the puppy for a walk without him running away.

'What are you thinking?' asked Seb, one bushy eyebrow rising higher than the other in a quizzical manner.

'I need some string for a lead.'

Seb eyed her thoughtfully. 'You'll need something. A collar too, no doubt. Now I'd better get on. I've got tools to clean. You stay here and play with Harry while I get that done. Where do you live?'

'The Vale. One hundred and sixteen.'

'Right. Well soon as I'm done I'll walk you home. It'll be getting dark soon.'

'I can find my own way home!' Joanna's outburst was sudden and caused Seb to look up from scraping the last clod of mud from his spade before smearing it with oil.

Seb's eyes softened. Poor little kid. Mother dead, father off to war and her left with a stepmother who had no time for her. Seb decided it would not be wise to push the issue.

'All right then. How about I walk with you as far as the bottom of The Vale?'

He saw her hesitation and knew that although she would relish the company she was too frightened to let him come with her. However, he did have an ace up his sleeve. 'Thing is I'll be going into that shed every day and if Harry was sick or something, I wouldn't know how to let you know so I need to know where you live.'

'I told you. It's number one hundred and sixteen.'

'All right then. I know where you live and nobody is going to see me walk with you as far as the bottom of the hill. Would that be all right?'

She agreed with a shy smile.

Dusk was falling by the time he left her at the bottom of The Vale. For a moment he watched her walk away, a waif-like form in worn-out clothes. She'd been as bouncy as a beach ball with Harry. Now, on her way home to a doubtful welcome, she dragged her legs. It didn't take a genius to know that she didn't want to go home.

As he made his own way home, he thought on this woman who was treating a child so badly. It wasn't until he felt a toothache coming on that he realised just how firmly he'd been clenching his teeth. The damned woman! No matter that Joanna had refused to let him anywhere near where she lived, he was overcome with the urge to know what her stepmother was really like. At some point he would achieve this but wouldn't let Joanna know of his plans. He was also unsure of what his daughter might say. Nevertheless, it was what he would do.

CHAPTER SIXTEEN

Christmas morning, two weeks later

Joanna shivered as she made her way down the stairs. Halfway down she heard the sound of snoring coming from her stepmother's bedroom. She stopped and looked up, waiting for her stepmother to fling back the door and cuff her ear just because she had a headache.

Nothing happened. The door remained shut and the snoring continued, so Joanna carried on. Even though it was Christmas Day, she still had a fire to light, though first she would get herself some breakfast.

The moment she pushed the living-room door open, her nose was assailed with the stench of stale food and drink. An empty bottle of sherry sat in the middle of the table surrounded by dirty plates. Remembering how it had tasted, she wrinkled her nose. The smell was bad enough. The taste was even worse and it made you sleep, and had given her a headache.

There were two plates on the table, both streaked with remains of the cottage pie their next door neighbour had provided for Christmas dinner. Now there would be nothing. Joanna's eyes filled with tears. She wasn't expecting to receive a Christmas present but knew she would get a beating if she didn't clear the table, wash up and put everything away.

Having to do her chores as usual wasn't her main concern. She had hoped to save a little of her own portion of cottage pie for Harry. Now she would have to find something else.

She couldn't even guess at the identity of the person who had eaten her portion of Mrs Allen's welcome gift, but guessed it was a man. Her stepmother didn't have any close female friends.

Never mind what her stepmother did, Joanna's first priority was to get to Harry as fast as she could. Before washing the dishes she scraped the remains of the cottage pie from the oven dish into a sheet of clean newspaper. It wasn't much but hopefully it would keep the little dog going.

A quick rummage through the pig bin and she found some pieces of bacon fat and rind. It was illegal to throw such things away, but her stepmother was too lazy to render them down for cooking. She didn't cook that much anyway. Elspeth ate in the factory canteen, taking the view that as she worked all day she deserved to be well fed, leaving Joanna for the most part to fend for herself. There was also a piece of cheese rind that shouldn't have been there either.

Joanna wrapped all her finds up, put on her coat and slid the food into her pocket. Carefully she opened the front door and left the house.

The night hadn't quite gone. The day was dull and thick with a mist that seemed to soak up both the light and the sounds of the day. In peacetime the church bells would have been ringing, but they wouldn't ring again until the enemy was defeated and peace had returned to the world.

She hurried down The Vale and along St John's Lane, through Victoria Park and down to the allotment. The solitary note of a steam train wailed into the morning mist, its steam adding to the whiteness already cloaking the air.

Harry peered over the top of his bed, shook his head so that his ears flapped, and got out to meet her. The food she'd brought was gone in a flash.

Joanna sat looking at him wondering what she could give him next. Perhaps Mrs Allen might have some leftovers she didn't want? It was worth a try. She resolved to knock on her door later and ask her.

'Right,' she said, sitting back on her haunches. 'Harry, it's Christmas. It's a time when people buy each other presents. I don't have anyone to buy for except you, so here it is.'

She got out a round package containing a red ball Mrs Goodson had found in her garden. Without her old dog she no longer refused to give balls back and, not having found the original owner, she'd given it to Joanna.

'Merry Christmas, dear,' she'd said the day before yesterday. She'd then rushed indoors dabbing at her eyes.

Harry made short work of the newspaper she'd wrapped the ball in, tearing it into shreds with his sharp teeth.

The ball bounced and Harry bounced after it.

Joanna also got out a piece of rough rope she'd brought with her. Today she intended introducing Harry to a lead. Once the weather improved they would be able to go out for walks and she was looking forward to it. Her only concern was that somebody she knew might see them together, but she'd already decided on a suitable excuse. She was walking the dog for a kind old man who lived close to the park. It was all she could think of to stop Harry being carted off to be killed. Seb was the kind old man she had in mind. Meeting him had come as a complete surprise and also a relief.

By late morning, Harry was worn out and ready to sleep. Once she'd made sure he had water, Joanna headed for home. There wasn't much chance of getting anything to eat, but her stomach was beginning to rumble. She'd had nothing since the bowl of porridge she'd prepared herself that morning.

As she let herself in, she heard a man laughing, then her stepmother laughing in turn. Her spirits soared. Her father was home!

'Daddy!' she exclaimed. Thinking that her greatest wish had come true she pushed open the door.

The smell of roast chicken came out to greet her. So did the sight of the man sitting next to her stepmother. Her stepmother's cheeks were flushed and her eyes had a glassy look.

'Where the bloody hell do you think you've been? I've a good mind to throw your dinner in the bin.'

'Now, now,' said the man, patting her stepmother's hand. 'Don't be a cow, Elspeth. It's Christmas. Goodwill and all that. Anyway, did you tell 'er about the bird? Come on. Get 'er some dinner.'

The man had a fleshy face and a scar running down one cheek. His lips were almost non-existent, as though at some point he'd sucked them in and swallowed them.

The way he looked her up and down made Joanna feel uncomfortable.

'Pretty little thing, ain't she. How about coming and sitting on my lap, Joanna? You can pretend I'm Father Christmas!'

The look Elspeth gave him was unreadable. She slapped his arm.

'Jack, leave her alone. The girl wants her dinner, don't you, Joanna? And we've got pudding afterwards.'

'You're just jealous,' he said, his wet lips grazing Elspeth's cheek, his eyes fixed on her stepdaughter.

Joanna sat down at the table, barely able to believe that her stepmother was setting down a plateful of food in front of her. There were roast potatoes, vegetables and slices of chicken all swimming in thick gravy.

Although she was very hungry, Joanna couldn't stop staring at the fleshy faced man sitting next to her stepmother. She knew her well enough to realise she was being affable only in order to impress Jack. Whoever Jack was, Joanna didn't like him and certainly didn't like the way he looked at her.

Her stepmother noticed her wary gaze. 'Joanna!' she snapped. 'Stop staring and eat your bloody dinner!'

Jack intervened. 'Hang on, hang on. Elspeth, where's yer manners? You ain't properly introduced me.'

Elspeth was all nervous laughter, determined to make a good impression. 'Jack Smith, you're big enough to introduce yourself.' She slapped his arm playfully.

Jack's expression seemed to freeze after she did that. 'Less of a heavy hand, if you don't mind, Elspeth.'

His voice had turned surly and although it lightened when he looked at Joanna, he still frightened her. The way he leered at her made Joanna feel slightly sick.

'So there you are, little lady. Me name's Jack Smith and you're Joanna Ryan. Now we've got that out of the way, we can all get on with our dinner. Then perhaps you can sit on me lap afterwards!'

Elspeth was about to slap his shoulder again, but on seeing his warning expression instead stroked his arm.

Both the chicken and the pudding went down well. Joanna was doubly surprised when her stepmother helped her take the dishes into the kitchen.

'There,' she said resolutely. 'Wasn't that nice of Jack to bring us that chicken? I bet there aren't that many people hereabouts having chicken for their Christmas dinner. Make sure you thank Jack for his present. Right? If you do sit on his lap, remember to give him a Christmas kiss. In fact, make sure you do.'

Joanna didn't like her stepmother's tone of voice. Neither did she like Jack Smith or the prospect of sitting on his lap and kissing him.

'I don't think Dad would like me to do that. So I won't.'

'You will do as you're told.'

'No. If you make me, I'll tell Dad as soon as he gets home.'

Alarmed by her defiance, Elspeth Ryan grabbed her arm. Joanna yelped at the pain of her fingers digging into her arms. Her stepmother's flushed face was inches from her own. 'He's my cousin. All right? You remember to tell your father that. It'll be the worse for you if you don't,' she hissed.

She straightened suddenly, her voice returning to uncharacteristic sweetness.

'Now. You be all right washing the dishes by yourself, will you?'

Joanna nodded and kept her head down. Anything was better than sitting on Jack Smith's lap and kissing him.

Elspeth seemed satisfied enough. 'I'm going in to have a drink and a chat about old times with Jack. I'll close the door so we can't hear the dishes. That's a good girl. Oh, and do what you can with the remains of the chicken. But tell no one,' she said in a conspiratory whisper. 'It has to be a secret.'

Joanna winced as her stepmother patted her head a little more heavily than was necessary. Once the door was closed she washed the dishes as quickly as she could, one eye on the remains of the chicken. There was some flesh left plus the cooked entrails and neck along with pieces of crisp skin.

Once the dishes were washed, dried and put away, she divided the chicken into flesh, bones, skin and entrails. The latter two items were wrapped up in newspaper along with the gizzard, the parson's nose and the neck. Harry would have his Christmas dinner and once he had, she would take him for a walk.

CHAPTER SEVENTEEN

'Are you sure you don't need any help with the planting? I mean, you don't need to go down there today, do you? It is Christmas.'

It was the third time Sally had asked her father if he needed her assistance and pointed out to him that it was Christmas Day. His response on this third occasion was even brusquer than on the previous two.

'Do you think I'm infirm or something? I do know how to plant a few carrots and vegetables, you know!'

'I only asked,' she said, raising her hands in submission. 'I was only offering.'

'You've got your own work to do, running this house.'

'Pierre is willing to help.'

His face darkened. 'No need. I can manage and, anyway, I like a bit of time to myself.'

Sally sighed and gave up. It had taken her some time to get her father to snap out of the melancholia he'd suffered ever since her mother had died. She'd lost count of the times she'd attempted to get him to take an interest in something – anything – that would help him become yet again the father she'd known. Things had improved, though he still had his moments.

It hadn't been their habit to buy each other presents at Christmas so it came as something of a surprise when her father handed her a set of embroidered handkerchiefs, blue forget-me-nots in each corner.

'It was the last they had,' he said, somewhat shyly.

'Oh, Dad.' All her reservations fell away.

He looked bashful when she kissed his cheek.

'I bought you socks,' she said handing him a small parcel wrapped in brown paper. 'It was the last they had too. I think I'll be knitting them from now on.'

Secretly she was glad he didn't want her to accompany him and she knew he was all right down at the allotment by himself. In the meantime she had her own life to lead.

'Dinner smells good,' he commented as he reached for his old army greatcoat.

'Stuffed bullock's heart, roast potatoes, cabbage and carrots. I had to queue for all of it. Must say I'm looking forward to the day when you're bringing vegetables up from the allotment.'

'They don't grow overnight, you know.'

'Pierre's aunt was in the same queue. She was expecting a chicken, but somebody broke in and stole the lot.'

'I had heard. Don Stone down at the allotment told me.'

She smiled. Her father was beginning to mix with people again.

So much had happened since the outbreak of war and she'd been looking forward to Christmas Day. She had hoped that Pierre would be dining with them, but he'd promised to eat with his aunt. She'd been invited too but had declined.

'I can't leave Dad by himself.'

'He can come too,' Pierre had offered.

'No. I think he might in time, but not yet. He's only just coming out of himself since Mum died and I don't want to upset him. Forcing him to do something out of the normal routine might do that.'

Pierre said that he understood, but deep down she knew he wanted to be with her; she certainly wanted to be with him.

Instead he agreed to call round for her mid-afternoon.

'We will go for a walk. I need to talk to you.'

Her heart had flipped, but she thought she knew what he was going to talk to her about. Would it be too early to be a spring bride? She loved the blossoms that appeared on the trees after a long winter, and though she could make a bouquet out of them, perhaps wear some in her hair.

Blushing at her thoughts, she forced herself to concentrate on getting dinner ready, including the pudding she'd made weeks ago adding a little sherry from their meagre supply.

After her father had returned from the allotment for his Christmas lunch and they'd listened to the King's speech on the wireless, he told her he would deal with the washing up.

Sally clamped her lips tightly together so she wouldn't say out loud what was on her mind. *Goodness! That's the second time this year!*

Pierre arrived about an hour after they'd finished lunch and he'd brought presents: a bottle of French brandy for her father and French perfume for her. He also brought his aunt's best wishes. 'She sent you these.' He handed over half a dozen eggs.

'Eggs and perfume! What a lucky girl I am.' She kissed him on the cheek. Her father set his tea towel to one side and shook his hand. 'And I have something for you.' She handed him a copy of *The Three Musketeers* by Alexander Dumas. 'It was a bit presumptuous of me, but for some reason I didn't think you had a copy – not in English anyway.'

He laughed. 'Sally, I confess I do not own a copy in English or French!'

She blushed when he kissed her cheek. His accent, his looks and his chivalrous manner all contributed to make her blush like a girl.

'It seems so poor compared to this,' she said, holding up the bottle of perfume. 'I'm a really lucky girl.'

A secretive look clouded his eyes. 'It was touch and go whether it got here. I've just discovered a hole in my pocket. It was quite small but it's getting bigger.'

'Give it to me. I'll mend it for you.

'That's very kind.'

'You're very kind too.' She frowned as a thought occurred to her. 'You didn't even know me before coming over from France, so how come . . .?'

He stood close to her. 'I've already told you. I just knew I was going to meet someone like you. It's Chanel. The very best.'

Sally took a deep breath. Never in her whole life had she owned such an expensive perfume. She planted a second kiss on his cheek. She would have kissed him more deeply but her father was in the room.

'This is so wonderful. Give me a minute and I'll put it upstairs. I don't intend wasting a drop.'

Eyes sparkling, she brushed his arm with her hand.

'She'll be ages,' Seb grumbled. 'Might as well take a seat and I'll make you a cup of tea.'

Pierre grinned. 'It is cold outside. Tea is very English, but as a Frenchman I would prefer brandy.'

Seb flashed an amiable expression and fetched the glasses. 'You fill them while I get my things ready to go back down to the allotment.'

Seb hadn't wanted Sally to go out with Pierre, not at first. Not because he was French but purely because the young man would undoubtedly come between them. At that point in his life he hadn't wanted anyone to intrude upon his relationship with his daughter. She was all he had left. Now, since coming across the four-legged friend living in his shed, he regretted behaving in such a selfish manner.

Seb folded his coat over the back of the chair, his boots to the side. The right-hand pocket of his coat sagged close to the floor.

Pierre poured the amber fluid into each glass. 'To a very happy Christmas,' he said.

'And here's to a more peaceful New Year,' returned Seb.

They clinked glasses in a toast and as their eyes met Seb wondered what it was he sensed about the man. It wasn't so much that he was a bad lot or anything, just that the Frenchman struck him as a man who kept secrets.

'What is this?' Pierre said, reaching over to the floor at the side of Seb's chair.

He held up a parcel wrapped in newspaper that had fallen out of his coat pocket.

'That's private,' said Seb snatching it back.

Pierre watched as he stuffed it back into his coat pocket.

'Is it a secret?'

'Yes,' snapped Seb. 'It is.'

'Is it for Sally?'

Seb shook his head. 'No. It is not.'

'I see,' said Pierre, smiling and nodding as though he understood perfectly well who the present was for.

Sally had told him about her mother dying and her father drowning in sadness. She'd also told him about how he had changed in the last couple of months. He was happier than he had been. To Pierre's mind it could mean only one thing.

'Your father has a lady friend,' he had told her.

Sally had burst out laughing and shaken her head vehemently. 'I can't believe that.'

'But you say he is changed.'

'There is no sign of him being friendly with a woman. Mrs Evans two doors along invites him in for tea and a piece of cake now and again. But that's all.'

Pierre prided himself on reading people. He wasn't always right, but judging by Seb's manner and the way he had shoved the package back into his pocket, he was convinced that he did indeed have a lady friend.

'I would prefer if you said nothing of this to my daughter,' said Seb.

'You have my word,' Pierre said. In fact, he felt a sneaking regard for the old man. A love affair! At his age! He could almost be French!

The moment and the suspicion were swiftly placed aside. He had made a decision on which both his future and Sally's depended. Today was not the ideal time to tell Sally of his intentions, but if he didn't declare his feelings today his courage might fail him. It had to be today and going for a walk together would be the best time to tell her he was leaving.

Victoria Park was oddly desolate. A white mist had descended, trailing between the bare branches of trees like a bride's veil. The air was chill but Sally felt warm. Pierre's hand held hers and their upper arms brushed against each other as they walked.

Sally once again thanked him for the perfume. 'It was so unexpected.'

Creases appeared at the corners of his eyes. He wound his arm around her shoulders and hugged her. 'Make the most of it. If Mr Hitler has his way French perfume could be difficult to obtain in future.'

She sensed wariness clouding his eyes, the smile persisting but lacking in softness.

'You're worried Germany might march into France.'

He nodded. 'It is a possibility.'

'What about the Maginot Line?'

She'd read about the concrete bastions that stretched from the Belgian border down into northern France.

'I am not sure that will stop him. It only protects a part of the French border and besides he could come marching through Belgium. It wouldn't be the first time. The Kaiser did the same in the Great War.' He gave her a quick squeeze. 'Let us talk of more pleasant things.'

'Or just walk in silent peace,' she suggested.

What with dusk descending and the swirling white mist, she could almost forget it was Christmas Day. She sifted through her thoughts, trying to guess what might be on his mind. He was here helping his aunt out with the menagerie she'd gathered around her, but somehow sensed it was not the only reason.

He was the right age to be called up to fight, but she wasn't sure which army he would be expected to join, after all he had both British and French ancestry. The question refused to go away. There was nothing for it but to ask him outright.

'Have you joined the French army?' Her blood turned chillier as she waited for the answer. She didn't want him to join *any* army.

'No.'

'I suppose you have two options. French or British.'

'You are quite correct. I am eligible for both.'

His pronouncement seemed very non-committal and she couldn't help getting the impression that there was something he was not saying.

'Will you go back to France?'

His jaw clenched and unclenched and he stared straight ahead as though seeking an answer in the middle of all that mist. She immediately knew the answer.

'You are!' The knowledge filled her with dismay.

'I think I have to,' he said.

They stopped and faced each other not far from the children's swings at the bottom of the park close to the railway line.

'Your aunt will miss you. *I'll* miss you.'

'Sally, my sweet,' he said, turning to her and cupping one side of her face with his hand. His look was intense and made her legs feel weak. 'Wait for me.'

Sally shuddered. It was exactly as she'd guessed. In her mind she could see the black-and-white newsreels she'd seen at the cinema, Hitler's army marching into Austria and then into Czechoslovakia. She imagined them marching into France. Did he know something she didn't?

'There's nothing I can do to dissuade you?'

He shook his head silently, his mouth in a firm straight line. Dark circles under his eyes that told her he'd had many a sleepless night thinking about this. She sighed, resigned to the fact that he had made up his mind and so had she.

'You will come back. I do believe that, and I will wait for you.'

Shrouded in mist they kissed long and deeply, eyes closed and lost in their own private world.

Seb gritted his teeth. The shed door was not locked and when he looked inside it was empty. Surely Joanna's mother hadn't locked her up again?

On checking the dog's food and water dishes, he knew it couldn't be so. There was water but only a few indiscernible scraps in Harry's food dish. *Good job I brought along a bit of brisket*, he thought to himself.

Pierre's aunt had donated the piece of beef.

'She would have given us a chicken but somebody broke in last weekend and stole the lot,' explained Sally.

Chicken stealing was definitely on the rise.

He determined to keep his ears open as to who might have been so lucky as to eat chicken for Christmas, though people were just grateful to eat regardless of the activities of thieves and black marketers.

Bending his knees, he took a closer look into the dog's dish. The puppy had made short shrift of whatever might have been in there. Poking around with his finger he came across a small dark piece of meat that was easily identified once it was between his finger and thumb and held against the light.

A heart. A chicken heart!

Pursing his lips, Seb got to his feet. He'd said nothing to his daughter about Joanna or the dog. Although she eyed him quizzically she had not yet asked him a direct question as to the reason for his change of mood in the past few weeks. He decided to ask Joanna where she'd got the chicken offal, though for now he would let it go. By the looks of things the kid had a hard-enough life without him intimidating her. But he would ask – in a roundabout way so she didn't get upset.

In the meantime he assured himself that she and the puppy had gone for a walk. His heart leapt with joy at the thought of it. The little lad was growing up.

Standing in the doorway he looked around but couldn't see her. A terrible sense of loneliness seemed suddenly to jump on his shoulders. So did doubt. Surely she hadn't left for good?

No, he assured himself. They've gone for a walk. That's all.

A sliver of doubt eased its way into the back of his mind. It was possible a nosy neighbour might have betrayed Harry's presence to the authorities, he thought grimly. If they had they would answer to him. He clenched his jaw at the same time as running his fingers over the small parcel in his pocket.

In an effort to take his mind off things, he walked around his allotment, checking the growing vegetables as he went. Soon there would be carrots, cabbages, onions, parsnips and swede. Once they were harvested he would plant peas and green beans. In the summer he would plant lettuce, tomatoes and cucumbers, once he'd built a makeshift cloche that is.

The fruit canes were doing well and so was the rhubarb. The only other people he saw dealing with their allotments were strangers and quite a way from where he gardened. One or two waved at him and he waved back.

Then he spotted a small figure emerging from the mist. He waved and was about to shout when he saw her alter course. She was going behind the sheds rather than in front of them. It was the long way round and he wondered why – then realised she didn't want anyone else to see her.

Leaving off scrutinising what was growing well and what was not, he slowly made his way to the shed, scraped his boots off outside then entered.

Joanna entered just a few minutes later and started while Harry leapt up and down, excited to see him.

Seb bent down to fuss him. 'Steady on there, young Harry! You got springs instead of legs?' He turned to Joanna. 'Been for a walk, have you?'

She nodded and held up her hand. 'Harry needed a lead so I could take him for a walk. I found some rope.'

Harry proceeded to shake his head and scratch at the rope that served as a collar as well as a lead.

'I've got a Christmas present for you.' Seb smiled as he reached into his pocket. He was certain that Joanna's stepmother wouldn't have given her anything. It pleased him no end that he had. 'Merry Christmas, young lady.'

He held out the parcel Pierre had quizzed him about.

Joanna's jaw dropped. Her eyes were round with surprise. 'What is it?'

'A Christmas present. Haven't you ever had a Christmas present before?'

'Yes. From my dad.'

'But not this year.'

His tone and expression were sombre. It was such a shame that a child like Joanna had received nothing at all. She deserved a proper home and a real Christmas.

Joanna shook her head, her gaze fixed on the parcel. 'No.'

'Well,' he said. 'Are you going to take it or do I have to take it back home with me?'

Gingerly, too surprised to speak, Joanna took the parcel. 'Can I undo it now?'

'Well of course you can,' Seb replied somewhat impatiently. 'It's your Christmas present!'

Harry played with the pieces of wrapping paper that dropped to the floor.

'Oh . . . oh . . .!' Joanna stared open mouthed at the collar and lead dangling from her hand.

'Do you like it?' asked Seb.

It felt as though her tongue was stuck to the roof of her mouth so she could only nod.

'Well say something then!' he exclaimed gruffly.

'It's beautiful. Really beautiful,' she finally managed to say.

'Better see if it fits him then, hadn't you?'

Excited at the sight of the collar and lead, Harry wriggled and jumped around before she finally managed to get the collar around his neck. Even then he tried to shake it off, his velvet soft ears flapping around his head.

'I don't think he likes it,' said Joanna.

'He'll get used to it. Now you'd better have this as well.'

He gave her a brown carrier bag containing a few beef bones plus some bits of fat and gristle and a portion of ox heart.

'Couldn't give you all of what was left because we need some fat to fry and bake cakes with. And there's a cooked sausage I bought for him that I saved from my breakfast. That lot should last him a few days.'

Since his change of mood, Sally had given him the job of midweek shopping. Although they had little meat themselves, Seb hadn't been able to resist buying a sausage and desisting from eating it for breakfast.

Seb glanced out through the window at the gathering dusk. 'Looks like time we were both heading home.'

Joanna unhitched the lead from Harry's collar and hung it on a free hook beside the gardening implements.

Harry continued to scratch at the collar and flap his ears, but once he had a beef bone to gnaw on, he settled down. In fact, he hardly noticed them leave.

'Tell me,' said Seb, as he slid the catch on the shed door. 'Do you go to Victoria Park school?'

'Yes.'

'I thought you might. And what's the name of your teacher?'

'Miss Hadley,' Joanna replied, as she sucked on a gobstopper he'd given her.

'Is that so. Do you like her?'

Joanna nodded. 'Yes. She's my favourite teacher.'

Seb felt an instant surge of pride. He realised now how offhand he'd been with his daughter since the death of his wife. Not only had he been distant and uncommunicative, he'd taken little notice of what was happening in her career. All he'd done was insist on not letting her out of his sight – as though that was going to solve anything.

Now he had to make amends and show her just how much he cared about her. Meeting up with Joanna and her dog would help him do that.

There was also the question of where the chicken came from. It was highly unlikely that anyone living in The Vale had the money to dine on chicken this Christmas and Joanna's home circumstances were such that her stepmother couldn't possibly afford one. Only people in the country who had the room to keep chickens dined so lavishly. So where had the bits come from that Joanna had fed to Harry?

'Did any uncles and aunts visit you this Christmas?' he asked her.

'No. I don't have any. At least I don't think I do. There was just me, Elspeth and her cousin.'

'Her cousin you say! What was his name then?'

'Jack. Jack Smith.'

Later that evening, once he and Sally were seated in their cosy sitting room, Seb asked his daughter about the little girl named Joanna Ryan.

Sally, still thinking of Pierre while she knitted, didn't seem to hear so he repeated himself.

'I met a little girl named Joanna Ryan. She said she was in your class.'

Sally's attention jerked up from the socks she was knitting. Knitting socks from wool unravelled from old jumpers for the brave fellows fighting gave her something to do while she wandered through her thoughts. 'Joanna Ryan? Yes. She's in my class. Where did you meet her?'

Seb tapped out the contents of his pipe into the hot coals in the grate. He would tell her all she needed to know – except with regard to the dog.

'At the allotment. Am I right in thinking she's a bit neglected by her parents?'

'By her stepmother,' Sally exclaimed, an angry flush coming to her face. 'Her mother died, her father remarried and now he's gone off to war. The woman's a tart!'

'Strong language!' Seb was taken aback. It wasn't often his daughter reacted so strongly. 'I take it you've met the woman.'

'Peroxide-dyed hair and her face plastered in makeup and takes care of herself. She certainly doesn't take care of Joanna, which is a great shame. Joanna is a lovely girl. Quite intelligent in fact. She used to come to school quite decently dressed and plumper than she is now. She's now a skinny little thing and a bit cowed. As for her clothes . . .'

'She's long grown out of them.'

His daughter sat back in her chair and sighed. 'I wish there was something more I could do to help her. I did visit the woman and gave her a piece of my mind. I should imagine she watched herself for a while, but I doubt she let it worry her for too long.'

'Is there nothing that can be done?'

Sally lay the knitting to one side. 'Well, I could report her circumstances to the children's welfare officer at the council, but I'm not sure I'd be doing Joanna any favours. Despite her stepmother's shortcomings, a children's home is not the best place for a child to grow up in. I was hoping her father would come home soon then he could see what's been happening and do something about it.'

'Hopefully he will,' said her father, and looked thoughtfully towards the window. Beyond the front wall of the house were the park and the allotments. His thoughts turned to the puppy that had brought him and the little girl together. 'I think we might have snow.'

CHAPTER EIGHTEEN

By the end of January, Harry was going out for regular walks on his lead. On the occasions when Joanna couldn't get there, Seb did the honours.

'Don't you worry. I'll bring him a bit of breakfast and he can share my lunch. I've got a lot of catching up to do, things to plant and what have you, or we'll all be starving.'

The end of February saw Pierre shipping out to France. At first both Sally and her father had presumed he had been offered the opportunity to join the British Expeditionary Force. Seb had asked him outright.

Pierre had responded that he had no wish to wear a uniform. 'Not until I have to.'

He admitted that he had chosen instead to make his own way across the Channel. The reasons he gave were commendable, but unaccountably vague.

'I want to be close with my people over there,' he had told Sally. 'Things are not going to get any better and at least part of my heart is in France.'

'What about the part of your heart that is here?'.

He stroked her face and looked at her with fondness. 'You do not need to goad me into words. You should know what is in my heart.

'I know it's selfish, not wanting you to go . . .'

'There will be a time for selfishness when this is over. In the meantime there are people dear to me who are likely to be in danger once the Germans march in. There are things I have to deal with. Important things.'

'You can't know for sure that they'll reach Paris . . .'

He'd shaken his head sadly. 'The German army is unstoppable. There are people over there I need to see for various reasons. Please do not ask me to go into great detail because I cannot.'

His statement had caused Sally some consternation. He wasn't joining the British army. Neither was he joining the French army. He was going over there to do his bit, though not outlining exactly what doing his bit might entail.

'I don't think I can help being selfish,' she'd said frowning.

They'd been standing beneath the railway bridge, droplets of water plopping onto the ground from the iron framework, Pierre awaiting the train that would take him away.

'I fear the demise of the army – French and British. But France must fight on and besides . . .' He held her close against him, her head resting on his shoulder. 'I know you would do the same if the circumstances were reversed. You would do what you could, even though you belong to no army.'

It was hard to imagine she would do any such thing until she thought of her father, the children at school, the nice neighbours she knew who didn't deserve to be intimidated and frightened.

'Freedom demands a high price,' she said at last.

They clung together soundlessly, her face buried against his chest, each tortured with frightening thoughts, and each wrapped tightly in each other's love just as strongly as they were wrapped in each other's arms.

Sally clung to him, wishing their kiss would never end, fearing that if she let go he would vanish at this very moment.

'Keep safe,' he said to her.

'Write to me,' she replied.

He avoided the look in her eyes, instead gazing over her head at nothing in particular.

'You have my address in Paris. I will be there for a short time. I will also give you an address of a café ran by an old friend I can trust. I will write to you from there – somehow – for as long as I can.'

From London he would take the boat train to the coast from where he would get a boat to France. It was still possible to do this, but for how long nobody could say. Men had been called up, drilled and sent over to France, but nothing was happening. France was still depending on its Maginot Line and Prime Minister Neville Chamberlain was looking ill, his cheekbones as seen on cinema newsreels more prominent, his eyes more deep set as though he were trying to hide from the horrors of the war he had declared back in September.

The station was crowded with other women seeing off their men. Most of the men were in uniform. Pierre looked a little out of place with his well-cut clothes and black Fedora, the brim pulled down jauntily over one side of his face.

His aunt had come too, hanging back as they said their goodbyes, her giving the excuse she needed a quick cup of tea.

'Goodbye, *mon cher*,' she murmured as he kissed each cheek in turn.

Although everyone around them was hugging, kissing and crying, Sally failed to shed a single tear. The truth of the matter was, she was in shock. Shocked that she'd fallen in love so easily, and shocked that he was now leaving her, off to do goodness knows what in a country that could be overrun by the enemy at any time.

Pierre, as though girding himself for the conflict to come, was suddenly brusque. 'Goodbye. Goodbye to you both.'

'*Au revoir*,' called Lady Ambrose as he bolted for the train.

'*Au revoir*,' Sally repeated, tears finally stinging her eyes and an empty feeling inside. Her voice dropped to a whisper. 'Keep safe.'

Lady Ambrose offered her a lift home, which Sally gratefully accepted.

Her ladyship sat ramrod stiff in the back of her car, her chauffeur sitting up front. Normally Sally would consider this very grand, but her thoughts were otherwise occupied. In a brief moment she dragged her thoughts back to the present. It struck her that today Amelia, as her ladyship had insisted she call her, was not dressed in the clothes of a working man but in a smart lavender-coloured suit.

The way she was staring straight ahead was worrying. Sally was in no doubt that she had something distinctive to say.

'Sally, I want to tell you a story. It's about a young couple falling in love in wartime. They were hopelessly in love and swore they would spend the rest of their lives together. War came and the young man went away to fight. The young woman thought he looked quite splendid in his uniform, every inch the hero. It never crossed her mind that anything might happen to him. Getting killed or seriously injured only happened to other people. Not to them. But . . .' Her voice dropped an octave and her chin trembled. 'He was killed at the Battle of the Somme. She didn't believe it at first, walking around like a lost soul, sighing his name, her health and her heart breaking with each passing day.'

Sally started when her ladyship's gloved hand touched hers.

'Place no faith in the saying that it is better to have loved and lost than not to have loved at all. Having loved and lost leaves a wound inside that can never heal. Let the parting be sweet, my dear, but put it behind you. Step back from loving and you feel his loss easier to bear.'

'You can't believe he will be lost!'

The look on her ladyship's face deepened into greater sadness. 'Every young man who marches off to be a hero believes it will never be him that is killed. Archibald thought that too.'

'Archibald?'

Lady Ambrose sighed. 'He was the love of my life and the reason I never married. That's why I keep so many animals, the replacement for the husband and children who might have been. The DeVere name belonged to my father. He was French. Ambrose was my mother's maiden name, hence my double-barrelled title.'

172

Stunned by her revelations, Sally quickly regained her composure. She stared straight ahead of her, her jaw set in determination.

'I can't stop loving just because I might lose him,' she said finally. 'I have to love him in spite of that.'

Shirtsleeves rolled up to his elbows, Arnold Thomas was placing a pot in the sink when he heard the bell. At first he tried to ignore it, scrubbing at the pot with more enthusiasm in the faint hope it would block out the sound.

The bell jangled and kept jangling, the sound guaranteed to get on anyone's nerves.

Clang! Jangle! Clang!

Friends and professional acquaintances had expressed their opinion that he had the patience of a saint. For the most part they'd been referring to his patience teaching at Victoria Park boys' school. Those who knew his wife considered him a saint. The woman was bedridden for the most part and although Arnold could afford to hire a day nurse to help him cope – even if only on a part-time basis – he had stubbornly refused.

In fact, he would have loved some help, but the truth was that Miranda refused to have another woman in the house.

'I know what you'd get up to once my back was turned,' she'd snarled when he'd dared suggest they employ someone.

When they'd first met he'd considered her as ethereal as Titania, the Queen of Fairyland. Her skin was pale as alabaster, her hair so fair it was almost white and her dark violet eyes glowed like blue flames and were in stark contrast to the shining light that seemed to surround her.

The bell continued to jangle on and on, grating on his nerves until he was clenching his jaw so hard that it hurt, until he was attacking the saucepan with renewed vigour, his knuckles and fingertips red raw from the effort.

He looked up at the ceiling as a loud thudding suddenly accompanied the jangling bell. Resentment surged deep inside as he imagined her sitting up there in bed, bell in one hand, walking stick in the other. *Jangle, jangle, jangle* and *thud, thud, thud*.

The pot entered the water with a splash. He reached for the tea towel and dried his hands, then rolled down his shirtsleeves.

'All right, Miranda. All right. I'm coming,' he shouted up the stairs.

She was sitting on the edge of the bed, her hair awry, her nightdress crumpled above her thin white knees. Her skin had always been pale, but now it was almost translucent, blue veins like skeins of silk thread just beneath the surface. Her eyes were like chips of obsidian in the midst of a snowdrift.

His smile was similar to the kind he might give a crying child who had fallen down and cut his knees.

'There, there,' he said soothingly. 'What's all this fuss about?'

'Fuss? Fuss? I'm sick. I'm dying. I've every right to fuss, you stupid man.' Her carping shriek was enough to set a saint's teeth on edge, but Arnold had got used to it.

'Now come on,' he said, just as soothingly as before as he attempted to lift her. 'Let's get you back into bed.'

Face contorted with rage, she lashed out at him with her walking stick. He caught its tip just before it made contact and prised it out of her hand. 'Now, now, my dear. There's no need for that.'

There was no anger in his voice, no emotion at all really, just a controlled politeness as though there was a glass partition between them through which no hurts could penetrate.

Sticks and stones may break my bones but words will never hurt me . . .

Arnold had got used to her tantrums, which were flung at him on a daily basis. It often amazed him how one could get used to the most grievous taunts without matching her violence. When it all got too much he just increased her medicine that little bit so she fell asleep a little earlier and a lot deeper.

'Let's get you decent,' he said as he straightened her nightdress, pulling the hem down to her ankles. She had very slim ankles that had once looked graceful in high-heeled shoes. He remembered stroking them all the way up her calves to her knees and beyond. Such wonderful days when she had enjoyed physical intimacy as much as he had. Such joy!

He was still reminiscing when he pulled her bodice across to cover her alabaster breasts. He wasn't ready for the clout she gave him with the brass bell she used to summon him to her presence. For a moment his head spun, but a moment was all he allowed himself.

'Now that was a silly thing to do, Miranda.'

After prising that too from her iron grip, he raised his hand to his forehead and felt a sticky trickle of blood.

'Silly? Silly?' she exclaimed. 'Better to be silly rather than a creeping vegetable like you! Look at you! Arnold Thomas, head teacher of a boys' school in a down-and-out area of the city. Wouldn't say boo to a goose! Well, I will, Arnold. Boo, boo, boo!'

'Drink this, Miranda.'

His voice was firm. Arnold never raised his voice even though it was like dealing with an unruly child.

Miranda raised one eyebrow as she eyed the drink he was offering her. She'd watched him pour medicine into her glass then top it up with a shot of whisky. She never refused whisky.

'It's your favourite,' he said to her.

She sniffed. Her smile was hesitant – until she took a sip, Arnold still holding the glass. Eyeing him over the rim with a look of pure contempt, she drank it all down. With his arm around her, he laid her back on the pillow, her white hair spreading like a fibrous halo around her head.

She closed her eyes, deep in a drug-filled sleep.

Arnold sighed and rubbed at his forehead. He was used to feeling drained, but today he didn't so much feel drained as buried alive. That's how much it had taken out of him being married to a woman like Miranda, a creature with whom he no longer shared a bed or had intimacy with – not even a kiss. That part of their relationship had died years ago.

As he looked at her, her face almost as white as the pillow beneath her head, he found himself hating her. As a consequence he harboured a great determination to go out tonight, to live again as he deserved to live.

Jaw firmly clenched, he closed the bedroom door and made his way to the bathroom. Once he'd washed the blood off, he put on his coat, checked the blackout curtains and left the house. Taking great gulps of fresh air was as good as drinking the finest wine. It was free, and so was he. For a time, at least.

Normal people. I need to be with normal people, he thought as he strolled down to the pub at the bottom of Redcatch Road.

Deep down he knew his need was greater than being with normal people. He desired company, female company most of all.

There was something about Elspeth that reminded him of Miranda. Maybe it was her hair, though Miranda's was natural. Elspeth's had the look of a bottle blonde, her complexion was flawless only with the aid of face powder, her lips were red with the application of lipstick. Overall she had a more substantial body than Miranda, but the fact that she laughed and smoked with the men, and seemed to like him especially, was attractive to him. It had been a long time since a woman had made it so obvious that she liked him and he needed that. He needed it very much. He hoped she'd be there at the pub alone. To his great joy she was.

She was lounging against an upright piano, singing along with whatever was being played. For a moment his hopes seemed dashed. The pianist had a cigarette dangling from one corner of his mouth and judging by the glint in his eyes he was obviously enjoying Elspeth's attention.

She too seemed to be enjoying herself, returning the pianist's saucy looks with some of her own. Until she saw Arnold, then suddenly all signs of brashness left her features, replaced by something almost demure in its composition.

He gestured that he was getting a drink for himself and did she want one.

Elspeth raised her glass and nodded, her eyes bright with expectation. She mouthed the words, port and lemon. A bit expensive, but he didn't care.

As he made his way to the bar, she came to join him. She was at his side just as the drinks arrived. They clinked glasses. She smiled up into his face. 'Hello stranger. Where have you been hiding?' Her lips were glossy, her eyes bright with welcome.

Happy to see her, he smiled broadly. 'Funny you should say that. I do feel as though I've been hiding, but there comes a time when you have to get out and about, don't you think?'

'Absolutely,' she said, clinking her glass with his one more time. 'You weren't hiding from me, were you? I won't bite you know.'

He shook his head and blushed. 'Of course not.'

She snuggled up close, her face upturned so their eyes could more easily meet. 'Though I might bite you, but only if you were willing,' she said softly, a twinkle in her eyes.

The moment she'd seen him, the evening she'd planned for herself and the pianist were jettisoned. Arnold had a car, a house and a bit of cash. He'd told her so himself about the car and the house.

'Though it's difficult to get petrol,' he explained.

The cash she'd added on herself. It peeved her that he hadn't been around for a while, but that was the way of things nowadays. Men were shifting in and out all the time. She knew he was a head teacher, and had an invalid wife. That was enough to keep him in one place.

Now he was here she had every intention of not letting him stray from her sight.

The night went well. Arnold drank three pints and a whisky. Elspeth downed more than him, thanks to a couple of drinks she'd been bought before he arrived, but was careful not to let it show.

When they left the pub Arnold insisted on seeing her home.

The offer pleased her. 'Well, aren't you the knight in shining armour!'

Drink had made him more confident. 'I don't have a suit of shining armour, but I do have a torch.'

He flashed the meagre beam onto the pavement.

Elspeth clutched her handbag tight to her side. She had her own torch among the rest of the detritus she carried around but she wasn't going to let him know that. She hugged his arm close and for a brief moment he caught her smile in the light from his torch.

'Good job I've got you then,' she said with a smile.

Elspeth breathed a sigh of satisfaction, enjoying the warmth of his arm linked with hers. It was a shame he'd dropped out of sight for a while, but he was back now and this time she wouldn't let him go.

So much for the privations of war, she thought to herself as they reached the bottom of The Vale. The great thing about the blackout was that on really dark nights like tonight, nobody could see anyone and that included her neighbours enclosed behind their blackout curtains. It was getting harder to remember how lights had twinkled in streets and from house and shop windows. But, she reminded herself, there were advantages.

'I missed you,' she whispered when they were halfway up The Vale. 'You can't imagine what it's like not having a man around, and not just any man. Somebody who makes me safe and warm.'

'I'm flattered.'

'How's your wife?' she asked him tentatively.

Arnold considered his answer. He had no desire to be a defendant in a divorce petition – God knows there were plenty of them going on nowadays. But Miranda was his wife in name only. He felt it gave him a right to stray from the straight and narrow, and anyway, she was sleeping a drugged sleep. She would never know. And I'm a normal man with normal desires, he thought to himself, but he couldn't find it in himself to lie.

'She's very ill and can be very difficult at times.'

Elspeth felt her breath catch in her throat. 'I see.'

'I wouldn't want you to think I make a habit of doing this kind of thing. I've never been unfaithful to my wife. I'd always hoped she'd get well again. Alas it hasn't happened and isn't likely to. And in the meantime . . .' His sigh was heavy enough to sink a ship.

Elspeth licked her lips and chose her words carefully. 'Life's too short to be lonely,' she said, her voice as husky as a screen siren she particularly admired. She gave his arm an affectionate hug, tugging it close to her breast.

Feeling relaxed in her company, Arnold opened up. 'I wish she was her old self but I've been wishing it for so long and now I've got to the stage where I accept that she's never going to be the woman I married ever again. The woman I loved left her body a long time ago. She's just a shell of her former self.'

Elspeth stopped and forced the torch up between them so it lit up both their faces. 'I understand, Arnold. I understand completely. If you ever need a shoulder to cry on, I'll be waiting.'

As they approached her house she advised him to turn the torch off.

'My neighbours are particularly nosy,' she said quietly. 'And we don't want them to see us, now do we? We do have our reputations to think about.'

'Of course.'

She stroked his face with her gloved hand, tracing a line from the corner of his eye to his jawline.

'Thank you for walking me home. I would ask you to come inside for a cuppa, but I think we both know it would be more than that. I will understand if you say no.'

'I think it has to be no,' he said, his courage having failed him at the final hurdle. 'Perhaps another time.'

'Next Wednesday? In the Redcatch?'

He found himself saying yes. As he walked away he felt both elated and guilty. He had taken the first serious step off the straight and narrow and wasn't at all sure he would ever regain that particular path.

At night it was Joanna's habit to lean out of the front bedroom window and gaze at the stars. Tonight there were no stars and the streets sweeping down over the hill, and on the hills on the other side of the main road, were like black blocks cut out of the earth.

Her eyesight was good and she'd spotted the faint light of a torch picking out the footsteps of two people walking up The Vale.

A few doors down from the house, they stopped and the torch shone upwards lighting the faces of the two people. On recognising her stepmother's features she pulled the window closed, but stopped when she saw the features of the man in her stepmother's company.

She pulled the window shut swiftly then left the front bedroom to return to her own at the back of the house. Already in her nightdress, she hid herself beneath the bedclothes where she shivered, afraid of what she had seen.

She'd got used to her stepmother going out with other men and kept out of her way if she dared bring one of them home. For the most part they were rough and common, but she knew the man Elspeth was with tonight, and he was far from being common.

Mr Thomas was the headmaster of Victoria Park boys' school. She instinctively knew it was a secret she must keep to herself.

CHAPTER NINETEEN

Seb Hadley knew every inch of the railway embankment next to the allotments.

He knew where the rabbit holes were and the best spot for catching a pigeon.

Trapping wildlife provided food for the growing puppy. Seb wondered why more people didn't do it, but put it down to laziness or ignorance. Having grown up in the country, Seb had learned how to fish, trap and hunt in order to put meat on the table.

'Tonight's supper,' he said to Harry, after skinning both the rabbit and the pigeon and putting both in a pot of boiling water.

Leaving the meat bubbling in a pan on top of a Primus stove, he left the allotment with Harry on a lead and headed for the park. As the children were at school it was fairly empty.

'We're going on a big walk today,' he'd said to the little dog on their way there.

No matter whether Harry understood or not, he was keen to be let off his lead to gambol and chase around the park, but Seb had other ideas.

His intention was to walk along Coronation Road. On one side of the road was the embankment falling down towards the river. On the other was a terrace of four-storey houses and offices above workshops, where coopers bent metal bands over oak barrels, and others weighed scrap metal on a scale or rags gathered in sacks and gone beyond natural repair.

Seb admired the coopers making the barrels. He spotted the sign advertising the garage owner's name and the tasks he was prepared to carry out. D.L. Brown sold, bought, mended and checked every motorcar anyone could ever think of, or had done before the war. In peacetime rich folk had taken their cars to be mended here. It had a huge workshop at the rear plus a storage facility where chauffeurs parked the limousines used by their employers.

Seb knew from local gossip that the workshop had been turned over to making munitions and other engineering items. Some of the people who worked there were coming out for a bit of fresh air, their tea mugs clutched in one hand, a cigarette in the other.

He heard a woman laugh and jerked up his head. She wore a turban but enough hair poked out for him to see her hair was bleached white blonde – like that Jean Harlow woman.

She saw him looking. Instead of wishing him good day her tone was downright belligerent. 'Had yer eyeful or want your penny back?' she shouted.

Seb turned quickly away. The woman looked like trouble.

Elspeth Ryan, for it was indeed she taking a break, tossed her head defiantly and went back to her tea and her fag. Today her temper was up. This morning she'd received a telegram to say her husband was on his way home.

By the time Seb and Harry got back to the allotment, it was gone four o'clock and the shed was full of the smell of cooked rabbit and pigeon.

Joanna was there waiting for them and had turned the little methylated stove off and taken some of the meat out to cool.

Her face was bright with excitement.

'My dad's coming home,' she said, as Harry jumped all over her, yapping excitedly and licking her face.

'Well, that's nice to know,' said Seb. 'Seems to me you might have need of these then.' He handed her a brown paper carrier bag containing a few early carrots and some sprouts. 'I expect your dad will enjoy them. Fresh from the garden they are.'

Feeling fit to burst, Joanna smiled and nodded, so full of happiness she couldn't speak. She'd told everyone in school that her dad had written saying he was on his way.

'We'll get another telegram soon with the exact date,' she'd told her friend Susan whose father was also away fighting.

After school, running from the school gates on her way to see Harry, she saw Paul coming out of the boys' school and told him too.

'Wish my dad was away fighting,' said Paul. Just for once he refrained from wiping his runny nose on the sleeve of his coat. Paul's father was too old to fight. He was also too lazy, and even when he wasn't in prison he was often out of work and the subject of criticism in the street.

It was Paul's mother who went out to work, initially as a cleaner but with the war on she also worked at the munitions factory, the same one where Elspeth, Joanna's stepmother, worked.

'Wait till you tell him about Lottie,' said Paul. 'Bet he'll be angry.'

Joanna's face clouded. Paul mentioning Lottie brought all the hurt back. The surprising thing was that she'd hardly thought of her cat since Harry had arrived on the scene. It made her feel guilty. She'd also kept Harry's existence from her friends. Sometimes she had been tempted to confide in Paul or Susan, but had held back just in case word got out and Harry went the same way as her cat.

'Do you think he'll bring his gun?' asked Paul enthusiastically.

'I don't know.'

'If he does and you tell him about what happened to Lottie he might shoot the person who did it.'

Joanna found herself brightening at the prospect. As far as she was concerned her stepmother was the guilty party and deserved to be shot.

'He might get you another cat,' Paul continued.

Joanna shook her head. 'I don't want another cat. Not now.'

She was just about to tell him about Harry when she spotted the headmaster of the boys' school coming their way.

'I've got to go,' she said, breaking into a run as she turned away. 'I'll see you tomorrow.'

She'd been right. It was definitely Mr Thomas she'd seen with her stepmother and her face coloured up with embarrassment.

Paul's suggestion that her father might shoot her stepmother stayed with her as she'd ran to the shed. Her spirits soared at the thought of it, thrilling at the prospect of telling him about Harry and showing him the puppy who had brought such joy into her life. She would also tell him about Lottie, of course, and how her stepmother had disposed of her, as though she were an old handbag, not a living, breathing creature who was loved, and capable of loving in return.

Yes. Everything would be different once her father got home and found out what had been going on.

'Did you have a good day in school?'

Seb's question interrupted her flow of thought. 'Yes. I told everyone about my dad coming home.'

'Even your teacher?'

Joanna nodded, the sparkle in her eyes gladdening Seb's heart.

He chuckled. 'No doubt I shall hear all about it tonight I shouldn't wonder. Do you know why that is, Joanna?'

Still smiling, eyes still sparkling, Joanna shook her head.

'Because your teacher, Miss Hadley, will tell me all about what happened in school today.'

He saw the mystified look on her face and finally told her who he was and who her teacher was.

'Miss Hadley's my daughter,' he said to her. 'And sometimes she tells me about her day. She takes a pride in all you kids – some of you more than others. You are one of her favourites, though I suppose I shouldn't say that.' He winked. 'But there you are. It's out now.'

'Wow!' she exclaimed, shrugging her shoulders up to her ears as the wonderful news flooded over her.

Once Harry had eaten and snuggled down in his bed, she said goodbye to Seb and ran all the way home, excited beyond belief at what Seb had told her. In fact, she was bubbling over with the news and desperately wanted to tell someone.

As she ran up The Vale, she looked in each garden on the way up, desperate to see somebody she knew so she could tell them the good news that her father was coming home and that her friend Seb was her teacher's father.

The afternoon was grey and cold. She saw nobody until she caught up with Mrs Allen walking slowly up the hill.

Mrs Allen's legs were bad, her ankles bulging over the rims of her shoes. A shopping bag weighed her down on one side and her hand was pink from the effort of carrying it.

Joanna hailed her brightly and offered to carry her bag.

'That would be lovely, dear. I'm getting too old for carrying shopping bags.'

Joanna took it from her, balancing it with the bag of vegetables Seb had given to her. 'It's not too heavy for me,' she said reassuringly.

'You've got the strength of youth,' said Mrs Allen kindly. 'I used to be strong when I was your age, but now I can't even get all the shopping I need. As for this rationing and having to queue for everything – well! It's too much for me. I would have liked some carrots, but my old legs won't let me stand too long. Have you had a good day at school? Bit late getting home, aren't you?'

'I've been with a friend. Did you hear that my dad's coming home?'

Mrs Allen chuckled. 'Well, well, well. That'll be nice for you. Tell you what, I'll make him a nice cottage pie when he gets back. Potatoes, onions and a bit of gristly meat I expect and if I can get carrots, I will. Just for you and your dad.'

'That would be lovely.'

Mrs Allen purposely didn't mention Joanna's stepmother. She wasn't one to gossip or criticise, but she disapproved of Elspeth Ryan, a woman who was rarely home and neglected a child.

'And if there's no hot meal for you when you get home, come round and see me. I've get a bit of stew on the go.'

Joanna looked down at her shoes and felt the weight of Seb's vegetables bumping against her legs.

There would be no hot meal on the table. Her main meal of the day was the one she got in school. Still, a hot meal at the end of the day would be most welcome. In fact, she'd found the smell of the pigeon and rabbit Seb had cooked for Harry quite appetising.

'I'll take it to your front door,' offered Joanna as they arrived at Mrs Allen's garden gate.

'That's lovely of you, dear.'

While Mrs Allen turned her key in the lock, Joanna placed Mrs Allen's shopping bag on the step and placed her own brown carrier bag beside it.

She was back at the garden gate before Mrs Allen noticed.

'What's this?' said a surprised Mrs Allen.

'Carrots,' shouted Joanna. 'And sprouts. They're a present.'

It seemed far more likely that Mrs Allen would make a decent meal of the vegetables. Her stepmother was unlikely to do anything with them unless she kept them for when her father got home.

Joanna reminded herself that her father wasn't coming home just yet and the vegetables might have gone rotten by the time he was.

Mrs Allen peered into the bag then looked up. 'Carrots and sprouts. Just what I wanted! Where did you get them?'

'They were a present.'

Mrs Allen heaved a big sigh. 'One good turn deserves another. Come on in and have a bowl of that hot meal I promised you.'

Warmed by the stew which was thick with vegetables and thickened with dumplings, Joanna told Mrs Allen about the man at the allotment who was also her teacher's father.

'He looks after my puppy when I can't get there to see him. My puppy lives in his shed.'

'A puppy! Well I never.'

'But you mustn't tell Elspeth about him. She had my cat destroyed. She'd have Harry destroyed too if she ever found out. You do promise to keep it a secret?'

Joanna's alarmed expression pulled at Mrs Allen's heartstrings. She'd so often seen this child looking thin and neglected, her face dirty with coal dust, specks of it sparkling in her hair.

'Of course I will,' she said softly. 'Have you told anyone else?'

Joanna shook her head as her spoon scraped the last vestige of food from her bowl.

'Not even your friends at school?'

Joanna shook her head again and wiped her greasy lips on the back of her hand. 'No. But I will tell them once I've told my father.'

Creases crowded around Mrs Allen's eyes when she smiled sadly. 'Well then, I feel really privileged.'

She meant what she said. The poor child had lost her mother and was missing her father. Whatever had the man been thinking of marrying a conniving cow like that dreadful Elspeth?

'Because my father's in the army do you think he might bring his gun home with him? Do you think he might shoot her when he finds out about my cat?' Joanna asked her.

Mrs Allen's jaw dropped, and then she laughed fit to burst. 'Well, I for one wouldn't blame him if he did!'

CHAPTER TWENTY

That evening, Seb Hadley sat down after his evening meal and decided the time was right to tell his daughter about Joanna and her dog.

Sally spoke first. 'I've still had no news from Pierre.'

'That's a shame.'

She headed straight for the sink and the washing up, a ruse he realised to hide her breaking heart.

'Leave that for now. I want to tell you something.'

'In a minute, Dad. Just give me a minute.'

Something about the way the light picked up the dark auburn of her hair threw him. So did her soft curves and the way she moved, purposefully yet gracefully. When was it she'd started looking so much like her mother?

For the first time in a while his thoughts brooded on the woman he had lost. So carried away with his thoughts did he become, that he didn't notice Sally's disappearance until she was gone.

He heard the sound of her moving around upstairs in her bedroom and thought about following her up there and telling her about Joanna and her dog, but something told him that now was not the time. '*Let her have a moment to herself,*' whispered a voice he recognised as his late wife's. '*Sometimes a woman needs to be alone.*'

Sally ducked her hand beneath the silk shade of the table lamp and turned it on. The lamp, its pale apricot shade warming the room, stood on her dressing table that doubled as a writing desk.

With a heartfelt sigh, she took the box of Basildon Bond lined letter paper from the right-hand drawer along with the matching envelopes.

An old friend had bought her the writing set two Christmases ago, and she'd been frugal about using it. It had turned out that she was right to do so. Paper was in short supply and quality letter writing material such as Basildon Bond was becoming difficult to get hold of.

The fresh page glared at her as though it were begging to be written on. Her pen was full of ink. This would be the sixth letter she had written to Pierre. So far she had received no reply and the obvious questions clutched at her heart.

Keeping busy, especially at school, helped enormously. Only then did she manage to push her concerns to a far corner of her mind so she could concentrate on the job in hand.

At night, or when her hands and mind were not busy, fear came creeping back.

Why hadn't he written? Was he hurt? Had he joined the army? Or was it just that absence, contrary to making the heart grow fonder, had destroyed his love for her?

She couldn't know anything for sure and hadn't expressed her feelings and fears to anyone.

The empty page loomed like a glaring challenge, almost to the extent that it stung her eyes.

'Write something,' she growled and somehow the verbal command travelled to her fingers. Her pen began to write.

My darling, dearest.

My diary tells me it is only two months since you left England, yet it feels like a lifetime. I wonder what it will feel like once this war is over and we have lived a lifetime together?

Every day I dash down to the letterbox in the hope that you have replied to my latest letter, so far to no avail.

I will not dare to think that you no longer wish me to wait for you because in my heart of hearts I do not believe this to be true.

I dread thinking that you are in a position where you cannot possibly write to me, that you are in some kind of trouble.

As yet the Germans have not marched into France and this 'phoney war', as people are calling it, makes us all hope that the real thing will never happen. I hope they never march into France and that you will return intact and uninjured – then perhaps we can attempt to have that lifetime together . . .

She read the letter through one last time before consigning it to a matching envelope on which she wrote the address he'd given her.

On Saturday she would take it along to Lady Ambrose as she had the others.

'I'm sending him some luxuries – plus socks and soap – just in case he can't get those there,' his aunt had told her. 'Might as well put the letters in with it.'

It had seemed a sensible enough action and Sally had not hesitated to agree to the idea.

After slipping the letter into her handbag, she went back downstairs. Her father looked up as she entered the room.

'Well. Are you interested in what I've got to say or what?' He sounded almost as grumpy as he used to before he'd started attending the allotment again.

Sally apologised. 'Sorry. I had to write a letter.'

Her father's face softened. 'To Pierre?'

She nodded her head.

Seb Hadley sighed. 'I should imagine things are getting a bit difficult over there. Panic breeds mayhem and I reckon there'll be a lot of that going on before very long.'

'Do you have to be so gloomy?' Sally snapped, annoyed at being reminded just how dangerous Pierre's predicament might be. 'There might not be a war – not a proper one anyway. Chamberlain said—'

'Like a lot of us, Chamberlain lived through the carnage of the Great War. He did his best to keep us out of this, but by my reckoning it's gone beyond that now. Best prepare yourself . . .'

On seeing the worried look on his daughter's face, Seb clamped his mouth tightly shut before choosing his words.

'It's bound to be difficult over there. Don't fret until you know something for certain. Now how about we have another cup of tea?'

Sally was in no mood for drinking more tea, besides which she was trying to make it go further.

'It's all right, Dad. I'm fine. Now what was it you wanted to talk to me about?'

Suddenly, wanting to tell her all about Joanna and her puppy seemed trivial. 'Never mind. You've got far weightier problems on your mind.'

Sally perched on the arm of his chair. 'I'm sorry for flying off the handle. It was inexcusable. Tell me what you wanted to tell me.' She kissed the top of his head.

'It's about two waifs I've met. A little girl and her dog.'

Her father began telling her about Joanna and the dog and his concerns for the girl's welfare.

'Though I understand her father's about to come home. I also understand she's already told you that particular piece of news.'

'Yes. She did. She's very excited and quite frankly I'm rather glad. Her stepmother is not the nicest person I've ever met. She works at that place along Coronation Road that used to be a garage. She strikes me as a right cow!'

Seb's eyebrows rose at her unexpected use of an expletive he'd never heard fall from her lips before. 'That bad?'

'Yes. She is. Peroxide-blonde hair and a very bad attitude.'

'So you've met her.'

'Yes,' she said, turning slightly and placing her arm around her father's neck. 'Joanna could introduce the dog to her father, but I don't rate its chances once his leave's come to an end. The dog will go the same way as the cat. Not that it really needs to. The government has backtracked and left the decision to pet owners – thanks to the intervention of the RSPCA.'

Seb pursed his lips. 'You're right. Trouble is the kid's bursting to tell her father, I don't think she'll be able to stop herself. And as you say, once her dad's gone back, that woman will do as she pleases.'

'She's mean and Joanna is a real-life Cinderella, hated and treated badly by her stepmother.'

Seb sat thinking for a while. 'Would it be all right with you that, if all else fails, the dog comes to live here? He's wearing Flossie's old collar and lead.'

'Well, that's as good a reason as any!'

Sally looked at him. Over the last few months she'd thought his getting over her mother's death had been a natural process and not dependant on any outside factors. Now, on mentioning Joanna and her dog, she knew better.

'You're a good man,' she said, stroking her father's white hair back from his face.

He looked up at her in some alarm. 'You won't tell Joanna I told you about the dog, will you?'

'Of course I won't.' Her expression disappeared along with her smile. 'And I don't think she should tell her father – under the circumstances.'

CHAPTER TWENTY-ONE

Spring flowers were dancing in the May sunshine when a telegram arrived, two days before the date Tom Ryan was expected to arrive home.

Joanna's stepmother was thrown into a whirlwind of activity. Together they cleaned the house from top to bottom. Elspeth had purchased a new coat, two dresses and a pair of shoes for Joanna.

'Don't want your dad thinking I've neglected you, now do I?' she said, a snarl of warning twisting the corners of her mouth. Joanna winced as Elspeth pinched her arm. 'And don't you go telling tales. Do you hear me?'

Mutely, scared to open her mouth, Joanna shook her head.

They'd also queued until late on Friday night to buy whatever food their ration books would allow.

'He'll probably bring a bit of something with him,' said Elspeth. 'I've heard the army don't go short of food.'

She also warned Joanna not to say anything about Jack Smith coming to the house or the fact that they'd had roast chicken for Christmas Day lunch.

Excited her father was coming home and uncaring about anything else, Joanna readily agreed.

It wasn't often so much food was in the house and Joanna found herself salivating. Elspeth warned her not to touch anything.

'At your peril!' she shouted, wagging her finger in front of the child's face. 'All this is for when your father gets home. In the meantime, we'll make do. Do I make myself clear?'

Bubbling with excitement, Joanna told just about everybody in school that it was finally happening. At last her father was coming home.

Paul was full of boyish curiosity and still wanted to know whether he'd be bringing his gun with him.

'I expect so,' Joanna said grandly, swinging her legs as she walked along so that her new coat swished against her legs. She was also wearing a new grey skirt and cardigan. Her shoes were new too and although they pinched and blistered her ankles, she would endure it all.

Her friend Mister Seb had told her that he would feed Harry his breakfast on school days. He had been the only person who knew of the puppy's existence, but now Mrs Allen also knew and gave Joanna the bones she'd used for stew, even though they were totally bereft of any meat.

There had been times when she'd wanted to tell Paul or Susan about Harry, but it seemed only right that her father should be told first.

Miss Hadley saw her beaming face and, although she knew the reason why, she wasn't going to spoil the moment.

'You're looking very happy, Joanna. And what's this? More new clothes and shoes?'

Joanna's eyes shone with excitement. 'My dad will be home on leave soon!'

'That's wonderful, Joanna.'

Neither of them mentioned the fact that Sally was Seb's daughter as though it were a secret in itself.

As she watched the little girl settle happily in her seat in class, she thought about how close she had come to reporting Joanna's circumstances to the children's welfare officer. While the child's father was home Joanna would be looked after. The only thing she had to do for Joanna that day was to provide plasters to cover the blisters caused by the new shoes.

Her stepmother should have done this, she thought to herself, her jaw holding uncomfortably firm as she ministered to

Joanna's needs. She was in no doubt that the minute Joanna's father had gone back to his unit, Joanna's lot would be what it was before. She badly wanted to tell her not to disclose anything about Harry the dog, but her father had sworn her to secrecy. It was wise to see how things turned out.

'Won't it be lovely when your father's home again? It's so different without a man in the house,' Sally said laughingly.

'Mr Thomas visits,' Joanna blurted, then bit her lip. 'Oh! I don't think I was supposed to tell. You won't tell Elspeth I blabbed, will you?' A worried frown creased the little girl's brow and her eyes were wide with fear.

Taken aback at the mention of the headmaster of the boys' school, Sally stared as she attempted to take in what Joanna had said. Mr Thomas had visited Joanna's home? Had she heard right?

'Are you sure it was Mr Thomas, Joanna? The head of the boys' school? Is that the man you mean?'

Joanna's bubbling excitement abated. She chewed her bottom lip and looked upwards with doleful eyes. 'I'm not supposed to tell.'

'You're not lying, are you, Joanna? Liars are not tolerated in my classroom. You do know that, don't you?'

Joanna nodded. It was all she needed to do. That and her doleful expression said it all. Arnold Thomas, the man saddled with a sick wife, had finally jumped over the traces with, of all people, Elspeth Ryan.

Still reeling with the shocking news, Sally attended a meeting at breaktime along with the teachers from both the boys' and the girls' school. Presiding over the meeting was Arnold Thomas.

The meeting was about the timetable for air-raid duties and refining the process of how the children should leave the school in the event of an emergency.

'We have been allocated a large shelter in Victoria Park. I think you all know exactly where it's located.'

Everyone said they did. The series of shelters was quite large and had been built at the bottom of Victoria Park close to the railway line beside the allotments.

Sally had made up her mind to have a word with Arnold Thomas regarding his liaison with Joanna's stepmother.

The signs had been there a while that he was lonely and in need of feminine company. She recalled the feel of his palm of his hand on her backside and gritted her teeth.

Lingering at the door she waited until everyone else was out and turned to face him.

He saw her and smiled. 'Miss Hadley. Is there something I can do for you?'

Sally kept her expression neutral. 'How's Miranda?'

'Oh,' he said, casually waving his hand before shuffling his papers into a neat little pile inside a brown manila folder. 'You know Miranda. She's got everything you don't die from.'

Though you wish she would. Sally contained the rogue thought.

'I did wonder seeing as I hadn't seen much of you.'

'You know me. I never stray far from the fold,' he said in a jovial manner.

'Everyone reaches a breaking point,' Sally said somewhat pointedly. 'I thought you might have taken a lover.'

Something flashed into his eyes before vanishing in the depths of their natural cloudiness.

'Goodness! Whatever made you think that?' His smile looked as though it might break his jaw. His eyes had a shuttered look, as if he had locked any thoughts that might betray him securely away.

Sally shrugged. 'When the cat's away, the mice do play.'

He became defensive, his shoulders stiffening, his stiff smile gone. 'Perhaps you can tell me what you mean by that.'

None of the old familiarity remained in his voice. Arnold Thomas, the mild-mannered man with the patience of a saint, had turned hostile.

'There's a war on, Mr Thomas. A lot of husbands are away fighting, leaving their women at a loose end. I thought you might have taken up the slack with one of them.'

His pale eyes suddenly blazed like liquid mercury and a pink dot arose on each pronounced cheekbone. 'How dare you! I want an apology right now!'

Sally clutched her folder to her chest and narrowed her eyes. 'It's always a great joy when one of those "cats" come home. The father of a little girl in my class is coming home shortly. Her stepmother's name is Elspeth Ryan. I'm sure the father is looking forward to being enfolded in her arms and told she's been faithful through thick and thin.'

She turned on her heels then, her face red with anger, surprised that she'd been so bold as to state it as it was to the headmaster's face.

Arnold Thomas stood like a block of salt, staring after her, his pink flush undiminished. How did she know about him and Elspeth?

Elspeth had admitted she was married and that her husband was away fighting.

'We don't see eye to eye any more,' she'd said to him.

He'd seen no evidence of a child at Elspeth's house. Though thinking back, she had once told him that she had a daughter. But there was barely any evidence of a child at the house, and in his desire he'd forgotten that she'd had one.

Overcome by the moment, he slumped onto a chair. Sweat erupted through the pores in his skin, trickling from his forehead and into his eyebrows.

There was his position to think of. The board of governors would not be best pleased. The relationship had to be terminated, yet he could not bring himself to do so.

Elspeth was so enjoyable, not just socially but in bed. It had been such a long time since he'd indulged in his marital rights that he'd thought he'd be rusty. Elspeth's actions were such that he now knew otherwise. She had reawakened his sexual feelings to a level that he had never experienced before. Some men were addicted to drink, but in his case he was addicted to sex with Elspeth Ryan. Giving her up might be the respectable thing to do, but he no longer cared about being viewed as respectable. Come hell or high water he intended keeping her acquaintance.

Who could say that at some time in the future – perhaps quite soon – they might both be free?

Her a widow.

Him a widower.

The two different facets ran into each other and became one. They both needed to be free but, although Miranda was very ill, it could be years more before she died. A lonely future stretched like a desolate wasteland in front of him. In the meantime . . .

At the sound of the school bell ringing he looked up and realised it was time for the boys in his charge and his teaching staff to go home.

Time for him to go home too. He grimaced at the thought of it.

Home to the unwelcoming charms of a sick wife, who took delight in goading him with nasty words, thrown crockery, a swipe from a walking stick and the ringing of a bell that she knew set his nerves on edge.

'You don't have to put up with it,' he muttered to himself.

CHAPTER TWENTY-TWO

Joanna was laughing and chattering with her friends Paul and Susan, running and jumping as they made their way up The Vale, over-excited at the prospect of her father coming home.

The day had been the brightest of her life. Nothing could daunt her spirits, not until Paul pointed out that a policeman was pushing open the garden gate of number 116.

'What's a copper doing there then?' Paul remarked.

Joanna began to run. Paul and Susan ran after her, lingering by the garden gate as she headed for the front door and the uniformed policeman standing there with his back to her.

'Nobody's in,' she explained. 'Elspeth's at work.'

The policeman bent his knees so he could see her better and smiled sadly into her face. 'Is Elspeth your sister, love?'

She shook her head. 'My stepmother. She's at work.'

'I see.' He jerked his chin in a nod of understanding. 'Is there any other adult I can speak to who might know where your stepmother works?'

A terrible apprehension coiled like a snake in Joanna's stomach. Keen to know what news he brought, Joanna took him along to Mrs Allen's house.

Mrs Allen came to the door wearing a wraparound flowered apron and curlers in her hair. After taking in the look on the policeman's face, she swiped at the trickle of snuff that had come down her nose and invited him in.

'Take a seat,' she said. 'You too Joanna, love.'

Feeling the coldest she'd felt all day, Joanna sat down, the colour draining from her face.

Mrs Allen offered the policeman a cup of tea, which he declined. To her mind that said it all. The news was bad. Very bad.

She settled herself in one of the battered Edwardian armchairs that had once belonged to her mother. Some of the horsehair protruded from one arm and the springs were gone. Mrs Allen could not afford replacing them.

Mrs Allen clasped her hands in front of her. 'What is it, constable? What's happened?'

The policeman looked at the little girl as he made up his mind whether to give the news he had come to give, or wait and give it to Mrs Ryan. It seemed only right to tell the wife first before the neighbour. There was also the child to consider.

When he asked, Mrs Allen gave him the address of the place where Elspeth worked which he wrote down with a stubby pencil in his little black book. 'Right. I'll go there and tell her.'

'Can you tell me what's happened?' pressed Mrs Allen, her arm now fully encircling Joanna's shoulders. The child's face was pale and her eyes wide with fear.

'She'll be all right,' Mrs Allen said when she saw him look at Joanna. 'I'll take care of her.' She peered at him quizzically. 'We already know something bad's happened or you wouldn't be here, so you might as well tell us what it is.'

The policeman looked from the child to the old lady before taking Mrs Allen to one side.

'I'm afraid there's been an accident on the railway. Private Ryan was one of those killed when a passenger train and a goods train collided in a tunnel. It was quick. He wouldn't have felt anything.'

Elspeth was just finishing her shift when a policeman called to tell her the bad news.

She stared hard at him for a few minutes as though attempting to take it all in. He offered her a handkerchief. She shook her head.

'No, thank you. Did any of his stuff survive? You know. His personal effects and all that.'

Discomfited by the avarice in her eyes and the total lack of tears, the policeman shrugged. 'I couldn't say, but I'll make enquiries and let you know.

'So what happens to the body?'

'That's up to you. His remains can be transported for burial back here or it can be done closer to where the accident happened.'

Elspeth lit up a cigarette and peered into the distance. 'How much will it cost if he's buried at the scene of the accident.'

'The railway will meet all costs.'

Elspeth nodded thoughtfully. 'He does have a life policy.'

She was doing the figures in her mind. It would be cheaper to have him buried where the accident happened. However, the neighbours would be likely to point the finger if she did that. Not that she cared too much what they thought, but as a widow she did have things to sort out. Still, a bit of extra money saved on the funeral would come in handy.

'Have him buried there,' she said bluntly. 'Where he gets buried don't make that much difference when you're dead. Now, if you don't mind, I have to get back to work. There's a war needing to be won.'

The policeman pushed at the rim of his helmet with two fingers as he watched Mrs Ryan sashay back to her workbench. He'd seen some widows shed buckets of tears when told of their husbands' demise. Others turned white with shock, holding back their heartbreak until they were alone with their thoughts and their memories.

Mrs Ryan's eyes had remained dry and her face had never lost colour. She didn't give a damn.

The burial of Tom Ryan took place later that month. The railway company laid on free tickets for the widow and the child to attend the funeral. There were no hymns, just a tired-looking vicar intoning the words of the service. There were no flowers either. There was no point. The only mourners were Joanna and her stepmother.

Mrs Allen had asked Elspeth what the arrangements were as a number of people wished to pay their last respects. She'd looked scandalised when Elspeth had told her that the railway company would only be sending two tickets.

'Family only. Just me and his kid,' Elspeth declared with an air of superiority before slamming the door in Mrs Allen's face.

Mrs Allen stood there outraged. Curtains were drawn in the houses all around and black-edged condolence cards stuck on the windows. It was what people did out of a mark of respect.

'Whatever is the world coming to?' she muttered, shaking her head as she made her way home. As for that poor child, what would happen to her now? She had no real mother. No father now either, and her stepmother didn't want her, using her purely for her own selfish ends.

Pure selfishness ran through Elspeth Ryan's veins. The only person she would ever look after was herself.

Once the funeral was out of the way, Arnold Thomas became a more frequent visitor, though now and again Jack Smith also paid a visit.

Joanna kept out of the way, especially when Jack Smith was around, though she heard him ask her whereabouts.

'Pretty little thing. And growing up fast I bet,' she'd heard him say to her stepmother.

'I think she's gone out,' she heard her stepmother say. 'But you can go upstairs to her bedroom and check if you like.'

She'd sounded amused.

Joanna was terrified and hid under the bed.

He was halfway across her bedroom floor before she heard her stepmother calling him from downstairs.

'Better not stay up there,' she shouted out to him. 'We don't want to get into any trouble now, do we? That little madam's likely to spin a tale to her teacher and you know what they're like.'

Heart in her mouth, Joanna heard Jack Smith's heavy tread doing back downstairs.

For now she was safe, but very frightened.

CHAPTER TWENTY-THREE

May turned into June. Elspeth Ryan only tolerated Joanna living in the house she now regarded as her own as long as she continued to do most of the cooking and cleaning.

Having her stepdaughter as a drudge meant she could spend her days at work and her nights out at the pictures, dancing, down the pub or once a week with Arnold Thomas.

It was still Arnold she was aiming to snare as her next husband. Once that was done she was set up for life. She'd even convinced herself that she would change her ways, learn how to speak better and dress more soberly, as a headmaster's wife should do.

Tom had been halfway a decent gentleman, but Arnold was a professional man with a good salary, and that appealed to her mercenary nature. Love had precious little to do with it.

The neighbours could gossip all they liked, but she was now a widow and if she cared to bring a man home for the night, she was free to do as she pleased. Mrs Thomas was in no position to find out about their liaison.

Despite doing her best to put him at ease, Arnold was still uncomfortable about coming to her house.

'I have a professional reputation to maintain. I'm a married schoolteacher. Headmaster of the boys' school and I cannot be seen . . .'

Elspeth placed her finger on his mouth, shushing him to silence.

'I'm a respectable widow,' she said, although that was in fact stretching the truth a fraction. 'And your wife is at death's door.' She paused, her eyes big and round, full of pleading. 'Isn't she?'

He found her hard to resist, but although he did accept her invitation to come in for a late-night drink, he refused to be seen with her in broad daylight. And he had started staying over less often, and his mood had changed. Where once he was ardent, matching her desire with his own, he had become of late more cautious, and their relationship in the bedroom had suffered. It was all to do with Miranda. She was getting worse, refusing to take her medicine and getting more and more violent.

'She's my wife. In sickness and in health. I have to do what I can,' he told her as he got dressed. He could not seem to look her in the eye.

'Oh, Arnold! I want you so.'

No matter what beguiling tactics she used, her hand against his member, her fingers undoing the buttons of his flies, his overnight stays became infrequent.

Elspeth was exasperated, but vowed the day would come when he would move in permanently and lie with her upstairs. After all, his wife was sick. She convinced herself that it was only a matter of time before he was free. In the meantime, seeing he was unwilling to commit, she indulged herself when he wasn't around.

Joanna sat with her arms around Harry's neck, her face buried in his silky ruff. Her tears had wetted his coat on many occasions since the death of her father.

Attentive to the sound of her sobs and the sight of her salty tears, Harry eyed her with his brown soulful eyes, his paw resting on her knee, his wet tongue licking the salt from her cheeks. It was as though he was trying to tell her that he understood.

When she went on too long with her crying, he prodded her tear-stained cheek with his cold wet nose. This was followed by another series of warm wet licks. For the most part Joanna kept her head buried in his neck. Harry was her only consolation. Without him her whole world would turn black.

'No good you sitting there crying all day long,' said Seb on one particularly fine sunny day. 'Your dad's gone and nothing is going to bring him back. But Harry needs you. That dog is in need of going for a walk. He likes his walk. All dogs like going for a walk.'

Persistent nagging finally dried her tears and he did manage to get her out of the door. Harry walked beside her, though not bouncing as he usually did when the opportunity to go out arose.

They clambered along the embankment, Joanna's legs aching on account of the slope. Once she was sure he wouldn't run away, Joanna let Harry off the lead. In the distance she saw Seb bent over his allotment, digging in a large amount of compost with each thrust of his spade.

Harry ran off in front of her before circling behind her, never straying that far.

Joanna sat down on a grassy tump, her sore face and red eyes turned in the direction of the railway line.

A train driver waved from his cab as he went by. Usually Joanna waved back but today she just didn't see him. Her heart was heavy, her mind absorbed with wishing she could bring her father back. Was there anything she could have done to prevent what had happened? If she had told the truth about Harry, about stealing food from the kitchen to feed him, would that have made a difference? She couldn't see that it would have.

Back at the shed Seb offered her a sandwich plus a cup of tea from his Thermos, but she declined.

'Oh well then,' said Seb, his shrewd eyes missing nothing. 'P'raps young Harry here will help me out. He does like a bit of cheese.'

Joanna fingered the edge of the workbench which was now crowded with young seedlings ready for transplanting.

'You might as well snap out of it,' said Seb. 'Being glum is not going to bring your dad back.'

Under the circumstances, Seb's outburst seemed almost cruel. The memory of her kind father would be with her for ever. She wouldn't forget him and was sure she would never feel happy again.

Joanna pouted. 'I don't want to be happy. I'll never be happy again.'

'Is that so, young lady? Well, might I remind you that dog of yours is only a youngster and needs looking after. That's your job. I'm only the man whose shed he lives in. But you found him. He's your responsibility and you're his very best friend. Just think of that. And think on this, you're both orphans now.'

CHAPTER TWENTY-FOUR

Miranda Thomas died at the end of September.

The whole school turned out for the funeral as well as relatives and neighbours. It was some weeks before Arnold Thomas was entirely alone and ready to recommence his life.

Aware of his loss, Elspeth, keen to take advantage of his newfound freedom, was there for him, snatching odd moments, though never long enough for her.

She'd also toned down her hair colour and her clothes. No longer was she the good-time floozy, but had adopted a more classic style.

Something seemed to be preying on her lover's mind and she wasn't sure what it was. Arnold finally told her that the car was his but not the house.

'Only half of it is mine. The other half belongs to my wife's brother. He's a solicitor and has told me he would prefer it to be sold. I have agreed to do so. In fact, I'm thinking of moving on anyway. An old friend has offered me a position in Scotland at a private school. I like the sound of it. I thought perhaps you and I . . .'

'When?'

'As soon as they confirm a starting date. In the meantime we have to live apart. My brother-in-law would not allow another woman living in his sister's house.'

Elspeth's dreams were shattered. Normally she would have blown a gasket, but she'd always held her tongue with Arnold, aware he wouldn't respond well to a raised voice and the ripe gutter language she was well capable of.

'We could live at my house,' she said timidly. 'Just the two of us. Until you know for sure that you've got the job in Scotland.'

Despite the fact that his relationship with his wife had been far from ideal, he'd worn a frown since her death, as though he was guilty about how he had treated his wife while she was alive.

At her suggestion the frown lifted slightly and a hint of a smile stretched his lips. 'Just the two of us.' He nodded. 'That would be nice.'

She linked his arm with hers. 'Everything will be quite straightforward and quite wonderful.'

She did not reveal that Joanna was still living there, having told him that as Joanna was her husband's daughter she had gone to live with relatives.

The solution was very simple. The girl had to be sent away for as long as possible, and when she came home Elspeth and her new husband would be living in Scotland. She would not be leaving a forwarding address.

CHAPTER TWENTY-FIVE

'You're to be evacuated. There's nothing else for it. The train leaves tomorrow. I'm taking the morning off work to take you to the station. A whole trainload of kids is being evacuated and you'll be just one of many.'

'No!'

Alarmed Joanna stood rooted to the spot. She knew of other kids who'd been evacuated, but this had come entirely out of the blue.

Her stepmother glanced at her reflection in the mirror and patted her hair. 'Your dad's dead and you're not my kid. We both need a break. I know I certainly do. Once the war's ended we'll take another look at things. Anyway, you'll love it in the country.'

'But what about school?'

'You'll still go to school, just a different school. In the country.'

'But I'll miss my friends,' Joanna said pleadingly, her eyes filling with tears.

'You'll make new ones.'

Joanna felt as though her whole body had been dunked into an ice-covered lake. In her heart of hearts Harry loomed larger than any of her school friends. What would happen to him?

'But I don't want to go,' she said, her voice breaking to the verge of tears. 'I won't go!'

Elspeth's face turned angry, her eyes blazing. 'You will do as you are told, young lady! Now get up those stairs and pack whatever toys or books you want to take. I've done most of your clothes. Now!'

A clip at the back of Joanna's head sent her stumbling in the direction of the hallway and the stairs leading up to her bedroom. Seeing all the signs of further anger and perhaps being locked in the coalhouse, Joanna ran up the stairs.

Eyes brimming with tears, she looked at the shabby suitcase lying open on the bed. There were no books or toys she particularly wished to take with her. She'd grown out of her tatty little collection some time ago. All she wanted was Harry.

It was too difficult to concentrate on anything else but her little dog. She was going away to goodness knows where, to live in the countryside with strangers. The countryside was that huge area where all the evacuated children went to live because it would be safe there when the bombing began.

But what about Harry? She wanted him to be safe too. It wasn't fair for him to be left behind to face the bombs alone. Yes, there was Seb to look after him, but she was the one who had rescued Harry. He was her dog and she was the one he loved best of all. Besides, she'd promised Harry they'd always be together.

And why couldn't he come to the countryside with her? He would love it there with all that grass, trees and farm animals. He'd make friends with everyone.

Slowly, as she thought it through, the countryside didn't seem such a bad place after all. The solution to them remaining together seemed obvious. She would take him with her.

The idea had come like a bolt of lightning and now formed into something solid.

Would the place she was to be evacuated take Harry in? She doubted that, so perhaps she should go off and find a place in the country herself where they would both be welcome.

Her mind was made up. There was nothing much else she needed to pack except food for Harry, which would not be possible until her stepmother had gone to bed.

After turning off the light, she got into bed fully clothed. She was ready for the morning. She'd need to find her own way to the country. Her stepmother was bound to show up at the station and there would be lots of grown-ups there writing up details, asking names and checking labels.

She wouldn't wear her label, the kind handed out to all evacuees. Neither would she take her gas mask with her. That night, her mind busy with plans, she only dozed and awoke long before dawn.

Slowly and carefully she swung her legs from beneath the bed covers and felt for her suitcase, found it and went tiptoeing across the squeaky floorboards to the bedroom door.

Before tugging it open, she laid her ear against it, listening for any sign that her stepmother was awake. A resonant series of snores sounded from the front bedroom confirming that she most certainly was asleep. And there was nobody in bed with her. That was unusual.

Holding her breath she opened the door, listened again then crept carefully down the stairs.

In the kitchen she threw what food she could into her suitcase.

In the pale grey light of dawn she shut the front door then the front gate behind her. Workers on their way to the early-morning shift were huddled around the bus stop at the top of the hill, but didn't appear to be looking in her direction.

Quickly, just in case they did see her, she darted down the hill keeping close to the privet hedges until she was sure they were safely behind her. From halfway down the hill she broke into a run and didn't stop until she got to the path leading into the allotment.

It was too early for Seb to be here and even Harry looked surprised to see her.

'We're leaving,' Joanna whispered.

Harry got out of his bed, stretched one back leg and then the other, and wagged his stumpy tail, his eyes bright with interest.

He was familiar with the times the old man and his good friend Joanna came and left, but having her visit this early was an extra and much appreciated treat.

If Joanna thought they were going to rush out straightaway, she was very much mistaken. Harry went to his dish, snuffling around its emptiness so that it moved over the floor eventually landing up at Joanna's feet.

Joanna sighed. 'I suppose you can have breakfast before we leave.'

She broke up some cold rabbit Seb had cooked the day before. The remains she wrapped up in newspaper and placed in her suitcase along with the other food she'd brought with her.

Joanna sat on an upturned bucket watching Harry gobbling down his breakfast. He was still a growing pup, his coat was glossy and his nose was wet, just as it should be. He'd become the centre of her world, the only living thing left in it that she really loved, and she would do anything to keep him safe.

Somehow she would get him to safety, but how would she do that? Where would they go? It had seemed a good idea to run away rather than be evacuated and separated from Harry. Getting to the shed was only the first part of her plan. Neither of them could stay here now, not if they wanted to remain together.

Joanna hung her head and although tears pricked her eyes, she refused to let them fall. She had to be strong for Harry's sake.

Once Harry had eaten his food and lapped up some water, Joanna cleaned the dishes and found space for them in the suitcase.

Harry jumped and yapped with excitement when he saw her reach for his lead and attach it to the collar Seb had bought him.

Cupping his head in her hands, she gazed lovingly into his eyes. 'We have to leave here, Harry. We're going to the countryside. It's the only way we can still be together.'

Harry's pink tongue lolled from the side of his mouth. He sounded breathless and looked up at her lovingly as though he understood every word.

To her his panting was more than breathless excitement. He seemed to be saying, *Let's go! Let's go!*

Joanna took a deep breath at the same time as telling herself to be brave.

Suitcase in one hand, dog lead in the other, she failed to close the door behind her, leaving it swinging open and banging against the upturned bucket.

That was how Seb found it when he dropped by later that morning.

Panic-stricken, he ran up and down outside calling the dog's name, hoping that somebody had discovered him and took him. Either that or the door had blown open and the dog had run off. But no. He had to face the brutal truth: Harry was gone.

Receiving no response to his frantic calls, he went back into the shed harbouring the daft thought that he might be mistaken, that the dog MUST be in there, perhaps hiding.

It was indeed a daft thought. There was nowhere for the dog to hide and, anyway, he usually came rushing out to greet his first visitor of the day.

What Seb did see was that the dog's food and water dish were gone. So was his lead. Everything had been here on the previous evening when Joanna and her dog had been playing and bouncing around outside.

His initial conclusion was that Joanna's stepmother had relented and she'd taken him home. A second possibility nudged the back of his mind: the dog had been stolen. The third was difficult to face, but he had to confront it. For some reason Joanna had taken the dog and run away.

'Think,' he muttered, leaning on the seed table, his eyes narrowed as he scoured the view through the shed's single window.

There was only one thing for it: he had to wait until Joanna made her way here after school. If she didn't come, then he would know she had taken him home. If she did come, then he would have to break the bad news that person or persons unknown had stolen Harry. Either way he was heartbroken. If she had indeed taken the dog with her and run away, he didn't know what he might do.

CHAPTER TWENTY-SIX

Sally Hadley had only just opened the register when the head-mistress tapped on the classroom door and beckoned her outside.

In her fifties, Miss Burton was a kindly woman of respectable appearance, her grey hair forming a halo of grey candyfloss around her head. Abstaining from marriage in favour of career, she was much admired for her dedication and kindness.

Teaching was regarded as a vocation and a female teacher who married was expected to leave the profession. In Miss Burton's case this situation had never arisen. She had become a teacher following the death of her fiancé during the Great War. Thus she had remained a spinster and would remain a teacher till the end of her days.

'Recite the twelve times table while I speak to the headmistress,' Sally instructed her class.

As the whole class intoned the twelve times table, Sally closed the door behind her so their litany became a monotone rumble.

'Good morning, Miss Burton.'

'Good morning, Miss Hadley.'

A look of tension pervaded Miss Burton's soft features. She held a scrap of paper in her right hand.

'I'm afraid you've lost another of your pupils. Joanna Ryan has been evacuated.' She waved the scrap of paper. 'The caretaker found this on the doormat earlier this morning. The woman must have posted it through the letterbox last night. I must say she could have given us more warning. The register needs to be changed and paperwork completed.'

Sally frowned. The paperwork was the least of her worries. Her father would be heartbroken. But what about the dog?

'Is that all it says? That Joanna will be evacuated?'

Miss Burton glanced down again at the poorly formed writing and the crumpled piece of paper. It looked as though it had been torn from a book, not an exercise book, but the fly leaf of one that was meant to be read.

'That's all she says. Have you met Mrs Ryan?'

Sally said that she had and that Elspeth Ryan was Joanna's stepmother, her natural mother having died and her father remarrying. 'Her father died in an accident about five months ago.'

Her frown deepened.

'You don't look as though you approve of the stepmother,' said Miss Burton.

'Let's put it this way. I don't think she's having Joanna evacuated for safety reasons. Mrs Ryan is not the sort to let the grass grow under her feet. In fact, I have heard she's been seen with someone I know. Someone we both know.'

Miss Burton's eyebrows arched. The two women looked at each other in mutual understanding. The headmaster of the boys' school had been regarded as a pillar of fortitude when his wife was alive, looking after her until the very end. He'd changed since his wife's death and, although he still did a good job teaching the boys, he didn't seem to have the same commitment as he'd once had.

'We will say no more of this,' said Miss Burton. 'We all go through bad patches in our lives.'

Sally agreed with her. She was currently going through one of her own.

She hadn't received a single reply to all the letters she had sent to Pierre via Lady Ambrose.

'Nothing,' she said to Sally each time she went there to check if she'd heard anything. 'Now my dear,' she'd said, taking hold of Sally's arm and steering her to a chair. 'Let me be blunt. There's no point in you putting your life on hold while my nephew is over there. Life is too short, my dear, and nothing is ever certain when there's a war on. Get out more. Enjoy yourself.'

Sally pretended to agree with her, but inside she ached. There was no way she could possibly go dancing or to the pictures with another man, not when her heart was in France.

At the end of the school day she piled up the children's exercise book for marking at home and slid them into her briefcase. Her heart was heavy. Once it had seemed that everything had knitted together in her life. Now it seemed the stitches were unravelling.

Pierre had not replied to her letters. Young Joanna had been evacuated, which meant her father would be devastated; he'd so loved that little girl. Perhaps he could keep the dog. She hoped so.

She looked around the empty classroom, thinking how silent it was, the only sound coming from outside as the children ran for the school gate and the way home.

Suddenly the classroom door was flung open and a blast of cheap perfume smothered the classroom smell of chalk dust and children's plimsolls.

'Where's that little cow!'

Elspeth Ryan was wearing a red-and-cream checked suit teamed with black court shoes and a black handbag. A red-and-cream hat with a stiff black veil perched like a stuffed bird on her head. Sally noticed she now sported her natural hair colour, mousier than the dyed blonde it had been.

Mrs Ryan was the sort who took a pride in intimidating more refined women. Sally knew instantly Mrs Ryan would have her crying if she could. She was about to find out that Sally Hadley was made of sterner stuff.

'To whom are you referring, Mrs Ryan?' her tone firm and unhurried.

'You know bloody well to *whom* I am referring. Joanna! The little cow was supposed to be on a train this morning with all the other evacuees. I took a morning off work to get her evacuated.'

Sally set her face firm and her jaw square. 'Joanna did not come to school this morning. I was told by the headmistress that a note was pushed through the letterbox last night saying she was being evacuated this morning. That, Mrs Ryan, is all I know!'

'You'd better be telling the truth or it'll be the worse for you.'

'I am a truthful person, Mrs Ryan. If you don't believe I am a truthful woman, ask Mr Thomas, the headmaster of the boys' school. He knows me well, though not as well as he knows you!'

Mrs Ryan's head jerked back as though Sally had slapped her. Her eyes flickered, her features slackened.

Sensing she had the advantage, Sally pressed on. 'Did you think nobody knew, Mrs Ryan? Gossip is as rife in a school as it is in a street.'

She discerned a shift in Mrs Ryan's manner. The pallor of shock appeared underneath Elspeth Ryan's pancake makeup.

'I need to find out where my stepdaughter is,' she said in a consoling manner. 'I'm worried about her. That's why I was sending her away to the country. I owe it to her father.'

Mrs Ryan's statement seemed somewhat out of character and Sally didn't believe her to be sincere. However, with no other option, she was forced to give her the benefit of the doubt.

'I can't help you, Mrs Ryan. I think you need to get in touch with the police.'

Seb Hadley was standing in front of the sink washing vegetables in a bowl of water. More vegetables sat on the draining board, dirt piled into a newspaper. Once each item was clear of mud, it was dipped into the water for a final wash.

Sally came in breathless, her face flushed. She took off her coat and threw it onto a chair along with her briefcase and her hat. The hat got squashed but she had more important things to worry about than a hat.

'Dad. Joanna Ryan has run away from home.'

He didn't turn round. 'That explains a lot.'

'You know? Yes. Of course you do,' she said, resting her hands on the back of a kitchen chair.

Her father rolled his shoulders, left what he was doing and turned round to face her, wearing a worried expression. No doubt he was going to tell her, all how shocked he was not to see her today and where he thought she might have gone.

'There's a letter on the mantelpiece. It's from France.'

All thoughts of Joanna Ryan flew from her mind. Pierre had written! At last!

She opened the letter with a butter knife, ripping it in places in her haste to get to it.

Pierre had written!

At first she speed read, noting a few particular words and sentences that leapt out at her.

My darling Sally,

My beloved Paris has fallen to the conquerors, but we stand with our heads held high. Liberty, equality and fraternity have to stand for something.

Despite the invasion, the Parisians are unbowed, the city's cafés are still full to capacity, the sky over Notre Dame is still blue and the girls are still wiggling their hips along the Champs Elyseé.

The Germans are everywhere and I am lucky I do not wear a uniform and never got round to wearing one before they invaded.

No doubt there are those who might put it down to lack of courage, but I myself do not see it that way. It is more as though I was holding my breath, as though I knew my anonymity was precious, that I had to hold on to it, until having it made me very precious to resisting the invading army.

I'm missing you tremendously and am surprised you have not written. My aunt tells me that things are very quiet in your part of England, although bombs have fallen elsewhere.

Alone at night with my thoughts, I ponder on why you have not written. Make sure you send your next letter to Café Claude, the friend's address I gave you. They know where I am. It should come to me direct.

My aunt was sending me warm clothes and packets of cigarettes. She should have known I preferred French cigarettes, but the socks are useful. Goodness knows when I will get any more.

Please write to me, Sally. And wait for me. I need to know you are there . . .

Sally ran her fingertips over his signature. He was imploring her to write, as though he had not received her previous letters. But Lady Ambrose had assured her she would place both her own letter and Sally's in a parcel she was sending to France.

'It will get there more quickly,' she had said to her.

The dying embers in the fireplace warmed the back of her legs and she frowned as she considered the implications.

Had Lady Ambrose forgotten to pack her letters to Pierre or was there some other explanation?

Her father interrupted her thoughts. 'I take it nothing bad has happened to him.'

'No,' said Sally, folding the letter up and slipping it into the pocket of her skirt. 'Just a few minor difficulties that he hopes will be overcome.'

'So what can we do about Joanna?'

'Has she taken her things from the shed?'

Seb nodded. 'Yes. The dog and everything of his.'

Sally sighed and hung her head. Her father had changed so much since meeting Joanna. Would he regress now Joanna had left? She hoped not.

'Joanna was supposed to be evacuated. Her stepmother had booked her on the morning train. She didn't make it. Her suitcase is gone, but she definitely didn't get on the train.'

Her father turned his head so he was looking at the far corner of the room. He was sucking in his bottom lip, a sure sign that he was upset.

'Dad. What about the dog? Where can she go with a dog?'

'She will be noticeable,' he said without looking at her. 'The dog's gone and so is the cold rabbit and pigeon I've been feeding him, but it won't last forever. At some point she'll have to get food for him.'

Sally sat down, her hands folded in her lap. She looked at her father. 'Her stepmother's gone to the police. You know what that will mean when they find her. And they will find her. You do know that don't you?'

'Of course I do,' he said, snapping his head round to face her. 'She'll be evacuated for real.'

'And if her stepmother gets her hands on the dog . . .'

Seb's face dropped. 'I know that too, but I won't let that happen!'

Sally strode purposely up Redcatch Hill. In her mind she rehearsed what she was going to say to Lady Ambrose and surmised what her answers might be. One question loomed above all others.

'My letters haven't been getting through to Pierre. Why is that?'

As for her answer to that particular question? She couldn't begin to guess. What possible reason could she have? There was no animosity between them, in fact Pierre had told her his aunt liked her very much.

It had to be some kind of mistake.

She paused at the gates of Ambrose House, gazing up the drive towards the imposing entrance. Nobody was in sight. Presumably her ladyship was out back with the cats and dogs.

She strained her ears for the sound of barking, but heard nothing. All was strangely quiet.

Sally made her way up the drive. Rather than chance knocking on the front door, she went straight to the kennels.

Lady Ambrose was leaning on the gate at the end of the stable block, staring at the enclosures ranged along either side in the adapted loose boxes.

Disquiet tightened in Sally's stomach. Were the dogs and cats still there or had they been taken away? Had the government's advice caught up with all of them?

'Lady Ambrose?'

Amelia Ambrose glanced over her shoulder but maintained her position, her gaze returning to the stable block interior and the animals in her care. She held a piece of paper in one hand.

'I thought I heard you.' She sighed heavily. 'I'll be as cheerful as I can, but don't expect too much. Today is not a good day.'

Sally frowned and held back what she truly wished to ask. 'What's wrong?'

Lady Ambrose passed her the piece of paper. 'The house has been requisitioned by the War Office for use as a convalescent home or billeting for soldiers. I can either move out entirely or confine my living space to two rooms and a kitchen.'

Sally quickly read the directive, which stated that many large houses were being requisitioned to provide troop accommodation and hospital services. Ambrose House was one of them. 'The main residence plus outbuildings . . . But surely they'd let you keep the stables! The animals have to live somewhere.'

Amelia slid her a sidelong look that said it all. The War Office didn't care what happened to the animals. They were not a priority.

'They'd probably use them for target practice,' Amelia said grimly.

'Don't say that, please. Not even in jest.'

Ill-informed as they were, she couldn't believe any civilised government would do that.

Amelia sighed. 'Humans take priority.'

Sally had to concede that she was right.

Even so, it wasn't like Lady Ambrose to give in so easily. Perhaps a little goading was needed?

Sally chose her words carefully. 'I understand your ancestors fought beside the first Duke of Marlborough.'

Amelia nodded. 'True. The first of the Churchills.'

'Surely that must carry some weight.'

A weak smile crossed Amelia's face. 'My dear girl, there is no way I can march up to number 10 Downing Street and demand old Winston retract the requisition and give my animals a chance.' She grinned suddenly. 'If I did I might ask him if he can give a home to an old bulldog. Owners resemble their dogs and a bulldog would suit him fine.' Her smile diminished. 'Take no notice of me. Pure fantasy, my dear. Pure fantasy. Still,' she said, slapping the top bar as she pushed herself away from the gate. 'You haven't come here to hear about me and my problems. A good hostess should at least offer tea. Come on.'

The purposeful stride Sally was used to was not quite so purposeful, but there was still an air of command in her ladyship's voice.

Sally followed her into the cave of a kitchen, warm thanks to the Aga and the range of saucepans bubbling away on top. She guessed most of the food being cooked was horsemeat and offal for the animals. Both came from the kennels of a fox hunt in South Gloucestershire.

'The help's off. But I can make tea. Now. To what do I owe this visit?'

Sally had been about to say it was purely a social call, but Amelia's tone inferred she guessed otherwise.

Eight chairs were set around a scrubbed pine table. Sally dragged one of them out and sat down, her hands clasped in front of her, elbows resting on the table. 'I've had a letter from Pierre.'

'Oh. That's nice for you.' Although Amelia smiled, Sally noticed a guarded look in her eyes.

'Apparently he hasn't received any of my letters.'

Amelia gave the appearance of concentrating on pouring the water into a blue-and-white Wedgewood teapot.

Sally frowned. 'Did you hear what I said?'

'Yes. I did. Milk? I worry about bone china cracking so I always pour milk in first.' Her attention became fixed on pouring milk into two bone china teacups.

Sally thought quickly. There was something very telling about Amelia's manner. She didn't sound terribly surprised that the letters hadn't arrived. Could it be that she'd forgotten to send them? Surely she hadn't held them back purposely?

Sally reined in her suspicions, willing to give her the benefit of the doubt. She chose her words carefully. 'Do you think they got there? I mean, you did remember to put them in with the things you sent him and your own letters . . .'

'No! I did not.'

Lady Amelia Ambrose had a very high forehead and the sort of skin that shone when caught in the light. It shone now, though it seemed more like perspiration, as though she were nervous or upset. Amelia was not the sort to be nervous and she was already upset about the house being requisitioned.

'I didn't send the letters because I wanted to split you two up.'

Sally's jaw dropped. 'What?'

'You heard me. I wanted to split you up and before you call me a mean old witch with a snobby attitude, there was a very good reason for wanting to split you up. I don't want you being hurt, Sally.'

Tea untouched, Sally sat across from the older woman feeling as though every last drop of blood had been bled from her body. Her throat felt as though she were swallowing thorns and her tongue seemed to be lying dead in her mouth.

When she finally found it, her voice sounded small and faraway. 'Why would I be hurt?'

Amelia fiddled with her teacup, looking into the pale tan liquid like a fortune-teller looking for the future. Only there was no future to be found there and she was no prophetess making trite comments about what was and what might be.

'Pierre is married.'

She took a swift sip of tea, eyes averted, her mouth set in a tight line as though she'd just eaten something particularly unsavoury.

It was as though icy fingers had traced frosty patterns throughout Sally's body – like the ones on the inside of windowpanes in the depths of a very cold winter.

Sally waited for Amelia to explain more. She was met with a silence she couldn't bear.

'Is she French?'

Amelia nodded. 'Yes.'

It wasn't enough. Sally's shock was swiftly turning to anger. Would knowing more placate that anger? She didn't know and didn't care. She *had* to know more.

'Tell me about her. About them. I want to know!'

Amelia's hooded eyelids lifted. Her pale blue eyes studied Sally with both pity and reluctance.

'I promise not to rant and rave. Nor will I burst into tears.'

Amelia shrugged. 'If you insist. What do you want to know first?'

'Her name would be a good start, as well as how they met and why they're apart.'

Amelia looked at her thoughtfully, pursing her lips before finally taking the plunge. 'Since I've opened the gate, so to speak, I might as well let the horses gallop through. Adele and Pierre grew up together. Their parents regarded them as childhood sweethearts and in a way I think the pair of them moulded themselves to what other people wanted. Anyway, Adele was expecting when they got married.'

Sally swallowed. Her throat felt as frozen as her body. 'Go on,' she managed to say at last, too shocked to say much else and certainly too far into this explanation to turn back. A child! This was the worst thing imaginable.

'Adele had a baby girl. Stillborn, I'm afraid.'

'They must have been devastated.'

'I assume they were, though Pierre never refers to it. In fact, he rarely speaks of Adele. I'm not sure of his exact feelings because on the occasions when I've broached the subject I've met with a blank wall. He almost told me something once, about Adele's political beliefs and her outlandish behaviour, but he clamed up almost as soon as he started talking. I have my own suspicions about that. Pierre refuses to speak of the baby and refuses to talk about Adele. And before you ask, I've no idea why. It grieves me that they haven't made a go of it. They used to be so close and I liked Adele very much – as much as I like you. Things seemed to fall apart about three years ago, but even before that . . .'

Sally stared down at her entwined fingers, tears stinging her eyes. Pierre meant everything to her and she'd truly believed they'd have a life together. All the dreams she'd built had turned to dust.

'He should have told me,' she said bitterly, digging her fingernails into her palms. The only folly on her part had been falling in love. As for Pierre, on his part there was only subterfuge. He'd lied to her by omission. She could never forgive him for that.

'I urged him to tell you. He told me the time wasn't right and that I was not to tell you either. He told me he wanted to see Adele before the German army invaded, before she . . . Well, how he's going to do that now they have is likely to be very difficult indeed. As for letters – well – that isn't going to be so easy from now on.'

Pierre's deceit had made Sally angry, but still she found herself wondering and worrying. Would she ever see him again now that the Germans were in France?

'He told me he was going to France to help fight the invader when they came. And now France is totally overrun. Our troops had their backs against the sea at Dunkirk. Pierre didn't get away back in May so God knows where he might be now. He might be waiting to kill himself some Germans. I don't know for sure.'

Amelia nodded in agreement. 'That might well be true. Pierre loves France and I hope he still loves Adele, though I doubt it. They've grown apart.' Amelia clasped her hands in front of her, her chin held aloft. 'Sorry, my dear, but I believe that marriage should be for life.'

There was little left to say. Amelia asked if Sally would like more tea. A biscuit perhaps?

She declined.

On the walk home she thought about the letter from Pierre she had lovingly folded between the pages of her diary, a letter waiting for a reply.

The moment she got back she would throw it into the fire or tear it into pieces. Pierre did not deserve any kind of response. He'd lied to her by his failure to disclose the truth of his marriage.

Back home she took the letter from inside the diary meaning to take it downstairs and throw it into the fire. She would very likely have done so if she hadn't been tempted to read it one more time.

Her gaze flew over the words, her heart fluttering in exactly the same way it had when she'd first read it.

Her eyes cloudy with unshed tears, her chin firm with resolve, she folded the letter in three parts passing it from one hand to another as she confronted her fears and her thoughts.

The bitter taste of his betrayal remained.

Why hadn't he told her the truth? Surely he must have realised that at some point his aunt would tell her?

Anger and despair surfaced in equal measure along with the most beguiling of his features, the way his brandy-coloured hair curled around the nape of his neck, the way creases appeared around his eyes when he smiled, the way his mouth moved when he spoke, the words delivered in a slight accent that made her spine tingle.

How could he have asked her to marry him when he was married already?

Yet he'd been so adamant. There had to be a genuine reason he had not told her the truth. *You're deluding yourself*, said a small voice in her head.

Another small voice protested equally vehemently. *No! I saw no deceit in him, no sign that he was lying. Now why would I do that?*

The truth exploded into her mind in letters three feet high. *Because you love him.*

On hearing the back door open and close, she returned the letter to her diary and went downstairs. She would decide whether or not to reply to Pierre later. She needed time to think.

Her father was sprawled on a kitchen chair, his legs straight out in front of him. He was still wearing the boots he wore when he was gardening. His head rested against the chair back as he did when he was dozing, but on this occasion his eyes were wide open and dark with concern.

She knew he was thinking about Joanna and the dog.

'Have they found her?'

'No. Nobody knows where she's gone. The police have checked if there are any relatives, but it seems not. Her father was an only child and her stepmother's background is dubious to say the least. Not that she wants her found.' He looked at his daughter. 'I think the only reason she went to the police was because she'd made the mistake of coming in to see you first. She'd truly believed that Joanna had gone into school as usual. It must have come as quite a shock when you told her she hadn't showed up.'

'I told her to contact the police. You think that was a mistake?'

He shook his head, his callused hands resting in his lap. 'You did the right thing. My opinion is that she wouldn't have got them involved if you hadn't suggested it. She'd have been quite happy to live her life without Joanna around, no matter what had happened to her.'

A heavy sadness washed over Sally as she sank onto a kitchen chair. Resting her elbows on the table, she cupped her face in her hands.

Today had been memorable, though not for the right reasons. On the one hand a sadly neglected child had run away from home. On the other hand she had found out that the man she loved was already married. Pierre was in France and Joanna goodness knows where. A letter to Pierre might shed some light on the reasons why he had asked her to marry him without him being free to marry her. But what about Joanna? Who could possibly know where she might have gone?

CHAPTER TWENTY-SEVEN

The country bus was single decker and the man who was driving also took the money and gave out tickets.

Joanna had eyed him nervously, Harry snuggling close to her legs, looking up at her imploringly.

'Twopence for you. Same for the dog. Anyone meeting you the other end?'

Joanna shook her head. 'No. Not at the bus stop anyway,' she said, instantly realising her mistake. The last thing she wanted was for the driver to question the fact that at the end of the journey she would get off the bus alone.

The driver was still regarding her with a puzzled expression. 'Where you off to, then?'

Joanna swallowed her nervousness and proceeded to lie.

'I'm going to stay with my grandmother. Her legs are bad so she can't come to the bus,' she added, a picture of Mrs Allen and her bad legs springing to mind.

The driver looked from her to Harry who was wagging his tail happily, his big brown eyes fixed on the driver's face.

'Oh well. At least you've got a bit of jolly company,' he said to her.

At the end of the journey the bus stayed where it was. Joanna walked off past the small post office that Paul had mentioned in his stories.

A woman came out from the village store and began cleaning the windows, stopping when she saw Joanna and her dog. 'Afternoon, young lady. Out for an afternoon walk?'

'Yes. I'm going to visit my grandmother.'

When it seemed as though the woman was about to ask more searching questions, Joanna quickened her pace.

A man wearing a flat cap, his shirtsleeves rolled up, a waistcoat and trousers tied about with string at the knees, alighted from a farm wagon. He said nothing, but merely glanced in her direction before disappearing inside the post office.

Joanna's heart had raced when challenged by the bus driver and the woman. Thankfully the man had only glanced at her, too committed to entering the shop and buying something.

The road was long and flat. The rank of terraced cottages, the post office and the village store were soon left behind. Just a few buildings, cottages and narrow lanes dissected the meadows where cows and sheep grazed. The day was fine enough but tonight the temperature would drop.

Suppressing a shiver, Joanna knew she had to find somewhere to shelter. She had to find the place Paul had slept at night after fishing all day.

Daylight was fading and it was getting cold by the time she came to the double gates Paul had described to her.

Joanna shivered. It was far colder than she'd expected it to be and she wished she'd grabbed the hat and scarf Mrs Allen had knitted her.

The double gates were made of corrugated iron, the pair of them held together with a rusty chain. He'd assured her it was never locked. All she had to do was walk over tumps of dried grass to get to them.

Harry was off his lead. He sniffed around quite happily while she attempted to push open the gates, the chain hanging loosely, the gates making a squealing sound as she pushed them open.

The grass field sloping down to the river was just as Paul had described it.

'Me and Charlie caught some really big fish along there,' he'd told her excitedly.

Joanna looked around across the river to where the bare branches of trees seemed to be scratching the sky. Daylight was fading and a frosty moon shimmered in an indigo sky surrounded by ragged clouds that also seemed touched with silver.

The old barn was exactly where Paul had told her, its old stonework and the bit of roof still remaining covered with ivy.

Loneliness suddenly overwhelmed her. There was not another human being in sight.

'Harry?'

Her heart seemed to stop. Without Harry, the reason for her doing this, there was no point in running away.

'Harry!' she called again, this time more urgently than before.

A sound of lapping came from where the river swirled against the adjacent bank.

Joanna's heart stopped racing. Harry was merely slaking his thirst.

The barn was very dark. Enough daylight remained for her to see where straw bales had been piled in the far corner.

Feeling her way over tumbled straw, she eased herself into a snug gap between walls made of bales. Harry followed her in, sniffing and snuffling at the straw all the way.

Once settled down on the straw, she groped in her satchel for the pieces of rabbit she'd brought with her. Harry wolfed them down while she nibbled her way through some bread and cheese. It wasn't much but would keep her going. Paul had told her there were fish here. Perhaps she could catch one for their next meal, though she'd never fished in her life.

Cold and tired, she snuggled down against Harry's warm body. To keep them extra warm she pulled some of the loose straw over them.

The day had been long and although she thought she had planned her escape well, she still didn't have any real idea of where to go.

It was late morning when she finally woke up. Harry was eating the last of his food. She got out a last piece of pie from Mrs Allen.

The day was spent ambling alongside the river. Joanna considered going back to the shop she had passed the day before, but she decided to wait. Something might turn up and there was still the prospect of fishing or catching a rabbit. She'd also had the foresight to bring a box of matches. She might be able to cook something and perhaps pick apples. There were bound to be some left somewhere.

Tonight she would sleep and consider her options in the morning.

In the morning a weak sun had broken through the sky turning it a dirty lemon colour. Ducks quacked on the river, welcoming the morning mist that rose like steam into their watery world.

Her arm wrapped around Harry's neck and snuggled close to his side, Joanna slept on.

Harry lifted his head. He had heard the ducks but was presently staring at the gates through which they had entered the field.

His nose quivered and his whole body stiffened, his gaze fixed on the direction from where the sound was coming.

Beyond the barn a tractor trundled its way through the iron gates. Its driver, Jim Sanderson, had farmed the meadows bordering the River Avon for years. His father had done the same before him and his father before that. He was lean and wiry, his weathered complexion etched with lines. Tired eyes peered out from beneath a flat cap and two days of hair growth bristled on his chin. In peacetime he had taken a shave each day. Nowadays he just didn't have the time.

A number of farm labourers had ditched working the land in favour of joining the armed forces. Some had been conscripted, leaving Jim with a heavier workload than he would normally have.

A few more days and the land girls he'd been allocated would put in an appearance. He'd held out against having them, arguing that women weren't as tough as men and wouldn't pull their weight. He'd had to reconsider once he was down to just two male labourers and they were all working from dawn to dusk, grumbling that the work was hard and if they'd been young enough they would be off fighting.

The trailer he was pulling behind the tractor was piled high with hay that he intended to store alongside the straw already in the barn. The cold depths of winter, when he intended moving cattle into the riverside field, were not that far away. At least here the cattle would have a straw bed and shelter if the weather did get bad. They'd also have hay if it should snow and they couldn't get to the grass.

By shunting the tractor backwards and forwards, he got the trailer lined up outside the barn entrance, making it easier to offload.

Satisfied he'd done that, he switched off the engine and clambered down.

The little girl stared at him, her arms around the neck of what looked to be a golden cocker spaniel.

Surprised, Jim nudged his cap with two fingers sending it further back on his head. 'Well I never! Now what might you be doing 'ere?'

The little girl looked terrified. A low growl rumbled in the dog's throat.

Jim smiled. He rather liked dogs and from what he could see he had indeed been right about the breed. An English cocker, once trained, was a very good gun dog.

'All right, buster,' he said addressing Harry. 'No need to get worried. I'm not going to hurt anybody.'

Something about his amiable smile and the way he spoke seemed to get through to the young dog. Harry stopped growling and eyed the farmer with interest.

Jim reached down and patted his head. 'Now,' he said, turning to Joanna, 'have you had any breakfast?'

Joanna shook her head. Running away was all very well, but the night had been cold and the little food she'd brought with her was already gone.

'Well, just you wait till I unhitch this trailer and we'll go get some. Bacon and eggs all right with you?'

Joanna, her stomach gurgling at the prospect of a proper cooked breakfast, something she hadn't enjoyed for a very long time, nodded enthusiastically.

For the first time in her life – and in Harry's for that matter – she rode on a tractor, cramped in front and sitting on the farmer's knees.

Harry balanced on a ledge to the side of the seat. His ears blew in the breeze as they trundled along the road, but the breakfast at the other end was worth any prior discomfort.

Meg Sanderson, Jim's wife, raised her eyebrows and put her hands on her ample hips when she saw her husband arrive back home early and with passengers on board.

Before going inside, Jim whispered in his wife's ear. Her pink face was merry enough but lit up even more when she smiled. She nodded that she understood.

'Leave it with me,' she said to him softly. 'You go and do what you have to do. Now,' she said, turning to Joanna. 'What's your name?'

'Joanna Ryan.'

'And what about him? What's his name?'

'He's Harry. We got lost.'

'Well, never you mind. First let's get some breakfast inside you and then we'll try to get you sorted. Nobody wants to stay lost for ever now, do they?'

She chatted as she fried bacon and eggs. 'Hope you like field mushrooms. Picked them this morning I did. Care for a sausage?'

Joanna stared at the plate that was placed in front of her. Bacon, sausage, egg and fried bread.

Harry got a plateful of dog biscuits and cold meat that looked to Joanna suspiciously like the rabbit he was used to. He'd finished what she'd brought with her the previous night.

Meg Sanderson saw her looking. 'We've got a lot of rabbits round 'ere. Vermin they are. Jim, that's my husband, shoots them. Got more rabbit than we know what to do with. Could do with a dog like you got to go shooting. Proper gundog that is. So where were you going, you two?'

Joanna was taken by surprise and instantly swallowed the mouthful of food. She used the same explanation she'd given the bus driver. 'I'm visiting my grandmother.'

'Really? P'raps I know 'er. What's 'er name then?'

Joanna pretended to concentrate on chewing a piece of crisp bacon while she thought of a suitable name. 'Thomas,' she said at last. 'Mrs Thomas.'

Where the name had come from she wasn't quite sure. She didn't know a Mrs Thomas, though the head of Victoria Park boys' school, the one she had seen with Elspeth, was called Mr Thomas.

Jim Sanderson had gone into the other room when she'd first sat down at the table. He nodded at his wife when he came back in. Meg gave him a pinched smile and Joanna detected a shifty look in her eyes. Meg Sanderson knew where her husband had been and what he'd been doing.

'That's a nice dog you've got there,' he said to Joanna as his wife poured him a cup of tea. 'I'd like a dog like that. If ever you don't want him, there's a home for him here.'

Joanna was defiant. 'He's my dog. Harry and me will be together for ever! We're orphans. Both of us.'

Jim's smile remained along with the look of pity in his eyes.

At the sound of a car pulling up outside, Mrs Sanderson wiped her palms down her apron and Mr Sanderson got to his feet.

'I'm sorry, my dear,' he said, looking down at Joanna. 'But your parents are likely worried out of their mind wondering where you are. You're going home. And so's that dog of yours, but if your parents don't want him, I'm willing to take him on. Just you remember that.'

Joanna looked up at him in dismay.

'You'll never have Harry! Never ever!'

CHAPTER TWENTY-EIGHT

Most kids would have been excited beyond belief to have ridden in a tractor and then in a motor car and all in the same day. Joanna was far from it.

The policeman at the station was very kind.

'Here you are. Cup of hot cocoa to warm you up. You were lucky Mr Sanderson found you. It was a cold night last night and likely to be even colder tonight.'

Even though she'd eaten a hearty breakfast, Joanna took the mug gratefully, her thank you barely audible. Her eyes remained downcast.

PC Crow was surprised that his jovial manner had not raised a smile on her pretty face. He was famous as being able to bring a smile to the solemnest.

Undaunted, and slightly miffed she hadn't responded as expected, he tried again. 'I expect your mum will be worried out of her mind you going off like that.'

The little girl's eyes flickered. Was it his imagination or had her face turned whiter than white?

Not all kids had good homes but not all admitted it. He prided himself on winning kids over, gaining their trust and getting at the truth of their home lives. To this end he bent low so his face was level with hers.

'Look, Joanna. If there's anything you want to tell me, it won't go any further. If there's anything worrying you . . .'

Her eyes blinked sharply wide. There was one thing above all others she was worrying about. 'Where's Harry?'

The policeman smiled, pleased that his efforts were half satisfied. He'd found the key to her heart. 'Your dog?'

She nodded.

'He's out in the kennels where we keep stray dogs. Sometimes we keep our own dogs there as well. Police dogs that work with us. Real clever they are. Ever met one?'

She shook her head.

'How about you get that cocoa inside you and I take you to meet one?'

She shook her head even more vehemently than before. 'No. I just want Harry. Harry is a clever dog. Better than any old police dog!'

The policeman, a family man with four children of his own, scratched his head. 'Was Harry the reason you ran away?'

Joanna thought about it. 'I was supposed to be evacuated. My stepmother said I had to now my dad's dead. I didn't want to be parted from Harry. He's my best friend – him and Paul and Susan.'

PC Crow felt an instant pang of pity. He presumed Joanna's father had fell at Dunkirk, though he wouldn't mention it. The kid was upset enough already. Fancy counting a dog as her best friend!

Joanna had almost finished her cocoa when one of the double doors to the police station crashed open. 'So there you are, you little minx!'

Startled, Joanna dropped the tin mug, which rolled over the floor ending up spraying her stepmother's shoes with what was left at the bottom.

Joanna cowered against the wall, half suspecting her stepmother would slap her face right there and then.

'I'll give you running off, my girl. Just wait until I get you home. Just you wait!'

Elspeth shook Joanna until it felt as though her teeth had loosened and would fall out of her head.

'Mrs Ryan, is it?'

The policeman who had been so kind to Joanna stepped forward, his broad shoulders and imposing presence physically representing the power of the law.

Elspeth stopped shaking Joanna and looked at him. Unwilling to upset anyone who represented authority, she pasted on one of her false smiles and patted her hair. 'Yes. It is.'

The policeman's eyes hardened. 'Perhaps we could have a little talk – in private.'

Elspeth decided it would be imprudent to disagree. 'Of course.' She threw Joanna an icy glare and pointed a warning finger. 'Don't you dare move from that spot until I get back.'

Elspeth Ryan regretted that she hadn't done herself up a bit more before coming to the police station, but she kept smiling. The policeman who sat across from her was a fine figure of a man. She judged him as one who appreciated good-looking women and wasn't immune to having a bit of fun on the side. Most men were like that.

'I'm sorry for putting you to so much trouble,' she said once she was seated on the other side of the table from him. 'My stepdaughter is getting to be a right little handful since her dad died and that's a fact!'

'Is there any other reason for her leaving home besides her father dying?' asked the policeman.

Elspeth was not been prepared for the policeman's question. 'Of course not.' She paused. 'She's always been a right little madam. I did tell her father that, but he wouldn't listen. Spoilt her, he did, and that's a fact!'

Tossing her head dismissively, she took a Woodbine cigarette from the packet in her handbag. She waited for the policeman to offer her a light but when he didn't bother she changed her mind. Now was not the time to smoke, not with him looking at her so accusingly.

'What about the dog?' he asked.

Elspeth pulled in her chin and frowned. 'What dog?'

'She had a dog with her. A cocker spaniel by the look of it. He goes by the name of Harry. She says it's hers.'

'Well!' exclaimed Elspeth. Despite being in the company of a very good-looking man wearing a uniform, the mask she usually adopted for such as he slipped from her face. 'I've no idea where she got that dog, but one thing I do know is the dirty smelly thing is not coming to live in my house!'

'So you want us to dispose of him?' The policeman sounded surprised.

'I really don't care what you do with him. I agree with the government that all pets should be put down in a time of war. In fact, I'd put all dogs and cats down if I had my way even when we're not at war. They're nothing but a nuisance.'

The policeman eyed her disparagingly. 'Might I remind you, Mrs Ryan, that we use dogs to apprehend criminals. They've proved very useful in their time. Dogs have walked with man since the beginning of time,' he stated in a lazy monotone, his eyes gazing into the distance. 'Hunting dogs to start with. Then guard dogs, blood hounds, etc. Chinese mandarins used to shove the Pekinese dog up their sleeves to keep warm. Then there were lapdogs, King Charles spaniels, and all manner of other dogs bred for a purpose. Not that having a pedigree makes a difference. All dogs have a degree of intelligence.'

He could see from her expression that the woman sitting opposite him was unmoved.

'I don't care what they do. All that I'm saying is that you can dispose of this one in any way you choose.'

PC Crow studied the hairs growing on his knuckles as he considered what to do next. If he couldn't persuade this woman to give the dog a home, then it was more than likely the animal would have to be put down. It crossed his mind to take him home himself, but he'd had to rehome the cat they used to have because one of the children was allergic to it. Who's to say Timothy, his youngest son, wouldn't also be allergic to a dog?

One look at Mrs Ryan and he'd weighed her up. She might try and appear a respectable married woman, but he guessed she hadn't always been that way. In fact, he had a sneaking suspicion he might have arrested her for soliciting some years ago. But that was then and this was now and they weren't here with regard to a criminal offence. This was all about a little girl and a dog.

'Is there anyone else who can take the dog in?'

'Nobody that I know of. Everyone's having a hard enough time feeding their families let alone looking after a dog.'

PC Crow nodded, his expression ably hiding what he was feeling inside. In this business you had to stick to the facts and appear even-handed and helpful. This was what he was aiming to do now. 'It seems you've made up your mind about the dog.'

'I certainly have,' Elspeth declared and tossed her head.

'And the child? What do you intend doing with Joanna?'

His look was steady but although Elspeth was unnerved by his manner, the possibility of remarrying – and a gentleman at that – outweighed all other considerations.

'She'll be evacuated to the country as planned. I've made enquiries and there's a train going at the end of the month. I'll get her on that.'

PC Crow didn't press her to relent because he knew her sort never did. The father and breadwinner dead, Elspeth Ryan was looking after herself. The child was just an encumbrance, one she wished to get out of her sight and mind as quickly as possible.

Shame about the dog.

CHAPTER TWENTY-NINE

All the way home from the police station Elspeth Ryan held Joanna's hand so tightly it felt as though the bones were cracking.

No matter how much Joanna cried and protested that she was hurting, Elspeth's grip was unrelenting.

'Harry! I want Harry!' Joanna sobbed through her tears.

'Harry can go to hell!'

By the time they got home, Joanna's arm felt as though it had been pulled from its socket and her fingers like they'd got caught in the mangle.

Proud of her scarlet nails, Elspeth had often given Joanna the job of feeding the laundry through the mangle, and sometimes her fingers had been caught between the wooden rollers that pressed the water from sheets. The experience had made her wary, though the mangle had never inflicted such pain as her stepmother was inflicting now.

Once in the house, Elspeth pushed Joanna through the door and continued pushing her all the way to the back of the house and the kitchen.

The flat of her hand beat into the middle of Joanna's back sending her sprawling.

Her stepmother stood over her, eyes blazing, hands on hips and legs akimbo.

'First things first. Wash up and tidy this kitchen. I want it spick and span. I've been at work most of the day – I say most because I got called into the police station to pick you up! You're a bloody nuisance and that's a fact. So make yourself useful and you can help yourself to some supper.'

Joanna got to her feet, wrapped her arms around herself and stood trembling in the middle of the kitchen. Her bottom lip quivered and although she was terrified of her stepmother, she found enough bravery to ask about her dog. 'What will happen to Harry?'

Elspeth stood by the stairs, one hand on the newel post, the other on her hip. Her smile was the cruellest Joanna had ever seen. 'He's going to be shot!'

With that she ran up the stairs to her bedroom, laughing all the way stopping at the top to shout down. 'And don't touch that pie. It's not for you. Find yourself something else.'

Tears welled up in Joanna's eyes and finally streamed steadily down her face.

The pie left on top of the cooker had the most golden of pastry. She recognised the pie dish as belonging to Mrs Allen next door. The pie smelled as wonderful as it looked, but although Joanna was hungry, she was too upset to eat. She had no appetite and wouldn't have until she knew Harry's fate.

Her tears trickled off her chin and into the washing-up water. There was a lot of washing up, indicating that her stepmother had not had visitors since she'd been away and had left them for Joanna to wash.

Joanna knew all the signs. Tonight her stepmother was expecting somebody.

Whoever it was, Joanna would not see them. She did not care to. Her world had been shattered, and all thanks to her stepmother.

First she'd had Lottie put down. Now it was Harry's turn and she was relishing the prospect. Joanna was in no doubt that her own punishment had been put on hold until she'd finished the dishes and tidied up.

The sound of her stepmother's footsteps thudding down the stairs in smart court shoes counted down the seconds until the moment of reckoning.

Joanna turned round, her back pressed flat against the sink, her knees shaking.

Her stepmother had reapplied her makeup and changed her clothes. She was wearing a tight-fitting twinset in royal blue, a checked skirt and her black suede court shoes. Pearls glistened from her earlobes and around her neck. She looked a lot less cheap than usual, almost as though age was making her more refined.

All the same her eyes shone with cruel intent, her red lips set in a tight smile proclaiming she had considered Joanna's misdemeanour and intended inflicting her favourite punishment.

Her voice was low and threatening. 'I'll teach you to make a fool of me, Joanna Ryan.'

The slap across her cheek stung, but Joanna knew worse was to come.

Grabbing Joanna's arm, Elspeth dragged her to the coalhouse. 'It's into the darkness for you. In with the dirt, the dark and the spiders!'

Fingers viciously biting into Joanna's arm, her stepmother pulled open the door and threw her in. The iron bolt rattled as Joanna fell back onto the heaped coal.

'And not a sound from you or I'll keep you in there all week!' Elspeth shouted from the other side of the door. 'That'll teach you!' The hard voice broke into raucous laughter. 'I bet you hate the dark. I hated it too but it did teach me to do as I was told. And you will do as you are told, Miss Joanna Elizabeth Ryan. And if you don't you'll spend more time in there because quite frankly, my dear, I prefer you out of my sight. Out of sight, out of mind, and out of my bloody way!'

Surrounded by darkness, Joanna raised herself onto her elbows. It was the first time her stepmother had mentioned anything about enduring the same punishment when she was young. What Joanna couldn't understand was if she'd been so cruelly treated herself, why inflict the same on others?

The darkness was total, just like the mines deep in the earth where the coal came from. Head resting on her knees, she wrapped her arms around her legs and closed her eyes.

Normally she would be counting by now, on and on until she was finally released from her prison. This time she couldn't concentrate. All she could think of was Harry and whether he was already dead.

Exactly one hour after her stepmother collected Joanna, Seb Hadley stepped over the threshold of the police station.

The news that Joanna and Harry had been found came to him via Joanna's friends Paul and Susan. They had told Sally after she'd found them chattering excitedly together after school.

'They've found Joanna,' they'd chimed excitedly, admiration for Joanna's adventure shining in their faces.

On arriving home, Sally had immediately told her father, who was busily washing vegetables he'd brought from the allotment. He was so taken by surprise that the parsnip he'd been scraping fell back into the water.

'I take it Mrs Ryan has fetched her home,' he said, his mouth set in a tight line.

Sally sighed. 'I suppose so.'

Her father reached for the hand towel, wiped his hands and reached for his coat. 'Where are you going?'

'I'm betting that bloody woman has left orders for the dog to be put down,' he said. 'Are you coming?'

Sally flung her briefcase into a chair, kept her coat on and swung out behind him.

November had brought its usual fog, not helped by the smoke billowing from thousands of coal fires, factory chimneys and steam driven locomotives and other machinery. They headed for the local police station hoping against hope that they would be on time. Both Sally and her father were under no illusion about what Mrs Ryan might have done. The woman seemed to enjoy maltreating the child physically and mentally.

Deranged, thought Sally, and shivered at the kind of life the little girl had endured.

There were lots of other children who lived with poverty and a certain amount of neglect and abuse, but Joanna's case was the worst she'd come across.

A dark-coloured van stood at the kerb outside with no driver in it.

The pair of them pushed past it without giving it a second glance, racing up the steps, hoping and wishing that they'd arrived in time.

PC Crow, the police constable who had interviewed Mrs Ryan and overseen the handing over of Joanna, was just going off duty when they arrived.

Seb rushed up to the arched aperture behind which sat the duty sergeant. PC Crow stood just behind him, buttoning his mud-coloured trench coat in preparation for going home.

Seb being breathless, Sally outlined the reason they were there. 'It's about the dog the child Joanna Ryan was with. We wondered what was going to happen to it.'

The sergeant smiled at the pretty face looking through the aperture, noting her breathlessness and the concern pinching her brow.

'Name?'

'Her name was Joanna Ryan. The dog's name was Harry.'

'Ah yes. I know the case.' The sergeant shook his head. 'The owner instructed the dog be put down and the deed is about to be done.'

Seb blanched. 'Done? What do you mean?'

Sally felt as though somebody had landed a punch in her chest.

The desk sergeant looked a little embarrassed. He couldn't help get the feeling that something here was not quite right. Besides that, he didn't relish the thought of telling this lovely young lady that the dog concerned was about to receive a bullet to his head.

Seb immediately put two and two together. 'Somebody from that van outside?'

They'd all heard of the van that came round collecting pets for disposal. The one outside matched the descriptions passed from one neighbour to another.

'Yes. Mr Wheeler. He's just gone to the men's room before—'

Seb slammed his fist down on the counter. 'You cannot do this!'

The desk sergeant winced, grateful it was the counter being hit and not him. 'I'm afraid we can, sir,' he responded, his manner now stiffly official. 'It's up to the owner, sir.'

'It's my dog!' Seb's voice rang around the dull little room that served as the public reception area for the police station. 'That woman's nothing to do with him!'

'Sir! That cannot be!' Exasperated at what he perceived was a lie, the sergeant threw down the stubby pencil he used to write down details in his big thick incident book.

'Excuse me.' PC Crow stopped buttoning up his trench coat, took off his trilby and stepped forward. 'You say it's your dog?'

Seb nodded. 'Yes. It is my dog. He lives in my shed down the allotment. I feed and water him. It was young Joanna Ryan's job to take him for a walk. Harry, the dog, helps me keep the rabbits down. As for her stepmother, well, she never even met the animal let alone lived with it!'

PC Crow's first impression of Mrs Ryan was that she was supremely selfish and a liar. She had seemed surprised when the dog was mentioned. In his opinion that meant the gentleman who had just arrived was telling the truth.

'I'll need your names,' declared the sergeant.

Names and addresses were taken, Seb and Sally fidgeting all the while, worrying if they were in time to rescue Harry who was definitely more than man's best friend. He was best friend to a lonely little girl who had nobody else in all the world.

Concerned that justice would be done, PC Crow patted the sergeant's shoulder. 'Fred, I'll deal with this if you like.' He turned to Seb. 'Let's go and have a word with Mr Wheeler, shall we?'

He turned and left through a door in the small general office. He was halfway through when they all heard the crack of a pistol.

Seb leapt for the door marked private on their side of the general office cubbyhole. After a moment, Sally followed him.

'Oi!' shouted the sergeant as they disappeared into the restricted area.

Seb had fought in the Great War and knew what a pistol shot smelled like. It was just a case of following his nose. The prickling sensation of the familiar smell filled him with fear and he prayed they were not too late.

They almost collided with PC Crow, who beckoned them on. Through one door then another and they were out in the backyard, a place walled in on all sides, screened from the outside world.

A man in a dark coat and hat stood in the middle of the yard. He was muttering something under his breath while fiddling with the pistol he held in his left hand.

Seb's gaze darted to Harry. He was muzzled, his front legs tied with rope to a drainpipe, his back legs to a railing. The poor creature saw him and whined recognition.

'What's up here then?' PC Crow asked.

George Wheeler, his surly look directed at his pistol looked less than pleased.

Seb ran over to where Harry was tied, relieved not to find him lying flat out with a bullet in his head.

'Harry! Harry, my boy. What are you trussed up like this for? For God's sake . . .'

The moment he took off the muzzle, Harry's whine turned into excited barks as Seb began to untie him.

PC Peter Crow frowned at the man with the gun. 'What's been going on? I heard a gunshot.'

Small eyes shaded by the broad rim of a trilby hat settled on Sally before the thin-lipped man faced the policeman.

'Bloody dog leapt at me and I misfired. Had to tie him up after that. I couldn't waste a second missed shot. Every bullet has to be accounted for. Now I've got to report to headquarters that I used two bullets. It won't go down too well at all, that won't. Not too well at all. Still, it's a job that has to be done. Now if everybody will just get out of my way . . .'

'Over my dead body!'

Seb stood between the shooter and Harry, the dog's lead clenched tightly in his fist, the timbre of his voice loud enough to shake the windows.

PC Crow placed a restraining hand over that of the gunman.

'I think you're finished here, Wheeler. There's been a mistake. It turns out the woman who gave the order for it to be put down had no claim on the dog. He belongs to this gentleman.'

The man named George Wheeler looked very put out as he lowered the gun. 'Are you saying I've wasted my precious time coming here?'

'That's about the size of it.'

'And what about my fee? The authorities won't be best pleased you know.'

'George, it's Sunday. A day of rest. Now unload that gun before somebody gets hurt and get home. Give us all a bit of rest!'

Sally smiled to herself as she walked alongside her father, who was strutting triumphantly on the walk home. Harry walked in a similar manner at his side, his nose in the air and his stumpy tail wagging.

Walking into the warmth of their kitchen helped dissipate the awful feelings she'd had that they might not have got to Harry in time. They had, and both she and her father were greatly relieved.

The smell of brisket and potatoes roasting in the oven enveloped them.

Sally sighed. 'It's so good to be home.'

Before taking off her coat she made up for lost time by putting the greens on to boil.

Harry licked his lips in anticipation of what was in the oven. After a few exploratory sniffs around the furniture, Harry chose the spot he preferred, lying stretched out in front of the fire.

'For you,' Sally said, as she placed the dog's dish in front of Harry's nose.

'I thought you had to save that fat for baking?' said her father, on noticing the plateful of fat, gristle and bone she'd given to Harry.

'Your teeth wouldn't get through gristle, Dad, and you dislike soup, so making stock from the bone is not an issue. Anyway, Harry was hungry.'

She paused, unable to think of a believable reason for giving Harry the gravy. 'He deserves a treat. He's been through a lot,' she said at last.

Sally made herself comfortable in the armchair her mother used to sit in on the left-hand side of the fireplace. Her father was sitting in the one opposite. When she looked at him she noticed that he too was staring into the fire.

'You're worried about Joanna.'

He nodded, his unlit pipe twirling between his fingers.

'When Joanna told me about being locked in the coalhouse, I had a great urge to go round there and give that stepmother of hers a good talking to. But Joanna is not my child. I shouldn't interfere.'

He glanced at his daughter, as lovely as her mother and just as patient. She'd been supportive all the time he'd grieved for his darling Grace.

He waited a moment before asking the question that was on his mind. 'Should I interfere?'

Sally leaned forward, her chin resting on her hands. 'Perhaps after you told me how she was treated I should have contacted the children's welfare officer. Perhaps I was wrong not to.'

'There was Harry to consider – or rather her feelings for Harry. She'd have been heartbroken being parted from that dog. At least she had some respite from her home life down in my shed with her dog. You ought to have seen her running along the embankment with him! So happy. Poor little thing.'

'Her stepmother will insist on her being evacuated as soon as possible. This time she'll be locked in before being sent away. I dare say she might enjoy being evacuated when compared with living with her stepmother.'

'It's her being separated from the dog that concerns me. The child's mental state is so fragile. Some kids clam up altogether after going through all that she's been through.'

Elspeth Ryan made faces in the mirror that hung over the fireplace. Her lipstick needed retouching. If she had had the money she would have bought a better brand.

Her grimace turned to a smile. Well, the time was coming when she would have more money. Arnold wasn't short of a bob or two. Just the thought of it made her smile at her reflection.

There was something about the way he knocked at the door that was different to anyone else's knock. First two hesitant, then three separate knocks one after the other.

She took one more glance at the mirror before going to the door and letting him in. He hugged and kissed her even before taking off his hat and coat, and once free of them ran his hands over her body.

Elspeth had certain priorities to deal with before she would let him take full advantage.

'Food first, you naughty boy.' She smiled as she slapped his hand playfully. 'I need to talk to you. We've got things to plan now that we're both free.'

Being a gentleman, Arnold went along with her wishes. He didn't seem at all surprised when she stated her intention to ditch the house and make the move with him to Scotland.

Arnold was pleased. He went on to tell her the finer details, about the house available to him until he could see his way to buying his own and how lovely the town was with a loch not far away.

Elspeth listened with a smile on her face as she dished up the pie the affable Mrs Allen had brought in. Well, sod the kid, though she might leave a bit for her depending on Arnold's appetite. After a day's work she was hungry herself but her sights were set on changing her life. The thought of being with Arnold in a place far away without any family encumbrance thrilled her.

Reining in her wandering thoughts, she tuned in again to what Arnold was saying. 'And we're not likely to be bombed seeing as it's a rural area.'

Having heard enough of his plans, Elspeth decided now was the time to cement her own.

'When is this move likely to be? I mean, I have to make plans. *We* have to make plans,' she corrected, slipping her arm through his and looking into his eyes. 'I have to give notice on this house,' she added by way of explanation.

Giving notice to the council was only part of her reason to press him for a definite date. She had to have some time to get Joanna evacuated for as long as possible. When and if the girl did ever return it would be to a house occupied by strangers. She had no intention of leaving a forwarding address or informing anyone of her impending marriage. Joanna must never find her. She wanted Arnold to herself.

The last thing she wanted was to scare him off, but she knew how to pace herself. She was using all the tactics she had used to snare Joanna's father. The old tricks never failed and once they were married it would be too late for him to change his mind.

'About a month,' he said to her. 'If that's all right with you? We can get a special licence tomorrow and be married by then.'

Elspeth kissed him, not minding sucking in pie crumbs that had stuck to his mouth.

'Mr and Mrs Thomas! I can't wait,' she squealed, resting her chin on his shoulder and hugging him tightly.

'Neither can I,' he answered, his voice husky with desire. There was just one thing holding him back.

'Your stepdaughter. Is she here?'

Elspeth was taken aback. 'Joanna?'

'Her teacher mentioned her. Joanna Ryan. That's your stepdaughter's name, isn't it?'

Elspeth's mind worked quickly. Damn that bloody Miss Hadley.

'Oh yes. But she's not here. Didn't I tell you? Joanna was very upset when her father died. I did arrange to have her evacuated, but then a relative offered to take her in. Joanna was given the option to stay with me or live with her favourite aunt. She decided to go with her aunt. I can't say I blame her. After all, blood is thicker than water. The child has to go with family and where she's happiest.'

'And you don't mind?'

Elspeth pouted and adopted a doleful look. 'A little. But she isn't my true daughter and, anyway, I've got a future with a new husband to consider.'

When he smiled his breath covered her face.

'So,' she said seductively, eyes shining, lips smiling. 'What would you like for dessert?'

The stairs above Joanna's head, which formed the roof of the coalhouse, creaked with the weight of footsteps before the house fell to silence.

Joanna felt very alone and very afraid. It was as though the world had disappeared. Not a sound did she hear and not a single chink of light found its way into the coalhouse.

Was being dead like this? Joanna shivered at the thought.

For a while she dozed and in her dream she was running along the railway embankment with Harry, who was chasing rabbits. One of the rabbits was very big and turned round to face them.

To Joanna's horror its face resembled her stepmother. Sensing her disquiet Harry barked at the rabbit, causing it to turn tail and run across the railway line into the path of a goods train. The noise was tremendous and everything was shaking as the train left the rails and thundered over her.

At least she thought it was a goods train, but when she found herself flung backwards and covered in coal dust, she knew it was not.

The coal had moved, flinging great clouds of dust into the air. She could feel its grittiness covering her skin, its taste on her tongue.

When she'd fallen asleep she'd been at the higher end of the coalhouse close to the door. She was now wedged into the narrowest part, where the stairs were at their lowest point at the hallway end.

Curling into a ball, she covered her head with her arms, coughing as she inhaled the coal dust that presently surrounded her in a dense cloud of grit and choking dust.

No heavy breathing steam locomotive could have done this. Reality replaced the dream and even though she was only a child she thought she knew what it was. The worst of the war had finally arrived. A bomb had fallen on her house.

As the coal dust settled she rubbed the dirt from her eyes and peered through the darkness. A slit of light showed at the very top of the coalhouse door. Although it was no more than a sliver, to her it was like the beam of a lighthouse.

Struggling onto her hands and knees, she made her way out of the lowest part of the coalhouse, the ceiling height increasing as she crawled over the heaped coal. Although it scraped at her knees and her hands, she gritted her teeth and kept her eyes focused on the sliver of light.

Pieces of coal rolled and tumbled beneath her hands and knees. Climbing up over a mountain of coal was far from easy, but Joanna was determined to reach that chink of light.

She coughed as she climbed, swiping at her gritty eyes and wiping her runny nose on her sleeve. Some of the coal had shifted against the door rather than away from it.

Joanna scrabbled up as far as she could, stretching in an effort to reach the top of the door. Time and again she stretched her arms, her fingers barely failing to fold over the top of the door.

Her calf muscles ached with the effort of standing on tiptoe, but still she couldn't reach.

A little more height. That was all she needed. And some air to breathe.

More coal would help.

With that in mind she felt for pieces of coal – big pieces that she could pile one on top of another so she could climb higher.

Despite the thin beam of light, it was still too dark to see. All she could do was feel her way and judge when the pile of coal was high enough.

She was tired, thirsty and dirty, but she kept going, piling pieces of coal higher and higher.

At last she judged that it was as high as she could make it. Carefully, so as not to disturb any of the underlying base of her coal mountain, she struggled to the top of the heap and almost cried out with joy when her fingertips folded over the top of the door.

A little more effort and . . .

Suddenly the coal gave way and her feet were sliding behind her until she was face down, blood trickling from a wound above her eye.

The bombing, the fear and the effort of trying to get out lay heavy on her small body. For the first time since her father died she began to cry and softly, very softly, she began to count.

One, two, three, four, five, six, seven . . .

* * *

Before the bombing raid, Sally Hadley and her father had just finished supper when Harry suddenly sat bolt upright. Raising his long floppy ears he began to whine, low at first then louder and louder.

Seb was concerned. 'What is it, boy? What is it?'

His whine intensified and was accompanied by a series of high-pitched barks. The hair around his neck formed a stiff ruff. Suddenly his fragile whines were joined by the thin wail of the air-raid siren, its whine intensifying to a high-pitched screech.

Seb exchanged a worried look with his daughter. 'It's for real. It's an air raid.'

The house shook as the droning of aircraft sounded from overhead.

Harry's ears, far better than that of a human, had heard the enemy aircraft before they'd heard the sirens.

Father and daughter grabbed what they could and headed for the shelter. Harry went with them. The shelter was hardly the most comfortable place in the world, though they'd done their best with camp beds, blankets, a flask of tea and sandwiches.

'It's going to be a long night,' said Sally's father.

He was right. The raid went on until the early hours of the morning when the all clear finally sounded. When her father ordered her to stay put, Sally was adamant she would do no such thing. 'If our house is still standing, I'm going to bed even if it's only an hour of sleep before I head for school.'

Seb didn't argue. Sally and the dog followed him out.

Gratefully he pushed open the shelter door, noting that it wasn't stiff so hadn't suffered any blast damage that might have wedged it in place.

The air outside had a particular smell about it. As Seb lifted his head and sniffed the air, old memories resurfaced. A bomb had fallen somewhere, though not on their house. Seb patted the old walls and muttered, 'Thank God.'

Outside in the street a number of people were running up and down blowing whistles.

'Please evacuate your houses. We have an unexploded bomb.'

After each warning those shouting resumed blowing on whistles.

Seb hailed one of them and asked where the bomb had landed.

The man pointed over to where figures barely distinguishable in the early morning light, were moving around in the park.

'There's an unexploded bomb at the bottom of a bloody big crater. We need to get everyone out in case it goes off before the sappers get here.'

Seb knew he was referring to the bomb disposal section of the Royal Engineers who were always called sappers.

'If you've nowhere else to go, everyone's gathering at the Methodist Hall.'

'Any other damage?' asked Seb.

'Not here, thank God. A house up in The Vale scored a direct hit though. Poor buggers in it didn't stand a chance.'

At mention of the direct hit being halfway up The Vale, something curled in Seb's stomach.

'The Vale you say. Any idea what number?'

The man shrugged. 'Not sure. You got relatives up there?'

'A friend. About halfway up.'

Even though there was no streetlight by which to see Seb's expression, the air-raid warden could tell he was worried.

'Hang on. I'll see if I can find out more.' He shouted to somebody further down the street. 'Ted. There's a chap here with friends up in The Vale. Any idea what number got hit?'

'Not sure of the number. Lower hundreds I think,' the man named Ted shouted back.

Nodding his thanks, Seb went back to where Sally was waiting for him, an enquiring expression on her face. 'We have to get out?'

Seb nodded. Being evacuated until the bomb was made safe didn't concern him so much as Joanna's safety.

'I heard him mention the Methodist Hall.'

Seb nodded again. 'Unless you've got somewhere else to go.'

Sally frowned. 'Where are you going?'

'The Vale. A house halfway up was bombed. The warden doesn't know the number, only that it was in the lower hundreds.'

Sally passed him Harry's lead. 'Hold this. I'll get my coat and bring yours out too. It's chilly and we might need it where we're going.'

'I'm not going to no Methodist Hall,' he shouted after her as she disappeared back into the house.

'Neither am I,' she said breathlessly on reappearing and shrugging herself into her coat. 'I'm going with you. We have to check on Joanna.'

CHAPTER THIRTY

The news of number 116 The Vale being bombed spread like wildfire. Neighbours began shifting debris before the rescue services arrived.

An ambulance, its bell jangling all the way, pulled up outside the pile of debris that had once been a house. The police and other people in assorted uniforms arrived to offer their help.

'The whole of the upper floor fell in,' said Mrs Allen in a shaky voice. Her nightdress was shredded, bits flying around her like so many ribbons. Her body was barely covered. She had however thought to put on her hat.

'What number did you live in?' asked a policeman, who was attempting to guide her towards an ambulance.

'Number?'

'What number was your house,' he repeated, more loudly this time.

'She looked at him in a daze. 'One hundred and fourteen. Everyone knows I live there, especially the rent man.'

The policeman recognised she was in shock. 'Can you tell us what happened,' he said gently.

'What happened? A bomb fell. I heard the noise. Didn't you heard the noise?'

The policeman tried again. 'Where were you when you heard the bomb fall?'

Suddenly she seemed to come to, a more knowing look brightening her eyes. 'I was out in the Anderson. I only had it put in a few days ago. Just a few days,' she said, her expression one of total bewilderment. 'Then I found I'd left my knitting behind and went back in the house to look for it. Couldn't find it though. I reckon somebody pinched it – after he'd dropped the bomb.'

The rescue workers helping her exchanged rueful smiles.

'Don't think old Hitler likes to knit,' one of them said.

'But Goering might,' returned Mrs Allen.

An ambulance man passed the policeman a blanket, which they placed around Mrs Allen's shoulders before leading her to the ambulance.

'What about next door, love?' asked the policeman. 'Do you know who lives there?'

'Joanna and that old cow her dad married,' Mrs Allen answered. She sounded tired out.

The ambulance driver got her to lie down. 'You have a bit of a rest love. It'll do you good.'

He didn't add that there was little chance her next-door neighbours had survived. Mrs Allen's house, 114, had been badly damaged. But 116 had been totally destroyed except for that single wall and the length of staircase rising above the rubble.

The policeman passed the information on to the rescuers. 'Apparently a mother and daughter lived in this one.'

The men who'd been clearing debris from where they estimated the bedrooms had been suddenly shouted.

'Over here!'

A group of rescuers picked their way swiftly over the mounds of brick and roof timbers, shattered doors and furniture. A kitchen tap suspended on its lead pipe dripped water and a gas pipe hissed before a man folded the lead piping over and hammered it flat.

'It's dark down here,' shouted the air-raid warden as he shone his torch into a black hole amidst the devastation. The beam from his torch picked out a figure.

'Looks as though she's dead. I reckon the first floor collapsed onto the ground floor. Whoever was in bed up there didn't stand a chance.'

A doctor approached and climbed down into the hole, though not before attaching a rope around his waist.

'The whole lot's a bit unsafe,' quoted the air-raid warden.

The doctor went down anyway. After making a quick assessment of the situation, he signalled to be pulled back up.

'Crushed to death I take it,' said the air-raid warden, his face sombre as he heaved the doctor out of the hole.

The doctor shook his head. 'The man died instantly. The woman was still alive. It looks as though she suffocated. Further examination will confirm that.'

He walked away, his face smeared with dirt, his eyes smarting from the dust that hung in the air. 'Damn this war,' he muttered to himself.

He wondered how long it would take to get used to this kind of thing. The woman lying in the double bed beside the man had indeed suffocated. Judging by her bleeding hands and broken fingernails, she'd beat and scratched at what imprisoned her until her last breath. A horrible way to go, suffocated and buried in darkness.

The rescuers discussed the information neighbours had given. Nobody knew the identity of the man but there were hints that Mrs Ryan was not stingy in her affections.

'And the child?'

'Somebody said she was evacuated, but we don't know for sure.'

'Hopefully she was. Just a minute while I check.'

Mrs Allen was still sitting in the back of the ambulance being tended by a nurse. The policeman sat down beside her. 'What about the little girl? Was she in the house?'

Mrs Allen was confused. Her memory had been knocked sideways by the shock but her mind was steadily clearing. 'Joanna. Mrs Ryan arranged for her to be evacuated a few days ago.'

Breathing a sigh of relief, the policeman thanked her for her help.

'It seems the little girl's been evacuated,' he said to one of the other rescue workers, a soldier home on leave.

The soldier, a member of the Royal Engineers, straightened and rubbed at the small of his back. 'Good for her. So we can go ahead and clear the site, though carefully. Everything's going to fall inwards so we all need to stand well back. For a start, that wall there will fall down.'

He pointed to the upper half of a set of stairs still clinging to a single standing wall.

'You see? Only half the staircase is visible and the fact that the bottom half is buried in rubble is probably the only reason it's still standing. It'll come down all at once, though we'll do our best to get it to fall in on itself rather than outwards. No damage done that way.'

The policeman and air-raid warden both agreed. 'There is only a coalhouse under the stairs. All these houses were built the same.'

Immersed in a thick fog of dirt and coal dust, Joanna swiped at the stinging in her eyes. Her chest felt tight. She needed air.

Balancing on the heaped coal got her nearer to the gap at the top of the door. Her head tilted back so her mouth was next to the gap, she took deep breaths.

Outside was almost as black as inside the coalhouse. Although there was nothing to see, she could hear people shouting. There were people out there. Perhaps her stepmother was out there too and would tell them where she was.

When she tried to shout, she found she couldn't. Thanks to the dust her throat was dry so her voice was small and squeaky. Worse still, when she did manage to emit a slightly louder sound, the jangling bell of an ambulance drowned her out. Everybody outside was shouting. Nobody could hear her.

By the time Seb, Sally and the dog arrived at 116 The Vale, a bulldozer had been brought in to help clear the site and make it safe. Roof timbers were piled to the back of the house, mainly where they had fallen.

'I think our next task is to get them stairs down before they fall down. We can't clear anything else from the site until they're out of the way. Start clearing a path through to it if you can,' the engineer ordered the driver of the machine.

Black smoke rose from the bulldozer's exhaust pipe as it shuffled forward, its shovel biting into the piles of brick, plaster and wood. With each load it turned round to load it onto a lorry that would take it to be dumped, possibly into the crater made by the bomb that had fallen in the park.

'Keep going like this and the stairs will fall in on themselves,' said the sapper. He looked as though he couldn't wait for it to happen. There was something very satisfying about demolishing buildings. If the bombing increased there was bound to be a call for that sort of work. He was seriously considering making a business of it once the war was over.

Joanna was terrified. The sound of the machine rumbled through the air. Dust cascaded over her, blocking her nostrils and sending her into a choking cough. There seemed now to be more dust in her chest than there was air.

'Help!' Her voice was still no more than a squeak and she hammered on the door until her knuckles were sore.

'Help.'

Sensing her efforts were useless, she slumped onto the coal, hot tears running down her dirty face.

Despair was replaced by resignation. She was only a child. There was nothing else she could do.

CHAPTER THIRTY-ONE

A brawny arm shot out across Seb and Sally's path as they closed on the site.

'This is a restricted area. Demolition in progress.'

Sally caught her breath. Dawn was breaking. A quick survey of the sight confirmed the very worst. She exchanged a knowing look with her father. 'It's Joanna's house!'

One of the rescuers heard her. 'Did you know the people in there,' asked the man.

'Yes. We did. I was her teacher,' Sally explained.

The man's attitude softened a fraction. 'We found a dead woman and a man, but no child. We were told by the neighbours she's been evacuated.'

Sally shook her head. 'No. She ran away. We were at the police station earlier. We know she ran away and was taken home by her stepmother yesterday.'

The man's tired eyes weighed up their resilience as he prepared to say what had to be said.

'The whole house came down. The man and woman were in bed. It stands to reason that the little girl was in her bed too. I'm sorry . . .'

Seb felt a tug on his arm. He looked down to see the dog straining on his four strong legs, nose quivering and eyes fixed on a point in the middle of the site where a single wall still stood.

Harry began to whine.

The man was about to walk away when Seb grabbed his arm. 'The little girl wasn't in bed. She'd put her stepmother to a lot of trouble and she was the sort to make her suffer for her disobedience.'

The man frowned.

'I'm telling you now. The little girl never went to bed. She's probably in there somewhere.'

'What's that machine doing?' Sally asked, her voice quivering.

'We're aiming to pull down that set of stairs and the wall before it falls down.

'You can't do that,' Sally shouted and lunged forward.

The man grabbed her. 'Oh no you don't!'

'Listen, you big oaf,' scolded Sally. 'The stepmother was in the habit of locking the little girl in the coalhouse under the stairs as punishment. The stairs are still standing. If you disturb them you'll likely kill a child!'

The man looked perplexed. He had a family of his own and found it hard to believe that anyone could do that. A spanking now and again was one thing, and only when thoroughly deserved. But locking a kid in the darkness under the stairs? That took some believing.

'Wait here. I'll see what the bloke in charge has to say.'

Harry was straining against his lead. His ears were raised as high as floppy ears could be. His eyes were fixed on what remained of the house and his wet nose quivered, a sure sign that he was dissecting all the different smells and had found one that interested him the most.

The bulldozer, its shovel full of rubble, was heading back to where the lorry waited.

Seb surmised that one more trip, one more attempt to dig around the stairs and the wobbly wall and staircase would all come tumbling down.

Harry barked, looked up at Seb and wagged his tail.

Seb understood. If nobody else was going to act in time, then it was up to him. He unclipped the lead from Harry's collar.

'Find Joanna!'

There were raised protests as Harry ran across the bombsite, avoiding the danger spots, his instinct sensing they were there.

Brawny arms reached out to grab him, but with his four legs he was far too quick for them. With a resounding crash, he leapt at the top half of the coalhouse door, yapping and scratching excitedly.

'What's that bloody dog doing there?'

The engineer was miffed. He liked being in charge of this and resented interruption.

The policeman who had helped Mrs Allen, plus a few other men, ignored him and dashed for where the dog was going crazy, yapping and springing on his hind legs so his nose was level with a thin gap showed at the top of the door.

While everyone was in uproar, Seb sprinted across the bombsite although it strained his joints and made him breathless. It had been many a long year since he'd moved so fast.

Once there he grabbed Harry's collar. 'Quiet now, boy. You've done your job. She's probably heard you, but we can't hear her. Joanna!' he shouted. 'Joanna! Are you in there?'

The rumble of the bulldozer's engine drifted across to the bombsite, drowning out any response.

'Shut that bloody thing off a minute,' shouted the policeman.

The engineer looked disinclined to comply, but was overruled. Everyone wanted to see if there really was somebody alive amid all this devastation.

The whole site fell to silence.

The men gathered around the upper half of the door placed their ears as close to the door as they could.

A man with brawny arms banged on it with his fist. Harry barked.

Suddenly they heard a sound, a small barely audible voice. 'Harry! Harry!'

Men with shovels were called for. Seb grabbed one and began to dig. The bulldozer was left standing still as an army of men carefully dug around the door until finally they could bust the hinges and break the panels of wood apart with their bare hands.

At first sight it seemed to be just a bundle of dirty rags lying on black coal in a black hole. Seb sucked in his breath as he took in the poor child's surroundings. How could anyone treat a child so badly?

'Joanna! Joanna! Can you hear me?'

The policeman gently pushed him back. 'Leave her to me, sir.'

Empowered with youthful strength, the policeman reached in to get her out, but Harry got there first.

Straining against Seb's hold on his collar, he dived in, his whole body wagging with excitement, squealing and yapping until he was standing over Joanna. Once he was there, legs squarely fixed on either side of her body he began to lick her face.

'Harry,' she whispered as she reached for him. 'Harry.'

Despite all that she'd gone through she smiled up at him, her face striped thanks to Harry's tongue leaving white tracks over her black face.

CHAPTER THIRTY-TWO

Sally held Joanna's hand, stroking it and telling her everything was going to be all right.

'Only cuts and bruises,' the doctor told her, 'though we are inclined to keep her in hospital for a night or two just to check there are no head injuries.'

'But she'll be all right?'

'She'll be fine.'

A question loitered in his eyes. 'You're not her mother are you?'

She shook her head. 'No.'

'I didn't think you were. You look too young.' Sally could tell he was genuinely interested, and not just in Joanna.

'I teach Joanna in junior school. She's an orphan. Her mother died some years back, her father just a few months ago.' Her jaw tightened. 'Her stepmother died last night – not that she gave a jot what happened to the girl.'

'Ah!' The doctor scribbled something in his notes. 'I'll contact someone with regard to her future. Leave it with me.'

Once she'd reassured Joanna that she would be back in to see her and that Harry was being taken care of, she made her way to the hospital exit.

Outside the ward she spotted the doctor talking to a rotund woman wearing dark green tweeds and a plain mustard hat. The doctor glanced at her then said something to the woman. Both looked in her direction so she knew immediately that this was something to do with Joanna. The doctor glanced down at his notes to check the name she had given before calling out to her.

'Miss Hadley.'

The round woman raised her gloved hand at the doctor, as though saying to him that she would handle whatever had to be done.

The doctor disappeared. The woman in the dark green costume strode purposefully towards her. The costume was well cut and made of bulky material.

'Miss Hadley.' The hand that shook Sally's hand was warm and meaty, the grip strong. 'I'm Miss Thorpe, children's welfare officer.'

With a wave of her hand, Miss Thorpe directed Sally into a small side room. The room was dull as well as small, brown paint halfway up the walls, then cream to the ceiling. The ceiling was high, far too high for the size of the room.

Miss Thorpe indicated a chair on one side of a desk. She took the other, her fleshy hands meeting and resting in front of her. 'I hear from Dr Jason that the Ryan girl is an orphan.'

'I'm afraid so.'

'Do you know if the child has any other relatives – aunts, uncles, grandparents?'

Miss Thorpe held her head high, the ends of her mouth downturned, her tiny eyes fixing on her from either side of a pair of flaring nostrils. Although she made her feel uneasy, Sally answered the questions as best she could.

She shook her head. 'I'm afraid not. As far as I am aware, she has no one.'

'I see.' The pugnacious-looking Miss Thorpe nodded curtly.

It was impossible to read the woman's thoughts, but Sally couldn't help being apprehensive. She was in two minds to offer to take Joanna home with her, but the possibility of Pierre returning held her back. Fostering a child was not something she'd ever considered before and she couldn't understand why she was flirting with the idea now.

Pierre had been her future and even though he was married she still entertained a fond hope that all would turn out well in the end. If so, they would have their own children. Like most men he was unlikely to welcome looking after someone else's child.

However, if her father could gain custody . . .

Never mind, she thought to herself. If all else failed, Joanna would be found a loving and caring foster home, perhaps one with children of her own age.

It wouldn't hurt to confirm that. 'I take it she'll be fostered.'

Miss Thorpe gave a short sharp laugh as though she'd just suggested they find the child a spare room at Buckingham Palace.

'There are too many orphans and evacuees for that matter, and not enough foster families. Joanna will be placed in an orphanage in Brislington.'

'Brislington! That's miles from here.'

Sally had been prepared for Joanna to be fostered fairly close at hand so she could still see Harry, and also so Sally and her father could visit. It would be enough of wrench for Joanna to be parted from Harry, but at least being on hand to visit would have softened the blow.

Sally eyed the fleshy face, the tiny eyes and the mean mouth. Was it her imagination or was Miss Thorpe enjoying her dismay?

'Is there nowhere closer?'

'I'm afraid not. Stanleybridge House is a very long-established orphanage. They are skilled in dealing with all kinds of children from broken backgrounds, though most are orphans.'

Sally fiddled with her gloves, her mind racing as she weighed up the implications of what Miss Thorpe had said. There was no foster parent and no chance of getting one by the sound of it.

'Can she not continue to be evacuated as her stepmother planned?'

Miss Thorpe shook her head. 'No. Circumstances have changed. Parents now have to pay a certain amount to the homes offered to evacuees. The Ryan child has no parent, therefore no money is forthcoming.'

Sally played with the fingers of her gloves, all the time trying to decide if what she was thinking would be acceptable. Never mind that Pierre might object to her actions, she had no option but to dive straight in. She might regret it later on, but it had to be done.

'What if my father and I took her in?'

Miss Thorpe, a local government officer who had no children of her own and didn't particularly like them, pulled in her chin and glared. 'Your father and you?'

I don't like you, thought Sally. She nodded anyway and adopted a neutral expression. Best first to see where this interview was going rather than responding to instinct. 'That's right. I am her teacher and my father treats her as though she's his daughter – or granddaughter. And then there's Harry to consider.'

Even to her own ears, Sally thought she sounded excited. She had failed to endow her voice with the same neutrality as her face.

'Harry? Is that her brother?'

Feeling slightly foolish, Sally shook her head. 'No. He's her dog.'

Miss Thorpe looked unimpressed. A friend managed the orphanage she recommended. The governing body paid five pounds for every child referred there, which her friend shared with her. Two pounds ten shillings was a very useful sum indeed.

'How old is your father?'

'Sixty-five, but very spry and I look after him very well, just as he looks after me.' Even to her own ears she sounded as though she were trying to impress.

Miss Thorpe's eyes narrowed. 'You're a very good-looking girl. I take it you have a sweetheart?'

Sally felt herself blushing. 'I really don't think that's any of your business!'

'What if we did pass the child into your care? If you get married, who will look after her then? Your father?'

'That is so unfair . . .'

'Your father is in his sixties. He will be way past three score years and ten, as it says in the Bible, when the child starts work. If you marry, the child will be left with him. If he dies she has no one unless you take her in. New husbands are not usually keen to take on other men's brats!'

Sally bristled. 'I dislike your tone, Miss Thorpe. In fact, I can't help but get the impression that you would prefer to place Joanna in an orphanage regardless of who stepped forward to take her.'

'Not at all.' Miss Thorpe was unbending, the sort of woman who holds on to her own opinion regardless of any arguments to the contrary. 'Children thrive in the company of other children. She will also receive a decent education. I'm sure you, as a teacher, would approve of that?'

'That may be, but my feeling is that Joanna would blossom in a family environment – a happy environment with those around her who love her – including her dog.'

'There are no dogs at Stanleybridge. They are not allowed. However it is my firm belief that Stanleybridge would suit the child very well.'

'Joanna. Her name's Joanna.'

'I'm sorry?'

'You keep referring to her as "the child". Not once have you used her proper name.'

Miss Thorpe shrugged nonchalantly. Her manner was dismissive. 'I have a job to do, Miss Hadley. Many children are referred to my department. I have to determine what is best for each one without becoming personally involved.'

Chair legs scraped the dull linoleum floor as Miss Thorpe got to her feet, signalling that the interview was over.

Seething, Sally did the same. Despite her resolve to be neutral and professional, she couldn't help herself. 'Perhaps you should consider giving them numbers,' she snapped disparagingly.

Miss Thorpe gave a weak smile. 'I do.'

CHAPTER THIRTY-THREE

Stanleybridge Orphanage was housed in a building not dissimilar to one of the mills its benefactor had owned. Built of red brick, its windows were small, its doors stout and the interior was starkly grim.

Being a man focused on practicality rather than beauty, Lionel Stanleybridge insisted that only browns, creams and greens were used to decorate its dour interior, the same colours used in the many woollen mills that he owned in North Somerset and West Wiltshire.

The mills produced the finest woollen cloth thanks to their proximity to the sheep grazing the Mendip and Quantock hills and the close proximity of fresh running water.

Joanna was taken to the orphanage on a bus. Miss Thorpe had tried to obtain the use of a council-owned motorcar for the journey just as she had before the war. She'd been told that her use of it did not have a high priority. She'd bristled at that and blamed the child she accompanied rather than the war for the council's decision. She'd never been refused use before.

On the bus Miss Thorpe insisted Joanna sit by the window then squeezed in beside her, her bulk filling two-thirds of the seat. Escape was impossible.

Joanna sought solace in the passing scenery, which went some way to helping her disregard the woman she was with and where she was going, though not entirely. She was still numb from the bombing and the aftershock of learning that Elspeth was dead.

No conversation passed between them until the journey was over.

'Your new home.'

There was a look of self-satisfaction on the face of the children's welfare officer as she eased herself sideways from the seat, snatching at Joanna's wrist just in case she decided to make a run for it.

Joanna was dragged from the bus, her meagre belongings, items of underwear and a new jumper that Sally had brought into the hospital taking up little room in a brown paper carrier bag.

Round-eyed, Joanna stared upwards at the towering height of the orphanage gates. Dark green in colour they were made of iron plate, each plate bound to its neighbour by iron rivets. To Joanna's eyes the rivet ends looked like large boils, as though if she pressed one it would pop.

When Miss Thorpe pulled on a long iron handle a bell clanged gloomily from the other side of the gates.

A door-size portion of the gate opened, and a woman with a pale face and severe bun appeared.

On recognising Miss Thorpe she invited her in unsmilingly. Miss Thorpe duly obliged, tugging Joanna in behind her, her grip undiminished. The two women exchanged few words and those only in regard to required paperwork. Turning swiftly on her heels, the woman led them up the path to the orphanage.

Joanna stared up at the prison-like facade of the building. She was unable to shake off the feeling that if she entered she might never ever leave. For ever! She might be in here for ever!

Even though Elspeth had been less than kind to her, the house in The Vale had been familiar, the only home she had ever known. Suddenly she missed it.

The pale-faced woman opened the huge double doors of the orphanage with an iron key and locked it again once they were inside. The interior was gloomy and cold; the walls painted a glossy brown halfway up and then green all the way to the ceiling.

Dull as the colours were, they'd been dulled even more by age, unpainted since the day the orphanage was built. The colours and paints were used simply because they didn't show the dirt and so needed no repainting.

A marble bust sat on a stone column to her right in an arched alcove. A brass plaque was set in the wall to one side of it with the inscription: LIONEL MERRYWEATHER STANLEYBRIDGE. BENEFACTOR.

On the opposite wall hung a painting of the same man, his ruddy face clashing with the dullness of his clothes. A silver pocket watch hanging from his waistcoat was the only other thing besides his pink cheeks to add colour to the painting.

'No time to stare,' snapped Miss Thorpe as she pushed Joanna through a door leading off the reception hall. The room she entered was wood-panelled and carpeted, a distinct contrast with the reception area.

As the door closed behind her with a dull thud Joanna rubbed at the wrist Miss Thorpe had finally released. Her attention was drawn to the woman behind the desk. The desk was huge and heavy. So was the woman. Joanna couldn't help but stare.

'The girl, Ryan,' said Miss Thorpe, pushing her forward.

The woman sitting behind the desk was enormous. Fat cheeks bulged over a triple chin and bulging neck, where a linen napkin was tucked. In front of her was a huge plate of food.

Joanna's stomach rumbled at the smell. She hadn't eaten since breakfast.

The woman's fat fingers set down the knife and fork. She continued to chew as she spoke. 'Well, you chose your time well! You should know by now that I dislike having my meal times disturbed, Thorpe. Decidedly bad for the digestion.'

Up until now the children's welfare officer had shown the confidence of a woman used to having her own way and being in charge. Her manner now changed.

'I do apologise, Miss Portman, but the council wouldn't allow me the use of a car. I had to come by bus. It's the war, you see.'

Miss Portman grunted something about having a stiff word with that man Churchill if she ever ran into him.

Miss Thorpe placed a brown manila envelope on the desk. 'Here's the paperwork. Would it be possible for you to sign the acceptance form?' The sharp tone of before had become a wheedle.

Miss Portman eyed Miss Thorpe with piggy eyes.

'I know what you're saying, Jane,' she said, letting slip Miss Thorpe's first name as a mark of disrespect.

They'd vowed always to use their professional names in front of outsiders. But Jane Thorpe had interrupted her meal and Miss Portman hated that. She also knew she was angling for her half of the money the orphanage received for giving space to yet another orphaned child.

Thorpe, having found out Miss Portman kept the fee for her own personal use, agreed to share, a fact Miss Portman resented.

'Come back on Monday. We can deal with the formalities then. In the meantime ring the bell outside. Dawson will deal with the child.'

Miss Thorpe knew better than to argue. Grabbing Joanna by the shoulders she turned her round to face the door and pushed her towards it.

'Come on. The sooner I get rid of you the better. I've got a long bus ride back.'

She marched purposefully to a table and rang a gleaming brass hand bell.

Joanna stood feeling helpless and alone, the strings of the brown paper carrier bag cutting into her hand.

The girl who appeared was older than Joanna and wore a pale brown dress beneath a white apron. Her face was as pale as the woman who had let them in and her eyes seemed too large for her face. She was also very thin and the dress she wore looked too small for her, scrawny wrists showing beneath the tight cuffs, the material faded from numerous washings.

'Dawson. This is Ryan. She is expected. Deal with her. I have a bus to catch.'

Without bothering to say goodbye – not that Joanna cared – the children's welfare officer was let out by the same thin woman who had let them in.

The slamming of the door made Joanna jump. She stared at it in dismay, fearing it might never open again, that she'd be incarcerated in this place for ever.

The girl referred to as Dawson spoke to her. 'Shall I take your carrier bag? Those strings can be a devil can't they.' Her smile was warm, a bright oasis in the wan face, and her voice was very soft. 'All the girls in your dormitory are around your age,' she explained as they mounted the stairs. 'They'll tell you the times of lessons and meals, though there is a timetable on the back of the door. But if you forget just ask. I take it you can read?'

Joanna nodded. In fact she'd been top in her class at reading, but she had no wish to tell this girl that. Somehow she didn't think it would go down too well.

They ascended four flights of stairs before entering a long room with four beds ranged along each wall, eight in all. Two dormer windows jutted out onto the roof. A small cupboard partnered each iron-framed bed. There were no pictures on the sludge-coloured walls and no curtains at the windows.

'This is yours,' Dawson said to her. She glanced over her shoulder to see if anyone was around before giving Joanna a quick hug. 'It's very hard when you first come here, but you'll get used to it, in time. My Christian name is Anne, but don't let Mrs Pig or any other adult hear you calling me that. Remember to call me Dawson when they're around.' She grinned. 'That's what we call Miss Portman. Mrs Pig. No need to ask why, is there?'

Something inside that had been totally frozen over seemed to shift slightly, especially when she saw that Anne was smiling. So many emotions seemed contained in that smile: sympathy, affection and pity.

'My name's Joanna Ryan.'

Anne nodded kindly. 'Yes, I know.'

Joanna tried to smile but found it hurt too much to do so. She didn't want to be here, though goodness knows she didn't have anywhere else to go.

Anne read her thoughts. 'We would all prefer to be elsewhere, Joanna. But we can't. We have to make the best of it. There's nowhere else to go.'

Joanna blinked back the tears. 'I miss Harry.'

Anne eyed her quizzically. 'Is Harry your brother?'

Joanna shook her head. 'No. He's my dog.'

Some people might have scoffed at that, but Anne had been here a long time and knew that love from any source was better than none at all.

'Lucky you. I've always wanted a dog. I think I remember having a kitten but it was such a long time ago. Look, I knew you were coming and might be hungry so I saved an apple from my midday meal. Supper isn't until seven.'

She handed Joanna an apple. She devoured it greedily.

'Make sure you hide the apple core. We're not really supposed to eat in the dorm, but it's not unusual for meals to be missed. There's a mouse hole over in the corner. Push it in there when you're finished and then you'd better change into your uniform.'

She pointed to a similar outfit to her own that was laid out on the bed. The pale brown looked just as washed out and Joanna didn't need to be told that it had once been worn by someone else, perhaps more than one person.

'Hide the jumper,' she said after taking a look in the carrier bag. 'You can keep the underwear, though I can't guarantee you getting it back after laundry. Everyone has to take what they're given.'

The other girls arrived in the dormitory at six, after completing their chores and their lessons. Unlike the children at Victoria Park, they didn't come in laughing and chattering, but kept their voices low.

Anne told her that schoolwork was always preceded and followed by chores.

'And we have to wash the dishes after supper,' a girl named Hilary Evans explained to her.

Hilary spoke in a Welsh singsong voice and had been in the home for three years.

'Since I was six,' she explained. 'At least I think I was six, though I might have been seven. Or five!' she added casually, as though numbers were unimportant to her.

She waved her hands about as excitedly as she spoke. Her hands were quite red in places and Joanna was intrigued. Hilary saw her looking.

'I talk too much,' she said, holding her palms outwards so Joanna could see them better. Red marks that came close to drawing blood crisscrossed her palms.

'When Miss Ogden, that's the thin woman who also tends to visitors, can't stop my chattering any longer she sends me to Miss Portman and she gets out her ruler. That's what she hits me with,' she explained, sounding oddly proud, as though pleased to see to Joanna's look of horror.

Anne whispered in her ear. 'Because she's so thin, we call Miss Ogden Miss Stick.'

Joanna managed a tiny smile.

Supper was vegetable pie served with thin gravy and potatoes. It was followed by suet pudding with a spoonful of jam. There was no tea, only water to drink.

Lights out was at eight o'clock. Joanna lay in the dark listening to the snuffling sounds of girls asleep and the sobs of those missing their former life. Even the old building creaked as it settled down for the night, sounding sadly in tune with the girls that lived there.

Thinking about Harry made her want to cry. Harry was her hero. He'd rescued her and she was desperate to get back to him.

She was also missing Sally and her father. If it wasn't for them, Harry might be dead by now. Seb would give him a good home, but she hoped he was missing her.

'I will get back to you,' she whispered into the darkness. 'I will see you again, Harry.'

The walls of the orphanage closed in on her, the big square rooms making her feel she was locked in a box. She made up her mind that she would not stay here. She had run away once and could do so again. It was just a question of waiting for the right opportunity.

CHAPTER THIRTY-FOUR

A nurse prevented Sally from entering the ward.

'Who are you looking for?'

Sally frowned at the empty bed recently occupied by Joanna.

'The little girl, Joanna Ryan. I've brought her some more clothes so she can come home with me. I only brought in a cardigan yesterday. Where is she?'

'I'm sorry, but she left this morning.'

'But she wasn't supposed to leave until this afternoon.' There was no holding back the dismay in her voice.

'I'm sorry. The children's welfare officer took us by surprise too. She was most insistent.' The nurse did not sound as though she entirely approved.

Sally's tone was grim and simmered with anger. 'I bet she was.'

Her intention had been to have another go at persuading Miss Thorpe to reconsider her offer to foster or adopt Joanna. The obnoxious woman had pre-empted her bid to do just that, dragging her away before she could do anything.

She returned home, feeling dejected and angry in equal measure. The conflicting emotions left her numb and solid in an odd kind of way, as though she had become a brick wall that divided one range of emotions from another.

On entering the house she shared with her father, she swept down the passageway leading to the living room at the rear of the house but found it empty.

She frowned, at first thinking he might be taking Harry for a walk in the park.

'Sally!'

He called to her from the front room, his wiry frame shifting between the right and left side of the doorframe.

His muddy boots and ruddy face was evidence that her father had only recently returned from the allotment. Harry had gone with him and now lay contented at his feet, until he saw Sally that is.

The lively ball of golden fur bounded forward, springing up and down as though his legs were made of elastic.

Sally bent down to fuss him. 'Harry. Calm down.'

Once Harry had calmed, Sally realised they had a visitor.

'Amelia!'

Her ladyship sat there wearing a lavender-coloured dress, a fox fur draped like a trophy around her shoulders.

Fear lurched from Sally's guts to her chest and for a moment she couldn't breathe.

Amelia's stern expression was every bit as good as a written or spoken message. 'I've just come from Whitehall. I know someone there.'

So that was the reason for the stunning outfit! 'Pierre?'

'He's all right, Sally. I've had word from his friends at the café in Paris that he's gone on the run. You see, he'd joined the resistance and they attacked a German patrol. A number of his compatriots were killed. A few were captured and interrogated but he managed to escape.'

A mixture of fear and surprise caused Sally to gasp so vehemently that her breath seemed to stall in her throat. There was something about the expression on Amelia's face that didn't ring true. She was hiding something.

Sally sat down, her eyes fiercely holding Amelia's. 'There's more. I can see it in your eyes.'

Amelia looked oddly crestfallen, as though what she'd set out to do had not come off, namely hiding what had really happened and what she was feeling.

'I feel guilty telling you about Pierre's marriage, though there's a lot more I thought it his responsibility to tell you about. But the situation being as it is . . .'

As her voice trailed away Sally felt a bolt of fear shoot through her.

'I take it it's something to do with Adele?'

Amelia looked down at the floor and her fingers beat a nervous tattoo on the chair arms before she found her voice.

'Adele has always been wild. There's no harm in her as such, she just can't help herself. Like many other men, Pierre was drawn to her as a moth to a flame. She's wild, exciting and incredibly beautiful, exuberant is a good description. The thing is, she's prone to spontaneous and ill-conceived affections and notions. She just can't help herself.' Amelia raised her eyes watching for Sally's reaction.

Although discomforted by the bold description of this Gallic beauty, Sally urged Amelia to go on. 'I have broad shoulders,' she stated, her tawny hair flying around as she nonchalantly tossed her head. Inside her stomach felt as though she'd dined on barbed wire.

'I hinted to you that Pierre and Adele became at odds over her political beliefs. Adele supports Hitler and all he stands for. Beautiful she might be, but her judgement is flawed. Her latest lover is a German general. It may be she had something to do with Pierre's escape. One can never tell with Adele. War or not, she is not one to abide by the rules.'

Sally swallowed, her thoughts very much her own. Pierre was married, yet she hadn't banished him from her heart. *I should be feeling guilty*, she thought to herself. *Am I wanton because I don't, in which case am I any better than Elspeth Ryan?*

'I need to see him again.'

She heard herself saying it, but Amelia's description of Adele was something of a salve to any guilty feelings she might – should – harbour.

'Do we guess as to where he's gone?'

'My guess is Spain. I was going to go there myself once to fight in the civil war. Strange that it's a neutral country now, though who knows what it's really like for the people living therein.'

Seb had been listening quietly, Harry was lying at his feet and making low noises in his throat as Seb stroked his ears.

'When did this happen?'

Amelia shrugged. 'The message was brought to England by the daughter of a friend, who had met up with Pierre at some point in France. Her father's English and a civil servant in the War Office. Her mother French.'

Seb frowned. 'How come she was in France at this late stage? Come to that, how did she get out?'

'I'm not sure of the whys and wherefores and got a very blank look when I dared to ask. I got the impression I was being warned not to enquire too deeply.'

Sally frowned.

Seb explained. 'Her ladyship means the young woman was on a secret mission. They'll be recruiting many people who speak fluent French and flying them in behind enemy lines.'

'I can't comment either way,' said Amelia. 'Except to say that Pierre is likely to be heading back to England in the hope that he'll get snapped up to do the same.'

Sally devoured the words. Suddenly it felt as though the weight of the world had been lifted from her shoulders. Pierre was on his way home, but what about his wife?

'Don't ask me about Adele,' said Amelia immediately reading her expression. 'I cannot say whether she'll come with him. They may be married but as I have already explained to you, Adele will suit herself. She belongs to no man. She never will. As for what her political allegiances might be now . . . I cannot say.'

Seb got up from his chair. 'I'll just put the kettle on. Cup of tea, your ladyship?'

'Amelia. Call me Amelia, Mr Hadley.'

Seb smiled. 'Only if you call me Seb.'

Amelia's attention switched to the dog. 'I've always liked cocker spaniels. Judging by the look in Harry's eyes, I would say he's of above average intelligence.'

'He rescued the little Ryan girl from a bombsite. Nobody else realised she was still there.'

'I read about him in the paper. He's quite famous.'

Sally felt an instant prick of pride. The *Evening World* had sent a reporter and a photographer along. Her father had been over the moon though insisted he would not be photographed. 'The dog's the hero, not me.'

Harry looked from one woman to the other and wagged his tail.

Amelia laughed. 'Yes, young fella,' she said, ruffling his ears. 'You know we're talking about you.'

Looking at him, Sally was reminded of Joanna's predicament. She'd made enquiries of the children's welfare department at the council offices, asking to see Miss Thorpe's superior if possible. There was no point in seeing Miss Thorpe. The woman seemed openly hostile.

'Are you a relative?' a female voice had asked on the other end of the telephone.

She'd wanted to lie, but couldn't bring herself to do it. Yet again she was told that the children's welfare officer concerned had made a decision and in the absence of a relative the decision would be adhered to.

Remembering brought a more sombre look to her face. The corners of her mouth turned downwards and her eyes filled with sadness.

Amelia yet again picked up on Sally's mood.

'Your father said the little girl is now an orphan. Has she any relatives?'

Sally shook her head. No matter how heartened she was at the prospect of Pierre returning, she still felt that somehow she had let Joanna down. But what could she do? Who could possibly help?

'Tell me,' urged Amelia.

Sally sighed, her hair falling forward like a veil around her face as she bent her head and began to explain.

Firstly she outlined Joanna's background, her mother dying some years ago, her father remarrying then getting killed fairly recently. From there it was a short step to the dreaded Elspeth, Joanna's stepmother. From there she explained about Harry.

'She found Harry in a sack somebody had thrown into a stream. Joanna rescued him but couldn't take him home. Her stepmother had already had her pet cat destroyed in the first week of the war.'

Amelia slapped her hands on her thighs. 'Damned government! They panicked everybody. I thought I'd never see the end of the stream of pets abandoned at my front gate.'

'Mrs Ryan told the police to put Harry down. Luckily we arrived in time. The woman's a monster. To say she wasn't kind to her stepdaughter is putting it mildly. The woman enjoyed bullying somebody who couldn't fight back.'

Amelia nodded sagely. 'I've met plenty like that in my lifetime.'

'She's dead now. She was buried alive in the bombing when Joanna was rescued.'

She didn't go on to mention that she was in bed with Arnold Thomas. The man was a separate case, not quite himself following the death of his wife and taken advantage of by a venal, grasping woman.

'I'm glad to hear it. Sorry,' she said, 'does that sound a bit harsh?'

Sally shook her head. 'I understand what you mean. Elspeth Ryan used to lock her stepdaughter in the coalhouse on a regular basis. Pitch dark, dirty and no food.'

'So where is Joanna now?'

'In an orphanage.'

'Really?'

Sally leaned into her hand which covered half her face as she went on to tell her about the attitude and decision of Miss Thorpe, the children's welfare officer.

Sally came out from behind her hand to see Amelia eyeing her strangely.

'What is it?'

'Are you sure she's been taken to Stanleybridge Orphanage?'

'Yes. Is there something significant about that?'

Seb interrupted them, returning with a tray of tea and a plate of homemade biscuits. 'Significant about what?'

'The orphanage,' said Sally, somewhat impatiently. She turned to face Amelia. 'Go on.'

Amelia took a deep breath. 'As a magistrate and a woman of substance, I am called upon to serve the community on many levels. One of the services I undertake is to sit on the governing body of the orphanage you mention. I am also a city councillor. The children's welfare office is currently under investigation regarding accusations of fraud, that is, placing children in private orphanages when council-run establishments are readily available, and, might I add, run with the good of the children in mind. Rumours are rife that money is exchanging hands and an audit is currently on going. Private orphanages are paid by the council to look after children, but quite frankly such establishments have had their day. Orphanages where religion and discipline is the order of the day belong to the past.' She sighed. 'Unfortunately old habits die hard. Some still believe in sparing the rod spoils the child.'

Sally's eyes brightened. 'Do you think you can help?'

Amelia pursed her lips. 'I've had a number of misgivings about Stanleybridge for some time. Your experience of Miss Thorpe's bullying attitude only serves to strengthen my feelings. I think the time is right for me to pay them a little visit.'

Stiff with concern Sally leaned forward, her hands tightly clasped and an intense look on her face. 'Do you really think you can help?'

Amelia tossed her head as though there was nothing she couldn't accomplish once she put her mind to it.

'I think I can cause an earthquake.'

CHAPTER THIRTY-FIVE

Joanna lay awake for hours that first night, trying not to make a sound though the tears streamed down her face.

Sobs came from a bed further along the dormitory. Whoever it was sounded as though their heart was breaking.

'Quiet! Miss Stick will hear you,' came a warning whisper from another bed.

Joanna hid her head beneath the bedclothes in case she too broke into unrelenting sobs and Miss Stick heard her.

Hidden from everyone and everything around her, this was where she could think and her chief thought was escape. How she would do that she didn't know, but something was bound to turn up. That's what she told herself before she finally fell asleep. Somehow she would escape.

The loud jangling of a hand bell jerked her from sleep. Rolling onto her back she rubbed at her eyes and knew that it was morning.

Wooden beams criss-crossed the ceiling above her. A thin thread of daylight penetrated from the dormer windows. A single light bulb hung in the middle of the room. She watched as a spider journeyed down the long wire by which it was attached to the ceiling.

The girl who occupied the bed next to her was already halfway to being dressed. She gave her a nudge. 'Don't just lie there. Quick get up or you'll be for it!' she hissed.

Dressed now, Joanna watched the other girls, ready to copy whatever they did. She saw them pull back their bedding after which they stood at the foot of their beds ramrod stiff.

The tall thin woman Joanna recognised as the one who had let her and Miss Thorpe into the orphanage yesterday strode between the rows of beds.

The clumping sound of her heels hitting the floor only ceased when she walked halfway down each bed, stopped and inhaled deeply.

Seemingly satisfied there were no nasty whiffs, she carried on down the length of the dormitory.

It wasn't until she came to the last bed it became clear that she had found what she was looking for.

'Jones! Wet again? That's the second time this week.' Her voice was as ear-splitting as the sound of metal scraping against metal, such a scary sound coming out of a skinny body.

The girl standing at the end of the bed began to tremble. Suddenly she broke into deep, heartrending sobs. Joanna was sure they were the same sobs she had heard the night before and thought how unfair it was to shout out what the poor little girl had done. She guessed she was only her own age, perhaps a little younger.

Nobody moved. Nobody smirked or murmured a sound.

Miss Stick came to stand beside the trembling girl. 'A wet bed yet again, Jones!' The tirade continued. 'If you go on like this you'll sleep on the floor, or we'll hang you up on the washing line with all the other wet sheets!'

A trickle of urine ran down the girl's leg and puddled on the floor.

'You disgusting child!' A bony hand slapped the girl's cheek, which resulted in louder sobs and more pee, some of which splashed over Miss Stick's shoes.

A look of disgust came to the pinched face.

Joanna felt her heart lurch in sympathy. Couldn't the woman see how frightened the poor girl was?

'Simmons! Fetch me a cleaning cloth.'

A girl with short brown hair ran to do as she'd been bid. In a second she came back with a cloth that she handed to Miss Stick. In turn the woman thrust at the sobbing girl.

'Clean it up!'

Still crying, the girl dropped down onto all fours.

The other girls were told to stay and watch as the girl attempted to wipe up the wetness.

'Let this be a warning to all of you too lazy to go to the lavatory.'

Having finished wiping the floor, the girl stood up, her red-rimmed eyes blinking with fear.

A cruel smile twisted the woman's hawk-like features. 'Now wash your face.'

Tear-filled eyes looked pleadingly from above flushed pink cheeks. The girl started to head for the end of the room where the washbasin was situated.

'No. Wash it with the cloth you have in your hand!'

Joanna was immediately filled with a sense of outrage. She'd endured her stepmother's neglect and cruel punishments, but this was far worse. She had never been humiliated like this in public. Her heart went out to the little girl. This was just not right.

'That's not fair!' The sound of her own voice filled her with surprise. She heard an intake of breath from the other girls.

Miss Stick turned angry black eyes in her direction and stripes of deep puce appeared on her cheekbones. 'You don't think so? Come here, girl.'

A long thin finger pointed at the floor.

Joanna walked the length of the dormitory feeling the eyes of the others following her.

The woman towered over her, a thin strip of humanity between her and the daylight beginning to seep through the window behind her. 'Ryan, isn't it?'

'Joanna Ryan.'

'So why don't you think it fair, Ryan?'

Joanna dragged up every bit of courage she had. 'She's probably lost her parents and her home and been through nasty things. We all have.'

'And what makes you think that, Ryan?' said the woman, her thin fingers tapping Joanna's shoulder.

'There's a war on. Nasty things are happening.'

Miss Stick dragged the other girl forward, the pee-soaked cloth dangling from her hand.

'Right, Jones, Ryan's spoken up for you so she can take your punishment instead of you. That should teach her never to do so again. Well!' She pushed the girl forward. 'Go on!'

The girl's pink face came close. Her lips moved. 'I'm sorry,' she whispered, her rosebud mouth quivering with fear.

Joanna held her breath and closed her eyes. Only a deep-rooted anger stopped her from crying. Why were adults so cruel to children and animals? These girls had lost their parents through no fault of their own. There was nobody to show them any kindness.

Later, as she sat at the breakfast table, the girl from the next bed to hers passed her a wet flannel, with which to wash her face out of sight beneath the table. 'Don't let Miss Stick see.'

'Don't you ever think of escaping?' Joanna whispered back, as she stirred her dish of unsweetened porridge.

'There's nowhere else to go.'

Dishes had to be washed before they trooped in a single file to assembly and then to their lessons. Their first lesson was history, which Joanna quite enjoyed. The teacher was called Miss Baker and was younger than the other women at the orphanage. According to her friend Edna from the next bed, she didn't live at the orphanage.

It turned out that Miss Baker taught just about every subject, except for religion and arithmetic. Neither did she oversee domestic science, which seemed to consist of polishing the brass door handles and plaques, cleaning the floors and dealing with the laundry.

'It's sunny outside,' Edna whispered to her. 'I'm hoping to get the job of cleaning the brass on the front doors. It's hard work but at least it's outside.'

It was Miss Stick who shared out the chores for the day. Her thin fingers pointed like twigs allotting jobs to each girl. 'You, you and you to the laundry.'

Then the twig-like finger pointed at Edna and Joanna. Joanna heard Edna hold her breath before sighing with relief. 'You two for cleaning the brass both inside and out. While the daylight holds, start outside first and work inwards.'

The two girls collected a wooden carrier containing polish and dusters plus a small brush for getting into the places where even a small finger couldn't push a cloth.

Joanna felt Miss Stick's eyes on her. She kept her own lowered, just in case she was capable of reading her plan to escape.

'Shall we put our coats on, miss?' asked Edna.

'There's no need. Polishing vigorously will keep you warm.'

Sleeping in the barn by the river had taught Joanna how cold a November night could be. Soon it would be December and it promised to be a hard winter. If the opportunity to escape did occur, a coat would have been of great benefit.

Then I'll have to run faster, Joanna told herself as she and Edna were let out of the main doors to begin their labours.

'I won't be too far away,' Miss Stick announced as she unlocked the door. 'Come in as soon as you're finished.'

The cold air nipped at their faces. Each of them grinned at each other and remarked how rosy their cheeks had become.

'Better get on,' Edna muttered. 'The sooner we're finished the sooner we're back in the warm and—'

Joanna was only half listening. Her gaze had wandered to the gates at the end of the drive. They were high and like the main doors locked against the outside world. They were also completely smooth and therefore impossible to climb over.

A tree stump to one side of the gates looked useful and there were other trees close to the high brick wall surrounding the grounds.

Bereft of leaves, the branches were easy to evaluate, and there were round holes in the trunk that would give easy footholds, the lower branches reaching down like welcoming arms. Climb those and she could make her way onto the top of the wall. From there she would have to seek footholds on the other side, or jump.

'Ryan!'

Edna's sharp tone broke into Joanna's wandering thoughts.

'Come on,' said Edna thrusting the tin of Brasso at her. 'I can't do this all by myself.'

Joanna took the cloth as if in a dream, her gaze remaining fixed on the metal gates and the trees.

Guessing what was on her mind, Edna sucked in her breath.

'You can't escape, Ryan,' she whispered, glancing over her shoulder as though fearing somebody was close by. There was no one. Everyone else was inside.

'My friends call me Joanna!'

Edna winced at Joanna's fierce expression and her resolute tone. She'd only seen that expression on the staff in this place, never on one of the orphans. She glanced towards where Joanna was looking.

Edna lowered her voice. 'You are going to try to escape, aren't you!'

Joanna kept her eyes fixed on the drive and the heavy metal gates but said nothing.

Edna tried again. 'Even if you did manage it, where would you go?'

Joanna sucked in her bottom lip. She had tossed and turned the previous night thinking it through. The other girls had been here longer than she and accepted their lot. But she would never in a million years accept the lot doled out to her. She would not stay here. Harry was missing her.

During the night she had asked herself the question Edna was asking her now. Where would she go?

'I mean, is there somebody out there for you? An aunt or something?'

Joanna nodded and a faint smile came to her lips. 'Harry.'

'Is he your brother?'

It wasn't the first time she'd been asked and the idea that he might be was growing on her. They were that close and in the absence of any brother or sister, he was as close as she could get.

'Kind of.'

She could have also mentioned Miss Hadley and her father, but a warning voice told her not to do so. If she did get away Edna would be questioned. The threat of being shut away or having the ruler across her hands would loosen her tongue. These people did not know where Harry lived and who he was. They would presume he was a brother, just as Edna had done.

'You're very brave,' said Edna, as she began rubbing the Brasso into the plaque. 'Now come on or we'll never get this done. Then we'll both be in trouble.'

Receiving no response, she turned round to see Joanna running across the damp grass towards the boundary wall, skirting bushes and her skirt catching on bare rose bushes and tangled shrubs.

Her breath caught in her throat. For a moment she wanted to run after her, but obedience and fear had become deeply ingrained. Her eyes glittered with that deep-seated fear and the need to make a decision. She could carry on here polishing the brass and pretend she hadn't seen Joanna run for the gates. Or she could shout a warning through the double doors that would bring Miss Stick running.

Edna had come to Stanleybridge before the outbreak of war. Her mother had died and she'd never known her father. Her grandmother had taken her in and for a while she'd been happy. On the death of her grandmother she had come here, to Stanleybridge, where she'd made a rule never to get too close to any of the other girls. She was alone in the world and had disciplined herself to accept it. Making an instant decision, she pushed on one of the mahogany doors so hard it banged against the wall.

'Miss Ogden! Miss Ogden!' she shouted. 'Ryan is running away.'

* * *

Her chauffeur having joined the army, Lady Amelia Ambrose sat gripping the wheel of her car on the drive to Stanleybridge Orphanage.

Seb Hadley sat next to her, his coat collar turned up around his face. The day was cold. The car had no heating. Every so often they stopped to scrape the ice off both the inside and outside of the windscreen.

Her attaché case took up a small portion of the back seat, the other half taken up by Harry and Sally.

Every so often, Seb glanced at the stern-faced woman sitting beside him. Seb decided he'd seen stone statues in the graveyard with softer expressions than hers.

The rest of the time he stared through the windscreen at the road ahead. Worrying about Joanna had made him turn inwards. He had no wish to discuss what they were about to do; it was bad enough just worrying about the outcome.

Sally too was sitting silently, her eyes gazing out of the window at the passing scene without taking anything in. Everything passed in a haze. She couldn't quite believe what they were going to do and what the outcome might be. It was hard to stay positive, but she did her best.

Harry lay with his head between his paws, not even looking up when Sally scratched his head. It was as though he knew they were on a particularly important mission, Sally thought to herself.

As they approached the orphanage gates, Sally was overcome with a need to break the silence. 'Do they know we're coming?'

'I phoned to say I was coming. I did not state my reason. Nor did I say that I was bringing company with me or that I would be bringing papers with me that would put an end to their cosy little world!'

Woe betide anyone who gets in her way, thought Seb. Boudicca had a chariot with knives on the wheels; Amelia had a sharp tongue and a piercing look.

Amelia poked the car's snub-nosed bonnet into the recess in front of the main gates, put on the handbrake and got out.

A young woman with soft brown eyes and a worried expression appeared in answer to the jangling of the wrought-iron bell pull.

Seb opened his window a fraction and strained forward to hear.

'Lady Ambrose! I didn't know you were coming, but I'm so glad you are here.'

'Nice to see you, Miss Baker. Might I ask you a few questions?'

'Of course.'

Amelia got out of the car, standing head to head with the young woman she'd addressed as Miss Baker.

Their conversation was animated and although Seb did his best, his hearing wasn't as good as it used to be.

Amelia got back behind the steering wheel and the young woman opened the main gate so she could drive the car through.

'Right,' declared Amelia. 'Into the breach my friends!'

Seb glanced over his shoulder at Sally, their eyes meeting in mutual agreement that her ladyship sounded even more determined.

'Is she a friend or an enemy?' Seb asked her.

'That was Miss Baker, the schoolteacher. She was about to jump ship but I've asked her to stay until things are sorted out. And in answer to whether she's a friend or an enemy, she's actually a witness. It's not just her job at the orphanage that's numbered, it's the orphanage itself!'

Sally looked over her shoulder. Miss Baker had left the gates open and was smiling as she followed them up the drive to the house. Sally guessed that she had broken a rule. Whatever it was, she was certainly looking very pleased about it.

Whoever was waiting behind the door had no doubt heard the car approach.

They all got out, leaving Harry on the back seat, though he was no longer lying down but sitting up, his eyes bright as though he knew the reason they were there and that Joanna was close by.

They were shown into the principal's office where the smell of recently eaten food caused Sally to wrinkle her nose.

'Lady Ambrose!' Miss Portman gushed welcome as her pudgy hands pushed her up from her desk. Her fat face was shiny with grease and Sally detected a sly sharpness in her piggy eyes.

Miss Thorpe also got to her feet, her jaw dropping as she recognised Sally from their brief meeting at the hospital.

Not noticing the alarm on the face of the children's welfare officer, Miss Portman went on unperturbed.

'I've arranged tea and biscuits.' Her eyes took in Seb and his daughter. 'Though I was only expecting one person . . .'

Her voice trailed away.

Amelia refrained from introducing them. 'We'll come to them later. They're only half the reason I'm here.'

There was a loud thud as Amelia slammed her attaché case onto the desk. She lost no time in bringing out the manila folder.

'I have here a set of accounts that passed between this orphanage and the child welfare office.'

The sheets of lined accounts paper were fanned out on the desk.

The colour drained from Miss Thorpe's face. She'd wondered why she'd been summoned here today. The reason was now abundantly clear.

The principal did her best to maintain a fixed smile, but Sally detected a worried look in her eyes.

'According to these records, Stanleybridge Orphanage has had twenty children placed here over the last six months when the council specifically ordered the establishment needed a thorough upgrade before *any* children were placed here. However, on checking the records, I see that the five-pound foundling fee was paid by the council for each of these children, yet none of that money shows in the orphanage accounts.'

Miss Thorpe attempted to explain. 'There was no room anywhere else and—'

Amelia turned accusing eyes on the trembling woman. 'And each of those children were placed here by you, Miss Thorpe. Nobody else. Can you explain what happened to each of those five-pound placement fees?'

Miss Thorpe's face reddened. Even Miss Portman looked taken aback, though only momentarily. Thinking it might be possible to lay all the blame at Miss Thorpe's door, she turned her fat neck and said, 'Jane! Surely there is some explanation.'

She turned back to see Amelia wearing an expression capable of turning flesh to salt. 'I have just said I have also a copy of the orphanage accounts to hand.' Her tone was cutting.

'They're none of your business!' declared Miss Portman, her pink face turning crimson.

'They are my business both as a member of the governing body, a councillor and, just as a little extra, a magistrate. You will recall it is required that a copy of the orphanage accounts is required to be submitted each year. This year they were a little early. You're in trouble – both of you!'

Recognising they were beaten, the two women put on a show of distancing themselves from each other.

Miss Thorpe pointed at the principal. 'It was her fault! She put me up to it!'

Miss Portman's fat hands slapped the desk. 'Judas! It was you. You were the greedy one! Always after more and here as soon as you knew the five pounds had been paid.'

A thin stick of a woman chose that moment to come in with a tray of tea. She had a sour expression that seemed to wrinkle on detecting the atmosphere she'd walked into.

'And now for the other matter. A child was brought here who had already been offered a home with Mr Hadley and his daughter. Their offer was rejected.'

Miss Thorpe immediately jumped in.

'Well, he is of a certain age and she is unmarried. What would she know about children?'

'She is a teacher! Joanna Ryan's teacher, in fact. She's ideal to foster and later to adopt the child and, before you argue, might I suggest that the five-pound foundling fee swayed your decision, not the suitability or otherwise of these good people?'

The thin woman with the tea was backing towards the door, a frightened look on her face. Before she could get much further, Miss Baker, the teacher they'd met at the gate, appeared in the doorway to provide a barrier for any further retreat.

She looked beyond Miss Ogden addressing Amelia directly. 'Joanna tried to escape. They've locked her away.'

Seb and Sally, alarmed at how it might affect Joanna, were up in a minute. 'Do you know where?'

Miss Baker shook her head. 'No, I'm afraid not. They have a variety of grim punishment places.' She shook her head. 'That poor child. This place is straight out of Dickens.'

Seb was already at the front door, Sally behind him. Amelia ordered Miss Portman and Miss Ogden to get their things together.

'And you stay where you are,' she ordered Miss Thorpe.

When they got outside, Harry was barking excitedly and pawing at the car windows.

'Go on, boy,' shouted Seb opening the car door.

Harry bounded out and ran as fast as his little legs could go, his tongue hanging out between bouts of excited barking.

Behind the door of the outhouse Joanna heard his barking and lifted her head.

'Harry?'

The barking continued.

'Harry! Harry!'

Soon he was scratching at the wooden door of the shed.

The door burst open and there they were, the people who loved her and, most of all, there was Harry.

CHAPTER THIRTY-SIX

Amelia drew in her chin so it rested against the thick neckline of the man's jumper she was wearing.

'Everything is arranged,' she said quietly. 'Joanna is coming home with you. I've persuaded the committee that you're the right people to take her in. Fostering at first until we see how things go, then adoption.'

Seb swiped at his eyes. He'd never believed in tears of happiness but he did now.

'All's well that ends well,' remarked Sally.

'This is not quite the end scene. There's still the paperwork to deal with.'

Sally shook her head in disbelief. 'I really don't know how you did it, I really don't.'

Amelia laughed. 'Once the serious provisions were being considered, I told the department that I did not dispute that a child needs a good education and the company of children of their own age. I pointed out to them she was a bright child and had been doing very well at school until she was taken away. She also had schoolfriends she was still in contact with. All she needed was love and that is where you and your father come in.' A secretive look lit up Amelia's face. 'I believe you and your father really will make her life complete – and Harry of course.'

Sally's gaze travelled to a group of girls hanging out of the front doors of the main house. They were oddly silent at first, but then began to cheer.

'And Stanleybridge? What will happen to the children?'

A self-satisfied smile lit up Amelia's face. 'You might say I have carte blanche to deal with this place and its unfortunate inmates. I have advised the council to dismiss the principal and also that Thorpe woman. An interim replacement has been arranged until some new blood is introduced. As yet I haven't broached the subject, but do you think you're up to the job, Sally? I mean as a live-in teacher. We could really do with that. I know it's a lot to ask, but I think you and your father could really help turn these children's lives around. What do you say?'

Sally's jaw dropped. Lady Amelia Ambrose was nothing if not forthright.

'Well!' Sally heaved a big sigh. Amelia's proposal had taken her by surprise. 'You certainly don't beat about the bush.'

'Never could stand prevaricating. Get to the point. That's me.'

'So I've noticed. But I'm only a teacher, I haven't had this kind of training.'

'You deal with children every day and they love you. I think that's training enough, whether it's in a school inside or outside this place. The children's lives will improve. I guarantee it. Oh, there's just one other thing. I'll be on site too.'

'I thought you might be,' she said laughingly. 'A lovely place for animals.'

'I didn't think you'd want the paperwork or the responsibility of actually running the place. That lot has fallen to me. I'm of the right age and right credentials. My father was a bit of a philanthropist. He gave a lot of his wealth to this kind of establishment and insisted I knew something about running them. He was old-fashioned and expected his children to learn from the bottom up, so to speak!'

Sally was speechless.

Amelia carried on. 'I've spotted a little cottage in the grounds and there are bags of outbuildings. The War Office can have my place for the duration, I'll have this one. More room for more animals. Until the war ends, then we'll see what we shall see as regards this old place and the children in it.'

'You don't think we can find homes for the children?'

Amelia shook her head. 'The bombing's barely started. There's going to be more orphans in need of a home. The authorities are going to be stretched as to where to put them, which means we're going to be busy.'

The days following Joanna being rescued swept past in a blur of activity and hope.

People listened to Lady Amelia Ambrose-DeVere, not just because she was titled but because she got things done and knew how to do things properly and with integrity. Things could not have worked out so well if it hadn't been for her.

There was just one more thing that would make everything quite perfect.

Sally rebuked herself for feeling slightly ungrateful. Yes, she liked the idea of helping Amelia to run Stanleybridge, and so did her father, who was to be employed as grounds man and gardener.

'Plenty of room for growing vegetables, and flowers. I miss flowers,' he said soulfully. 'Might as well add a bit of colour to the old place. And the children could help.'

Amelia's ulterior motives regarding requisitioning part of the orphanage's extensive grounds to house abandoned cats and dogs came as no big surprise to Seb either.

'The children will love it. And so will Joanna and Harry. This old place is going to change for the better. The kids might all be orphans but they'll be happy here.'

Sally certainly couldn't argue with that.

Everything was perfect and she should be supremely happy. Instead, the hole that remained in her life woke her in the middle of the night.

There had been no word from Pierre except for that letter received just before her ladyship had informed her that he was married. She'd replied anyway, not that it was likely to have reached him, things being the way they were.

Lying there in the dead of night she tried to visualise where he might be.

Some people claimed to have psychic powers where loved ones were concerned, knowing instinctively whether they were dead or alive.

Such things are nonsense, she told herself. You didn't wake up because you thought you heard him call you, you woke because you've got things on your mind. Including him.

Of course she did. Psychic powers were nonsense, she told herself. She felt no sense of either his well-being or his whereabouts. All she did was visualise him hidden in a hay barn, perhaps staggering over a mountain pass or dirty, wet and tired on a leaking boat in the middle of the sea.

No word. No letter. Nothing.

The visions she had of him were nothing but the residue of hopeful dreams.

CHAPTER THIRTY-SEVEN

On first being shown her bedroom Joanna had stood round-eyed she tried to take in what she was being told. 'Should I really be here?'

Sally frowned and smiled at the same time. 'Of course. You're part of the family now.'

Joanna looked puzzled. 'But what about the others? Will they become part of a family too?'

Sally shook her head. 'I wish I could say it will happen, but there are so many children who've lost their parents, so many homes destroyed. All we can do is to make their lives as comfortable and happy as possible.'

Joanna looked down at the floor as the harsh memories of her first night at Stanleybridge came back. The girls in that draughty attic bedroom, the niggardly food portions and the cruel treatment meted out for a nervous child wetting the bed.

Sally bent down so her face was level with that of Joanna's.

'We can't fit all the girls into this wing of the house, but they're still under the same roof. They'll be better looked after than they've ever been. We can't adopt them all into our small family, but we can make this a happy home, all of us under one roof.'

Sally's smile was reassuring. The tension left Joanna's shoulders but a quizzical look came to her eyes. 'Does this mean Seb is my father?'

'Your adoptive father. Yes.'

Joanna's mouth puckered into another question, one that had sprung into her mind and was as bright as a buttercup. 'Does this mean you're my sister?'

Sally smiled. 'Yes, I suppose it does.'

*   *   *

The grey days of winter slowly but surely turned into spring. Wildflowers brightened pieces of waste ground that had not yet been put under the plough. Flowers had disappeared from many gardens, each individual doing their best to produce food to feed the nation, or at least their own families. On top of that the railings from around Victoria Park had also disappeared, the metal required to make aircraft so they'd been told.

The spring of 1941 brought brighter weather but the bombing of British cities, especially London, grew ever more intense.

Everything seemed to be sprouting and that included Joanna and Harry. Joanna was filling out and her cheeks were rosy now she was getting enough food. The scared look had vanished from her eyes, at least during daytime. Being locked in dingy places no longer posed a threat, but the experience would take some time to get over.

Harry was no longer the floppy puppy he'd been when she'd first found him in the stream that day a year and a half ago. He had grown into a handsome dog, and although Joanna was his closest friend he found time for the other kids too, in fact, he was in his element. Harry loved all those who loved him.

Seb had thrown himself into making the extensive gardens and greenhouses around the sombre-looking house productive again. An army of adoring assistants helped him in this task.

'Any of you done gardening before?' he'd asked.

Some nodded but the majority, kids from London's docklands, shook their heads. Just the look of them touched Seb's kind heart. Judging by their scabby faces they hadn't eaten vegetables for a very long time, let alone seen them growing.

One day he found Joanna fingering the petals of a bright yellow daffodil, a faraway look in her eyes.

He laid his hand on her shoulder. 'Penny for your thoughts.'

She didn't look up at him. In fact, her head drooped further.

'What's the matter? Come on. Out with it.'

When she looked up at him he could see her eyes were tear-filled. 'There weren't no flowers on my dad's grave.'

Seb looked surprised. 'None?'

Joanna shook her head, her small lips quivering as she turned her gaze back to the dancing daffodils. 'Elspeth said we had to go to the funeral so we'd get the money. Other people took flowers, but she didn't.'

Seb felt the pain Joanna was feeling. His sharp eyes, shadowed by thick white eyebrows, looked over her head to a pretty little spot beneath a birch tree. The trunk of the tree glistened silver in the pale sunlight. In front of it was the remains of a stone cross, its features weathered and softened by rain. Rumour had it there used to be an abbey here at one time.

He'd had a mind to ring the base of the tree with bulbs which would have hidden the old cross from view. Now he had an idea.

'How about we set up a memorial to your dad – and to your mum, for that matter. What say you I carve their names on that stone over there and we plant flowers in front of it?'

Joanna looked up at him. 'Does it matter that they're not buried there?'

'No.' Seb shook his head. 'They're both in heaven. Both together now. So if their names are here and you're remembering them, then that's where they are. Wherever your heart is, that's where they will be.'

After finding a decent hammer and chisel, Seb etched the names of Joanna's parents onto the old stone. Once it was finished he stood back from it to admire his handiwork. 'Not a bad job,' he murmured to himself.

The flowers he'd planted would take some time to come up, so with that in mind he handed Joanna a large bunch of wildflowers interspersed with daffodils.

'For you to lay in front of your mum and dad's memorial,' he said gently.

Joanna took the bouquet in her trembling hand and looked up at him for guidance.

'Go on,' he said. 'Go and put them in front of their stone, so they'll know you haven't forgotten them.'

Joanna swallowed nervously. 'Aren't you coming with me?'

He shook his head. 'No. They're your parents and likely as not there's plenty you want to say to them.'

'Do you speak to your wife?'

A lump came to Seb's throat. 'Every day. Everywhere.'

Seb was enjoying himself because he was doing what he loved doing and the kids filled the hole in his life Grace had left when she'd died. He was doubly happy when a dozen yellow chicks arrived.

'Every one's a layer,' he'd boasted, as he placed the fluffy yellow bundles in the wooden coop he'd built them, complete with a wire-covered run. The sturdy wooden structure was placed in a cosy corner of the barn, where an old horse Amelia had found abandoned chewed hay.

Those who heard his declaration hoped he was right. A white egg with a yolk in the middle was a luxury, scrambled eggs made from the dried variety being the norm nowadays and not much liked.

'I could live in here myself,' Seb confided to his daughter as he surveyed the high rafters and the piles of hay and straw.

'You have a bed in the house, Dad.'

'I might have to sleep out here. There's foxes to consider.'

A range of pigsties at the rear of the property had been converted to house the overflow from Lady Amelia's animal refuge. Two donkeys, a goat and a Shetland pony had joined the unending parade of dogs and cats left at her door. These munched their way through the orchard, where the long grass and fallen apples that hadn't been found added to their diet.

The Hadley house near Victoria Park had been let to people whose own home had been destroyed in a bombing raid.

Despite her new surroundings, Sally still awoke in the middle of the night hearing her name being called. Sometimes the unmistakeable timbre of Pierre's voice reverberated in her head, so strong, so believable, that she answered, 'Pierre? Is that you?'

There was never any reply.

For a while she would lie there listening to the old house creaking and groaning as it settled down for the night.

Tonight it was Joanna who woke her. 'No! Let me out! Let me out!'

Sally grabbed her dressing gown and raced along to Joanna's room.

The child was sitting up in bed, her eyes staring at the far wall.

Sitting herself on the bed, Sally hugged her close.

'It's all right, Joanna. It's all right, darling,' she said, her soft fingers caressing Joanna's head. 'Did you have a bad dream?'

Joanna's eyes blinked into wakefulness as she looked up into Sally's face.

'I thought Elspeth was here. I thought she was going to lock me up in the dark.'

Sally continued to smooth the girl's hair as she laid her own head against that of the child.

'Elspeth's dead. She can't hurt you any more, Joanna. Not ever.'

CHAPTER THIRTY-EIGHT

It turned out that Seb was right about foxes. The chicks were no longer small and fluffy but growing plump and sprouting feathers.

Joanna and Harry walked with him to the barn, Joanna carrying chicken feed and Seb carrying a pail of water as there was no facility close by. Suddenly Harry shot off, barking loudly and heading straight for the barn's wide open door.

They saw a sudden flash of rusty red as the fox ran, belly close to the ground, Harry right behind him.

'Just as I thought,' muttered Seb. 'He'll be back. Seems tonight I'll be swapping my bed for a bundle of hay.'

Alarmed by what might have happened, Joanna counted the distressed chickens.

'There's one missing. Oh no! Oh no!'

Seb turned at the sound of her dismayed voice. 'Are you sure?'

He counted himself then shook his head. 'You're right. Blast that fox!'

Grumbling threats of what he would do when he found that fox, he found the place where the sly creature had stuck his snout into the chicken run followed by his sleek red body.

More wire, a hammer and some nails and it was quickly repaired. All the same, he promised himself that he would definitely be out here tonight. 'Don't you worry,' he told Joanna. 'I won't let him take another. I'll be out here waiting for him.'

Lady Amelia had given him a gun for just such an occurrence as this and Seb couldn't wait to give it a go. It had been a long time since he'd fired a gun and swore he would never do so again until it was absolutely necessary. This was an occasion he deemed necessary.

Sally was less convinced. 'Are you really sure it's the only way?'

Seb assured her it was. 'A fox will keep coming back until he's had the lot – even if he isn't hungry. He'll bury them in the ground for when the hunting is scarce. Call it part of the war effort – conservation of food and all that.'

'You'll catch your death of cold.'

Seb took no notice. Three days later he was in bed with a cold.

'Stay there and drink your cocoa,' Sally ordered him, though he grumbled and swore the fox would know if he wasn't around. Her father did not make a good patient.

Joanna sat on the end of his bed, Harry as usual at her side.

'Are you sure he'll be back,' Joanna asked him, her arm looped around Harry's neck.

'Bound to be. And who's going to deal with him if I'm not around? Tell me that, will you!'

Sally folded her arms and sighed. Her father could be so stubborn. The orphanage had become his world and the animals were a very great part of it.

Even Joanna couldn't imagine living anywhere else now, though being adopted and living apart from the other children was difficult to get used to.

Stanleybridge was changed beyond recognition and the new regime showed in the happy faces of their changes.

Reassured of her situation. Joanna joined in with the others at play and attended the lessons provided by Sally and Miss Baker. Setting up a proper school was a provision her ladyship and the new children's welfare officer had insisted on.

Seb continued to grumble about the fox.

Sally and Joanna, the latter having made the cocoa herself, looked at each other.

Sally's mind was made up. 'I won't sleep out there, but we have the gun if needs be. Will that suit you?'

Joanna took all this in. She loved Harry most of all, but she also loved Sally and Seb. The Hadleys had taken her in and she owed them a lot. Perhaps this was the time to repay some of that kindness. Seb wasn't well and needed to stay in bed.

Her eyes danced when the idea popped into her mind. She would sleep out in the barn and Harry would sleep there with her. Together they would outsmart that wily old fox!

She considered telling Sally her plan but decided against it. Sally would not allow it, but if it meant Seb – her new dad – staying in bed, then surely it had to be a good idea.

That night Joanna went upstairs to her own bedroom in the quarters set aside for the Hadleys, which took up one half of the west wing of the house.

Joanna's room was cosy with a pale pink rug and a window looking out over the orchard at the back of the house. There was a bathroom between her room and the one where Sally slept. Seb's room was on the same side but a bit further along. A corridor ran between the bedrooms, a rank of windows looking out over the front of the house.

Although Harry had his own basket, he slept on the end of Joanna's bed. Tonight was no different.

She didn't know what time it was when she woke up until she heard the church clock striking three in the morning.

Sometimes when she woke up it was because she was afraid that Elspeth was in the room and that she hadn't really been killed when the bomb was dropped on the house. Despite Sally's reassurances, her stepmother's presence was only slowly fading away. Tonight she felt no such presence.

'Shhh,' she said, holding her finger against her lips. 'We're off to nab that fox, but you'll have to be quiet.'

Once she was sure everyone was asleep, she dressed quickly, grabbed a blanket and crept out. Holding her shoes in one hand so she wouldn't make a noise, she negotiated the stairs and the door to the outside. Harry followed, sounding breathless with excitement.

Thanks to the blackout, the house was in total darkness.

A sudden creaking put Joanna on her guard. The sound seemed to come from overhead. Another followed that seemed to come from another quarter of the sprawling old house.

In the dim light she saw Harry look up at her then wag his tail. She took a deep breath. If Harry wasn't frightened then neither was she.

Having had the presence of mind to put on her coat, she didn't feel the cold. Once she'd put on her shoes she turned the handle on the door that led outside and made her way to the barn.

The barn had big double doors at both end but a smaller one set into the stonework. This was the door Joanna would go through.

The night air made her cheeks tingle and a slight breeze ruffled her hair and chilled her ears. She took out the torch in her pocket, turned it on and shone it towards the ground.

Harry's breath escaped in clouds of steam and his tongue flopped over his jaw.

He wasn't looking at her but with great interest at the door she was pulling open.

Joanna had come to know her dog very well. She eyed him intently and whispered, 'What's up, boy?'

Harry had gone rigid. He was looking straight ahead, the roots of his floppy ears seeming to tighten against his head. All the signs were there that Harry perceived something or someone was inside the barn that shouldn't be there.

'Is it the fox?'

It surprised Joanna when she saw his stumpy tail wag once or twice, as though he were in two minds whether the intruder should be welcomed or sent packing.

The darkness inside the barn was total, the smell of hay sweet and warm.

The old horse nickered in a comfortable manner, as though to say he was happy and content and did they really have to disturb him at this time of night?

'It's all right, Benny. It's only us.' Joanna called to him in a low voice as she closed the door behind her.

She had earmarked a spot close to the roosting chickens where she could sleep in safety and warmth until the fox put in an appearance.

She hadn't brought a gun but she had brought Harry. Harry was a hero. He would know exactly what to do and the fox would run away.

She flashed her torch over the chicken run, apprehensive in case the despicable creature already been and taken another bird. To her great relief nothing had been disturbed. The chicken wire was still taut where Seb had carried out the repair.

A grunting snort, something like the sound Seb made when he woke up from dozing, came from the stack of straw bales piled next to Benny's stall.

In response the horse whinnied and stamped his feet.

Up until now Joanna had felt excited at the prospect of sleeping out. Now she wondered if it had been such a great idea after all.

'Harry,' she whispered. 'Where are you?'

Straw rustled and suddenly there was a rustling sound, as though bales of straw were tumbling down.

Harry began to bark, a long outpouring of barks, sharp, high and excited.

The fox, thought Joanna. *He is here! He is really here!* What would she do if it came her way?

Harry. Harry will deal with it.

'Be brave,' she said to herself, focusing the torch to where the piles of hay and straw were stored. Among the bales she perceived a dark shadow, close to the ground at first, then suddenly rising up from the tumbled bales.

Elspeth! Elspeth has found her!

Joanna screamed and dropped the torch. Harry barked frantically, his legs darting in and out of the beam of light.

Up at the house, Sally heard the frantic barking and got out of bed, reaching for her dressing gown and searching out her slippers with her feet.

A distinctive bark. Harry!

The dogs in the kennels joined in, at first one or two, then a cacophony of sound.

Sally rushed out onto the landing knowing before she even got there that her father had also heard the noise. So had some of the other members of staff and children, flowing in a human tide down the stairs.

Seb was out on the landing in his pyjamas, a hat on his head and his feet bare. He was carrying the shotgun. Sally grabbed it off him.

'Oh no you don't! Get back to bed this minute.'

'That fox!'

'I'll get him.'

'You'll miss.'

Sally won the battle for the gun. The fox had to be dealt with, but as she headed into the dim light at the top of the stairs a more important thought hit her. It was Harry she'd heard first. Wherever Harry was there also was Joanna!

'Where's Joanna?'

Seb understood her meaning and immediately flung open Joanna's bedroom door and switched on the light. Her bed was empty.

'I'll get my coat.'

Gun broken down so it wouldn't go off accidently, Sally tucked it under her arm and headed downstairs. Just before she reached the barn she snapped the two halves firmly together, clenched her jaw and prepared to shoot the intruder.

As she reached the barn door, the noise from the kennels fell away and she could no longer hear Harry barking his head off.

She slipped inside the barn, her heart dancing the samba.

She couldn't see a thing. Damn it! She'd forgotten to bring a torch.

'Who's there? Come out or I'll shoot.'

Not realising her mouth was dry, the words came out rasped when she'd meant it to be shouted. Her hands shook as she aimed the gun, her finger wavering on the trigger.

'Get down, Joanna. I'm going to fire!'

'Don't do that!'

Somebody crashed into her, knocking her off balance.

The gun went off, the muzzle springing upright. Feathers floated down and a barn owl squawked before it bid a hasty retreat. Harry yelped and Joanna cried out.

A pair of strong hands wrenched the gun from Sally's grasp. 'I think I had better take this.'

Sally had the immediate urge to pinch herself. Was she in a dream? She hadn't heard that voice for so long. 'Pierre!'

He brought up the torch Joanna had brought with her, which he'd retrieved from the floor. The light endowed their faces with deep shadows and gold light. His kiss was instant, failing to give her the chance to even check her breath let alone to ask questions.

Voices, some excited, some questioning, sounded from outside.

'Harry! Where's Harry?'

'Where's Joanna?'

Lines of tiredness were etched into Pierre's face made more severe in the light of the torch. His mouth was still voluptuous, his eyes somehow darker. Later he would tell her he'd seen things he never wished to see again. But for now he nodded at the scene outside the barn door.

'I think we need to see what's going on out there.'

The children and staff who'd gathered outside lifted paraffin lanterns and torches. Joanna appeared, but she looked frantic. 'I don't know where Harry is!'

Everyone wanted to know if Sally had shot the fox and the identity of the tramp standing at her side.

'No fox,' said Pierre. 'Only me.'

'Are you hurt?' It was a small girl who asked, her eyes as round as marbles.

'Trust me. I am not hurt. Not at all.'

Seb entered the barn still wearing his pyjamas and hat, plus his trusty work boots.

Joanna was calling for Harry who was nowhere to be seen. The other kids began doing the same, a chorus of 'Harry's rising into the night.

'Well,' said Seb before noticing Pierre. 'I'm going to write to that farmer who's been after buying Harry as a gun dog.'

A multitude of sucked in breaths followed. Surely he wasn't going to let the farmer have Harry.

Pierre shone the torch onto Seb's animated face.

Seb grinned. 'Harry can't be a gun dog. Looks like he's run off. Obviously he's none too keen on the sound of guns.'

Sally gripped Pierre's hands, noting how rough they felt and how tired he looked. 'What are you doing out here? Why didn't you come up to the house?'

'It's been a long journey. I've been out of touch so I went to Ambrose House first but found it requisitioned by the War Office. I found out my aunt was here and so were you. I can't believe it. I can't believe I'm here.'

He hugged her so tightly she could barely breathe, her face tight against his shoulder. Sally closed her eyes and said his name over and over again.

His explanation poured into her ear. 'I was determined to get here but didn't arrive until about an hour ago. I did not wish to wake anyone up at this time of night. I intended sleeping in the barn until the morning.'

Sally tilted her head back and looked into his face. 'I can't believe we thought you were the fox.'

A smile brightened his face. 'Monsieur Reynard?'

Tears in her eyes, her face lit with smiles, Sally nodded. 'So much has happened.'

'I can believe that.'

'I have a new sister,' she whispered close to his ear. 'She came out here to guard the chickens from the fox and found you.'

'Lucky for you that you have such a sister. What's her name?'

'Joanna. Her name's Joanna. She's gone to find her dog. His name's Harry.'

'Party's over! Everyone back to bed,' shouted Seb. He could tell by the looks passing between his daughter and Pierre that they wanted to be alone.

Children and staff began to fall away. Joanna had found Harry and was speaking to him softly, telling him everything would be all right.

'How about me and Harry sleep in the barn and chase the fox off when he comes?'

Seb threw her a direct look. 'How about you get to bed so you're up for school in the morning?'

Excitement over, everyone made their way back to the house and their beds, and the old building went back to its creaking, groaning silence. The night air and the interrupted sleep had made everyone tired – with the exception of Sally and Pierre. She led him to the kitchen and made him sit at the table while she put the kettle on to boil.

Despite the kiss in the barn, an awkward silence hung between them.

Sally scrutinised the scarecrow of a man who sat dirty and dishevelled at the kitchen table. His face was haggard, his hair dirty and in need of a cut. A week's growth of beard bristled on his cheeks.

He was wearing a seaman's duffel coat, the dark cloth sparkling with dried salt. He smelled of fatigue, dry sweat and the sea.

'I'm weary,' he said.

The old sparkle was there in his eyes, but something else was there too; something darker, as though he were harbouring a sore memory that would not lie down.

The dream of the fishing boat came back to her. So did the memory of when he'd kissed her earlier. She'd thrilled at it while also curbing her enthusiasm to kiss him back. He was not her husband. He could never be her husband and, despite what Amelia had told her, she needed to hold on to her respectability. She could not have an affair with a man who was committed elsewhere. Old-fashioned, perhaps, but that was the way she felt. Perhaps her parents' long marriage had some bearing on the matter. Whatever it was, she couldn't help it.

The way Pierre was looking at her, she guessed he knew what she was thinking. The silence between them had to be broken. They had to move on with their relationship – even if it only stayed a friendship.

She poured his tea and placed two slices of buttered toast in front of him. 'Was it very bad over there?'

'Yes,' he said simply and finally. He quickly devoured the toast and drank the tea. Realising she was observing his gluttony he slowed down, apologised and explained. 'I haven't eaten since yesterday evening on the boat. We crossed into the area of Spain called Galicia then I was taken by fishing boat out to sea. It took us four days to cross Biscay.'

Sally's heart lurched in her breast. 'The sea was rough.'

He nodded. 'Very rough.'

'I dreamed you were in a rough sea.'

He looked surprised. A weak smile lifted his expression and his eyes were a warm brown in the salty roughness of his face.

'I dreamed of you too. You were confronting a man who once fancied you. He'd moved on to somebody else and I dreamed you told him exactly how despicable he was.'

For a moment she couldn't quite grasp the identity of the person he was talking about. Then she remembered Arnold Thomas.

The fact that they had dreamed about each other made her tingle. She shivered.

'Yes,' said Pierre on noticing her shiver. 'It makes you feel like that. Fate is telling us that we're made for each other. Soulmates.'

'Pierre . . .'

'Hear me out. This war is going to last for a very long time. I am not always going to be around. I will not ask you to commit yourself until I am free. French law being the way it is . . .' He shrugged. 'Adele was a mistake. While in France we met up and agreed to go our separate ways, but I cannot ask you to wait for me. Any commitment I had to her has been replaced with one to my country. I will be away quite a lot. Whatever our relationship is to be is up to you.'

His tired eyes failed to meet hers.

As well as his tiredness she felt the change in him. The terrible scenes he'd been witness to had altered him for ever. Before he'd gone away he'd informed her that he was the one for her, stated they would share a future. Now he was actually leaving the decision to her. He'd asked her to marry him, wanted her more than any woman alive, but wanted to be fair to her given his situation.

Sally pondered how much she'd been longing for his return regardless of his marriage to Adele.

She also thought of Joanna's father, marrying Elspeth in order to give his daughter a mother. Not the right reason to marry at all. And then there was Arnold Thomas, living under a cloud for years before hitching up with Elspeth, closing his eyes to her true nature because he was fed up of being lonely.

The world was in chaos and normal rules were no more.

'Yes,' she said quietly. 'I will wait for you.'

Pushing the kitchen chair behind him, he staggered to his feet, falling on her as if he would pass out if she failed to give her support.

When he kissed her his beard growth was rough on her skin. Both of his hands rested on hers, much rougher than they used to be.

Nothing, she thought, *will ever be soft again.*

She looked down at them, thinking of the time ahead when they wouldn't be together.

'I need a memento of our time together.' She raised her head, her eyes moist with fear and longing. 'I can't wait back here with nothing to remind me of you.'

He opened his mouth to interrupt and kissed her palm when she laid her hand over his mouth.

'I don't mean a photograph. Pierre, I want more than that.'

He nodded and looked at her in wonder as what she was suggesting sunk in. 'I understand.'

Knowing she would not wish her father or anyone else to hear, he took hold of her hand and led her out of the door and back to the barn.

'The hay is soft. I well recommend it,' he said to her softly.

The night air was chill around them, but even after removing their clothes they were warm, the sweet-smelling hay forming both the mattress beneath them and a warm covering.

Sally shivered. 'I've never done this before.'

Reining in his passion, Pierre took his time, kissing her lips, her nose, her face, his hands stroking her body until her flesh cried out for him.

'I have dreamed of this time,' he said softly, his beautiful accent pouring into her ears along with his hot breath.

The smell of his sweat, the salty taste of his body, would be his personal memento to her, a reminder of this moment to sustain her when he was away. His hands were hot on her breasts, slightly abrasive as they travelled under her nightdress, loitering over the silky softness of her inner thighs.

When he entered her she held her breath and was tense at first until slowly sliding into pleasure, moving her hips in time with his, gasping and arching her back until an incredible spasm shot through her body.

'I wish you didn't have to go,' she whispered when they finally lay replete and happy.

Pierre kissed her head, breathing in the scent of her hair.

'Neither do I. But I am ordered.'

He was called away two days later. Sally didn't ask where he was going. Deep down she knew he would be parachuted back behind enemy lines, though the actual destination was secret. All she could do was hope for his safe return and the day when they would finally marry.

A few days later she was still absorbed in thoughts about him and their night in the barn. Her mood was glum and she found it difficult to smile. Every small moment alone was taken up thinking about Pierre.

She was watching the red glow of sunset when she saw three figures coming towards her, no more than silhouettes against the glowing sky.

One of them was her father; another was Joanna. The third was Harry, his stout legs covering the ground between them.

Her father brushed past her followed by the other two.

Joanna was laughing and talking about the rabbits they'd found in the rough grass beyond the vegetable gardens.

'Dad's going to trap them. He would have shot them, but Harry doesn't like guns.'

Sally smiled absentmindedly. 'I wish everyone felt like that.'

Her father's eyes narrowed. She could tell he wanted to say something more but held off until Joanna was gone to bed and they were alone.

Sally made a pot of tea, frugally using the tea leaves from the previous brew in order to make their ration last.

Her father took a sip of tea then set his cup back in the saucer. Sally sensed he was about to give her a good talking to. Instead he burst into song.

'Jerusalem, Jerusalem. Lift up your head and sing. Hosannas in the highest . . .'

Sally's jaw dropped. She'd never heard her father sing before.

Harry, who had been flat out in front of the fire, sat up and howled along with the tune.

The sound of footsteps came down the stairs, preceding Joanna's appearance.

Thinking she'd had another nightmare about Elspeth returning, Sally sprang to her feet.

'Are you all right, Joanna?'

Joanna laughed. 'I heard Dad singing and then Harry howling.'

When Seb finally finished, Joanna clapped enthusiastically before wrapping her arms around Harry's neck.

She looked up at Seb. 'Dad, I didn't know Harry could sing. And that's such a good song. I like that song.'

Dad! Something jerked in Sally's mind. The first time Joanna called her father 'dad' hadn't really registered, but it did now. It seemed so apt after everything that had happened. Joanna belonged here. With them. They all belonged here. Together.

She blinked under the intensity of her father's eyes.

'We all have to be brave,' he said, quietly addressing his comments to Sally. 'I was downhearted for a while after your mother went, but now I realise I was selfish. There were other people worse off than me.' Reaching down, he rubbed Harry's ears. Harry closed his eyes in response and made cosy noises. 'It took a dog to shake me out of my selfishness.'

Sally smiled and narrowed her eyes to prevent the tears from falling.

'I'll come up and tuck you in,' she said to Joanna.

The little girl beamed from ear to ear.

Before she had chance to close the door, Harry had bounded up the stairs to make in himself comfortable on Joanna's bed.

Sally sighed. She didn't really approve, but if the dog gave comfort, so what?

Before going back downstairs she thought about what her father had said about being selfish. She'd known immediately what he meant. It was no good her being downhearted while Pierre was away. She owed it to him to be brave and she would wait for him. She most certainly would.

Joanna hurried with the chattering throng of children armed with buckets of food for all the animals.

A terrible racket ensued once the animals heard their approach and Joanna joined in with everything that was going on.

Seb trailed behind them carrying the heavier buckets and making sure the smaller children didn't get left behind.

Keen to do her bit, Joanna emptied her bucket first.

'Already?' said Seb, his eyes twinkling with fun.

'Yes, Dad!' Joanna breathed a big sigh of satisfaction. 'Everyone's been fed. We've all done our bit.'

Seb's eyes turned moist. She called him Dad all the time now.

He watched her as she met up with Harry, the glossy-coated cocker spaniel, the latter wagging as the two of them collided in a loving embrace.

He listened as she spoke to him while rubbing his ears.

'See, Harry? We've got a great big family now. We're not orphans any more!' Seb smiled. 'No,' he whispered, his eyes sweeping over the chattering throng of children. 'You're not.'

Can't get enough of Lizzie Lane?

Turn over for an extract from

HOME SWEET HOME

Available from Ebury Press

EBURY
PRESS

PROLOGUE

Sumatra, September 1942

John Smith eased over on to his side, wincing as he did so. Every bone in his body, every wasted muscle, cried out from the effort. Oh, for a bed with proper springs! Just a dream. Something he'd once enjoyed and nothing like he slept on in this hellhole!

A proper bed! Even a mattress! What he'd give for a feather bed or even a mound of moss in the middle of an English field. Or a Scottish, Irish or Welsh one. A place where the air was cool and his bed soft. Not like this bloody thing, no more than wooden slats banged together with iron nails. And only a few slats at that.

Thanks to burrowing insects and the skin-soaking humidity, the slats rotted quickly and needed frequent replacing. Where slats had not been replaced, only the iron nails remained on the struts sticking up to trap the slack skin of the man who lay on it. It took a great deal of effort to pull them out. Iron nails provided currency, a poor currency maybe, but anything one could barter or sell was like money in the bank. Taken out and hammered straight, they could be exchanged for food, a cigarette, or an extra ounce of rice. You needed a lot of nails to barter for anything like that.

1

Even here nails had a use: they were needed to form secret compartments in an inmate's bed, or used to form a box which was then buried deep in the dirt floor – anywhere hidden from the Nips – their slang for the Japanese and Korean guards. Everyone kept a little cache of something precious that could be bartered or merely treasured: jewellery, watches – anything that hadn't been taken off them.

Johnnie had originally been interned in Changi – heaven compared to this place, which was surrounded by hot, humid jungle, the air a perpetual swamp of sticky heat.

Leather boots fell to bits, the stitching that had fastened the uppers to the soles rotted away along with the rough bits of string that had long since replaced army issue boot laces.

Men rotted here too. Their uniforms, once proudly worn, were either a mass of ragged patches or completely gone, replaced by a sarong knotted at the waist and obtained in exchange for the last precious item a man might own – a cigarette lighter, a wedding ring, a lucky coin – not so lucky here.

Photographs were vulnerable to both insects and humidity. And photographs were the most precious of all: each photograph contained a memory, a reminder of a life once lived before ending up as a prisoner of war on the other side of the world.

After making sure nobody was watching, John eased the photograph of Ruby Sweet from the tobacco tin he kept it in. The sun was going down and there wasn't much light left. What with the stink of sweating men and the crowded surroundings, it was hardly the most romantic setting in the world. However, he'd made a habit of studying her photo before he fell asleep. In that moment he forgot his dire surroundings. Looking at her kept him sane, gave him hope. He'd received no letters from her since he'd become a POW, but then, he conceded, it wasn't her fault. None of the other blokes had received letters either. The only one he had was the one he'd received before Singapore had fallen. He'd read it until the folds broke, the paper softened with moisture. Still he kept it; and kept reading it, even though he could recite it almost word for word by now.

The letter contained a recipe. He'd read that recipe over and over again, salivating as he did so. In his mind's eye, he could see her giving one of her cooking demonstrations. Those memories always made him smile.

The photograph had been taken by an official of the Ministry of Food for propaganda purposes. He'd been lucky enough to persuade the photographer to make an extra copy for him. He'd forgotten to tell Ruby about it, but he was glad he had it.

Gazing at the photograph, he remembered everything about their time together. In fact, he went over each occasion in his mind as often as he could just so he wouldn't forget that he'd once known her in another life.

Another life. In this one, fear had become a tight band around his chest. Hopefully, he would return to that other life. He held on to the hope that he would survive his incarceration, that the war would end and Ruby would be waiting for him. He imagined her cooking an evening meal, just for the two of them, husband and wife. The future he imagined with her might be a leap too far, but a future in which they would be together was the only thing keeping him going.

What would she say about that? he wondered, and couldn't help smiling. They'd never expressed anything definite. They'd just flirted. Sometimes they'd argued, but they'd been slowly getting closer. And then there was that day in the field close to the railway station. I mean, you can't get much closer than that, he thought to himself.

He sighed, rolled on to his back and held the photograph to his chest with both hands. If it wasn't for his memories of Ruby, he would go mad. If he didn't cling to the hope of better things to come, he would give up and die.

Hope had surged in his chest a few days ago when the Japanese guards had come round with postcards for them to fill in. It was whispered that the cards would be passed to the Red Cross, who would in turn send them to their loved ones. The camp commandant confirmed it. The prisoners, starved, despondent and abused, had received such promises before. But then no cards had materialised. The conclusion had been that their captors had been playing with them, giving them hope in exchange for them behaving themselves.

But this time the cards had actually materialised. They dared to hope that it wasn't just a ruse. Hopefully, the postcards really would be handed over to the Red Cross and sent home.

Like the other blokes, John had avidly filled his in. There had been a fight over the few pencils they'd been handed and he'd made the mistake of getting involved. The butt of a Japanese rifle had connected with his forehead. His eye had been half-closed as a result of it, blood trickling down his cheek. It wasn't the first time he'd been beaten. Everyone had. Bleeding was a consequence of being a prisoner of the Japanese.

He'd ignored the blood and kept writing what they'd told him to write:

I am well. I am being well treated. The Japanese are winning the war.

Nobody dared deviate. It stuck in his craw that he had to write the lies dictated to them. He so wanted to tell Ruby the truth about how cruel their captors could be. But how?

In the past, early on in the war, he'd got round the army censors by adding a cryptic note in his letters that left her in no doubt of where he was and what was going on. That was what he wanted to do now, but it wasn't easy, not here. The guards were watching him closely. The camp commandant and his aides were carefully scrutinising each card. Those whose English was poor merely counted the words, comparing one card with another.

How to let Ruby know the truth?

A droplet of blood had fallen on to his hand from the cut above his eyebrow where the rifle butt had split the skin, and for a moment he had stared at it as though surprised there was any blood left in his body, he was that thin.

A number of flies began to buzz around the spilled blood. Another droplet fell on to the card as an idea formed in his mind.

He glanced swiftly around him. The coast was clear. The prisoners were concentrating on writing their cards, the guards on collecting the finished articles and reading what they had written.

Nobody saw him press his thumb into the droplet of blood that had fallen on to the card. Was it too obvious? He didn't think so. No more than a smudge, almost like mud – unless one looked very closely.

It was done! Now all he had to hope was that nobody would notice it.

His heart had been in his mouth as the postcards were snatched and flicked like a pack of cards by an officer who could read English. He might see the right number of words, but he was holding them at the corners. The imprint was hidden. After that they were placed into a box marked with the Red Cross insignia. The cards were taken away for despatch – at least he hoped they were.

Now John lay back on his hard bed. From outside the tent he heard the chattering of monkeys, the droning of insects; and inside there was the sobbing of a man a few beds down from his. Groans, murmured prayers and whispering voices were background noises he'd grown used to.

Despite everything, he still felt incredibly elated. His message was there on the postcard, printed in blood. Never mind the reassuring words that he was well and being taken care of. The bloodied fingerprint would tell the truth. But would Ruby see it and understand? He sorely hoped that she would.

CHAPTER ONE

England

On the day Mary Sweet finally left Oldland Common for good, the train journey to the east of England seemed to take for ever. It had been bad enough the first time round when she'd fled in haste to visit Michael in hospital. Fear and apprehension had travelled with her, and the dull weather had done nothing to raise her spirits. She had left early in the morning in autumnal darkness, a darkness that had only lightened to grey thanks to the gloomy sky and pouring rain.

Just like now, the train had passed acre after acre of ploughed-up fields, the monotony intermittently relieved by a green oasis of pastureland where cattle or sheep still grazed. Even though they passed close to Newmarket, the heart of British horse racing, she didn't see any horses. Grassland was precious; horses were a luxury, though they were also a valuable alternative to cattle. Horse steak wasn't dissimilar to beef, though she hadn't tried it herself.

Leaving home for good had left her with an empty, cold feeling inside. It wasn't just leaving her family and the village she'd grown up in; the prospect of what she would have to face at the other end of her journey also concerned her. She'd seen Michael's bandaged hands and torso on

7

her last visit. Now he was due to have his bandages finally removed.

She'd thought herself prepared for the event, but still her stomach rolled nervously at finally having to face the extent of the injuries that Michael had endured.

Michael's job was necessary to the war effort, but extremely dangerous. She had to face that. But how injured was he? She'd been told he would fly again and not to worry, but what did that mean? People would say anything to help her get over the shock. She didn't blame them for doing so, but despite their reassurances she couldn't help imagining it being worse than they admitted to.

They'd explained all this to her on her previous visit. Only some of it had sunk in. Questions remained. How badly scarred would he be? Could he still walk? Yes, he must be able to walk otherwise they wouldn't have said that he would still fly once he'd recovered. But his hands? His beautiful hands? Would he be able to feel her when he touched her?

All those questions still hung in her mind on this journey through the flat Lincolnshire countryside. Before she'd left, her father had taken her to one side and reminded her of where she needed to be. 'Your place is with him. By his bedside.'

'I should have moved there when he asked me to,' she'd replied.

Her father had looked a little sad at the prospect of losing her, but had said, 'He's your husband, Mary, and it's only right that you should be living with him, not here with us.'

It was dark by the time she'd alighted from the train at a branch station. The sound of a whistle screeched before the name of the station – the one she'd travelled to on her last visit – was shouted out. A dim blue lantern, similar to the dim bulbs they used in the railway carriages nowadays, cast just enough of its cold, blue light so people could see where they were going. Apart from the lantern, the unfamiliar surroundings were as black as a coal pit.

Shouts and laughter fell on to the platform as a whole battalion of army privates bundled out of the train carriages making jokes and laughing, their burning cigarettes glowing red in the deep black night.

On the train, one of them had told her that they were on their way to important east coast bases. The south and east coasts would be the front line should the enemy invade and had been packed with troops since the outbreak of war – more so now the Americans had arrived.

She had looked at the faces of the private and his companions, bright and cheerful despite the gloomy compartment, young faces that would soon turn old and worldly wise once they'd experienced what a war really was.

What the station lacked in light it made up for with other noises besides those of the men in uniform. Their boots clattered over the platform and clouds of steam hissed from the underbelly beneath the locomotive and the funnel on top.

In her heavily pregnant state, Mary's sense of smell was extremely acute, sickeningly so sometimes. Damp wool, men's sweat, cigarettes and smoke smelling of cinders from the steam engine formed an acrid brew that made Mary gag. Swaying slightly and closing her eyes, she placed her hand over her nose and mouth.

The crowd pressed on around her, a human tide surging towards the ticket inspectors and the exit, the former only serving to slow the flow but determined to do their job.

Once the throng had largely dissipated and she had room to breathe, she placed her case between her feet, took a deep breath and looked around her. Last time she had come here, Mike's friend Guy had been waiting for her and taken her straight to the hospital, where she had stayed until it was clear Mike was out of danger. Then she had returned to the only home she'd ever known, to pack up and return.

The light from the lantern threw a pool of light immediately in front of her. Whoever had been sent to pick her up would see her here, picked out by the poor light and close to the station clock. She looked up at it, saw its Roman figures. Nine o'clock. It had indeed been a long day, though according to some on the train, fifteen hours to cross from one side of the country to the other was quite normal.

Emerging from the gaping blackness of the exit, a figure paused to flash his identification at one of the ticket inspectors. Like a shadow that had come to life, he made his way to her, the only woman still on the platform. It wasn't Guy.

'Mrs Dangerfield?'

The light played tricks with his features, but his uniform was that of a member of RAF ground crew. He was of average height and build, not a prepossessing man at all, though there was something odd about one side of his face. At first glance, she put it down to the dark shadows thrown by the blue lantern. On second glance, she knew the cold light was not to blame.

Fear and a creeping sickness tightened her stomach. The skin on one side of his face resembled a mask, a cruel mask that made it seem as though his face had been torn apart then reassembled from the wrong pieces. The skin of his right cheek looked paper thin, one eye slanting downwards, his mouth uneven from a silky patch of skin that seemed to have been sewn on to his upper lip.

Her mind raced and her blood ran cold as the man in front of her saluted smartly and offered to take her case.

'Yes . . . yes . . . of course.'

'My name's Sergeant Paul Innes. It's a bit late to go straight to the hospital, so I have strict orders to make you comfortable tonight and take you to the hospital tomorrow.'

Mary tried not to let her mouth hang open, but it wasn't easy. It was difficult to take her eyes off the damaged side of his face. Suddenly she became aware of her bad manners.

'I'm sorry,' she said apologetically and tried to sound light-hearted, as though nothing was out of the ordinary and his face was unblemished.

My voice sounds shaky, she thought. My smile is too stiff, and as for my hands . . .

She curled the fingers of one hand into her perspiring palm. Luckily she was wearing gloves otherwise she would have left red crescents behind. Her teeth ached with the effort of smiling and pretending that nothing was wrong.

Sergeant Innes didn't appear to notice, or if he did, he hid it well. It was no good. She just had to apologise properly.

'I'm sorry. I don't mean to stare.'

He smiled a lop-sided smile. 'Oh, don't you be sorry about that, Mrs Dangerfield. I'm afraid it's a legacy of a burning Hampden bomber. I'm still alive. That's all that matters. The wing commander sends his apologies, Mrs Dangerfield. He would have collected you himself, but he's on Ops tonight. I've been ordered to take you to your cottage. I've got you some food in and lit the fire.'

He was affable and kind, but she shuddered as she wondered how many times he'd had to carry out this duty.

After placing her luggage on the back seat, he helped her into the car. They moved off, away from the town and into a dark, flat landscape. It took about an hour travelling along unlit country roads before they finally arrived at Woodbridge Cottage.

Once out of the car, he grabbed her luggage from the back seat, helped her out from the front seat and switched on a torch. They followed the flashlight's circular beam the length of the garden path.

'Where are you from, Sergeant?' Asking a question helped to keep their conversation light and friendly, away from the taboo subject of Michael's injuries.

'Birmingham.'

She couldn't help remarking that he was a long way from home, simply because she felt she had to say something, however innocuous.

'We're all a long way from home, Mrs Dangerfield.' Sergeant Innes didn't seem to have noticed her anxiety. 'But that's the nature of war. All hands to the pumps, no matter where they come from. Right. Open sesame.'

The beam from the torch picked out a bird box on the right-hand side of the cottage door. She couldn't remember it from her last visit but then she'd spent so little time here. It had been just somewhere to sleep after spending most of her time with Mike at the hospital. A huge iron key hung on a hook just below it.

'Here it is,' he said. He took the key and swivelled the torch ahead of them to pick out the keyhole. Now she noticed that the cottage had a sweet little front door. The key clunked as it turned in the lock.

Although the sergeant wasn't that tall, he had to duck to enter, and the top of her head barely missed the frame too. She smiled at the thought of Michael hitting his head on its low oak lintel. A pang of regret clutched at her heart. If only she'd come here sooner. They could have enjoyed some time together, talking about the baby, walking through the surrounding countryside. On the first visit she had stayed here all alone. Hopefully on this visit she wouldn't be alone for too long.

Precious as it was, some time together was all it would have been if she had come up earlier. Nothing she could have done would have prevented what had happened.

Because it had been dark, she hadn't seen much of the garden and had been too preoccupied to notice anything on her first visit. Tonight she smelt damp green leaves and fertile earth and imagined that in summer it was a riot of smells and colour thanks to sweet-scented stock, honeysuckle and lavender. Although the countryside was flatter than at home, the smells at least were the same.

The door opened directly into the living room, where a welcoming fire glowed in the grate. Once the blackout curtains were pulled, Sergeant Innes switched on a table lamp. The room echoed the look of a summer garden with its chintz-covered armchairs and flowery curtains. Despite the fact that the seats of the chairs sagged a little, they looked comfortable.

The sergeant offered to take her suitcase upstairs for her.

'There's no need. I can manage.' She wanted him to go. Her legs felt terribly weak. She reached out and grasped the back of a chair.

Sergeant Innes reached out as if to steady her. 'I think you need to sit down, Mrs Dangerfield. You've had a long journey in your condition.'

'Oh, don't worry about me,' she said, attempting a light laugh. 'You surely have more important duties with the air force.'

'Not at all. That's what I'm here for, Mrs Dangerfield. Would you like me to make you a cup of tea before I leave?'

'No,' she said, managing a weak smile. 'I'm quite fine now.'

There was kindness in his eyes. 'Now this here's the kitchen,' he said. The door he opened was almost a mirror image of the front door, planks of pine nailed to two cross braces.

'I remember,' said Mary.

'Ah, yes. Of course you do. Well, there you are. It's small but cosy. I've got you in a few tinned things, your bacon ration and some eggs. Had a hard job getting those,' he said to her. 'But where there's a will there's a way – and a farmer over the back field willing to gamble just about anything in a game of cards.' He winked. The corner of his damaged right eye drooped downwards, giving him a strange, almost roguish look. 'Trouble is he isn't much of a gambling man. Oh, and I persuaded Mrs Catchpole, who does a bit of cleaning for the officers, to make a nice toad in the hole. Not that there's likely to be many toads in it, but I guarantee it'll be tasty.'

For the first time since seeing his injured features, Mary controlled her fear and looked him directly in the face.

'Thank you, Sergeant. I think I'll be very comfortable here.'

'No bother, Mrs Dangerfield. Not sure what time I'm to pick up your husband, but don't count on it being too early.'

'Whatever time is fine. It gives me a chance to settle in.'

Once the door had closed behind him and the big iron key was hanging on yet another nail to one end of the fireplace, Mary sat down and thought about things. Just as she'd composed her expression to face Sergeant Innes, she'd have to do the same for her husband when she saw him tomorrow. It wouldn't be easy and she thought about it long and hard, so long that she hardly noticed that the only light in the room was from the glowing fire and the meagre table lamp. Dancing shadows played over the walls, but they didn't worry her. Today was almost over. It was tomorrow she was worried about. How would she cope?

She took a deep breath. Control yourself. Be calm.

The words popped into her mind and she took instant notice. The best thing to do is to keep yourself occupied.

Determinedly, she got to her feet. Sergeant Innes had gone to a lot of trouble. It was only right that she should enjoy what he'd arranged for her. She recalled Michael telling her that although far from town, the cottage had some degree of electricity downstairs.

'Upstairs it's candles or oil lamps,' he'd told her.

Her first stop was the kitchen. Besides the eggs and bacon Sergeant Innes told her about, she found bread and cheese, tinned meats and fresh vegetables set in the middle of a simple pine table. She couldn't help wondering whose ration card had been used.

A covered pan containing the toad in the hole was keeping warm on top of a cast-iron range. The coals in the fire bed glowed hot and red. Despite the iron cover, the smell escaped, made her nose tingle and her stomach rumble. However, eating could wait. This was the cottage Michael had earmarked to be their home for the duration of the war – or at least as long as he was stationed here.

There was no gas stove. Not surprising, really. They were in the midst of fertile agricultural land, some of the best in England. She guessed there was no gas for miles. As long as she kept the kitchen door open, the range would heat the house and cook the food. Hunger hadn't been much of an issue the first time she'd been here as she was so worried about Michael. But now he was coming home and she had it in mind to make sure the house was well presented. In the morning, she would explore the garden and pick some flowers, even if she had to put them in jam jars around the house.

After placing the tinned things on to a dresser and the rest into a metal meat cupboard, she wandered back into the living room.

Downstairs, the cottage had only the two rooms, the kitchen and the living room. The large inglenook fireplace took up one third of a wall, and while the furniture was shabby and the carpets worn, the atmosphere was warm and cosy. The smell of polish lingered in the air, evidence that someone cared for the cottage and was doing what they could to make the old furniture last that bit longer.

Armed with a wax candle she'd found in a kitchen drawer, she made her way upstairs. The candle flame flickered in the draught as she explored the two bedrooms. The front bedroom, the largest, held a double bed with a plain wooden headboard and smaller, matching footboard. The floors were of bare wood, a rag rug in pink and red to one side of the bed, a smaller green one close to the window. The curtains were of a Paisley-patterned fabric in matching colours. A wine-coloured satin eiderdown sat on top of a faded candlewick bedspread that might once have been yellow but was now a very pale lemon.

The second bedroom had a small square window, a chest of drawers and a single bed with a patchwork cover. She opened the window at the exact same time as the moon chose to emerge from behind a navy blue cloud. The air was crisp and cold. The flat land of Lincolnshire was spread out before her like a patchwork counterpane.

The blackout curtains were not drawn. She wondered at that, then recalled that Michael had said something about the pilots using the escaping light from this cottage as a kind of marker buoy, situated as it was at the very end of the runway. 'Against blackout regulations and all that, but we don't get many enemy bombers up here. Too far and not too much for them to bomb when they get here. Except us, that is.'

He'd laughed at his own joke, at least she'd thought it was a joke. Perhaps that business about bombers being able to see a light from ten thousand feet was rubbish.

The sight of the moon stirred a vein of anger inside her. She slammed the window shut and pulled the curtains, blotting out its silvery light. She didn't want to look at the moon, the bomber's moon, as Michael had described it.

'It's great for navigation,' he'd told her. 'The moon shines on a river, the water reflects light so we follow water or a river all the way to our target. Once we get there we can see everything.'

He'd been more reticent about adding that because they could more easily see the ground, those on the ground could also see them. After she'd challenged him, he'd admitted that there was a greater chance of being hit by an anti-aircraft gun on a clear night such as this.

Just for once in her life she found herself hating the moon, yet there had been a time when she'd loved it. She didn't know for sure whether the moon had been shining on the night Michael had been hit, but she couldn't help hating it in case it had aided his plane being shot down.

She managed to eat some of the toad in the hole, and left the rest for the next day. In the morning, she ate only a slice of toast and drank a cup of tea, and even had trouble keeping that down. Yes, there was the usual feeling of nausea, but this morning it was coupled with a sickening fear that lay in her stomach like a bag of rocks.

Closing her eyes, she willed it to pass and uttered a heartfelt prayer. 'Please, God, don't let him be too badly scarred. Please!'